the heart of Spain

Vale mas morír de pie que vivir de rodíllas

La Pasionaria

Anthology
of fiction
non-fiction
and poetry

the
heart
of
Spain

Edited by ALVAH BESSIE

VETERANS OF THE ABRAHAM LINCOLN BRIGADE

The Veterans of the Abraham Lincoln Brigade express their deep gratitude to the authors and publishers who have so kindly granted permission for the use of the material in this anthology, including the following.

One Small Detail reprinted from FREEDOM'S BATTLE by J. Alvarez del Vayo by permission of Alfred A. Knopf, Inc. Copyright, 1940, by Julio Alvarez del Vayo.

The First Days from IN PLACE OF SPLENDOR by Constancia de la Mora. Copyright, 1939, by Harcourt, Brace and Company, Inc.

"Down With Intelligence!" from BURGOS JUSTICE by Antonio Ruiz Vilaplana, by permission of Alfred A. Knopf, Inc. Copyright, 1938, by Alfred A. Knopf, Inc.

Spanish Sequence from THE FOURTH DECADE by Norman Rosten. Copyright, 1943, by Norman Rosten. Reprinted by permission of Rinehart & Company, Inc., Publishers.

They Fly Through the Air from THIRTEEN BY CORWIN by Norman Corwin. Reprinted by permission of Henry Holt and Company, Inc. Copyright, 1942, by Norman Corwin.

Andalucia from SLOW MUSIC by Genevieve Taggard. Copyright, 1944, by Genevieve Taggard. Reprinted by permission of Harper & Brothers.

Veterans of the Abraham Lincoln Brigade from LONG VIEW by Genevieve Taggard. Copyright, 1946, by Genevieve Taggard. Reprinted by permission of Harper & Brothers.

"The Ancient Christian Traditions" from the book *Un Año con Queipo* by Antonio Bahamonde y Sanchez de Castro published 1939 in English by United Editorial Limited, London, with the title MEMOIRS OF A SPANISH NATIONALIST.

The Last Days from THE EDUCATION OF A CORRESPONDENT by Herbert L. Matthews. Copyright, 1946, by Harcourt Brace and Company, Inc.

How Do You Sleep, Franco? from COLLECTED EDITION OF HEYWOOD BROUN. Copyright, 1941, by Heywood Hale Broun. Reprinted by permission of Harcourt Brace and Company, Inc.

This book is dedicated to the memory of eighteen hundred Americans who died in the ranks of the International Brigades during the second war of Spain's independence.

Their sacrifice to the preservation of American democracy has received no official citation. The enduring love and gratitude of their people has been theirs ever since the first American volunteer—Ben Leider—was shot out of the sky over the front lines at Madrid on February 18, 1937.

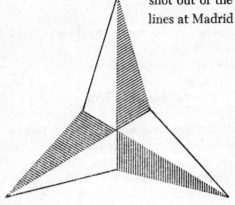

"The rifles you will never hold again,
In other hands will speak against the night. . . ."

SPAIN 1873-1874

Out of the murk of heaviest clouds,
Out of the feudal wrecks and heap'd-up
_ skeletons of kings,_
Out of that old entire European debris,
_ the shatter'd mummeries,_
Ruin'd cathedrals, crumble of palaces,
_ tombs of priests,_
Lo, Freedom's features fresh undimm'd look forth—
_ the same immortal face looks forth;_
(A glimpse as of thy Mother's face Columbia,
A flash significant as of a sword,
Beaming toward thee.)

Nor think we forget thee maternal;
Lag'dst thou so long? shall the clouds
_ close again upon thee?_
Ah, but thou hast thyself now appear'd to us—
_ we know thee,_
Thou hast given us a sure proof, the glimpse
_ of thyself,_
Thou waitest there as everywhere thy time.

WALT WHITMAN

TABLE OF CONTENTS

DRESS REHEARSAL (1938)

THE CONSCIENCE OF THE WORLD (1939)

"MADRID WILL BE THE TOMB OF FASCISM"
(1939-19——?)

The Veterans of the Abraham Lincoln Brigade deeply regret the omission from this anthology of John Howard Lawson's screenplay *Blockade*. Permission to reprint a portion of it was naturally granted by Mr. Lawson and, just as naturally, refused by United Artists, which controls the material.

Blockade was the first commercial film ever made in the United States to utilize the war in Spain as background and motivation for its story and the only film that attempted to say what that war was about and marshal support for the Republic.

At the time of its release (1938) it was attacked as "subversive" propaganda and it later figured as an item in the dossier on John Howard Lawson, presented by the House Committee on Un-American Activities as evidence of Mr. Lawson's dangerous ideas.

Refusing to surrender the Bill of Rights to J. Parnell Thomas, Mr. Lawson and eight of his motion picture colleagues, pilloried by that Committee, went to prison and are blacklisted by the motion picture industry.

An Introduction

DOROTHY PARKER

I WAS IN PARIS IN 1937, a year when "Not Valid For Travel in Spain" was stamped across American passports. So I went to our embassy to see what I might do to have my passport so altered that I might visit Spain.

The American embassy in Paris was—and, surely, still is—a lovely place, calm and spacious and dignified, and as you came through its massive portal, you had the feeling that all was to be done for you, that you would be served with courtesy, with understanding, almost with compassion.

Deep inside the building, one of the most courteous young men in the world listened to me. He wore admirable clothes, not new—oh, God, not new!—and the freshness of the handkerchief four-pointed in his jacket pocket was less like snow than like snow-drops. He was called—this I gathered from other young men who kept running in and out of the stately room—Pinky. But maybe my memory is wrong there. He may have been Binkie. He had the tidy face that you see atop the fine, hard, sedulously tended bodies of the young men like him, with whom he went to prep school and to college; young men who are always young men and, no matter where you see them, in whatever calm and spacious places their careers lie, are always at prep school and at college; the tidy face that you cannot for the life of you remember ten minutes after seeing it.

The young man with the tidy face and the admirable clothes was gentle and soft and patient with me; and patience, with its implication of time, was no easy matter for him. For those were tough days in the American embassy in Paris in the summer of 1937. There was tension in the air; there was strain and uncertainty and anxiety. The golf team of the embassy was about to set forth for Brussels, to play the team of our embassy to Belgium. My young man, high man of his team, had yet to do his packing; hell brewed. You knew what he was laboring under, and so his courtesy was doubly to be commended.

Fortunately, the matter of the passport was simple. It was just the business of taking a look at it, and then telling me where to go to have it approved for Spain. The young man looked at it, wrote something on something, and then said to me, "Oh, by the way"—for such young men keep conversation going by such phrases as "by the way"—"which side of this Spanish fuss do you want to go in on?" He said it with a little laugh, as who should imply, "These formalities—but after all, tradition—"

I said the Loyalist side; and I am not at all sure that I did not add, for such young men reduce me, and you, too, to the texture of a milk pudding, "if you don't mind, please."

He looked up then. "Really?" he said. "Well. Well, if that's what you think you want. But of course, you'd have much more fun on the Franco side."

I have not followed farther the track of the young man of the embassy. I cannot tell you, heaven help me, if his team won its match. I cannot tell you what ever happened to him. My guess would be: nothing. But I can tell you what happened to me. I went to Spain, on that side of the fuss where there was less fun, and I became a member of the human race.

I stayed in Valencia and in Madrid, places I had not been since that fool of a king lounged on the throne, and in those two cities and in the country around and between them, I met the best people anyone ever knew. I had never seen such people before. But I shall see their like again. And so shall all of us. If I did not believe that, I think I should stand up in front of my mirror and take a long, deep, swinging slash at my throat.

For what they stood for, what they have given others to take and hold and carry along—that does not vanish from the earth. This is not a matter of wishing or feeling; it is knowing. It is knowing that nothing devised by fat, rich, frightened men

II

can ever stamp out truth and courage, and determination for a decent life.

It is impossible not to feel sad for what happened to the Loyalists in Spain; heaven grant we will never not be sad at stupidity and greed. To be sorry for those people—no. It is a shameful, strutting impudence to be sorry for the noble. But there is no shame to honorable anger, the anger that comes and stays against those who saw and would not aid, those who looked and shrugged and turned away.

Well. I have stood too long between you and this book, this record of men and women who did not turn away, who looked and felt and acted. But before I go, I want to give over my words to better ones; to those of as fine a writer as lives.

They are from a letter to as brave a man as lives, Dr. Edward K. Barsky. Dr. Barsky was in Spain, healing and fighting. And ever since the war there ended—that curious word "ended"—he had gone on working for the anti-fascists. He had seen to it that Loyalist refugees have got to Mexico and to Africa, to get another starte at living; he had seen to it that those hundreds of thousands of them still left in France behind barbed wire had food and shoes and medicines.

For these works, he was pronounced subversive. By a process of reasoning too convoluted for the humble layman to trace, it was decided that his labor of saving fine, valuable human lives was evidence of some desire of his to destroy the Constitution of the United States and so he has served a term in prison. This letter to him was written by Sean O'Casey:

"I wish every success to your appeal for funds, to help those wounded in the fight against fascism, and to provide means to oppose and defeat any attempt to sanction the fascist spirit, evil spirit, in any effort, office, or activity linked with the life of man. Out of the flame and dust of fascism's fall, a few wriggling things have crept, which, in dark corners, hope to grow again to influence and power. Wherever they show themselves, these new-born fascist wrigglers should soon become the newly-dead. Indeed, it is a shame to think that fascism's foster parent, Franco, should still sit at peace, sunning himself in the orange groves of lovely Spain; the abiding wretch who trained, at Guernica, the apprentice hands of Hitler and Mussolini, and made them proficient in the fuller destruction of Europe. There must be no admission to life of another breeder of what we now know fascism to have been; no other breeder of such an evil while time lasts and men live. . . .

"We must be able to put our arms round our children, when it is time for us to go, and say unto them: Looka, young ones, we hand life over to you better and stronger than when we found it, because we have lived through it thoroughly and well."

Hollywood, California, December, 1951

Editor's Preface

This is a partisan anthology. It proceeds from the conviction that life, decency and progress were on the side of the Spanish Republic; obscenity, retrogression and death, the stigmata of its enemies.

There were few writers and artists of any stature, in any language or medium, who did not find their sympathies and talents engaged in the struggle that went on in Spain from 1936 to 1939—and which still continues. Almost without exception these artists were partisans of the Republic; and almost without exception they found their talents sharpened, broadened, deepened and enriched by their understanding of the significance of that struggle and their emotional identification with it.

As a small but infinitely significant index of this phenomenon, the following facts are adduced: in 1938 the League of American Writers polled its colleagues. The question, put by the League's then president, Donald Ogden Stewart, was: "Are you for, or are you against Franco and fascism? Are you for, or are you against the legal government and the people of Republican Spain?"

Four hundred and eighteen American writers replied. Ninety eight percent favored the Republic and its people; 1.75 percent declared themselves "neutral," and one writer favored fascism. This writer therefore represented twenty-five hundredths of one percent of the total.*

If there are any readers, however, who feel that there *are* two sides to this question and that the fascist viewpoint has a

---

* Cf. *Writers Take Sides*, published by the League of American Writers, New York, 1938.

"right" to be expressed, they are referred to the bibliography. It is alphabetical and it lists the majority of those books published in English on the subject. No effort has been made to separate them into categories: pro- and anti-Loyalist, or "neutral." Let the reader examine as many of these works as he will. Let him compare the words with the fruit those words have borne in actual life. He will find the truth and he will find the lie.

The reader will determine for himself the stature of those writers who supported the Republican cause; the reasons for their allegiance; the heights of felicitous expression they achieved; and, collaterally, why no contribution in this anthology expresses the fascist point of view. Any "literary" expression of the fascist viewpoint—which in Spain inaugurated the first systematic mass murder bombings of civilians and since Spain has caused the deaths of over thirty million human beings in wars, tortures and barbaric atrocities—belongs not to an anthology but to a museum of fascist horrors together with other examples of fascist "art" such as lampshades made of human skin.

The criterion employed in selection for this volume is primarily the writer's adherence to the cause of the Spanish people. The selections have been made from works written or translated into English; works not readily accessible to the reader; works directly contingent on important aspects of the Spanish struggle; works—whether poetry, fiction, drama, essay or reportage—of as high a literary or human quality as it was possible to find.

The reader will find many omissions for reasons of limitations of space. These are regrettable since there is sufficient material to compile an anthology of several volumes. But aside from space limitations there are some well known works which are not represented here. We would particularly like to explain to the reader our reasons for the omission of work by Ernest Hemingway. It was felt that Hemingway's talent and the personal support he rendered to many phases of the Loyalist cause were shockingly betrayed in his work "For Whom The Bell Tolls" in which the Spanish people were cruelly misrepresented and leaders of the International Brigade maliciously slandered. The novel in its total impact presented an unforgivable distortion of the meaning of the struggle in Spain. Under the name and prestige of Hemingway, important aid was thus given to humanity's worst enemies.

There are some writers who supported the cause of the Spanish people when it was fashionable and not entirely unprofitable to be outspokenly anti-fascist. Many of them today are fearful and silent. But the proudest single fact about our contributors is that the large majority of them are still as fiercely passionate in their writing and public activities in behalf of social progress, democracy and peace, as they were during the struggle in Spain.

Something more remains to be said. The crucial weapon that defeated Spain was the Hitlerian lie that Spain was a struggle between Christianity and Communism. The contents of this anthology will demonstrate what was actually the truth. But Spain *was* lost because of this lie, just as the German republic was destroyed by it, Italian freedom was strangled by it and American democracy and world peace itself are jeopardized by it today. The "Red Menace" is still the strongest weapon in the fascist arsenal.

It is true, however, that a great many members of the International Brigades were Communists. It is also true that the Spanish Communist Party increased its membership during the war, from perhaps twenty thousand to five hundred thousand.

It could never have achieved such prestige had not the people of Spain observed the obvious fact that the Spanish Communists were truly united with their fellow citizens in the struggle for common democratic ideals—just as Communists throughout all Europe provided the backbone and much of the leadership for the resistance movement in every nation occupied by the Nazis.

The unity which existed in Spain between Communists and non-Communists, and the international character of the Brigades, foreshadowed the greater unity achieved in World War II. Here again we found Communists and non-Communists united on a world-wide scale in defense of democracy.

VII

The lessons of this unity and what it can achieve have not been lost on the majority of the people of the world, much as our American reactionaries—and fascists everywhere—would like to obscure the reasons for it and distort its motivation and objectives.

It is therefore important at this time, when the ideals of human progress, decency and even peace are under official attack as "Red," "subversive," and even "treasonable," to present such a volume as this; a volume that was designed to gather in one place exalted expressions of a great human struggle which, as Albert Einstein evaluated it, is "the only thing . . . that can keep the hope of better times alive within us . . . the heroic struggle of the Spanish people for freedom and human dignity."

For the presentation of this book which, it is hoped, will be a further weapon in that continuing struggle, the editor wishes to acknowledge the cooperation of the many authors represented, as well as that of their publishers.

Appreciation is also expressed for the active collaboration of Irving Fajans; to the Executive Board of the Veterans of the Abraham Lincoln Brigade and Moe Fishman, its Executive Secretary; to my wife, Helen Clare Nelson and to Harold Smith, for invaluable editorial assistance and sound critical advice; and to Jessie Rella, who spent innumerable hours in research and in preparation of the manuscript.

ALVAH BESSIE

San Francisco, California
December 15, 1951

prelude to treason

"When Ferdinand III captured Seville and died, being a saint he escaped purgatory, and Santiago presented him to the Virgin, who forthwith desired him to ask any favours for beloved Spain. The monarch petitioned for oil, wine and corn—conceded; for sunny skies, brave men, and pretty women—allowed; for cigars, relics, garlic, and bulls—by all means; for a good government—'Nay, nay,' said the Virgin, 'that never can be granted; for were it bestowed, not an angel would remain a day longer in heaven.'"

RICHARD FORD:
Gatherings From Spain, 1846

In Spain the army is a caste, a social class similar to the military caste of the Kings of Prussia in the eighteenth century. The Spanish Army is not national, it is a Praetorian Guard.

BLASCO IBANEZ

It is no accident that the Apostles of Christ were workers and not generals like Mola.

JOSE BERGAMIN

Franco and his people have no other ideal than their God and Fatherland.

CARDINAL GOMA Y TOMAS,
Primate of Spain

Aide-Memoir

W E, THE UNDERSIGNED, Lt. Gen. Emilio Barrera, in his personal capacity; Don Rafael Olazábal and Señor Lizarra, on behalf of the 'Comunión Tradicionalista,' and Don Antonio Goicoechea, as leader of the Party of 'Renovacion Española,' have drawn up this document so that there may remain on record what happened in the interview which they had at four o'clock this afternoon, March 31, 1934, with the head of the Italian Government, Signor Mussolini, together with Marshal Italo Balbo. The President, after carefully informing himself from the answers, which each of those present gave to his questions, of the present situation of Spanish politics, and the aspirations and state of the Army and Navy and the monarchist parties, declared the following to those there assembled:—

1. That he was ready to help with the necessary measures of assistance the two parties in opposition to the regime obtaining in Spain, in the task of overthrowing it and substituting it by a Regency which would prepare the complete restoration of the Monarchy; this declaration was solemnly repeated by Signor Mussolini three times, and those assembled received it with the natural manifestations of esteem and gratitude;
2. That as a practical demonstration and as a proof of his intentions he was ready to supply them immediately with 20,000 rifles; 20,000 hand grenades; 200 machine-guns; and 1,500,000 pesetas in cash;
3. That such help was merely of an initial nature and would be opportunely completed with greater measures, accordingly as the work achieved justified this and circumstances made it necessary.

3

Those present agreed that for the handing over of the sum previously referred to, a delegate of the parties should be chosen, Señor Don Rafael Olazábal, and he should take charge of these funds and place them in Spain at the joint disposal of the two leaders, Conde de Rodezno and Antonio Goicoechea, for its distribution (here there is a word which is illegible) between the two, in the form and at the time and in the conditions on which they may decide.

In the same way it was agreed that with regard to the distribution of the first quantity of arms, the leaders in question should have what was necessary for the part proportional to the charge undertaken by each group and also for its transport to Spain. Rome, March 31, 1934.

(Signed) Emilio Barrera
Rafael Olazabal
Lizarra
Antonio Goicoechea

From Searchlight on Spain,
by the Duchess of Atholl,
London, Penguin, 1938

Remembering Spain

LOUIS MacNEICE

And I remember Spain
    At Easter ripe as an egg for revolt and ruin,
Though for a tripper the rain
    Was worse than the surly or the worried or the haunted faces.

With writings on the walls—
    Hammer and Sickle, *Boicot: Viva: Muera;*
With café-au-lait brimming the waterfalls;
    With sherry, shell-fish, omelettes.
With fretwork that the Moor
    Had chiselled for effects of sun and shadow;
With shadows of the poor,
    The begging cripples and the children begging.
The churches full of saints
    Tortured on racks of marble—
The old complaints
    Covered with gilt and dimly lit with candles.
With powerful or banal
    Monuments of riches and repression,
And the Escorial
    Cold for ever within like the heart of Philip.
With ranks of dominoes
    Deployed on café tables the whole of Sunday;
With cabarets that call the tourist, shows
    Of thighs and eyes and nipples.
With slovenly soldiers, nuns,
    And peeling posters from the last elections
Promising bread or guns
    Or an amnesty or another
Order, or else the old

Glory veneered and varnished
As if veneer could hold
The rotten guts and crumbled bones together.
And a vulture hung in air
Below the cliffs of Ronda and below him
His hook-winged shadow wavered like despair
Across the chequered vineyards.
And the bootblacks in Madrid
Kept us half an hour with polish and pincers,
And all we did
In that city was drink and think and loiter.
And in the Prado half-
wit princes looked from the canvas they had paid for;
And Goya had the laugh—
But can what is corrupt be cured by laughter?
And the day at Aranjuez
When the sun came out for once on the yellow river,
With Valdepeñas burdening the breath
We slept a royal sleep in the royal gardens.
And at Toledo walked
Around the ramparts where they threw the garbage
And glibly talked
Of how the Spaniards lack all sense of business.
And Avila was cold
And Segovia was picturesque and smelly
And a goat on the road seemed old
As the rocks or the Roman arches.
And Easter was wet and full
In Seville, and in the ring on Easter Sunday
A clumsy bull and then a clumsy bull
Nodding his banderillas died of boredom.
And the standard of living was low
But that, we thought to ourselves, was not our business;
All that the tripper wants is the *status quo*
That hands a pass to trippers.
And we thought the papers a lark

6

With their party politics and blank invective
And we thought the dark
    Women who dyed their hair should have it dyed more often.
And we sat in trains all night
    With the windows shut among civil guards and peasants
And tried to play piquet by a tiny light
    And tried to sleep bolt upright,
And cursed the Spanish rain
    And cursed their cigarettes which came to pieces,
And caught heavy colds in Cordova, and in vain
    Waited for the light to be right for taking photos.
And we met a Cambridge don who said with an air
    "There's going to be trouble shortly in this country,"
And ordered anis, pudgy and debonair,
    Glad to show off his mastery of the language.
But only an inch behind
    This map of olive and ilex, this painted hoarding,
Careless of visitors the people's mind
    Was tunnelling like a mole to day and danger.
And the day before we left
    We saw the mob in flower at Algeciras
Outside a church bereft
    Of its images and its aura;
And at La Linea while
    The night put miles between us and Gibraltar
We heard the blood lust of a drunkard pile
    His heaven high with curses;
And next day took the boat
    For home, forgetting Spain, not realizing
That Spain would soon denote
    Our grief, our aspirations;
Not knowing that our blunt
    Ideals would find their whetstone, that our spirit
Would find its frontier on the Spanish front,
    Its body in a rag-time army.

From POEMS FOR SPAIN, *Hogarth Press, London, 1939*

The Wonderful White Paper

RUTH DOMINO

A<small>T THE EDGE</small> of the province of La Mancha, on one of the huge sandy plains somewhat withdrawn from the great highways leading to Madrid, stood a little village called Cueva. On the horizon before and behind it rose bald mountains of reddish stone which, toward evening when the sun went down, shone in lilac hues.

The village was exactly like every other poor village in the land. The houses were small and white with flat roofs; and in summer when the heat seemed inescapable, they had sackcloth curtains instead of doors. The biggest space in every house was the courtyard which, enclosed by the henhouses and goatsheds and living quarters, was like a room surrounded by four walls. This courtyard had the same trampled clay floor as that in the living quarters. The peasants, too, were exactly like those in the other villages. They wore black shirts which hung over their trousers. In summer they wore large broadbrimmed straw hats, and the whole year round canvas sandals with matted soles and a cloth around their neck.

The women had black dresses and black headcloths. It was as if they went constantly in mourning in their white houses because hundreds of years since the water had dried from their fields together with the trees in the woods. On the other side of the village was a small river whose bed was usually dried up in summer, exposing gray rocks like weather-beaten tombstones.

The priests had told the people that the dearth of water came from their sins. So they bore the heat, the drought, the flies and their poverty as the curse of God, and thought no more about it; they sinned and brought children into the world who, as long as they were tiny, crept about naked on the court-yard clay.

The peasants had dark brown faces, the older ones with many wrinkles and deeply wrought furrows. Their skin hung like supple leather, though not like tired flesh, about their joints. And in that, too, they were exactly like poor peasants the world over whose fat poured from their bodies, together with their sweat, as they bent over the earth. And finally—like peasants everywhere—they had a passion: they sang. They sang after their work when they sat by the side of the road; the women sang in the evenings in their tiny rooms, and the young girls on Sundays when they tied a colored ribbon in their hair. Their songs were called *flamencos*. They were wild monotonous melodies that suddenly soared and swelled out of their throats. The heads of the singers lifted high as if about to fly from their necks. Then the voices would subside again. The more suddenly and fiercely the song mounted, the more highly esteemed was the singer's art. On Sundays the people of the village would sit about such a leader and as he sang shrill and loud, they would clap hands and cry, "*Olé, olé, olé!*"

The words of the songs were very simple, generally only one short sentence, "The landlord is powerful, he does with us what he pleases." Or, "The earth is dry and quivers like a fish on dry land." And the young girls sang that they were so poor the sun and the moon belonged to them, but nothing on earth; there was no man who would look upon them.

Only one thing was more remote from these peasants' imagination than a moist earth with constantly flowing streams: that was a land without colors, in which the sky did not appear blue and the earth was neither red nor violet. Faced with such a prospect they would certainly have replied that the people who lived there must be much poorer even than themselves.

Though the rich gentlemen still sat in their castles, the King had already been turned out of the country. Gradually teachers went into the districts to instruct the children; and to Cueva there came a young man, Fernando.

Before this when the monastery was still occupied, a few children had gone there to study, but they were the exception. Fernando brought with him maps that were very colorful. The children realized with astonishment that the land on the maps was only a plain without mountains. Moreover the mountains were shown in folds, brown like the earth; the rivers were as blue as the heavens and as sinuous as a goat's limb; the cities were thick black points like goat turds and the villages little black points like flyspecks.

The children learned that on the map their village lay directly to the right of the capital of Madrid, that the land near Valencia looked so green because it was a valley with abundant water and many green plants and that behind it, like unending and multitudinous rivers, was the sea. And the teacher taught those who already knew a few letters that the various curves and lines in the letters of the alphabet imitated objects in nature; and that when, for example, they placed a large O on its back or stomach, it resembled the shape of a lemon, only without the little nose. And he taught those who knew no letters that, conversely, lines and curves could be joined together to form letters. He distributed colored crayons, water colors and paint brushes to the children.

For their first lesson they all drew a lemon which the teacher had laid on his desk as a model.

Suddenly a titter swept over the class. The teacher, who was reading a book, looked up in surprise. Then the children held their painted lemons high and waved them like yellow drapes toward the desk. Fernando laughed too. There was not a child in the class who was bored.

After a few drawing and painting lessons the teacher divided his class. He asked his most diligent pupils to set down on paper objects out of their own imagination. He told them also that in the evening their older brothers and sisters, if they had time, could come to school. A few of the children tried to portray Bible stories in pictures, others attempted to make maps.

At home the mothers clad in black made the sign of the cross when they saw the paintings. To be sure, they had learned how to embroider in their youth but they had not drawn objects from nature. They had made patterns which had no meaning, or which depicted the cross of Christ and the loose swaddling-clothes of a Christ child on his Mother's lap. The fathers, for their part, gazed long at the maps. The children explained that the blue lines represented flowing water and that where there was much water everything was green, and that near Valencia there were three crops in the year.

To reproduce mountains, rivers and fruits on a small white piece of paper so that one could recognize and find meaning in colors and spaces as easily as in words, even if one could not read or write, that fascinated everyone. But then began what the priests and the authorities later called "the plague."

In the houses where there were boys, a colored map soon hung next to the oil painting of the Virgin Mother and the calendar of the Saints. Water-color paintings of biblical events were pasted over the sleeping-places of the girls. And where there were both boys and girls, colored drawings were grouped both to the right and the left of the Virgin.

Little Juanita wanted to show the rain of manna in the wilderness. But since she was unfamiliar with manna and tomatoes seemed to her good, tasty food, a gift of God worthy of the unfortunate Jews, she let tomatoes rain down from heaven. So her paper was filled with many beautiful, red tomato plants. Nine-year-old Angelita had a weakness for matches so she made an angel walk from star to star, at the coming of night, with a burning match in order to light the star spots which by day were colorless.

Not far from the village lay the landlord's house. The peasants had to bring payments to him for the arid little fields they rented from him. The tribute consisted of vegetables, eggs and a little wine. But the vineyards bore badly in the years of drought and exacted much toil. The landlord's house stood on the same broad expanse as the village; white rectangular, it faced the high red mountains. It had an outer courtyard and an inner courtyard around which the living quarters were grouped. At each of its corners was a spire. The peasants knew only the outer courtyard where the bailiff stripped them of their food payments. But once little Pedro, peering from behind his father's black shirt, had glimpsed the inner court. There in the center stood a well with magnificently embossed iron troughs. A stream of water jetted forth and fairly flooded the surrounding flower beds. It struck him as the height of earthly splendor: water which was not laboriously drawn by bending over a thousand times, water which did not have to be stolen from the sparse rains, water which poured lavishly forth and yet was neither river nor rain!

When the teacher placed colored crayons at Pedro's desk, he chose a blue one. Then he drew a white, wavy rectangle with pointed spires at the corners. And in the middle he drew a blue stream gushing high and away over the walls and over the brown fields, right into the middle of the village. At home he laid the sheet of paper on the table. His mother wrung her hands; his father took the picture in his hands and murmured in his black beard, "Is this not the landlord's castle?" His wife asked, "What are you saying, husband?" But Pedro's father fell silent again, so the matter was left as if unspoken.

And therewith, the priests and authorities later said, sin came to the village because of the plague of the drawings.

In the evening before the sun had completely set, the father said to Pedro, "Give me a piece of paper and the drawing pencil!" And he sat himself in the yard, not by the edge of the road as was his custom, and drew his house and the blue stream of water which he let fall on his field behind the house.

That night it rained mightily, and the pails that had been set out were filled to the brim with water. The next morning the leaves were crisp and green.

"The Holy Virgin is pleased with the picture," said little Pedro's mother. Word spread throughout the village. "The Holy Virgin grants us water and painting to the children," the people said. Pedro's father did not listen to the women's prattle;

12

and before the sun went down he again sat in his courtyard and painted a garden to his house, and colored his field green, red and blue. The blue came from the water of a little river which he depicted leading through canals and then flowed richly through all his fields. He painted the red of tomatoes and the green of the vine and the onion plant. The next day he sat down again and added a few more hills covered with vineyards, to which a little path led from his house.

The news of the painting by Pedro's father did not remain secret, and the neighbors with whom he used to sit before the house now came and watched over his shoulder. They liked the joyous colors of the garden and especially the water in it; and since their children also had crayons at home, one after the other began to sketch and paint his house with a big garden beside it and much water—in short, everything which did not in reality exist. And since they did not have much water, they copied from the stream which Pedro had sketched in his painting of the landlord's house. They made their little fields and gardens abundant in water and added vineyards which rose higher and higher, almost as high as the red mountains but in green. They extended their painted fields so much that they soon came close to the landlord's house. And now instead of singing *flamencos,* the peasants sat on Sundays before their houses and painted. Even those who could not write thus gave expression in paint to their desires on this earth. Fernando the teacher, who sometimes strolled in the evening through the village streets, would correct here and there an uneven line by one of the artists. He also showed them how to use water colors.

Then one evening a peasant said, "Yes, we're really painting our fields too big; the land no longer belongs to us."

Pedro's older brother sketched a white rectangle with spires and made it quite small next to the many-colored fields and blue canals. But no one yet said aloud to whom the great fields really belonged and what kind of a house that white rectangle with the ornamental spires was.

It seized them like a wild wind from the fields. Almost

everyone painted; and if it was not a father, then it was his sons and small daughters who painted the white rectangle with spires as well as they could. Some painted the Egyptian plagues, and huge grasshoppers rained down over the little white rectangle with spires. The rectangle remained unchanged, as little Pedro had first drawn it. Some painted the Flood like a mighty blue pinion which started in one corner of the paper and moved down to the other where stood a small white rectangle with spires, tottering and wavelike. And there was a second picture, "After the Flood," in which green plots of ground with houses and fruit orchards rose up; one who could also write drew an inscription on the green plot of land, "Fields of the peasants of Cueva, the village is swimming far behind."

After two months the supply of drawing crayons and paper was exhausted, so the teacher went into the city to get new materials. The proprietor of the stationery store told Fernando that he did not have so many supplies in stock and asked him what he was doing with so much paper and so many crayons. Fernando replied that he was only the teacher of the village of Cueva and that his pupils and several of the peasants were now actively painting.

"And what do they paint all the time?"

"They paint water, always water, so much water that it almost drowns out the landlord's house," smiled Fernando.

But the merchant did not smile. He remarked that that was very serious, but Fernando did not agree with him.

In the evening at the tavern the tradesman told the mayor and the doctor of the town, and they all shook their heads. They had never bothered with the village of Cueva because none of the peasants there had ever brought them any money. But now times were uncertain in the country, they said, and even churches and monasteries had been burned. The monks had long since been driven from the district of Cueva and undoubtedly the peasants no longer went to church, and now this young and worldly teacher—the authorities should really begin to pay attention to the village now that insubordination was so rife among the people. On Sunday they even voiced their opinions to the priest.

And that Sunday the peasants of Cueva sat before their houses and Pedro's older brother sang a *flamenco* with a new text. He sang, "Oh wonderful white paper, you are getting fruits and fields! Oh wonderful little white paper, the water flows blue on you and the vineyards grow. Little white paper, you will be bigger than the house with the spires facing the red mountains!"

The peasants were silent a moment after the song had ended, then they cried loudly, "*Olè, olè, olè!*" They clapped their hands and sang, "Little white paper, oh wonderful white paper."

The following week a priest visited the schoolhouse and inspected the children's paintings on the walls. He wrung his hands and hastened back to the city.

The next Sunday there came four men of the *Guardia Civil*. It was about noon. They had revolvers and swords in their belts. They strode through the village streets until they came to the schoolhouse which was closed. They knocked. The young teacher looked out of the window. What did they want? Just let him open the door, he'd see soon enough! He opened the schoolroom. The many pictures of the children and grown-ups hung roundabout on large thick nails.

"Who has painted these pictures?"

"The children," answered the teacher.

Didn't he know that the pictures were subversive? And they placed handcuffs on him. Two of them began to tear the pictures down from the walls. The children came running to the schoolhouse. They pressed themselves against the classroom door. Suddenly little Pedro sprang forward and cried, "Leave our pictures alone!" And he grasped the gendarme by the arm to stop him. When the man tried to shake him off, Pedro bit hard into his arm.

"*Now* will you!" the gendarme roared.

A gust of wind blew into the schoolroom and drove the pile of pictures into the street. The children watched with eyes wide open. Now the men of the village stood behind them; they too stood silent, their eyes staring.

15

Meanwhile the soldier had hurled the child from him with a powerful blow. The small body fairly flew across the room and lay on the threshold, stunned by the impact of his fall. His head hung down, his eyes were closed.

"That is my son," said Pedro's father taking a step toward the child.

"And so much the worse for you," shouted the soldier, "for he is the son of a dog!" Provoked by the silence of the children and the men, he kicked the senseless child from the threshold.

At that Pedro's father clenched his fist and held it ready for a blow. But the gendarme drew his saber and made as if to strike the peasant over the head. Perhaps he meant to use only the flat side. Pedro's father tried with his other hand to ward off the up-stretched arm, but the blade turned and fell downward, slashing him right across the face. Blood spurted forth and gushed on his new sandals. He staggered toward his son. The gendarme, still more infuriated, pointed to the red drops in the sand. "There you have colors to paint with!" Then all four of the *Guardia Civil* turned to go, dragging the handcuffed teacher after them. A cry arose from the crowd of peasants. But the four men soon disappeared around a bend of the village street.

Perhaps it was this cry, a long echo, grown audible, of the drops of blood in the sand—all of them suddenly had the oppressive feeling that they had been robbed, and that still more would be stolen from them. So they went swiftly home, and those who had paintings took them from their walls and hid them in the darkest corners of their closets.

Early next morning a party of horsemen drew near the village. A few children, seeing the glint of harnesses in the sun, ran into the fields to tell their fathers. The peasants dropped their implements at once and ran back with their children. The vanguard of the riders had already entered the village. They rode on beautiful white horses that shimmered even more brightly than the little white houses. Then they shouted to the men and women that they must hand over those accursed pictures or else they would soon see what would befall them. And they set about searching the bedding and the few pieces of furniture, smashing them to bits. The men stood silently by but when a soldier found a picture, they would unfold their arms and leap furiously at him.

That lasted about an hour. When the soldiers left the village, they dragged behind them ten peasants in chains.

In the afternoon three dead men lay outstretched on the square before the schoolhouse. Among them was Pedro's father. The blackclad women stood at the foot of the biers staring into the faces of the dead. Then Pedro's mother and another woman stepped forth and loosened something from the stiff hands of the corpses. They were fragments of the torn pictures. They smoothed them with loving care and brought them home. Then they again hid the bits of paper in the darkest corners of their closets.

From STORY MAGAZINE, *March-April,*
New York, 1943

Ballad of the Spanish Civil Guard

FEDERICO GARCIA LORCA

Their horses are black.
Black are their iron shoes.
On their capes shimmer
stains of ink and wax.
They never weep because
their skulls are of lead.
With their patent leather souls
they ride down the road.
Crouched like hunchbacks and dark
wherever they pass
they spread silences of murky rubber
and fear of fine sand.
They go by, if they wish to go,
concealing in their heads
the vague astronomy
of abstract pistols.

Oh, city of the gypsies!
On the corners, banners.
The moon and pumpkins
preserved with gooseberries.
Oh, city of the gypsies!
Who could see you and not remember you?
City of grief and of musk
with towers of cinnamon.
When the night came
that nightly comes nightly,
the gypsies at their forges
forged suns and arrows.

A horse with a mortal wound
knocked at door after door.
Glass roosters crowed
toward Jerez de la Frontera.
The naked wind swirled
round a corner of dismay
in the night-silver night
that nightly comes nightly.

Saint Joseph and the Virgin
lost their castanets
so came looking for the gypsies
to see if they could find them.
The Virgin comes dressed
like a village Mayor's wife
in tinfoil from chocolate candy
and necklaces of almonds.
Saint Joseph swings his arms
under a silken cape.
Behind comes Pedro Domecq
with three sultans of Persia.
The half moon dreams
an ecstasy of cranes.
Banners and torches
invade the roof-tops.
In the looking-glasses sob
dancers without hips.
Water and shadow,
shadow and water
toward Jerez de la Frontera.

Oh, city of the gypsies!
On all the corners, banners.
Put out your green lights
for the Civil Guards are coming.
Oh, city of the gypsies!
Who could see you and not remember you?

Leave her far from the sea
with no combs for her hair.

Two by two, they ride
into the city in fiesta.
A rustle of straw-flowers
invades their cartridge belts.
Two by two they ride,
a shadow-show but doubled.
To them the sky is nothing
but a window full of spurs.

Swept clean of fear, the city
multiplies its doors.
Forty Civil Guards
burst through them like a storm.
The clocks all stopped
and the cognac in the bottles
put on a November mask
to arouse no suspicions.
A flight of screams unending
rose among the weathervanes.
Sabres cut the air
that horses trampled.
Through the dusky streets
gypsy crones fled
with drowsy nags
and crocks full of coins.
Up the steep streets
mounted sinister capes
followed by a fugitive
whirlwind of scissors.
At Bethlehem's manger
the gypsies gather.
Saint Joseph, covered with wounds,
shrouds a young maiden.
All through the night

stubborn guns sound sharply.
The Virgin heals the children
with star-drops of saliva.
But the Civil Guard
advances sowing sparks
that set fire to imagination,
young and naked.
Rosa de los Camborios
sobs on her doorstep,
her two breasts cut away
and put on a platter.
Other girls flee
pursued by their tresses
through the air where black roses
of gun-powder explode.
When all the roof-tops are nothing
but furrows on the earth,
dawn shrugs her shoulders
in a vast profile of stone.

Oh, city of the gypsies!
As the flames draw near
the Civil Guards ride away
through a tunnel of silence.

Oh, city of the gypsies
Who could see you and not remember you?
May they seek you in my forehead,
a game of the sand and the moon.

Translated by LANGSTON HUGHES,
from "GYPSY BALLADS," *Beloit Poetry
Journal, Wisconsin, 1951*

Serenos y alegres,
Valientes y osados,
Cantemos, soldados,
El himno a la lid. ...

HIMNO DE RIEGO

One Small Detail

JULIO ALVAREZ DEL VAYO

B Y MIDNIGHT on the 16th of February 1936 the election results
which were coming in from the provinces were decidedly
in favor of the Popular Front.

The campaign had been a hard one. Many of the best Left-
wing fighters were, for all practical purposes, eliminated from
the struggle, having been in prison or in exile ever since the repression which followed the anti-dictatorial movement of 1934.
Thus the whole weight of the campaign fell on people like ourselves who, more by luck than anything else, had escaped the
reprisals made during that first attempt to turn Spain into a
totalitarian state. . . .

After a period of reaction known as "the two black years"
Spain turned again to a life of freedom with amazing zest. In
their attempt to stamp out the democratic régime in Spain, the
Government of Gil Robles and Lerroux, against whom the Spanish people had rebelled in 1934, had carried out such far-reach-
ing reprisals that even in our own ranks many doubted the
possibility of a rapid revival. Some forty thousand were imprisoned; thousands had had to flee the country. I heard more
than one of our leaders say that the Republic was doomed for
ten or twenty years. But one of the qualities of the Spanish people is their astonishing vitality, and it is this vitality that enables
them to recover from a period of repression in much less time
than might be logically expected.

In the rural districts especially, this popular awakening

was hailed with a most encouraging enthusiasm. The villages of Spain had always been, at every election, a dead weight on the democratic parties. The Spanish peasants, subjected to a régime of exploitation and usury which had no counterpart in any other European country, were faced with two alternatives: to vote for the candidate nominated by the landlord, or to suffer the economic consequences of defying one who not only was owner of their land, but who considered himself, not without reason, the master of their souls.

At this election every tiny village was a flame fanned by the desire for freedom. "We will vote for our own man, even if we have to starve for it": this was the pledge, afterwards so bravely kept, which ended all the election meetings—meetings held against the picturesque moonlit background of the village square, filled at a late hour of the night by crowds eager to listen to the message of freedom.

The struggle between the Popular Front and the combined forces of Spanish reaction could not have been more one-sided. Our first obstacle was the lack of money. It appealed to the subtle Spanish sense of humour when the reactionary press spoke of Russian gold being handed over in large quantities to the Left-wing parties in order to secure a Stalinist victory. "We could do with as much in copper, if only to pay for the posters," the trade-union treasurers would exclaim, their coffers drained dry after eighteen months of giving assistance to the victims of the October reprisals. In the second place, the Government of Señor Portela Valladares, under whose auspices the elections were held—and in Spain the expression *"hacer elecciones"* (literally "to make elections") has always conveyed the idea of engineering results—followed the time-honored tradition of employing the whole machinery of State to prevent the triumph of the popular parties. The difficulties with which the Republican and Socialist candidates had to contend in order to carry on their propaganda were so great, and the manner in which they were treated so arbitrary, that one day just before the elections Señor Azaña, who at that time was marked out for Prime

Minister in the event of a Popular Front victory, suggested, I remember, that it might be preferable to boycott the elections rather than risk the defeat which he considered inevitable if such methods continued.

The Spanish episcopate, with honorable exceptions, marched in the vanguard of the frenzied campaign against the Popular Front. "It is sinful to vote for the Popular Front. A vote for the conservative candidate is a vote for Christ," publicly declared the Bishop of Barcelona; and from their pulpits the clergy, both high and low, consigned to eternal damnation all those who did not do everything humanly and divinely possible to bring about a victory at the polls for the forces of reaction.

The morning after the elections the Popular Front victory was fully confirmed. At noon Señor Largo Caballero and I, as elected members for Madrid, called on the Prime Minister to protest against the first of the Fascist assaults, which had taken place that very day in the streets of Madrid. (Members of the Falangist organization had fired on a demonstration, chiefly composed of women, who were marching to the prison to bring the political prisoners the good news of the election.) Señor Portela Valladares received us with courtesy, and said unhesitatingly: "In you I greet today's victors." A year later, during the war, Señor Portela Valladares, when he attended a meeting of the Cortes in Valencia for the express purpose of proclaiming to the world that the Parliament formed after the elections, over which he had presided, was "truly representative of the nation's will," disclosed that our call on the Prime Minister had not been the most important he had received that day. "At four in the morning on the day after the elections"—I quote Señor Portela Valladares—"I was visited by Señor Gil Robles" (leader of the Right-wing coalition), "who proposed that I should assume dictatorial powers, and who offered me the support of all the groups defeated in the elections. At seven that evening the same suggestion was made to me by General Franco himself."

In these words, spoken by the leader of the Government which conducted the elections of February 1936, lies the key to the military rebellion. They give the lie categorically to the mistaken belief, so widely held outside Spain, that the death of Señor Calvo Sotelo—undoubtedly the strongest leader among the Government's adversaries—on July 13, 1936, was the starting-point and principal cause of the revolt, a revolt whose instigators were naturally at great pains to represent to foreign opinion as a natural and legitimate reaction against the Popular Front "terror." In point of fact, Spanish Fascism, encouraged and supported by Italy since 1934 at the very latest (as witness the interview which took place in Rome between Mussolini, Señor Goicoechea, the Spanish Monarchist leader, and the future rebel General Barrera, in March of that year), was ready to impose itself by force. If it won the elections, it would set up a dictatorship with an appearance of legality on the following day; if it lost, it would rise in revolt against the elected Government. From the first moment of the Popular Front victory a *coup d'état* became the one objective of the Fascist forces defeated in the elections, an objective worthy of their every effort. . . .

In the new Parliament there were 268 Popular Front and 140 Right-wing members (this was slightly changed by the Cuenca and Granada run-offs involving nineteen seats), while the remainder were independents or members of Centre parties. The Republicans dominated the Popular Front majority. The Socialists came next in number, while there were only fifteen Communists out of a total of 473. The Government was presided over by Señor Azaña, and consisted solely of Republicans; nine of the Ministers belonged to Señor Azaña's Left Republican Party and three to the Republican Union, a party led by Señor Martinez Barrio, the Speaker of the House; while a non-political general was War Minister. From the Front bench the Prime Minister constantly employed his well-known eloquence to convince the opposition that the triumph of the Popular Front would not bring with it any persecutions or reprisals. . . .

In itself the Popular Front program could not have been more moderate. We Socialists, who were without question the most efficiently organized and disciplined party in the country, had sacrificed many of our oldest and most important claims to the need for forming a wide democratic front uniting all anti-Fascist elements. In the new political constellation the Communists were too small a group to exert any decisive influence. With the exception of the amnesty for the victims of the "two black years," which had been the outstanding feature of the Popular Front campaign, the other points in the Government program could be summed up as a desire to re-establish the Republic—a most justifiable desire, seeing that it was the Republicans who had been returned to power. This involved respect for the Constitution; reorganization of the legal system in order to ensure its independence; and a continuation of the Agrarian Reform begun in 1931. This Agrarian Reform by no means implied the nationalization of land; on the contrary, it was governed by the principle of indemnifying the proprietors, whose large uncultivated estates, survival of a medieval system of agriculture, not only condemned the peasants to a life of misery, but also hindered the normal development of Spanish economy. . . . The other planks in the Popular Front platform were the protection of small industrialists and traders; a vast plan of public works; and the creation of new schools and educational centres. This last was the first concern of a Republic which had inherited from the old régime a state of affairs in which one third of the population could neither read nor write, and in which the universities and other centres of learning had to struggle with the deficiencies of an antiquated and entirely inadequate educational system. For the rest, the Popular Front program embodied the program of the Republic when it first came into being except for the plank on collectivization of large estates originally sponsored by the Socialists. This plank was rejected by the Popular Front, with the acquiescence of the Socialists, although to do so cost them many votes. Any other liberal party in Europe would have been amazed that such a program of State reform should have been necessary in the third decade of the twentieth century. It was a program which offered every guarantee that the inevitable changes in the political and social spheres would take place without endangering the existence of the Spanish bourgeoisie.

The more intelligent members of the bourgeoisie realized this. "The elections which have just taken place in Spain," said *La Vanguardia*, the most moderate of the important Barcelona newspapers, on February 18, 1936, "have two main characteristics: they are a conclusive manifestation of the popular conscience, and they have taken place in conditions of perfect discipline and normality. Faced with a phenomenon of this type, there is nothing to do but yield democratically. National sovereignty resides with the people. The Spanish people have said what they want. They have said it clearly and with extraordinary calm. The only reply which can be made to them is this: 'Let your will be done.'" *El Debate*, however, saw things in a very different light. "The issue," commented the organ of the Clerical-Fascist alliance, "was one of revolution against law and order, with Socialism as the real enemy."

Unfortunately the latter point of view predominated. Instead of respecting the will of the country, Spanish Fascism prepared to obtain by force what it had been refused by popular vote. It was during the debate on the Ministry of Agriculture's bill providing for restitution to the municipalities of their ancient common lands that Señor Calvo Sotelo revealed, with impressive frankness, the die-hard position of the defeated Right wing. "The only hope for agriculture," said Señor Calvo Sotelo, "is not in this Parliament or any other that could be elected, nor in this or any other Popular Front Government, nor in any political party; it lies in the Corporate State. Only by the Fascist revolution can the middle classes defend themselves against proletarianization."

In this way Parliament was used by Señor Calvo Sotelo and his friends merely as an agitator's platform. The debates in the House became more and more heated. Those who had been defeated in the elections talked as though they had been victorious, as though they had the whole country behind them. Responsible for a state of increasing disturbance, they yet held themselves up as the only sponsors of law and order. On May 6 Señor Casares Quiroga, Minister of the Interior, was cheered by his supporters when he counter-attacked Calvo Sotelo. (The latter had replaced Gil Robles, who was considered by the Right wing to be too greatly contaminated with parliamentarism and too mild in his attacks as leader of the opposition.) "Disarm?" exclaimed the Minister; "*we* are disarming; we have rounded up thirteen thousand firearms in Granada, seven thousand in Jaen. But these belonged to the Right. It is the Phalangist gunmen in the motor-cars, and not the workingmen, who are causing the bloodshed."

The Right wing were not daunted by this partial confiscation of the war material which they had carefully accumulated against an electoral defeat. They relied on the army generals and pinned all their hopes on a military rising. From Berlin and Rome came messages of encouragement, together with good news of the reception given to the various emissaries sent to solicit support from the two great Fascist powers when the signal for attack should be given. Ever since February 4, before the elections, when General Sanjurjo, and José Antonio Primo de Rivera, the Phalangist leader, under the pretext of an innocent winter-sports visit to Partenkirchen, arrived at the Kaiserhof, Berlin (a hotel reserved for guests of the German Government), the bonds between National Socialism and Spanish Fascism had been sealed. . . .

The idea of a *coup d'état* was not a hasty improvisation or conceived in a sudden fit of rage. In 1935 the violent departure of Gil Robles from the War Ministry had upset a vast and elaborate plan for imposing Fascism from above. A meeting held at the time in the house of General Fanjul, who a year later led the Madrid insurrection from the Montaña Barracks, had to be adjourned because of the unexpected speed with which the Cabinet crisis arose and was overcome. But Señor Gil Robles had lost no time at the War Office. All the generals on whom the honor of the 1936 rebellion was to fall were given key positions in the army. General Franco was appointed Chief of Staff, General

Goded, Director of Military Aviation, and General Fanjul, Under-Secretary for War. General Mola was given command of the army in Morocco. When on one occasion even the lukewarm and condescending President Alcalá Zamora referred to this preference for generals well known for their anti-Republican sentiments, Señor Gil Robles answered that he had chosen the most capable ones. . . .

An army does not serve its purpose, however, merely by maintaining a fine group of generals. It must be well trained, and as the enemy against which Señor Gil Robles was preparing his military machine was the Spanish people themselves, the chief objective of the maneuvers which took place during his period of office as War Minister was to familiarize the men with the territory where the rebels might expect to encounter the greatest resistance. Thus in the summer of 1935 General Aranda, Military Commander of Asturias, had the honor of being warmly congratulated by the War Minister and by General Franco, Chief of Staff, when these gentlemen attended the maneuvers which he had organized in that region. It was here that the Asturian miners had, in the previous October, given proof of so much bravery and strategic ability that Franco was forced to bring over from Africa sufficient Moroccan soldiers to carry out a campaign of extermination. The northern maneuvers, like those which took place in the same year in the Guadarrama Mountains, when the problem of an attack on Madrid was studied in all its aspects, formed part of a plan which had for some time been maturing in the minds of the Spanish Fascist leaders and which took concrete form after their defeat at the elections.

Towards the end of February the Popular Front Government appointed General Franco Military Governor of the Canary Islands. If the Government had no desire to keep him in Madrid, where they considered his presence unduly disturbing, at the same time they could not bring themselves to dispense with his services. Before leaving, General Franco, General Mola, and other military chiefs met in the house of Señor Delgado, a member of Parliament, and agreed upon the general plan of at-

29

tack. Franco did not leave Madrid without attempting to intimidate the Government, in visits which he made to Señor Alcalá Zamora, the President of the Republic, and to the Prime Minister, Señor Azaña. He represented Spain as about to fall a victim to the worst extremist excesses, and hinted that if his prophecies came true, he could render greater service to his country by remaining in the Peninsula than by going to such a distant post as the Canary Islands. President Alcalá Zamora, to whom he complained of the lack of army equipment and of the difficulties which would be encountered through lack of supplies in the event of a Bolshevik rising, consoled him by recalling how the Asturian movement of 1934 was easily suppressed, thanks chiefly to the valuable co-operation of General Franco himself. After all, he said, the Canaries are not so far away, and one can soon get back in an airplane. Prime Minister Azaña, on his part, replied, with his usual confidence, that he had no fear of a rising on either side. He knew about the Sanjurjo rebellion in the summer of 1932 long before it took place. He could have prevented it, but he preferred to let it take its course in order that it should end, as it did, in disaster and so bring ridicule on its leaders. Franco profited by this lesson and took the necessary precautions to ensure that his projected rebellion should not give Señor Azaña the slightest pretext for indulging his caustic irony at the expense of the army generals. In the meantime the fiction of a rising of Left-wing radicals (whom Franco was the first to make fun of among his friends) supplied an excellent red herring to draw across the trail.

The U. M. E. (*Unión Militar Española*, Spanish Military Union) now came into action. This was a military organization on trade-union lines, whose members were army officers inclined to conspiracy, and a continuation of the former "Defense Councils," whose activities during the monarchy, and more especially in the reign of Don Alfonso, had constantly endangered the existence of any government tinged with the slightest shade of liberalism. The officers discharged from the army after General Sanjurjo's abortive rising in 1932, or given posts with which they were dissatisfied, found their natural allies in the ten thousand officers who in the first years of the Republic had been pensioned off on full pay by the Government. The reason for this retirement scheme was to put an end to a completely anomalous situation in which there was one general for every one hundred and fifty soldiers, and to a state of affairs in which the army consumed in peace-time thirty per cent of the national budget. Unfortunately the majority of the officers who profited by that unprecedentedly generous pension scheme were enemies of the Republic and took advantage of a privileged position, in which they were paid for doing nothing, to use their leisure to plot against the Government. . . .

A Council of Generals was formed to lead the movement. It was originally composed of General Rodriguez Barrio, Inspector-General of the Army; General Franco, Military Commander of the Canary Islands; General Saliquet, who held no active command at the time; and General Goded, Military Commander of the Balearic Islands. The need for a central command, however, was responsible for General Mola's being entrusted with the main organization of the rebellion. While on May 29 General Sanjurjo, by reason of the part he had played as leader of the first revolt against the Republic, was given the principal role and formally appointed leader of the movement, it was in reality General Mola (undoubtedly the most intelligent of them all) who acted as head of the conspiracy in the Peninsula as soon as Franco had left to take up his new post in the Canary Islands.

From the very first day of his arrival in Pamplona, where he had just been appointed Military Commander—so writes his biographer and secretary, Iribarren—General Mola began his work of organizing the insurrection. The local papers, all extremely reactionary, obeyed instructions and mentioned him as little as possible. His appointment as Military Commander was given two lines tucked away in the society columns. . . . A few weeks after his arrival in Pamplona he held all the threads of conspiracy in his hands. Through Lieutenant-Colonel Seguí he was in permanent contact with the African garrisons (where the year before he had taken advantage of his position to work upon the Moroccan army); he was in touch with the Phalangist organization through the intermediary of an officer who had easy and regular access to the Alicante Prison (where José Antonio Primo de Rivera was in a better position to send orders to his followers than if he had been at liberty); and he was certain, when the time was ripe, of being able to rely on the Carlists, the most influential group in that region, without having to keep them informed of his plans long beforehand. . . .

The future insurgent generals had an unquestionable talent for dissimulation and deceived the War Minister most deplorably. For them their word was by no means their bond. Because he trusted General Mola's word of honor, General Batet, his immediate superior, was shot by the rebels a few hours after the outbreak of the rebellion. On July 16 General Batet had an interview with Mola, who swore to him that neither he nor the army would consider for one single moment breaking their oath of loyalty to the Constitutional Government. "On your word of honour?" asked General Batet. "On my word of honour," replied Mola. Forty-eight hours later Mola rose against the Government, imprisoned Batet, and gave orders for his execution. Franco acted in the same way. But the man who really surpassed all others in the art of tricking the War Minister was the Military Commander of Saragossa, General Cabanellas. As late as July 19, when Saragossa was in open rebellion against the Government, he replied to the official summons from Madrid with the most fervent protestations of loyalty and the assurance that everything in the city was as calm as a mill-pond.

We ourselves were naturally more sceptical regarding the word of honour of the generals. As Member of Parliament for Madrid, and Vice-President of the local Committee of the Socialist Party, I headed workers' delegations to Señor Azaña, the Prime Minister, on various occasions, to express our great concern at the underhand work of the army leaders. Señor Azaña would smile benevolently. Our tendency to believe these tales of banditry seemed to him a trifle childish. We were not, how-

ever, discouraged by this from sending the Government all available information concerning the growing activity of the enemies of the Republic.

Concurrently with this organization of revolt, the forces defeated at the elections were applying the same terrorist methods as those used by the Nazis in the summer of 1932 on the
eve of Hitler's seizure of power in Germany, with the object—
in Dr. Goebbels' own words—of creating an atmosphere of continual insecurity and of waging a "war of nerves" against the
authorities. On March 11 some Phalangist students made an
attempt on the life of Señor Jiménez de Asúa, Deputy Speaker
of the Parliament and Professor of Criminal Law at Madrid University. On the 15th of the same month an attempt was made to
murder Señor Largo Caballero. On the eve of April 14, the anniversary of the Republic, Don Manuel Pedregal, the magistrate
who had presided at the trial of the would-be assassins of Professor Jiménez de Asúa, was killed by the Fascists.

The policy of creating a permanent atmosphere of uneasiness was furthered by certain industrialists of Fascist sympathies,
who declared a series of lockouts in order to force the workmen
to counter with the strike weapon. There are people, even in the
Socialist Party, who since the war have endeavored to draw from
the Spanish struggle the moral that it is dangerous to press
working-class demands too far, and who attribute the rebellion
to the large number of strikes which took place in Spain in the
months following the general election. Documents found in the
Phalangist headquarters after the revolt failed in Madrid prove
that in point of fact some of the strikes at that time were the
work of *agents provocateurs* in the trade unions. Not that I
deny that some of these strikes—such as that of the builders—
went on too long, against the advice of those leaders with the
greatest experience and political acumen. I well remember the
efforts made by the Socialist Committee of Madrid and myself
to dissuade the C.N.T. (*Confederación Nacional de Trabajo,* National Confederation of Workers)—a trade-union organization
with Anarchist tendencies—from declaring a general strike after

the scandalous Phalangist attack of April 16. . . .

In actual fact, because the Spanish people, with their fine political intuition, were aware of the impending danger, they gave proof, in the months between the elections and the insurrection, of splendid discipline and common sense. Only on one occasion was there any intense popular excitement, and that was when an amnesty was demanded on the two days following the elections. Impatient crowds attacked the prisons to set free the October prisoners, many of whom had been kept for eighteen months without trial, and whose immediate release was one of the principal planks of the Popular Front platform. But not even in those impassioned days of February was there any serious incident. Señor Azaña's Government, before the wave of popular agitation for the release of these thirty thousand political prisoners, very wisely issued an emergency decree, in accordance with the Constitution, which, with a single signature, cut through all the bureaucratic red tape. Apart from this, complete order was maintained, in spite of the fact that those men who had been provincial governors up to the elections abandoned their posts after the great Popular Front victory without waiting for successors to be appointed.

With the exception of this spontaneous and natural mobilization of the masses to demand an amnesty, nothing happened until the month of July to justify the accusations of anarchy and chaos levelled against the Government by the Fascist conspirators, the better to cloak their own subversive activities. What did happen was, in fact, largely a concomitant of the preparations for the rebellion which were going on actively from the week following the elections. *Agents provocateurs* abounded. After the rebellion many of them were to boast of their exploits in the spring months in sowing the disorder which the leaders of the rebellion regarded as an essential part of their preparations. . . . But the violence of these months has been greatly exaggerated and repeatedly men like Gil Robles and Calvo Sotelo, engaged in actively preparing the rebellion, stood up in Parliament and read inflated lists of church burnings and other supposed outbreaks as a part of their revolutionary propaganda. An event of such political importance as the impeachment of the President of the Republic, Señor Alcalá Zamora, for having violated the Constitution took place without the slightest disturbance. On May 1, a day on which the temperature of a country can easily be gauged, all the foreign correspondents in Spain reported "perfect order."

Neither could the Right-wing extremists at that time bring any allegations of diabolic influence against the Soviet Embassy, for there was no Soviet ambassador in Spain, nor had there ever been one since the Russian Revolution. When the rebellion broke out, Republican Spain was maintaining normal diplomatic relations with every country except the U.S.S.R. The Republic did not recognize Soviet Russia until 1933. At that time I was Spanish Ambassador in Mexico, and was appointed to the Moscow Embassy. While I was on the way to Russia, however, the Azaña Government fell, and I handed in my resignation; the next Ambassador in Moscow, Dr. Marcelino Pascua, subsequently Ambassador in Paris, was not appointed until I became Foreign Minister in September 1936, two months after the outbreak of the rebellion; and the first Soviet Ambassador did not arrive in Spain until the end of August of that year.

With their weakness for symbolic dates, preferably of a religious character, the insurgent leaders had planned their revolt for the period between St. John's and St. Peter's days, June 24 and 29. It was postponed, however, on instructions from General Mola, who at the same time ordered that as from the 15th of the following month everyone should be at his post and ready for the signal of attack.

On the evening of July 13 Largo Caballero and I were in Paris, on our way back from the International Trades Union Congress in London, when we read in *Le Temps* of the death of Señor Calvo Sotelo. His corpse, with a bullet in the head, had been left at midnight, by persons unknown, in one of the depositories of the Madrid cemetery, and was identified some hours later. The day before, Señor Castillo, the well-known Republican officer of the Assault Guards, had been killed by Fascists while standing arm-in-arm with his wife at the door of their home. The connection between these two events was not difficult to establish.

We took the first train back to Spain. Madrid was charged with electricity. Various Right-wing newspapers had been suspended for the barefaced effrontery with which they accused the Prime Minister of being almost personally responsible for the death of the principal leader of Spanish Fascism. A meeting of the Permanent Committee of the Cortes, which took place two days later, gave an opportunity to opposition members to launch a broadside attack on the Government. Señor Gil Robles made what was undoubtedly the most insolent and aggressive speech of his whole political career. It was interspersed with Biblical phrases, one of which, reproduced the following morning in the reactionary press, was afterwards found to be a warning to the conspirators that the decisive hour was approaching. Over that meeting the threat of violence hung like a heavy cloud.

Government circles, however, remained confident. On Friday the 17th the Socialist members left Madrid as usual to tour the provinces during the week-end and to take part in the various propaganda meetings organized every Sunday by the party to counteract the intensive demagogic campaign of the enemies of the Popular Front. It so happened that, as we had not been expected back from London so soon, no arrangements had been made for me to speak anywhere. Thanks to this, I escaped the fate of many of my colleagues in the Parliamentary Group who found themselves in rebel provinces when the revolt broke out, and were immediately shot by the insurgents. . . .

With the strong conviction that that week-end would be the last that I should enjoy in relative quiet for many months, and having no meeting on the Sunday, I left Madrid for France, where my wife and children were spending the summer in a seaside place near the frontier. Before setting out, however, I obtained official assurance that there was nothing to indicate that it would be unwise to go away until the following Tuesday, when a lively

Parliamentary debate was expected. . . .

I had scarcely passed the frontier when the *Gazette de Biarritz* published the report of a military rising in Morocco. Since the proclamation of the Republic all this part of southern France had been the refuge of die-hard Spanish Monarchists. These men, although they had never been persecuted or interfered with in their own country, showed their hatred of the new regime by living in voluntary exile, where they alternated their golf and tennis with the easy sport of playing at conspiracy from foreign territories, without in the ordinary way cherishing any great hopes or unduly disturbing their placid existence. The relish with which that afternoon on the terrace of the Bar Basque in Biarritz they devoured the news of the local papers, the noisy merriment with which they passed remarks from one table to another, and the various outspoken comments which I overheard in passing, were eloquent proof that to some at least of those gentlemen of Spanish Coblenz, the revolt in Africa came as no surprise.

My suspicions were confirmed at once. In order to get in touch with Madrid as quickly and discreetly as possible, I went to the Post Office and asked for my own telephone number. The telephone lines were cut. I hailed a taxi and drove to the first Spanish village on the other side of the frontier. A large crowd, among which I recognized various old Socialist and Republican friends, was listening with obvious excitement to the radio at the door of a bar in Behobia. The U. G. T. (*Unión General de Trabajadóres,* General Union of Workers) was giving orders from the Madrid station to be prepared for any emergency, and to declare an immediate general strike in any towns where the local garrisons should attempt to aid and abet the Morocco rising.

There was no doubt about it. The rebellion had surprised the Government in the sweetest of slumbers. And, what was worse, even with the aid of such an ear-piercing alarm clock it had difficulty in waking. The Civil Governor of San Sebastián, whom I managed to get on the telephone, told me that the revolt was confined to Africa, that the Government was confident of being able to suppress it in the course of a few hours, and that there was perfect order in the rest of Spain. Provincial officialdom was as intoxicated with optimism as the ministers in Madrid.

The truth was that the rising, after four and a half months of preparation, took place in most parts of Spain with only a slight difference in hours. At half past two on the morning of the 18th Franco received in the Canaries a cable from Melilla reporting the first rebel triumphs. He had made plans well in advance to proceed to Morocco and from thence to the Peninsula. On July 11—that is to say, two days before the death of Señor Calvo Sotelo (and here is further conclusive proof that the violent disappearance of the Fascist leader was not, as has so often been said since, the cause of the rebellion)—the British aviator Captain Bebb, under special contract from a Franco agent in London, flew from Croydon to Las Palmas to pick up the rebel leader. Captain Bebb has since described* that historic flight with many interesting details, and has recounted how, on July 18, he smuggled Franco through the French customs and took him to a country-house in Casablanca where his liaison officers were awaiting him.

The military rising, planned with the complete agreement, and promise of support, of Germany and Italy, and carefully organized from the moment the Popular Front came to power at the February elections, spread like wildfire. Its leaders were convinced that within a few hours, or at the most a couple of days, they would be masters of the country. Everything had been carefully arranged.

But these generals, who have never been distinguished for their political acumen or knowledge of mass psychology, had overlooked one small detail when they drew up their plans with so much care.

They had forgotten the Spanish people.

---

* *News Chronicle*, London, November 7, 1936.

From FREEDOM'S BATTLE, *excerpted from Chapter I*

the people

(1936)

A people which has arms and fights
cannot be defeated.

JACINTO BENAVENTE

"I swear in the name of the beings who
are most dear to me to dedicate my life
to the democratic Republic, to the cause
of the people, to justice and social
progress. I swear by my blood to fight
with determination and ruthlessness, to
accept victory with joy and adversity
with dignity. If I do not keep this
pledge, may contempt, dishonor and the
inevitable punishments of military law
come upon me."

OATH OF THE SPANISH PEOPLE'S MILITIA

The Spanish national war is a holy war, the most
holy war registered by history.

PAMPHLETS DISTRIBUTED BY THE
SPANISH CATHOLIC CHURCH, JULY 1936

Q. How long, now that your coup *had failed in its*
objectives, is the massacre to go on?
A. There can be no compromise, no truce. I shall
go on preparing my advance to Madrid. I shall
advance, I shall take the capital. I shall save
Spain from Marxism at whatever cost.
Q. That means that you will have to shoot half Spain?
A. I repeat, at whatever cost.

GEN. FRANCISCO FRANCO

In interview granted at Tetuan, July 29, 1936
and published in the London News-Chronicle

Danger! To Arms!

· DOLORES IBARRURI (*La Pasionaría*)

WORKERS, ANTI-FASCISTS, and laboring people!
Rise as one man! Prepare to defend the Republic, national freedom and the democratic liberties won by the people!

Everybody now knows from the communications of the government and of the People's Front how serious the situation is. The workers, together with the troops which have remained loyal to the Republic, are manfully and enthusiastically carrying on the struggle in Morocco and the Canary Islands.

Under the slogan, "Fascism shall not pass, the October butchers shall not pass!" communists, socialists, anarchists and republicans, soldiers and all the forces loyal to the will of the people are routing the traitorous rebels, who have trampled in the mud and betrayed their boasted military honor.

The whole country is shocked by the actions of these villains. They want with fire and sword to turn democratic Spain, the Spain of the people, into a hell of terrorism and torture. But they shall not pass!

All Spain has risen to the struggle. In Madrid the people have come out into the streets, lending strength to the government by their determination and fighting spirit, so that it may utterly exterminate the reactionary fascist rebels.

Young men and women, sound the alarm! Rise and join the battle!

Women, heroic women of the people! Remember the heroism of the Asturian women! And you, too, fight side by side with your menfolk, together with them defend the bread and tranquillity of your children whose lives are in danger!

Soldiers, sons of the people! Stand steadfastly as one man

41

on the side of the government, on the side of the working people, on the side of the People's Front, on the side of your fathers, brothers and comrades! March with them to victory! Fight for the Spain of February 16!

Working people of all political parties! The government has placed valuable means of defense into our hands in order that we may perform our duty with honor, in order that we may save Spain from the disgrace that would be brought upon her by a victory of the blood-thirsty October butchers. Not one of you must hesitate for a single moment, and tomorrow we shall be able to celebrate our victory. Be prepared for action! Every worker, every anti-fascist must consider himself a mobilized soldier!

People of Catalonia, the Basque country and Galicia, and all Spaniards! Rise in the defense of the democratic republic, rise to consolidate the victory won by the people on February 16! The Communist Party calls upon all of you to join the struggle. It calls upon all working people to take their places in the struggle in order completely to smash the enemies of the Republic and of the freedom of the people.

Long live the People's Front!
Long live the alliance of all anti-fascists!
Long live the People's Republic!

Madrid, July 19, 1936

The Bull in the Olive Field

SOL FUNAROFF

With the first banderillas of daybreak
the darkness lowered its head,
a drip of bloody snot in its nostrils,
and Madrid awoke,
toreador in overalls:

A storm of people poured like rain
upon the face of the streets,
thundering with firearms
across barricades:

Against the darkness bearing
dust winds from the desert,
hot blasts in the mouths of cannon,
drouth and carnage in the olive land:

Death, in his black cassock,
bull with the black hide,
hooded, gold cross at the neck,
fat and in folds like velvet;

his crotch full, a purse with coins,
rutted with the cows,
the whores of the old world,
rotted with the disease
in the rotten lands,

and unloosed the blessed bastards,
the young bulls, aristocrats, all of them,
raised in the sanctuaries of the dons,
bred in the stables of
Salamanca, Rome, Berlin.

The fields filled with bullfire
and the hatred of beasts; their breaths

scorching siroccos,
hot winds burning hatred against US:

the layers of water,
bidders for water rented for dry land,
haulers of water in jars at the village well,
blind mules turning the water mill,
circling the centuries in ciphers of debt.

The fields sickened
in the hate of dry winds:

the hate hot in the mouths of clerks,
the gatherers of taxes under
the smoking rifles of civil guards;

the hate hot in the brand of latifundia,
seal of state stamped in the arroyos,
hooves in the gullies and stone-choked soil;

the hate in the dust of documents
drifting in the hot winds
in the buzzing mouths of officials
breeding swarms of idlers
like flies on our bread.

Breeding illness of their idleness:
horrors on the path to the bullring,
beggars in the path of the bull:

trees sick with spore diseases,
tubercular, stunted,
the bark parched and peeling,
trunks gored and their wounds
swathed in bandages of lime;
their limbs tortured, lifting up
bare branches of their poverty,
twisted in agony like christs in the grove.

From EXILE FROM A FUTURE TIME, *Dynamo, New York, 1943*

Madrid, que bien resistes,
Madrid, que bien resistes,
Madrid, que bien resistes,
Mamita mia,
Los bombardeos.

The First Days

CONSTANCIA DE LA MORA

JULY 17, 1936. Three o'clock.

A military uprising in Morocco. Ignacio had gone to the War Ministry. I was alone in the house. It was very hot. I pulled aside the blind and looked into the street. Down the block a little peddler pushed his cart. Otherwise nothing. The sun beat on the pavements. Madrid was quiet.

July 17, 1936. Four o'clock.

Ignacio would call very soon. He would say: "It is nothing. The traitors are all under arrest." Then we would leave day after tomorrow or the day after that for the seashore, to lie under the sun and watch the breakers foam over the rocks.

July 17, 1936. Five o'clock.

The house is so quiet, so empty. Now surely Ignacio will call very soon. A military uprising in Morocco. But suppose it was part of a great plot? Ignacio had expected it. Suppose the garrison in Madrid revolts? The people will defend the Republic. Spain will never be fascist—not while the people live.

July 17, 1936. Eight o'clock.

The heat hangs on. My face is damp with the hot winds. In the street there is more movement now, people passing quickly, talking. I can hear their voices, but no words. Are they talking of the uprising? What do they say?

Nine o'clock.

Our host, Freddie Bauer, returns. He has been making the

45

rounds of the cafés. The best-known leaders of the Ceda* and the Monarchist party are sitting in the Molinero restaurant, their usual meeting place. Freddie thinks this is a good sign. Surely the Government would have arrested the fascists if the uprising were serious?

I look at him across the supper table. "You think so?" I ask.

Freddie stares at his plate. "Well, they were looking very jubilant," he says bitterly; "they were ordering champagne and making toasts. They acted as though they were celebrating something."

We eat in silence. Finally Freddie bursts out. "The people will defend themselves—if only the Government gives them a chance."

July 17, 1936. Midnight.

How can it be that Ignacio has not called? He must know that I am sitting at home in the empty, quiet house, waiting for his voice to reassure me. He would have called. I know he would—if he had the chance. So he must be working furiously. Then the uprising is serious.

July 18, 1936. Four o'clock in the morning.

I sit beside the window in the drawing room, staring into the empty streets. Freddie comes home again.

"Ignacio has not returned," I say.

"Go to bed, Connie," Freddie replies. "There is no news."

I lie in bed, but I cannot sleep. When the light comes I get up and bathe and dress and drink coffee. The little maid brings in the early morning newspapers. The headlines are black —but meaningless. The uprising in Morocco is not serious. The Government has the situation under control. The Government has taken precautions.

Taken precautions. I sit beside the window again, dizzy with fatigue, watching the people go out to work. Do they seem strange this morning? Are they talking of the revolt?

July 18, 1936. Eleven o'clock.

---

* C.E.D.A. (*Confederación Española de Derechas Autónomas*), reactionary party headed by Gil Robles, nucleus of the 1936 opposition.

The empty house trembles with the blatant loud ring of the telephone.

"Ignacio! Are you all right? What is happening? Are you not coming home? Is the uprising. . . ."

His voice, sharp and staccato, cuts me off. "I am at the War Ministry now. I have been at the airport most of the night. I must keep all my loyal pilots standing by for orders."

"But what's . . ."

"Connie!" Ignacio's voice was loud. "I want you to promise me something."

"Yes, but . . ."

"I want you to absolutely promise to stay inside the house. Do you understand? Do not go out, under any circumstances."

I was bewildered. "Ignacio, why not, what's going on?"

But Ignacio hung up. I was furious. I had yet to learn that commonplace of wartime: that there are times when one cannot speak over the telephone.

July 18, 1936. Four o'clock.

I slept a little, awaking still fatigued. The heat grew. The radio in the house was broken. We could not find a mechanic to repair it. But the Government ordered all radios turned on permanently, and loud enough for neighbors to hear. Through our open windows floated the magnified voice of the Government announcer. *"People of Spain! Keep tuned in! Keep tuned in! Do not turn your radios off! Rumors are being circulated by traitors. Wild stories are causing panic and fear. The Government will broadcast day and night—learn the truth from this station. Keep tuned in! Keep tuned in!"*

Across the street from Freddie's house, a little soft drink and sandwich stand installed a radio. People sat sipping cool drinks at the small painted tables in the diminutive garden— listening. Crowds stood around the counter—listening.

Freddie and I could not sit in the empty house. We needed people around us. We walked out into the evening and sat quietly at one of the tables, listening to the blaring voice from the radio and listening to the talk of the people.

"The Republic has the situation in hand," the Government

announcer said.

"Ha!" a little man sitting next to me told his stout, good-natured-looking wife. "This time we'll really give it to those vermin! The Army! Every general, every last one of them, ought to be shot." His wife nodded.

"*President Azaña has moved from his residence at El Pardo to the National Palace in Madrid.*"

A tall, immaculately dressed dandy standing just in back of me snorted. "So! The Government has things in hand! But Azaña has to move. So!"

My neighbor stood up. "Say it again, you dirty Monarchist." The crowd turned from the loud speaker. "Where's the king-lover?" somebody yelled. The well-dressed man slipped discreetly away.

"I can't make head or tail of it," Freddie said. "What in heaven's name is going on?"

I shook my head. If only Ignacio would come.

At midnight Freddie left me and I went home to bed. I fell asleep with the voice of the announcer still pounding at my ears.

Next morning I woke with a start. It was very early. Through my open windows floated the voice from my neighbor's radio.

"*Attention! People of Spain! The Government will now briefly review the military situation.*"

I sat up in bed, wide awake. "*The rebellion against the Republic, led by a handful of traitorous generals, began with the Moorish troops. They persuaded their soldiers, by the use of the most vicious lies, to rise against the Republic. Some of the Moorish troops have been transported to the peninsula, where they are attacking—unsuccessfully—Republican troops.*

"*In the meantime, other members of this conspiracy against liberty have incited isolated regiments in the north and south to rise against the Republic. Fighting is still going on in these cities but we feel sure of the outcome. Málaga has been attacked and is in flames. Government forces and rebels are fighting in the streets of Barcelona.*"

I began dressing hastily. The news made more sense now. The plot had been carefully laid. Garrisons all over Spain apparently were to rise at the signal of the rebellion in Morocco. But the Rebels had not taken the Republicans completely by surprise. Comparatively few garrisons had risen. The Republican troops, barring accidents, would be able to handle the situation.

I ate my breakfast reading the headlines, feeling more confident by the moment. For I did not know, nor did Ignacio at the War Office, nor did the people of Spain know, that even as we all awoke and went to work that morning of July 19, 1936, in Berlin and Rome two dictators were giving the orders for the invasion of Spain by fascist troops, airplanes, cruisers, transports, technicians, Army officers, ammunition, guns, and money. The unequal battle—Spain against Germany and Italy, with England and France and the United States handcuffing my country's fighting arms—had already begun. But we did not know it.

About ten o'clock, the Government broadcast the news that General Francisco Franco, the hated general who sent the Moors to rape and kill in the Asturias, had flown to Morocco from the Canary Islands where he had been stationed after his removal as Chief of Staff. Now the pieces of the plot were beginning to fit together. Ignacio had always said that Franco was a very ambitious man—General Goded was more intelligent; General Mola a better soldier; but Franco was the most ambitious.

Ignacio came home Sunday morning at five o'clock. He had not slept or eaten a proper meal since he left the house Thursday afternoon. He looked haggard, thin, and so tired that I took pity on him and put him to bed without a single question.

A few hours later I woke again to the sound of the radio. I closed our windows hastily. Ignacio must sleep. But I stole out into the street and listened. The Government of Casares had resigned. *"Martinez Barrio will head a new Government. Listen in! Keep tuned in! The names of the new Cabinet Ministers will be announced shortly."*

Ignacio woke in an hour. At breakfast, Freddie and I bombarded him with questions. Ignacio talked fast as he ate. The revolt was much more serious than anyone had expected at first —anyone except himself and most of the Republican Army officers in Spain. The plot was a careful one, designed to bring all the converging Rebel troops from the provinces into an attack on Madrid. The Government must stop this converging process. But the only forces which could be used with complete trust were the workers belonging to trade unions and Popular Front parties. The Republican Government, however, did not wish to arm the people. Therefore it had resigned, to be replaced by a more moderate government which intended to make peace with the Rebels.

"Peace?" I cried, jumping up from the table. "But that means fascism? And the people will never. . . ."

Ignacio grinned. "Don't get so excited, Connie," he said, gulping coffee. "I don't think it's all over yet—not by a long sight. Martinez Barrio doesn't realize the situation; he can't make peace with the fascists. He doesn't know it yet, but he can't. You should see the crowds outside the War Ministry. Thousands of them. They've been there since Thursday night. Just standing quietly, or sleeping in the garden and on the curbs, holding their trade union cards in their hands. Waiting for arms. Just waiting."

We listened in for almost an hour, but the Government announcer had nothing else to say about the Martinez Barrio government. Ignacio prepared to leave for the Ministry. But before he went he made me promise I would not go out on the streets. Fascist snipers had been picking off workers, known Republicans or mere passers-by. He could not have a moment's peace while he worked at the War Ministry if he thought I was in danger of being shot in the back. . . .

After Ignacio left that morning, the house seemed very quiet again. The radio was still silent—no news of the Martinez Barrio Government.

Freddie offered to go and find out what was being said in town. About three o'clock he rang me up from a public telephone. "There's a huge demonstration against surrendering!" His voice was so excited I could hardly make out the words. "The people of Madrid say they won't have a Martinez Barrio Government. They want a Popular Front Government, and arms to fight the Rebels. Connie, you should see it! It's wonderful!"

For the plain people of Madrid, thousands upon thousands

strong, had marched to the Puerta del Sol, the heart of the city. Their ranks were orderly. Their air was full of dignity. They were very determined. No surrender to fascism! Arms for the people!

While many a Republican leader still saw the four-day-old revolt as a sort of military rumpus, the people of Madrid, the plain workers, the small clerks, knew better. They were, even in July, determined to fight fascism to the bitter end—and they forced the wavering Republicans to bolster the defenses of Spain. The Government was hastily revamped again. Premier José Giral took office together with several members of the previous Casares Cabinet. It was not yet a Popular Front Government for only members of the Republican parties held office. Nevertheless, the people had won a point. . . .

That night I heard that the people were storming the Montaña barracks. They were unarmed, with only an old cannon which they shifted from spot to spot with lightning speed—to make the fascists think they had a whole collection of light artillery.

The next morning I was awakened by the sound of bombs—for the first time in my life. I rushed to the terrace and found Freddie already there in his dressing gown, watching two old planes circle the city. While I watched, I saw two puffs of smoke and heard two more rumbles—the sound which I grew to find so familiar, so constant, so unimpressive that a year later I would not look up from work or awaken from sleep, unless a bombardment were remarkably heavy.

But on this July morning, the whole population of Madrid rushed to its windows and roofs to see the bombers, for they were our Government planes attacking the Montaña barracks. All night long the Government loud-speakers had ordered the fascists barricaded inside, to surrender—all night long the people had besieged the troops. Now, with Rebel forces planning a march on Madrid it was obviously impossible to allow hostile troops within the capital limits. The bombers went up to force the fascists to surrender.

We watched the bombers circle three times and then disappear. A few minutes later our phone rang. It was Ignacio, announcing the people's victory. The men and women of Madrid had forced the gates and seized the arms within the Rebel nest! The capital was safe.

That Monday was exciting. We had no sooner finished lunch than the radio announced a further Government victory in Barcelona. The Rebels were crushed in Catalonia. General Goded, their leader, was a prisoner. General Fanjul, another fascist notable, had been arrested in the Montaña barracks in Madrid.

A few hours later, the radio announced the death of General Sanjurjo, who had been killed in an airplane crash as he flew from Portugal to join the Rebels. Foreign newspaper correspondents, prompt to seize on dramatic items, rushed into print with the news that Sanjurjo had been scheduled to lead the revolt. "Leader Dies on Way to Command Rebel Army," some of the items read.

Spaniards, of course, could only smile at this dramatic announcement. The old general, dating from the Primo de Rivera dictatorship, was known to have used all his energy and enterprise in affairs of a purely personal, nay, sentimental kind. Even in 1926, when he was at the "height" of his military career (he once won an engagement with a tribe of practically unarmed Arabs) all Spain knew the doughty General Sanjurjo for the country's most famous *"bon vivant,"* to put it politely. In fact, there was a famous joke to the effect that Sanjurjo might not know Moors but he certainly knew women. After the Republic commuted the death sentence he had so richly deserved when he led the Monarchists in a revolt against the infant democracy, the lady-loving general retreated to Portugal where he acted as liaison man between the Nazis and the Spanish generals. He was probably slated to be some sort of a figurehead in the Government the Rebels had planned to set up. . . .

Madrid itself seethed with excitement—and tragedy. Families separated for the summer months were in many cases separated forever. In some cases wives and children in vacation resorts were killed by fascists as fathers and husbands agonized in Madrid for news of their families. Ramon Sender, the well-known journalist and writer, lost his young and beautiful wife in just such a way. She was alone at a country place near Madrid and the fascists, who had heard that her husband was vaguely left wing in his political sympathies, slaughtered her in front of her two babies as she recited the prayers of the Catholic Church.

At first I had been easy in my mind about my Luli, away at a summer camp in the Escorial. The radio reports seemed to be clear on Government victory there. But as my friends began to report the terrible tragedies of separation and death, I began to grow uneasy. A report, which I afterwards learned was untrue, hinted that the Escorial region was fascist. Suddenly I became panic-stricken. I rang up a friend and borrowed a car. I called Ignacio and told him I was driving down at once to bring Luli home. "You can't!" he said over the phone. "It's impossible. Wait a little. I'm sure she's all right."

I waited in growing terror. Luli! I began to blame myself for having sent her to a summer camp at all. If the fascists found out who her foster-father and mother were! Or if they bombed the camp!

And then, in an hour, Ignacio called. Luli was quite safe. The Government controlled the Escorial. The children didn't even know about the revolt. Their camp counselors had decided not to frighten them. Luli was well and happy—and getting very sun-tanned!

I sat down heavily and mopped the tears out of my eyes. . . .

After lunch I somewhat gingerly stepped out on the street. I knew that snipers were still at work, and although the Government had warned the newly armed militia not to fire in reply, I had heard that cars full of patrolmen roaming the streets were still somewhat careless with their unusual weapons. I walked to the bottom of our block, past an apartment house under construction. The street was nearly empty. Suddenly I heard the terrible sound of a machine gun. My throat closed with tight fear. I stood perfectly still, no doubt presenting a perfect target to the fascist snipers across the street in the half-finished building. But I couldn't walk. My knees trembled too much. The machine gun rat-tat-tatted again. I don't know if the bullets came very near me or not. I know they were aimed at me, for I was the only person anywhere near the building.

I kept thinking that I must run. But I didn't. I turned my head, very slowly, cautiously towards the building with its scaffolds. I saw no one. Suddenly an automobile tore around the corner, just as the machine gun started again. The car was full of militiamen, kneeling on the floor, aiming rifles as they came. The machine gun spit more bullets. The militiamen returned the fire. I heard the whine of bullets.

A few hundred feet down the street I saw a newsstand, overturned in the gutter. Slowly and stiffly, while the rifle and machine gun fire whined and rattled all about me, I walked to the flimsy wooden stand and slowly I bent my knees and crouched behind the little wooden barricade. The machine gun stopped. The militiamen dashed into the half-finished building and returned, without a captive. The fascist had apparently disappeared. After several minutes I stood up again. I saw the bus coming. The bus stopped. Just as the door opened, the machine gun started again. The driver waited until the noise of the bullets stopped, and then put the bus in gear.

The bus was crowded—I immediately spotted my friend Isabel Palencia and her young daughter, Marisa, who had just graduated from the University. They were the center of attention in the friendly, even jocular group on the bus. Everyone knew that Isabel Palencia was a famous Socialist leader and the workers listened attentively while she told them we must all be calm and not answer the provocation of the fascists still not arrested. I thought of my experience of ten minutes before—but I knew she was right.

"The fascists are only trying to provoke panic and alarm with this shooting from terraces and windows," Isabel said.

The last stop on the bus was at the Plaza de la Cibeles, across from the Bank of Spain. We got off to walk the rest of the way to the UGT headquarters. I had just stepped down the bus steps when we saw a crowd of men and women running for the subway entrance. We heard shots all around us. We dived for the subway with everyone else.

It was very crowded underground and more people kept storming in every moment. The trains were not running; the subway had become a place of refuge. I suddenly realized that my heart had not stopped thumping since I left the house—and I knew, all at once, what it must mean to the workers and little clerks and shopkeepers of Madrid to keep going to the office and factory every day, with the fascist snipers keeping up the vicious, cowardly attack on people's bodies and nerves.

A weeping woman came down the subway steps. She seemed to be half fainting. Her hair fell over her contorted face. Two young men, obviously strangers to her, supported her. Isabel had never seen her before, but in that crowded underground station, we were all friends.

"What's the matter?" Isabel asked the woman.

At first the woman could only cry—her sobs were terrible, broken, rasping from the heart. Then she began to talk. "I was walking with my brother past the Palace Hotel, only a little way from here, when a shot came out from nowhere, and then . . ." She hesitated.

One of the young men said softly, "Dead."

At the word, the woman began to cry again, pitifully.

"He was very young," she said loudly, "very young." . . .

A cordon of policemen and militiamen surrounded the trade union headquarters. Isabel showed her card and we three stepped into a sort of orderly madhouse. The UGT building was crowded to the very doors. Men sat on wooden benches, squatted on the floor, slept in corners. Endless queues waited outside the offices of the masons, the steel workers, the electricians, and all the other member unions of the UGT. We heard a word—new to us—passing as a sort of greeting from one man patiently standing in line to another man leaving. The word went from one group to another, was repeated loudly and softly all around us—"Salud! Salud! Salud!"

"*Salud!*" The greeting of the Popular Front. We heard the word and each of us inwardly rolled it on the tongue and added it to a vocabulary suddenly growing under the pressure of war. "*Salud!*"

Isabel tried to see the leaders she knew personally but the task was quite hopeless. Hundreds were waiting to see every trade union executive. So we settled down on the wooden benches to wait our turn to speak to the official in charge of women volunteers.

The crowds at the Casa del Pueblo were sweaty and disheveled. It was hot, very hot, that July in Madrid and most of the men were wearing the uniform adopted as suddenly as the word "salud"—a sort of overall we called *mono*. Men went out to the front in these *monos* and the first battles were fought between uniformed Rebels on one side and a grim line of overalled men on the other.

But the crowd at the UGT headquarters made me feel proud and self-confident. For although many looked tired and had the same expression of silent worry that Ignacio had worn for many days, they were not hysterical, nor noisy, nor even filled with bravado. These men who had stormed the Montaña barracks, gone without decent food or a full night's sleep for more than a week, waited quietly for orders. The Spanish people began to learn discipline.

I began to learn it, too. For when our turn came, the official who met us was polite and gentle, but quite firm. He would give a job to Isabel if she felt she could not be more useful in another place, but her daughter and me he could not help. The trade union could only send its members to assignments. I was irritated for a moment—and then I saw the justice of the rule. The trade union must not send spies or fascists to man the factories and telephone offices and street cars and buses. They must answer for the women they sent to take men's jobs. As for the hospital jobs—that was a very delicate matter. The hospitals were closely connected with military work. Surely we must understand how cautious the trade union had to be? We understood. We walked out of the building no less determined to find jobs, but much impressed with the dignity and discipline we had seen in the UGT headquarters.

Our bus back home was filled with men in *monos* riding home to pick up a few things and leave for the front. We talked cheerfully all the way to my corner, and as I stepped off the bus, the men waved, and I ducked the inevitable sniper. At home the little maid handed me a telegram from my parents in Paris —wanting to know if I were safe.

I looked at it bitterly. For some time Ignacio and I had suspected that my father was playing an important role in the preparations for the military plot. His electric company had all kinds of connections with Nazi Germany and he had let enough indiscreet remarks fall to indicate that he played some sort of a rôle as a go-between in the Spanish-German plot.

Of course, it may have been only a coincidence that he had taken the family abroad just before the rebellion broke out. Still, I answered the telegram with poor grace. I knew that whether my father had played an active role in the rebellion or not, he had most certainly helped to finance it. His money paid for some of the guns the snipers used. I wired him that I was safe—and suggested postponing his return for a few days until the Government had restored order in Spain. He replied that he was bringing my mother and brother back to our country place through Portugal.

This was the last direct word I ever had from my parents. . . .

The telegram depressed me. I sat home that night, turning over plans in my mind. I was determined to get a job and be part of the movement of the people to overthrow fascism. But what job? Where?

Next morning early, I rang up Maruja, the wife of Fernando, one of Ignacio's best and most trusted pilots. She was alone all day and night, too, and although she had four children she decided to leave them in the care of her two maids and start out with me looking for something we could do for the Republic. Together we went to call on Teresa Gonzalez Gil. . . .

We found Teresa, who had never much courage in any event, very depressed. Her husband had left the Army after the Republic had come in and founded a co-operative airplane factory. He had just won a national prize for the design of one of his newest planes and the rebellion found the young couple just beginning to sight prosperity. Now Teresa's husband had left everything, his factory, his beloved wife, and gone off to the front with a regiment of men recruited from his workers. He was in the Guadarrama mountains, defending the outposts of Madrid against the approaching fascist columns.

We had some difficulty rousing the frightened Teresa from her profound depression. Her husband was her life, she said. She felt in her heart he would be killed. Perhaps he was already dead? What could she do without him?

We urged her to work—it would help her forget and after a long conversation she declared herself ready. Next we rallied to our group another pilot's wife, Trini, a very pretty but rather frivolous and useless girl, and Concha Prieto, the eldest of Prieto's daughters and the most warm-hearted, self-sacrificing and intelligent of his children.

With my regiment formed, I next stormed the Republican officials. I rang up a woman I knew at the Committee for the Protection of Minors, a department of the Ministry of Justice, and asked what was being done about the children who until then had been taken care of by Religious Orders.

These children deserve a little explanation. The charity foundations for the care of children, which had existed under the Monarchy, had been taken over, little by little, by the Government. Not because the Government wanted to, but because they had to. For one of the first steps the rich Monarchists and fascists took under the Republic was to refuse to support the orphanages and pauper schools they had always kept up before. Let the Government do it, they said cynically. Why should we care for the poor? Let the Republic take care of its own. So the Ministry of Justice had to provide the funds for the maintenance of these pre-Republican orphanages. But curiously enough —and this was only a small example of the hesitancy of the Republican Government—the Minister of Justice in the Republican Cabinets followed a flat rule: the orphanages were supported by the Government but their operation remained in the hands of the people who had administered the establishments before.

I happened to know a little about these wretched homes and schools for the poor children of Madrid. Most of the insti-

tutions were housed in buildings without plumbing and hardly
fit to shelter animals. I remember particularly one small convent in a suburb of Madrid called La Guindalera, housing eighty
boys from six to twelve years of age. I visited it in 1935 with an
Austrian journalist who wanted to see "social welfare" work
in the Spanish capital.

The boys were the first things we saw. They were covered
with scabs and filth. Their ragged clothes hardly covered their
dirty bodies as they played on the mud and dirt heaps in the
courtyard. We rang the bell. An old nun opened the gate of
the garden and led us into the house. The windows of the main
room were broken and covered with burlap.

The old, short, fat Mother Superior came to meet us. Her
lined and wrinkled face quivered and twitched as she spoke,
and her words were hardly distinguishable, for she had no teeth.
"This foreign journalist would like to see how the orphan Spanish
boys live," I told her, but she did not seem to understand.

We pushed our way into the schoolroom. The walls of the
classroom were covered with filth of all colors and kinds, difficult
to imagine and impossible to describe in print. The desks were
also used as eating tables, and I doubt very much whether they
were ever used for much else. In the adjoining kitchen the
floor was littered with plates, covered with old, hardened food,
garbage, discarded paper, and the like. Cockroaches walked
freely on the floor and climbed the tables. My head swam and I
felt sick.

I wanted to show the journalist the contrast between the
old institutions and a new boys' club which we had recently
started, in the same neighborhood. It was a simple club, typical
of the ones we were opening in all the working-class districts of
Madrid, a club where boys could spend their hours after school
or where boys who had no school to go to, could spend the long
hours of the day; under roof during the winter, playing in the
garden during the summer. There were books and games in the
club, and boys could learn carpentry or music or painting. They
all worked in the garden, too, and played with a big dog we had
installed as mascot.

I found that the contrast was much more than I needed to impress the journalist. I felt shocked and ashamed that in 1935 such things could still exist in our country and in the heart of Madrid. But worse still: the orphanage we had visited was one of those that the rich had threatened to close if it did not get a Government subsidy. The Ministry of Justice, through its Committee for the Protection of Minors, paid for the maintenance of the eighty boys. Later, when a terrible scandal took place in that same orphanage, we heard as an excuse that the Sisters of Charity, who were in charge of the building and the boys' "education," were old and senile nuns who could not be used anywhere else and were sent there as a sort of asylum in which they could wait for death. But that was hardly an excuse for what I had seen.

This convent at La Guindalera was not much different from the places that housed three thousand orphan children in Madrid alone. Of course, after the Popular Front victory in February, 1936, a few changes had taken place. Some of the children had been moved to pleasanter buildings and the nuns who were still in charge of the youngsters were ordered at least to teach their charges to read and write.

But with the war the whole situation changed. For some of the nuns fled and others abandoned their children while they prayed night and day. The Government itself was finally forced to take care of the children of the poor. . . .

I had heard that the nuns were abandoning their orphans. So I took my newly recruited band of women to the office of the Protection of Minors department. The executive secretary, a handsome gray-haired man, received us very graciously—and then forgot all about us. We sat in his office for an hour, while a procession of militiamen in their *monos* marched in to report this or that orphanage abandoned and to ask, "What shall we do with the children?"

The office was in the greatest confusion—as a contrast to the UGT headquarters. The staff of the department, many of them still left over from the days of the Monarchy or the first Republican Government, dashed about madly, doing nothing. The executive secretary, not very sure of himself, tried to impress me, the wife of an Air Force officer—for he owned land and was hated by the peasants of his native Valencia.

Finally I heard the secretary shout in desperation: "I don't know what we can do. We have plenty of empty buildings and hundreds of abandoned children, and nobody with a sense of responsibility to take care of them."

I jumped up in exasperation. "That's what we've been trying to tell you all morning. We came here to offer our services."

"Very nice," he replied, bowing, "but we need women to cook and scrub floors and wash the dishes. All the buildings we have taken over are in a terrible mess. And one of our problems is that we have no money. We have already spent most of this year's budget and this is hardly the moment to ask for a new appropriation."

I tried to interrupt, but he held up his hand. He had a little speech, apparently, that he intended to deliver, willy-nilly.

"Not only," he began, with great precision, "do we have to care for the children abandoned by the nuns, but we must also find homes for the thousands of street urchins who sell papers and lottery tickets and so on. They can't be left at the mercy of the snipers. Many have been killed already, poor children."

His face became a mask of grief. "Yes, but . . ." I began.

But he wasn't finished. "The trade union people came to see me yesterday. There are thousands of other children whose fathers have gone to war and whose mothers have been drafted to take their places at work. We must find homes for them, too. The trade union people are planning on starting homes with their own funds. But we are a Government agency. We must supervise everything. We must set the example." He sighed and turned back to his papers, adding, "But how? How? I am very over-worked. I do not know where to turn."

This time I talked. "Look here, we are five strong women. We all have children and know how to care for them. Maruja and Teresa are excellent cooks and it won't be the first time I've scrubbed floors."

The secretary smiled and shook his head. We sat down

stubbornly. He made little jokes about the situation. We looked blank—unamused, like the English Queen. The secretary began to worry. He thought we were very influential ladies. Every time he looked at Concha Prieto he trembled. So finally we had our way. A militiaman led us to the Travesia del Fucar. . . .

We hesitated at the doors of the convent—and then suddenly the whole neighborhood surrounded us. People appeared at doors and windows, a dozen women trotted up the block to talk to us.

"Why did the nuns leave? Were they threatened?" I asked.

A stout, good-natured woman in a cotton kimono, chuckled. "Oh, no, *compañera*, nothing happened to them; no one asked them to go. But they heard rumors from their friends and relatives and their chaplain told them to leave."

"What are you coming here for?" a woman sang out from her window. "Maybe you're related to the nuns? Maybe you've come to get what's inside the convent?"

A man on the street took the cry up. "The Government owns everything in there now. Don't touch it!"

We laughed. The militiaman introduced us to the whole block. The women all began to chatter.

"You mean you're going to take care of children without being paid?"

"Can I send my two children who drive me crazy and spend all day playing in the gutter?"

"The girls who went to this school paid for the board; it was not a school for the poor. Will you charge, now?"

And then they all began to say: "We will help. Call on us if you need us."

When we told them that we hoped our new charges would play with their youngsters, we became friends of the whole neighborhood. They could not believe that the convent, so long isolated, was to become part of the block, part of their lives. Ever after that day we had only to appear at the door to get a salvo of "saluds!" and waves and smiles.

The militiaman found the key and we entered the hall of

the old convent. After the nuns had left, the place had been searched for arms. There were four ugly chests in the hall and their drawers were all pulled out and the contents spilled on the floor—mostly Catholic journals, dusters, and electric light wires and fixtures. We passed on and found that the building was very spacious but old fashioned and dilapidated. The kitchen was a distressing sight. The nuns had left the remains of their last meal. Three days in the hot month of July was enough to ferment the food left on the dirty plates. The red tiled floor of the kitchen and adjoining pantry were simply carpeted by cockroaches.

I glanced up at the faces of my friends. I could feel myself turning pale as the cockroaches moved in a thick wall towards the corners as we approached.

"Are we not the wives of heroes?" Maruja said, somewhat weakly. And with that, good humoredly, we started to work. . . .

That first evening fifty children arrived. The first group of twenty came in a big bus and were brought in by an official from the headquarters of the Institution who had gone to fetch them from a convent in the outskirts of Madrid where the children had spent most of their lives. Most of them looked frightened when they arrived. Some were crying silently and one older girl of about seventeen years was shrieking hysterically. They all wore dirty, cheap, black flannel dresses, ungracefully cut, with long skirts and long sleeves. Their faces bore signs of sleeplessness, tears, and smudges; their lifeless hair looked dirty, colorless, and unkempt; each child carried over her shoulder a white cotton bag containing a few miserable belongings. They moved like sheep and talked among themselves excitedly but in very low subdued tones.

I could not prevent the tears coming to my eyes. I had never seen a more pitiful sight than our first group of children. But it was no time to become sentimental. If we were to calm all these children and cope with their fits of hysterics we had to appear natural, to give them the impression that what was happening was nothing abnormal. We took them into one of the parlors leading from the hall, which must have been used by the nuns to receive their most important visitors. It was a large, square room with two sets of stiff-backed uncomfortable sofas and chairs of flimsy legs and undefined tapestry, a round three-legged table, with a white hand-embroidered doily under a mangy plant. Two large scenes of the Passion of Christ faced each other on the wall.

The children were obviously awed to be in such sumptuous surroundings. I had to say a few words to them. None of my companions would speak; had they not just made me the *Directora*? I swallowed hard and tried to smile at the children, controlling as best I could my inopportune tears. "We hope you are going to be happy here with us," I began, "and there is no need to talk in such low voices, because we are not afraid to hear you talking or laughing. Oh, we hope you will soon laugh and play! We have a lovely garden, you know! And more children will come tomorrow, and you can leave your bags in this room for the time being, until you go to bed tonight. Now you can all wash your hands. And then we will all have some supper."

The children looked dazed. Three or four of the most daring ones began to ask timid questions.

"Are we to live here forever, now?"

"Then it is not true what the Sisters said. . . ."

One little girl began to cry. "Don't tell her what the Sisters said. Don't tell her!"

But a chorus of voices answered. "The Sisters said you would be very cruel to us and beat us and they said the *milicianos* would rape us."

The ugly word sounded strange and horrible coming from these little girls most of whom were not yet twelve. This explained the hysterics of the oldest girl, poor Ana Maria whom Concha Prieto was trying to quiet in the adjoining parlor. The Sisters had departed, leaving their charges without food or care, and with the final warning that within a few days they would be ill-treated and abused by the wicked people of the Popular Front. No wonder our new charges were pale and tear-stained, frightened and nervous!

We felt a sudden wave of anger. Even if the misguided Sisters had believed such ridiculous tales, surely it was unnecessary to leave little children alone with terror.

Our dinner was a great success. It was very simple, we thought, and we had been afraid the children would think we would never give them any better food. But we had a salad—none of them had ever tasted such a thing before, and they were delighted. Then the dinner wound up with a rice pudding with milk and sugar, which they praised endlessly. And above all, we allowed them to talk during their meal—remembering my own convent days, I could understand their delight.

Bathing our girls that night was something none of us ever forgot. The convent had an old-fashioned bathroom in a sort of low-roofed shack attached to the back wall. Two bathtubs stood in the bathroom and twelve foot-baths were fastened to the walls. We decided it was possible to bathe all the girls that first day—but we had reckoned without our children.

We called two of the older girls and told them to bathe in the two tubs, while we started to work on the babies in the foot-baths. But the two girls stood demurely beside the bathtubs, obviously reluctant to undress. Finally they told us they had never had a bath in their whole lives. We found two screens and hoped for the best.

We never dreamt we would encounter the same difficulty with the younger ones. I picked a sweet, black-haired little girl with great black eyes for my first attempt. I unbuttoned Enriquetita's filthy black flannel pinafore, peeled off her thick black stockings and worn shoes. But then came the battle. As I tried to unfasten her dirt-encrusted chemise, she began to struggle wildly, shouting something I could not quite understand—she lisped. Finally I made it out.

"It is a sin against modesty!" she wept. Enriquetita was four years old! . . .

From In Place of Splendor,
excerpted from Part IV

Mediterranean

MURIEL RUKEYSER

O N THE EVENING OF July 25, 1936, five days after the outbreak
of the Spanish Civil War, the Americans at the Anti-Fascist
Olympic Games were evacuated from Barcelona at the order of
the Catalonian Government. In a small Spanish boat, the *Ciudad de Ibiza,* which the Belgians had chartered, they and a
group of five hundred, including the Hungarian and Belgian
teams as well as the American, sailed overnight to Sète, the
first port in France. The only men who remained were those
who had volunteered in the Loyalist forces: the core of the future
International Column.

I

At the end of July, exile. We watched the gangplank go
cutting the boat away, indicating: sea.
Barcelona, the sun, the fire-bright harbor, war.
Five days.
      Here at the rail, foreign and refugee,
we saw the city, remembered that zero of attack,
alarm in the groves, snares through the olive hills,
rebel defeat: leaders, two regiments,
broadcasts of victory, tango, surrender.
The truckride to the city, barricades,
bricks pried at corners, rifle-shot in street,
car-burning, bombs, blank warnings, fists up, guns
busy sniping, the town halls, towers of smoke.
And order making, committees taking charge, foreigners
commanded out by boat.

I saw the city, sunwhite flew on glass,
trucewhite from window, the personal fighting found
eyes on the dock, sunset-lit faces of singers,
eyes, goodbye into exile. Saw where Columbus rides
black-pillared: discovery, turn back, explore
a new found Spain, coast-province, city-harbor.
Saw our parades ended, the last marchers on board
listed by nation.

I saw first of the faces going home into war
the brave man Otto Boch, the German exile, knowing
he quieted tourists during machinegun battle,
he kept his life straight as a single issue—
left at that dock we left, his gazing Breughel face,
square forehead and eyes, strong square breast fading,
the narrow runner's hips diminishing dark.
I see this man, dock, war, a latent image.

The boat *Ciudad de Ibiza*, built for 200,
loaded with 500, manned by loyal sailors,
chartered by Belgians when consulates were helpless,
through a garden of gunboats, margin of the port,
entered: Mediterranean.

II

Frontier of Europe, the tideless sea, a field of power
touching desirable coasts, rocking in time conquests,
fertile, the moving water maintains its boundaries
layer on layer, Troy—seven civilized worlds:
Egypt, Greece, Rome, jewel Jerusalem,
giant feudal Spain, giant England, this last war.

The boat pulled into evening, underglaze blue
flared instant fire, blackened towards Africa.
Over the city alternate lights occurred;
                                    and pale

in the pale sky emerging stars.
No city now, a besieged line of lights
masking the darkness where the country lay.
But we knew guns
bright through mimosa
singe of powder
and reconnoitering plane
flying anonymous
scanning the Pyrenees
black now above the Catalonian Sea.

Boat of escape, dark on the water, hastening, safe,
holding non-combatants, the athlete, the child,
the printer, the boy from Antwerp, the black boxer,
lawyer and communist.

> The Games had not been held.
> A week of Games, theatre and festival;
> world anti-fascist week. Pistol starts race.
> Machine-gun marks the war. Answered unarmed,
> charged the Embarcadero, met those guns.
> And charging through the province, joined that army.
> Boys from the hills, the unmatched guns,
> the clumsy armored cars.
> Drilled in the bullring. Radio cries:
> To Saragossa! And this boat.

Escape, dark on the water, an overloaded ship.
Crowded the deck. Spoke little. Down to dinner.
Quiet on the sea: no guns.
The printer said, In Paris there is time,
but where's its place now; where is poetry?

> This is the sea of war; the first frontier
> blank on the maps, blank sea; Minoan boats
> maybe achieved this shore;
> mountains whose slope divides

one race, old insurrections, Narbo, now
moves at the colored beach
destroyer wardog. "Do not burn the church,
compañeros, it is beautiful. Besides,
it brings tourists." They smashed only the image
madness and persecution.
Exterminating wish; they forced the door,
lifted the rifle, broke the garden window,
removed only the drawings: cross and wrath.
Whenever we think of these, the poem is,
that week, the beginning, exile
remembered in continual poetry.

Voyage and exile, a midnight cold return,
dark to our left mountains begin the sky.
There, pointed the Belgian, I heard a pulse of war,
sharp guns while I ate grapes in the Pyrenees.
Alone, walking to Spain, the five o'clock of war.
In those cliffs run the sashed and sandalled men,
capture the car, arrest the priest, kill the captain,
fight our war.
The poem is the fact, memory fails
under the seething lifts and will not pass.

Here is home-country, who fights our war.
Street-meeting speaker to us:

> ". . . came for Games,
> you stay for victory; foreign? your job is:
> go tell your countries what you saw in Spain."

The dark unguarded army left all night.
M. de Paîche said, "We can learn from Spain."
The face on the dock that turned to find the war.

III

Seething and falling black, a sea of stars,
Black marked with virile silver. Peace all night,

over that land, planes
death-lists   a frantic bandage
the rubber tires burning   monuments
sandbag, overturned wagon, barricade
girl's hand with gun   food failing, water failing
the epidemic threat
the date in a diary   a blank page opposite
no entry—
however, met
the visible enemy heroes: madness, infatuation
the cache in the crypt, the breadline shelled,
the yachtclub arsenal, the foreign cheque.
History racing from an assumed name, peace,
a time used to perfect weapons.

If we had not seen fighting,
if we had not looked there
        the plane flew low
        the plaster ripped by shots
        the peasant's house

if we had stayed in our world
between the table and the desk
between the town and the suburb
slowly disintegration
male and female.
If we had lived in our city
sixty years might not prove
        the power this week
        the overthrown past
        tourist and refugee
Emeric in the bow speaking his life
and the night on this ship
the night over Spain
quick recognition
male and female.

And the war in peace, the war in war, the peace,
the faces on the dock
the faces in those hills.

IV

Near the end now, morning. Sleepers cover the decks,
cabins full, corridors full of sleep. But the light
vitreous, crosses water; analyzed darkness,
crosshatched in silver, passes up the shore,
touching limestone massif, deserted tableland,
bends with the down-warp of the coastal plain.

The colored sun stands on the route to Spain,
builds on the waves a series of mirrors
and on the scorched land rises hot.
Coasts change their names as the boat goes to
France, Cost Brava softens to Côte Vermeil,
Spain's a horizon ghost behind the shapeless sea.

Blue praising black, a wind above the waves
moves pursuing a jewel, this hieroglyph
boat passing under the sun to lose it on the
attractive sea, habitable and kind.
A barber sun, razing three races, met
from the north with a neurotic eagerness.

They rush to solar attraction; local daybreak finds
them on the red earth of the colored cliffs; the little islands
tempt worshippers, gulf-purple, pointed bay.
We crowd the deck,
welcome the islands with a sense of loss.

V

The wheel in the water, green, behind my head.
Turns with its light-spokes. Deep. And the drowning eyes
find under the water figures near
in their true picture, moving true,

the picture of that war enlarging clarified
as the boat perseveres away, always enlarging,
becoming clear.

Boat of escape, your water-photograph.
I see this man, dock, war, a latent image.
And at my back speaking the black boxer,
telling his education: porter, fighter, no school,
no travel but this, trade-union sent a team.
I saw Europe break apart
and artifice or martyr's will
cannot anneal this war, nor make
the loud triumphant future start
shouting from its tragic heart.

Deep in the water Spanish shadows turn,
assume their brightness past a cruel lens,
quick vision of loss. The pastoral lighting takes
the boat, deck, passengers, the pumice cliffs,
the winedark sweatshirt at my shoulder.
Cover away the fighting cities
but still your death-afflicted eyes
must hold the print of flowering guns,
bombs whose insanity craves size,
the lethal breath, the iron prize.

The clouds upon the water-barrier pass,
the boat may turn to land; the shapes endure,
rise up into our eyes, to bind
us back; an accident of time
sets it upon us, exile burns it in.
Once the fanatic image shown,
enemy to enemy,
past and historic peace wear thin;
we see Europe break like stone,
hypocrite sovereignties go down
before this war the age must win.

VI

The sea produced that town: Sète, which the boat turns to,
at peace. Its breakwater, casino, vermouth factory, beach.
They searched us for weapons. No currency went out.
The sign of war had been search for cameras,
pesetas and photographs go back to Spain,
the money for the army. Otto is fighting now, the lawyer said.
No highlight hero. Love's not a trick of light.
But. The town lay outside, peace, France.
And in the harbor the Russian boat *Schachter;*
sharp paint-smell, the bruise-colored shadow swung,
sailors with fists up, greeting us, asking news,
making the harbor real.
                            Barcelona.
Slow-motion splash. Anchor. Small from the beach
the boy paddles to meet us, legs hidden in canoe,
curve of his blade that drips.
Now gangplank falls to deck.
                            Barcelona
everywhere, Spain everywhere, the cry of Planes for Spain.
The picture at our eyes, past memory, poem,
to carry and spread and daily justify.
The single issue, the live man standing tall,
on the hill, the dock, the city, all the war.
Exile and refugee, we land, we take
nothing negotiable out of the new world;
we believe, we remember, we saw.
Mediterranean gave
image and peace, tideless for memory.
For that beginning
make of us each
a continent and inner sea
Atlantis buried outside
to be won.

From U. S. 1, *Covici Friede, New York, 1938*

> *Every man is a people.*
> ANDALUCIAN PROVERB

"I Could Never Get Angry . . ."

B IDDING FAREWELL to my wife and children, we set out into the night. The nearest stretch of Government territory lay some miles to the East, but it was difficult to reach as all the roads on the Fascist side of the front were strongly guarded and many people were known to have been shot trying to get across. So we decided to try the South, where the front was much less clearly defined. But the journey this way was a long one and to find the road was not easy.

The first part of our journey lay across bare, open country, with no trees anywhere. We made for the house of a friend in a village four or five hours from our own. He was a wine merchant by trade. We knew him to be a strong Republican, who would not give us away. In the early hours of the morning we reached his cottage.

Our friend offered us the best hospitality, fed us during the day and, when evening came, led us beyond the limits of the village to show us the way. "You see that bright star on the southern horizon?" he said. "Follow that for six nights and you will come to the Tagus. Cross it and you will be safe."

All that night we followed the star.

In the morning, when the daylight came, we lay down and hid in a hollow. When it was dark once more, the bright star rose and seemed to beckon us on to safety. We again set forth into the night.

All that night we walked and the next night, too. By the third morning we had come to wooded country, which gave us cover to continue our journey by day as well.

74

But finding the road by day was not so easy. We had nothing to guide us. We went on through the woods, yet for all we knew we might have been going not to safety, but to our death. About midday we heard a shepherd calling his sheep. I decided to risk everything and ask him the way.

"Can you tell me in what country we are?" I asked. The man looked at us before answering.

"I will not ask if you are going to save your lives," he said with a smile, "but over there lies the Tagus. On this side Fascism rules, on the other the Government. Take the path between yon two hills and follow it straight as a die. And you will be saved."

At night we continued our journey and sure enough the path lay as the man had told us. We followed it until dawn and then lay down and rested. At noon we set forth once more. In the late afternoon it became difficult to see, for the sun had fallen down below the level of the treetops and shone straight in our eyes through the leafless branches of the oaks. Suddenly, a few paces ahead, we heard a man singing the Phalangist anthem. It was too late to avoid him, for a break in his singing told us that he was already aware of our presence. I walked up to him. "Can you tell me in what country we are?" I asked. Then I added, "We have just escaped from the Reds and are trying to find our way to Orihuela to join up with the Fascist army."

"Very well," answered he, "take this path over the hill to the left and in half an hour you will reach the village of Alcoroches. Ask there and you will be shown the way to Orihuela. Adios."

We waited until the man had gone his way, and then we took the right fork, leaving Alcoroches at a safe distance to our left.

It grew dark once more and we followed the star. By morning the countryside had changed from low wooded hills to steep rocky mountains. The going was hard and our feet were sore and blistered.

We went on and on, but there was no one to tell us the way,

and for all we knew, we might have been retracing our steps. Our food supply, which had lasted us five days, had run out.

We might have wandered in these mountains for weeks without finding the way out, so we decided to go back and to risk asking the first person we met where the Tagus lay. We had not gone an hour when we came across a woodcutter's hut. There were two men standing beside it. My companions ran to the nearest stream to drink, while I walked up to the men. "Can you tell me in what country we are?" I asked. "We have often helped people like you," one of them said with a smile. "If you climb that highest peak, you will see the Tagus beyond you at your feet. Once you cross it, you are safe." These men gave us food in their little hut and told us that they, too, had been members of the village council deposed by the Fascists in July. Nothing had happened to them so far, but arrests had been going on in the Province of Teruel also. They had been wondering whether to escape and after talking to us decided to do the same.

We went as far as the foot of the peak they had indicated and there we lay down and slept, for it was already dark and the mountain too steep to climb except in daylight.

At dawn we made our way up to the top and sure enough, as they had told us, the Tagus lay like a ribbon at our feet. We went down the steep cliff and waded across a shallow part to the other side. Our journey was not ended, for we had to walk all that day until we reached Tragacete, the first Government village.

In Tragacete we were received by the villagers and by a number of troops as well, who prepared a banquet for us. It was the first proper meal we had had for six days, but not one of us three could eat it. A week of semi-starvation had got us out of the habit of eating and the sight of food made us feel quite sick.

It was several days before our appetite returned. Yet everywhere we went large meals were prepared by people who knew what we had been through. We could eat none of them. From Tragacete we went to Priego and from Priego to Cuenca.

I am still here in the town of Cuenca. My two friends are fighting at the front; I often get letters from them. I wanted to join up too, but they told me I was too old. I am fifty-five.

I have always tried to live a good life, to be fair to everyone. I worked from morn to night on my little plot of land, living on the proceeds of what I produced. When my neighbors were in distress I lent them money. I never took any interest, and if, when the time for repayment came, they were still in difficulties, I told them to wait and pay me back when times were better.

The people of the village wanted to make me their mayor, but I refused. For I knew that a mayor had to get angry on occasions and I could never get angry.

As for my wife and children, I do not know what has become of them. They may be alive and unharmed or they may be dead. For if anything has happened to them, I cannot save them by writing. And if they are safe and well, a letter from me might prejudice the authorities against them. Time alone will tell of their fate.

From Voice of Spain,
London, February 1939

Spain Within My Heart

PABLO NERUDA

INVOCATION   To a beginning, to lay upon the rose
pure and parted, to lay upon the origin
of sky, land and air, the wilfulness of a song
made of explosions, the desire
of an immense song, made of a metal that
    gathers
war and naked blood.
    Spain, crystal chalice, not diadem
but crushed stone, combated tenderness
of wheat, leather and burning animal.
Tomorrow, today, a silence
in your footsteps, an amazement of hopes
as an older air: a light, a moon,
dead, useless moon, moon of hand upon
    hand,
bell upon bell.
    Natal mother, fist
of hardy oats,
    planet
bloody and dry with its heroes.
Who? along roads, who,
who, who? in blood, in shadow, who?
in the sparkle, who? Falls

BOMBARDMENT   ash, falls
iron
and stone and death and lament and flames,
who, who, Sacred Mother, who, and where?
Plowed-under fatherland, you shall maintain
your right to your own earth in your ashes

like a flower of perpetual water,

your right to let fall from your thirsty mouth
petals of bread to the air, spilling inaugurated
tassels of corn. May they be cursed, cursed,
    cursed
those who with serpent and axe came to
    your earthly
sands, cursed those who awaited this day
    to open
your door to bandit and Moor: what have
    they gained?
Bring, bring the lamp, see the soaked earth,
    see
the little black bone eaten by the flames,
    the vesture
of executed Spain.

    Cursed those who one day
watched not, cursed blind cursed men,
those who refused their solemn fatherland
a bread without tears, cursed
uniforms stained and cassocks
of acid, stench-ridden dogs of hide and
    sepulchre.
Poverty rode through Spain
like horses full of smoke,
like stones dropped
in the spring of sorrow,
cereal earth without opening,
secret cellars of tin and azure,
ovaries, doors, closed
arches, profundities
that wanted to produce, and all this
lorded over by tri-corne Civil Guards
with heavy carbines, by priests
the color of sad rat,
by lackeys of the king with the immense

hind-end. Hard Spain of pine and apple
land,
they stood on the roads before your nomadic
people:
Kept you from sowing, from mining, from
mounting
the cows, from thinking of tombs, from
visiting
each year the monument to Columbus.
You never built schools nor made the earth's
crust
crackle with plows, nor filled the granaries
with
wheatly abundance: pray, beasts, pray that
a god
with an immense behind like the king's behind
awaits you:
"There you shall have soup, my children."
In the nights of Spain, through the old gardens

TRADITION   tradition, full of dead mucus, seeping pus
and
pestilence was passing with its tail in the mist,
phantasmal and fantastic, dressed in asthma
and hollow blood greatcoats, and its expression
all deep-sunk eyes were mooning and green
and eating
tomb, and its toothless mouth was biting
each night
the still-born tassels of corn, the mineral
secret,
and was walking under its crown of green
thistles,
sowing wandering bones of death and daggers.

MADRID   Madrid solemn and alone, July surprised
1936   you with
your poor hornet-nest happiness; clear was
your street

and clear your dream.
          A black hiccough
of generals, a wave
of rabid cassocks
burst forth from between your knees
their quagmire waters, their laughter of
          phlegm.
With eyes still wounded by dream,
with carbine and stone, freshly wounded
          Madrid
defend yourself. You ran
through the streets
leaving trails of your sainted blood,
uniting and calling with a voice like an
          ocean,
with an expression forever changed in
          bloody light,
like an avenging mountain, like a hissing
star made of knives.
When your burning sword pierced the
          gloomy districts,
the sacristies of treason, nothing was heard
but the silence of daybreak, nothing
but your bannered step,
and an honorable drop of blood on your
          smile.

A dish for the bishop, masticated and bitter,
A plate with remains of iron, with ashes,
          with tears,
A sunken dish of sobs and fallen walls,
ALMERIA A dish for the bishop, of blood of Almería.

A plate for the banker, a plate with cheeks
Of happy children of the South, a plate
With detonations, mad waters, ruins and
          fright,

A plate with parted axis and trampled heads,
A black plate, plate of blood of Almería.

Each morning, each disturbed morning of
　　　your life
You shall have it hot and steaming on your
　　　table:
You shall shove it off a little with your
　　　soft hands
So as not to see it, not to digest it over again:
You shall shove it off a little between your
　　　bread and grapes,
This plate of silent blood
That shall be there forever every morning
　　　every
Morning.

A dish for the Colonel and the Colonel's wife,
In every feast, in every party, celebration
Sitting over the oaths and the spittle, in
　　　the wine-colored light of dawn
So that you may see it trembling and cold
　　　upon the world.
Yes, a plate for all of you, the rich from
　　　everywhere,
You table companions, ambassadors, ministers,
Mistresses of comfortable seat and tea:
A spoiled dish, overflowing, filthy with
　　　blood of the poor,
For each tomorrow, for every week, for-
　　　evermore,
A plate of blood of Almería, always before
　　　you, always.

Translated by Lloyd Mallan;
From War Poems of the United Nations,
Dial, New York, 1943

> *Man is as God made him, and often worse.*
> CERVANTES

Blood Flows In Badajoz

JAY ALLEN

THIS IS THE MOST painful story it has ever been my lot to handle: I write it at four o'clock in the morning, sick at heart and in body, in the stinking patio of the *Pension Central,* in one of the tortuous white streets of this steep fortress town.* I could never find the *Pension Central* again, and I shall never want to.

I have come from Badajoz, several miles away in Spain. I have been up on the roof to look back. There was a fire. They are burning bodies. Four thousand men and women have died at Badajoz since General Francisco Franco's Rebel Foreign Legionnaires and Moors climbed over the bodies of their own dead through its many times blood-drenched walls.

I tried to sleep. But you can't sleep on a soiled lumpy bed in a room at the temperature of a Turkish bath, with mosquitoes and bed bugs tormenting you, and with memories of what you have seen tormenting you, with the smell of blood in your very hair, and with a woman sobbing in the room next door.

"What's wrong?" I asked the sleepy yokel who prowls around the place at night as a guard.

"She's Spanish. She came thinking her husband had escaped from Badajoz."

"Well, didn't he?"

"Yes," he said, and he looked at me, not sure whether to go

_____
* Elvas, Portugal

83

on. "Yes, and they sent him back. He was shot this morning."

"But who sent him back?"

I knew but asked nevertheless.

"Our international police."

I have seen shame and indignation in human eyes before, but not like this. And suddenly this sleepy, sweaty being, whose very presence had been an added misery, took on the dignity and nobility that a fine dog has and human beings most often have not.

I gave it up. I came down into the filthy patio, with its chickens, rabbits and pigs, to write this and get it over with.

To begin at the beginning, I had heard dark rumors in Lisbon. Everybody there spies on everybody else. When I left my hotel at 4:00 p.m. August 23, I said I was going to Estoril to try my luck at roulette. Several people noted that down, and I hope they enjoyed their evening at Estoril.

I went to the Plaza de Rocio instead. I took the first taxi. I drove around and around and finally picked up a Portuguese friend who knows his business.

We went to the ferry that crosses the Tagus. Once on the other side we told the chauffeur, "Elvas." He looked mildly surprised. Elvas was 250 kilometers (about 150 miles) away. We streaked through an engaging country of sandy hills, cork oaks, peasants with side-burns and women with little bowler hats. It was 8:30 o'clock when we pulled up the hill into Elvas, "the lock nobody ever opened." But Elvas knows humiliation now.

It had been nine days since Badajoz fell on August 14th. The Rebel armies had gone on—to a nasty defeat at Medelin, if my information was correct, as it sometimes is—and newspapermen, hand-fed and closely watched, had gone on in their wake.

Nine days is a long time in newspaper work; Badajoz is practically ancient history, but Badajoz is one of those damned spots the truth about which will not be out so soon. And so I did not mind being nine days late, if my newspaper didn't.

I know Badajoz. I had been there four times in the last year to do research on a book I am working on and to try to study the operations of the agrarian reform that might have saved the Spanish Republic—a republic that, whatever it is, gave Spain schools and hope, neither of which it had known for centuries.

We began to hear the truth before we were out of the car. Two Portuguese drummers standing at the door of the hotel knew my friend. Portugal, as usual, is on the eve of a revolution. The people seemed to know who the "others" are. That is why I took my friend along.

They whispered. This was the upshot—thousands of Republican, Socialist and Communist militiamen and militiawomen were butchered after the fall of Badajoz for the crime of defending their Republic against the onslaught of the Generals and the landowners.

Between fifty and one hundred have been shot every day since. The Moors and Foreign Legionnaires are looting. But blackest of all: The Portuguese "International Police," in defiance of international usage, are turning back scores and hundreds of Republican refugees to certain death by Rebel firing squads.

This very day (August 23) a car flying the red and yellow banner of the Rebels arrived here. In it were three Phalangists (Fascists). They were accompanied by a Portuguese lieutenant. They tore through the narrow streets to the hospital where Señor Granado, Republican Civil Governor of Badajoz was lying. Señor Granado with his military commander, Colonel Puigdengola, ran out on the Loyalist militia two days before the fall of Badajoz.

The Fascists ran up the stairs, strode down a corridor with guns drawn, and into the governor's room. The governor was out of his mind with the horror of the thing. The director of the hospital, Dr. Pabgeno, threw himself over his helpless patient and howled for help. So he saved a life.

We drove to Camp Maior, which is only seven kilometers (about four miles) from Badajoz on the Portuguese side. A talkative frontier policeman said: "Of course, we are handing them back. They are dangerous for us. We can't have Reds in Portugal at such a moment."

"What about the right of asylum?"

"Oh," he said, "Badajoz asks extradition."

"There is no such thing as extradition for a political offense."

"It's being done all up and down the frontier on orders from Lisbon," he said belligerently.

We cleared out. We drove back to Elvas. I met friends who are as much Portuguese and vice versa.

"Do you want to go to Badajoz?" they asked.

"No," I said, "because the Portuguese say their frontier is closed and I would be hung up."

But they offered to take me through and back again without complications. So we started. Suddenly we drove out of the lane on to a bridge that leads across the Guadiana River into the town of Badajoz. Now we were in Spain. My friends were known. The extra person in the car (myself) passed unnoticed. We were not stopped.

We drove straight to the Plaza. Here yesterday there was a ceremonial, symbolical shooting. Seven leading Republicans of the Popular Front (Loyalist), shot with a band and everything before three thousand people. To prove that Rebel generals didn't shoot only workers and peasants. There is no favoritism to be shown between the Popular Fronters.

Every other shop seemed to have been wrecked. The conquerers looted as they went. All this week in Badajoz, Portuguese have been buying watches and jewelry for practically nothing. Most shops belong to the Rightists. It is the war tax they pay for salvation, a Rebel officer told me grimly. We passed a big dry goods shop that seems to have been through an earthquake. "La Campaña," my friends said. "It belongs to Don Mariano, a leading Azañista (follower of Manuel Azaña, President of Spain). It was sacked yesterday after Mariano was shot."

We drove by the office of the Agrarian Reform, where in June I saw the Chief Engineer, Jorge Montojo, distributing land, incurring naturally the hatred of the landowners, and, because he was a technician following strictly bourgeois canons of law, the enmity of the Socialists, too. He had taken arms in defense of the Republic, and so—

Suddenly we saw two Falangists halt a strapping fellow in a workman's blouse and hold him while a third pulled back his shirt, baring his right shoulder. The black and blue marks of a rifle butt could be seen. Even after a week they showed. The report was unfavorable. To the bull ring with him.

We drove out along the walls to the ring in question. Its sandstone walls looked over the fertile valley of Guadiana. It is a fine ring of white plaster and red brick. I saw Juan Belmonte, bullfight idol, here once on the eve of the fight, on a night like this, when he came down to watch the bulls brought in. This night the fodder for tomorrow's show was being brought in, too. Files of men, arms in the air.

They were young, mostly peasants in blue blouses, mechanics in jumpers. "The Reds." They are still being rounded up. At four o'clock in the morning they are turned out into the ring through the gate by which the initial parade of the bullfight enters. There machine guns await them.

After the first night the blood was supposed to be palm deep on the far side of the lane. I don't doubt it. Eighteen hundred men—there were women, too—were mowed down there in some twelve hours. There is more blood than you would think in eighteen hundred bodies.

In a bullfight when the beast or some unlucky horse bleeds copiously, "wise monkeys" come along and scatter fresh sand. Yet on hot afternoons you smell blood. It is all very invigorating. It was a hot night. There was a smell. I can't describe it and won't describe it. The "wise monkeys" will have a lot of work to do to make this ring respectable for a ceremonial slaughter bullfight. As for me, no more bullfights—ever.

We passed a corner.

"Until yesterday there was a pool blackened with blood here," said my friends. "All the loyal military were shot here and their bodies left for days as an example."

They were told to come out, so they rushed out of the house to greet the conquerers and were shot down and their houses looted. The Moors played no favorites.

Back at the Plaza. During the executions here, Mario Pires went off his head. (Mario Pires is a Portuguese newspaper correspondent who had been entirely favorable to the Franco Rebellion before his visit to Badajoz.) He had tried to save a pretty fifteen-year-old girl caught with a rifle in her hands. The Moor was adamant. Mario saw her shot. Now he is under medical care at Lisbon.

I know there are horrors on the other side aplenty. Almendra Lejo, Rightist, was crucified, drenched with gasoline, and burned alive. I know people who saw charred bodies. I know that. I know hundreds and even thousands of innocent persons died at the hands of revengeful masses. But I know who it was who rose to "save Spain" and so aroused the masses to a defense that is as savage as it is valiant.

"But they didn't burn the jail." I had read in the Lisbon and Seville papers that they had. "No, the brothers Pla prevented it."

I knew Luis and Carlos Pla, rich young men of good family, who had the best garage in southwestern Spain. They were Socialists because they said the Socialist Party was the only instrument which could break the power of Spain's feudal masters.

They harangued the crowd that wanted to burn the three hundred Rightists in the jail just before they entered, saying they were going to die in defense of our Republic, but they were not assassins. They themselves opened the doors to let these people escape.

"What happened to the Plas?"

"Shot."

"Why?"

No answer.

There is no answer. All these people could have been allowed to escape to Portugal three miles away, but they weren't.

On the moon-drenched streets there was a smell of jasmin, but I had another smell in my nostrils. Sweet, too horribly sweet.

So back to Elvas.

There in the white Plaza by a fountain, a youth leaning against the wall with his feet crossed was playing his guitar and a soft tenor sang a melting Portuguese love song.

At Badajoz in June boys still sang beneath balconies. It will be a long time before they do again.

Suddenly through the square shot a car with a red and yellow flag. We halted. Our drummers came to meet us.

"They are searching the hotel."

"For whom?"

"Don't know."

We shall go away, as soon as it is light. People who ask questions are not popular near this frontier, if it can be called a frontier.

Chicago TRIBUNE,
August 30, 1936

The Arrival

EMILIO PRADOS

I have come back. And I thought I should know this street
lined with poplars.
                    Trees, that when I was young—
yesterday—spoke my tongue:
have you no word to greet
and welcome me, returned?

What has estranged us? Which of us forgot?
Did not your sap in spring mount through my vein?
Or is my mind confused? Speak: are we not
blood-brother, you and I, poplars of Spain?

You speak. What foreign words are these? What language
    have you learned?

            The wind is cold
            for the time of year . . .
            what freezes here?
            It is my hot heart!
            What bell is that
            (no belfry's near)
            of something dear? . . .
            It tolls in my heart!

            Silence!—accurst,
            funereal bell.
            You rock my blood
            in your long swell
            till my veins burst.

I am in danger!
What must I fight?
What watches me?
Are my eyes shut?
My eyes are cut
by the slashing wind . . .
I cannot see.

Ebb!—loud flood,
from my veins. Trace,
Memory, for me
the once-known road.

O hostile, kind
and sinister place—
my loved abode!
welcome a stranger
with a blind face.

No. I sleep and I dream. And in my dream I move no more
than a river dried in its bed.
How should I find the thing I knew before,
that neither live nor am dead?

Bird without wings and sad,
my dreaming self, like a ghost through the garden,
    through the city, along the harbor you go.

Five flames are nailed to your breast and stream upward
    and roar;
but as for you, you are voiceless; you are thinking of nothing;
    the sun warms you, but you cast no shadow. What is it
    that you lost? What is it that is here no more?

        Friends, I come from red Málaga,
        red Málaga on the bay;

and my sleep still smacks of salt and fish
and glory, and the dazzling spray,
and the sun that blazed all day.

(I was filled with flags when I set forth!
Why is the sun's face hid?
What evil dream was trotting north,
that dogged me into Madrid?)

Friends, I have much to tell you;
I bring good news from the coast!
And I find you well! I find you all
alert, and each at his post!

But no. But where is Federico?
Why is Federico not here?
I have wonderful news for Federico!—
news for his private ear.

Did he answer me? No. It was the wind in the poplars.
    It spread
from tree to tree. Bowed head after bowed head
they spoke. I do not believe what they said.

No, no. I sleep and I dream. I will not inquire
of the searching moon
what she has lost.
Were the trunks of the olive trees so twisted with anguish
    always?—I will not inquire.
        I have learned to my cost—
Federico! Federico! Too soon!—
how wise it is to cool the hot desire
for truth. Ah, cleanly tossed
from the crest of the wave like spray
let all my questions break and fall,
till I doze through the warm day

Emilio Prados

knowing nothing, that dared to know all.
It is in vain.
Not even in sleep can I endure this pain.
Where are you, Federico? Did you hear what I heard? I do not
  believe it, not I!
How they hurt me, how they hurt me, these bullets surrounding
your memory!

> There are fishes of steel in Málaga Bay!
> great fishes with a million eyes,
> guarding the harbor of Málaga
> from attack, and the town from surprise!
> And from Málaga the red to Granada,
> red kerchief and iron ring,
> the gypsies and fishermen march all day.
> They have a gift to bring,
> Federico, to your black jailers!
> From Málaga the red to Granada
> an army of gypsies, and sailors
> from fishing-boats in the bay—
> can you hear them, what they say?
> do you hear them, what they sing?—
> It is, "Death to your black jailers!"
> It is, "Death to your black jailers!"
>
> Federico, wait for me! Wait!
> I must talk with you! Look! We send
> from Málaga into Granada
> marching lines without end!
> I have so much to tell you, Federico!
> Wait for me! Wait my friend!

Translated by Edna St. Vincent Millay,
from AND SPAIN SINGS, *Vanguard, New York, 1937*

Lights! Camera! Action!

IVOR MONTAGU

DEAR MR. ZANUCK:

You are one of the most enterprising of the producers in the United States today, and so I am not at all surprised to read that you are preparing for immediate production a film on the siege of the Alcazar. Its heroism has thrilled the world, you are reported as saying. It was very heroic. But I wonder if you've heard who the heroes were.

A hero, I believe, is a man who fights against odds. It would be right to use the word hero for the people, the ordinary men-in-the-street, who, with empty hands and in the first flush of their surprise and indignation, overcame the generals and their machine guns in Madrid and Barcelona. Bare-handed they overcame them, the oath-breakers, in their barracks.

But in Toledo, the generals and their cadets had no ordinary barracks. They had a fortification that had withstood the armies of centuries, and held stores and arms for all the province. Few men they had, but for every man more than one machine gun.

If they were so armed, why did they run into their fortress? Liberators, national patriots, surely with such an abundance of stores they could have armed the populace that welcomed them and marched victoriously forward!

Curiously enough, the population didn't welcome them. Not one echo of sympathy did they meet among the good folk of Toledo, who, as one man, set about the investment of their citadel.

The cadets were few, their besiegers many, fit material for an heroic tale. You guessed it! The tale of traitors, armed to the teeth and with ample stores, cowering behind walls fourteen feet thick, while the man-in-the-street, a peaceable bloke like you and me, took off his coat and, in shirt sleeves and armed with a fowling piece, set about their punishment.

Just think of it! Walls fourteen feet thick with machine guns through every loophole and on the other side, shot-guns and blunderbusses taken from old trophies off the walls.

But now there's another thing it would be a pity to leave out. It happened before the siege started, but we who make films know that before the big scene starts you have to get a personal story built up. Well, I think this is just the personal bit you need. It gives us the motive, too. It wasn't just abstract indignation at treachery. No, it was a motive much more like the traditional one that has sent many an American father or brother or sweetheart reaching for his shotgun since long before films began. Let me explain.

The revolt of the army began. All this bloodshed and what not in Spain. They may have been right, we won't discuss that here. *What we do know,* and they and their friends have said it a hundred times themselves, is that they began. This means (mind you put it in your film) that that afternoon when it started the good people of Toledo didn't suddenly get excited and drive the cadets into their fortress. The cadets, *knowing that what they were about to do would meet the unanimous indignation of the people,* withdrew into their barracks, *knowing they would be cut off for a long time.*

Now what do soldiers want who are going to be cut off for a long time? Think, Mr. Zanuck. Not ammunition, they had plenty. Not food; when they prepared they had also seen to that. Something else, Mr. Zanuck. They took their womenfolk, some of them—we have heard a great deal of the women and children of the Alcazar—*but it was not only their own womenfolk they took.*

On that afternoon of rebellion, the cadets, hurrying to the shelter of the citadel of the Cid, paused in their flight to snatch these women. Shall we call them "hostages"? It was a holiday afternoon, and in the sunshine couples sat spooning. Others strolled along the lanes that ran by the hill on which the fortress stands. Sometimes the boy was knocked senseless. Sometimes, perhaps because he did something idly (shall we call it heroic, Mr. Zanuck?) he would be shot or stabbed with the bayonet.

That might make another good shot. And as a scenarist myself, I don't think it makes a bad set-up in general. There they are, the fathers and the brothers, who till now have spent their lives behind their desks and counters. Some have guns, perhaps, and others—yes, I can find you people who have seen it—have only sticks, but all of them, hatred in their hearts, crouch peering between chairs and tables piled in the street, at those walls of fourteen feet of stone and brick that hide from them those whom perhaps they fear ever to see again. Will you come into their headquarters, a chemist's shop round the corner, and see the militia officer (terrible name, isn't it, almost Red, but he was the chemist himself before the patriot heroes took him from his filling of prescriptions)? There on the wall behind his head, you will see the portraits of girls, last available family photographs on outings and the like, with beneath them a description and the circumstance of their capture. "Try to look out for these and save them when the citadel falls," is the legend on the wall.

But you've always got your happy ending. Not perhaps the conventional happy ending, which is no doubt what makes the subject appeal to so daring and innovating a mind as yours. I suppose the usual film ending would show merit rewarded, and injured virtue recovered, but as all the world knows, it hasn't worked out like that. Not yet at least. When those cowering heroes saw their bastions falling, when even those giant walls crumbled beneath simple miners' dynamite and the bare hands of the wronged populace, when these heroes at last felt vengeance at their breasts, then these who in all Spain could find no Spaniard to lift a hand for them were rescued by mercenaries, by Moors, by the riff-raff of the Foreign Legion, by Nazis fresh from the massacres of June 30th and Italian Fascists fresh from their mustard gas victory over the Red Cross.

But this isn't a happy ending at all, you may protest. **Oh, yes, it is.** The thoughtless girls of that holiday afternoon may, it is true, be missing when you're seeking for the facts. *But their families do not mourn them now.* Why? Ask your own newspaper. Ask Jay Allen. Ask those who saw the Moors celebrate the release of their Alcazar "heroes" by tossing hand grenades up and down the hospital wards before they set the hospital afire.

You must have that in. No one will be sad in the audience, when they know there's no one left now to worry about the sad things in the picture.

So you see what a fine picture you can make. I congratulate you once again on deciding to make it authentic. Not many film producers would have the courage.

> NOTE: *Mr. Montagu is a well-known British screenwriter, director and critic. The Zanuck production to which he refers in this open letter was abandoned after considerable protest from American, French and Mexican film workers. It had never reached the sound-stages, but a script had been prepared. This letter first appeared in* New Theatre and Film, *London, March 1937.*

"The Voice of the People..."

FATHER JUAN GARCIA MORALES:
Radio Madrid, Sept. 14, 1936

COMRADES OF THE world, and my brothers! You must know that many Spanish priests are on the side of the people and with the people's cause, that they wear the honored uniforms of the popular Militia, and that they stand opposed to their brothers in the priesthood who have left the Body and Blood of Christ Jesus on the altars, have taken up rifles, and have trampled underfoot the commandments of God's law, to hurl themselves like tigers on the working people of Spain.

We cannot do less than protest when millions of pesetas are discovered in the palaces of the bishops, while the poor perish of hunger, beg alms, or go to gather the leavings of the meals in the barracks. A cross of two sticks, a threadbare cassock, and a tin ring would have sufficed to permit a bishop to fulfill his function. The hatred of the people is not directed at God nor at the Church; it is turned toward their "ministers."

All we Spanish Catholics are anxiously waiting for the words of our Holy Father in Rome. In these moments of our country's agony the voice of the Representative of Christ on earth will be like the voice of the angels at the birth of the Messiah: "Peace on earth to men of good will. . . ."

The Holy Father in Rome must be well informed of the rebellion. There are plenty of people in Rome who will advise His Holiness on whatever occurs in Spain. Nuncios who have dealt only with Dukes and Marquises, and know nothing of the people. Directors of Catholic Social Action in Spain, who have drawn blood out of stones to assure the triumph of Capitalism. Most Holy Father, we do not want diplomacy. We are sick of diplomacy. All these things lead nowhere: useless actions and scraps of paper. Diplomacy serves no purpose: Your Holiness is the Representative of God Who was a carpenter and a poor man—and in the Name of this God Who died on the

Cross for just men and sinners, you must condemn those military chiefs and clergy who have taken up arms against a legally constituted Government.

On my knees, making my profession of Catholic faith, I wait for the voice of Your Holiness, hoping that tomorrow it will prove itself a light to lighten the understanding of the rebels, so that they may be convinced of their crimes, and laying down those arms which they have taken up against the people, they may smite their breasts and say a solemn "Miserere."

> FATHER LEOCADIO LOBO, Vicar of San Gines:
> *Radio Madrid, Sept. 20, 1936*

I AM A CATHOLIC and a Spaniard. I maintain relations with the Holy See and with my Bishop, who is now absent from Madrid.

My gospel is good news for the shepherds, for the fishermen, for the publicans and the tax-gatherers, for the adulterous woman and the woman of Samaria: the miracles of my gospel are the loaves multiplied by Christ Jesus for those who are hungry, health for those who suffer, light and life for the blind and the dead.

Will you tell me that the people do not believe, that they have turned pagan, that—I have heard it with my own ears—they are riff-raff, and rabble, and a Marxist mob? I do not curse, for the Gospel restrains my tongue from cursing: but I say they are not a mob, not riff-raff, not a rabble. *You, Catholics of Spain, officers who have taken arms against the people, conservative classes who have raised a wall and dug an abyss between the people and yourselves: you are not right. The Spanish people has been and always will be a GOOD people.*

They do not believe, you say? They have become pagan? They are Marxist? Ah, then your duty and my duty is to love them more than ever, to go out and seek them in the highways and byways of life, to tell them that their legitimate and just aspirations are Christian, though they do not know it: to remind them that the world, as Chesterton said, is full of Christian ideas run mad, and to be found everywhere: we must tell them this, and more: but above all, we must give them bread to appease their hunger, and love to fill their hearts.

They are against an absurd and brutal economic system? Then I am with them, for the Church has long been with them in this.

They demand social justice, the lessening or the total disappearance of the infinite gulfs between those who have all and those who have nothing? Then they are right, and because they are right they must demand, and claim, and insist, and prevent the continuance of this wrong state.

And when the people were roused to demand their rights; when they asked for the universally claimed transformation of the land-owning system, when they asked for access to the great heartless machine of industry to humanize labor there—then we stopped our ears; we gave them a few crumbs in the name of charity, and refused to envisage the solutions which reason and justice forced on every Christian conscience. And there appeared immediately in the midst of the conflict a word lacking all meaning and reason for those who were to use it as a terrible weapon of attack. In the midst of Spain's struggle appeared the word "Order." There were people who stood for "Order," and classes who stood for "Order," and political parties "of Order," and a Press "of Order": they talked of the "established Order," and fortifying and defending themselves against the workers they called them with infinite scorn "enemies of Order." "Let everything go on as it was," was the supreme aspiration of those who were comfortably placed in life, who were little if at all perturbed by the existence of the *disinherited,* yes, "disinherited," a term and a conception which fill the mind with horror, so clearly do they speak of fratricidal and anti-Christian cruelty.

This biased vision of the world which was characteristic of the conservative classes in Spain was profoundly shocked by an event both natural and logical, namely that those *disinherited classes* should become revolutionary, and manfully oppose the perennial existence of the "established Order."

"Why change," they said, "since we are so well off and satisfied?" *They wished to keep their wealth, their privileges, their power over things and people. Instead of trying to create a Catholic, Christian order, in which Spain might recover her racial historic feelings of essentially democratic liberties and rights, they tried (with partial success) to unite the Catholics in an organization of conservative outlook and bourgeois origins.*

But they have done worse. Official favor has partly succeeded in corrupting the Catholics, so that they may be persuaded to hand over the Church to the State on the plea of obtaining for her support, protection and defense.

The final move, the last word of madness in this state of things, was the rising of the army leaders and the Fascists against the people of Spain. I cannot hide the truth, and the truth is this. The attack was begun by the military and the Fascists: revolutionary or not, the Spanish proletariat maintained an attitude within the law, and was content to shape little by little the so-called Pact of the Popular Front, which in those circumstances and at that time should, as I understand it, have been upheld almost completely by the Catholics of Spain.

Therefore, the responsibility, the tremendous moral and material responsibility for this struggle without precedent in history, rests with those who provoked it, who in public and private obstinately maintained that the Spanish problem could only be solved by force of arms, exploiting the discontent of the military leaders; it rests with those who exasperated the combative attitude of our youth, those who insanely applauded inhuman and brutal repressions, those who provoked crises because the death-penalty was not exacted, those who forgot the whole history of Spanish thought and loosed this tide of frenzy and violence.

The Spanish people cry out that they, the rebels, shall not pass. And they shall not pass, for neither reason nor justice is with them, for they have confounded together things that are utterly opposed, Christ and Mahomet, violence and religion, Fascism and Spain!

I ask you to think. Fascism, disguised or not disguised, is essentially Anti-Christian.

JOSE BERGAMIN, director of the Catholic review, CRUZ Y RAYA: *Radio Madrid, Sept. 20, 1936*

WITH GREATER AUTHORITY than mine a true Catholic priest has spoken to you from this microphone. In his words, vibrant with the noblest of human emotions, which is that of truth, the pure truth of a Spaniard and of a believer, many of us have heard, for the first time since this war of fire and blood overwhelmed us, the authorized voice of the Church. A voice which supports and upholds our deepest conviction as Spaniards and believers, that conviction which brings us today so close to the people of Spain that we cannot and will not separate ourselves from them: we feel ourselves one flesh and one spirit. *It is thus that I understand my independence as a writer and my liberty as a Christian Catholic believer*: united inseparably with the people, who have suffered for justice throughout the centuries and are now fighting gloriously, giving their lives for their truth—their liberty, their independence—which is also *our* truth and *our* life. Let all men understand this: the voice of the people is the voice of God.

The clearest of all truths here in Spain, clearer than ever before, even in the blood and fire which envelop us, is this: that on one side is the Spanish people, all the people of every part of our land, knowing themselves, with their tradition and their history, their past and their future clear and bright as never before in the truth of their life and their hopes: *while on the other side a handful, a mob of desperate traitors who have had to call in outside help, foreign, barbarous, anti-Spanish, to fight against us*, provoking this war which is suicide for them but which they hoped might be suicide for Spain. Cast your eyes for one moment on that tragic pyramid of grotesques: generals, bishops, Moors, Carlists in red berets—they are like some fantastic mumming-show of Death.

They entrust the defense of their Spain to Moors and soldiers of the Foreign Legion, for they have no Spanish hands and bodies to defend themselves. This is the truth of Spain in these bloody hours. *We* are the Spaniards: they are a handful of traitors with some thousands of barbarian mercenaries at their command, with some weapons of war bought on credit out of the spoils to which they would reduce our land. And in these they put their trust, or rather their desperation.

By such barbarians some of the dignitaries of our Church seek to defend their impostures—dignitaries of the Church which they have taken from the people, which they have corrupted, prostituted, shamed with avarice and spotted with our blood, the blood of the Spanish people. Listen to this, if you are listening to me, unfaithful shepherds, traitors to Christ! You have placed in the barbarous hands of Legionnaires and Moors the sacred vessels, the riches and treasure which you never offered to your people, the poor, the disinherited, the hungry. And you either give these things as sacrilegious booty, or to convert them into weapons dealing death to your people and your flock. I know you well, bishops who dabble in politics, who chatter of politics. Listen well, for this is an accusation which I make. You, the dignitaries of the Spanish Church, have betrayed that Church, and have robbed the people!

> PIUS XII, in pastoral letter read in all Spanish churches, *March 1939, after fall of Spanish Republic*

WITH GREAT JOY WE address you, dearest sons of Catholic Spain, to express our pastoral congratulations for the gift of peace and victory, with which God has chosen to crown the Christian heroism of your faith and charity, proved in so much and so generous suffering. . . . We give to you, our dear sons of Catholic Spain, to the head of the State and his illustrious government, to the zealous Episcopate and its self-denying clergy, to the heroic combatants, and to all the faithful, Our Apostolic Benediction.

In Spain it is enough to be a mother.
SPANISH PROVERB

Bombing Casualties

HERBERT READ

Dolls' faces are rosier but these were children
their eyes not glass but gleaming gristle
dark lenses in whose quicksilvery glances
the sunlight quivered. These blenched lips
were warm once and bright with blood
but blood
held in a moist bleb of flesh
not spilt and spattered in tousled hair.
In these shadowy tresses
red petals did not always
thus clot and blacken to a scar.

> These are dead faces.
> Wasps' nests are not more wanly waxen
> wood embers not so greyly ashen.

They are laid out in ranks
like paper lanterns that have fallen
after a night of riot
extinct in the dry morning air.

From POEMS FOR SPAIN

NOTICE: *Orphaned children. A lady announces that she is willing to adopt two boys, and another family offers to take in a little girl. They must be orphans and fulfill the following conditions: The children, the two boys and the girl, to be two to three years of age and in good health. Their father to have died fighting for his country against Marxism. The future of the children will be assured by those who adopt them. For particulars apply to Gervasio Villaneuva, priest. Address the Maternity Home, Navarre.*

Notice in DIARIO DE NAVARRA, *fascist territory, Aug. 27, 1937*

"Down With Intelligence!"

RUIZ VILAPLANA

I ONLY HAD a superficial acquaintance with Antonio José. He was introduced to me a few days after my arrival in Burgos, and I realized that here was an interesting personality, very much out of his element in that cold, grey atmosphere.

He had a real passion for music and was absolutely devoted to it, but his restless spirit used also to roam in the field of literature. I read several of his literary productions, and in all of them the modern mood was conspicuous. I did not know his musical compositions, but I was aware of the fact that in Barcelona and Madrid he had something of a name, and had won for himself a reputation, particularly as an authority on folklore, which was richly deserved.

Antonio José was distressed at the lack of interest on the part of Burgos society in artistic matters. He had endeavored, but without success, to rouse them out of their lethargy, but convinced that all his efforts were in vain, he was looking forward to getting away to Madrid or Barcelona where he would find a more congenial environment. I encouraged him in his projects, holding out to him the prospect of a bright future away from that inhospitable region where he was not appreciated and where he was wasting his youthful energies.

One afternoon, on the way up to the castle, he told me of his plans and how he proposed to carry them out. I was quite right, he said, and he was going to leave Burgos and go to Barcelona where he thought he would stay for awhile. In Barcelona particularly he had had a great success with his folklore compositions, and had received attractive proposals of assistance and encouragement. After that he intended to go to Paris—to travel, improve his mind, and make Spanish music known wherever he

105

went, especially the old, popular songs of Castile.

He talked of these things with burning enthusiasm. How he loved Spain, and most of all Castile! . . . He was a fervent admirer of the latter's rich, artistic patrimony, of its old songs, the basis of all his musical compositions.

In love with his art, wrapped up in his folklore studies, shut up in his ivory tower, he lived entirely remote from politics and social problems. Now and again in conversation he would laugh at his own ignorance of those matters—to the extent of confusing the different parties and even the names of their leaders. Nevertheless, although knowing nothing about politics and remaining completely aloof from them, his kindly and generous nature instinctively inclined him toward the working classes, causing him to regard sympathetically all that was humble and lowly.

Perhaps the influence of his folklore studies, the authentic voice of the plains, reflecting as they did the simple griefs and passions of the people; the virile, dramatic accents of the mountains; the deep tenderness of the valleys that he knew and loved so well—all this stirred his emotions and brought him close to the heart of the people. His greatest joy was talking with countrymen and shepherds who taught him their old legends and melodies, and on his return to the city we would hear him deplore the moral and material conditions in which these poor folk lived. I used to call him ironically the "Baudelaire" of Castile.

When the people's *Ateneo* was established Antonio José took on the organizing of musical evenings and lectures. Knowing nothing of the political and trade union significance of the club, and only seeing in it a haven of refuge for the people, the worker and the peasant, he put his whole heart and soul into the job.

Besides giving concerts he managed to organize an *Ateneo* choir whose rendering of choral Mass was his especial pride. From among the workers in the mines and on the railway, from the laborers on the farms and the young shepherds, he recruited an *ensemble* which, developed under his artistic training and direction, attained quite a high standard. With this choir he used to journey on Sundays and local feast days to the various towns and even into the villages, introducing everywhere the gaiety and freshness of a new era, a new spiritual outlook.

The embittered, melancholy Castilians were gladdened by these songs and melodies which expressed so poignantly their innermost feelings. Those grey afternoon hours in the fields were cheered by the sound of the old refrains:

> *Ya se murió el burro*
> *Que acarreaba la vinagre.*
> *Ya lo llevó Dios*
> *De esta vida miserable.*
> *Que tururú . . .*
> *Que tururú . . .*
> *Que tururú . . .*
> *Que tururú . . .*

Wrinkled old women and pallid-faced girls from those arid plains shed tears for the first time in their lives—reluctant tears, forced from their long-suppressed emotions, as they listened to the tender, melancholy strains of those mountain airs:

> *Ya se van los pastores*
> *A la Extremadura . . .*
> *Ya se queda la sierra*
> *Triste y oscura! . . .*

Antonio José, who had had his days of triumph in Barcelona, with a public musically intelligent and instructed in matters of art, who was planning ambitious tours in the East, ingenuously confided to me that nothing had ever affected him so deeply as those Sundays among the people when, as a peddler of art, he scattered his wares along the highways and byways, sometimes receiving a chicken or a basket of fruit by way of payment from the grateful countryfolk.

The well-to-do elements in Burgos, however—the panjandrums of the Casino—did not look with approval on Antonio José: his aloofness from the ordinary bourgeois and official life of the city drew down upon him the hostility of all who had any connection with officialdom, and in particular that of the Church. They had done their best to get him into their own camp, but confronted with his independent and rebellious spirit, gave it up and proceeded to make him the particular target of their resentment.

Antonio José's triumph in Barcelona, recorded in all the local papers, the news of his plans for the future and, above all, his ascendancy over the poorer classes and the affectionate regard in which he was held by them had the effect of fanning the flames of their hostility. And there was an additional source of rancour. Several young men who shared the same ideas and enthusiasms and who were, like Antonio José, of a somewhat restless nature, managed after great efforts to save up enough money to launch an illustrated periodical entitled *Burgos Gráfico*. This was a modern production which, although non-political, did not conform with the prevailing conservative doctrines. Antonio José only wrote on music or on literary topics which had no connection with local affairs. Nevertheless, people criticized him for his association with that "irreligious" publication.

Then, owing to an event of the greatest importance, the paper came to an end after a brief existence. It was all to do with a scandal that had occurred at Estépar, a village in the neighborhood of Burgos. The local priest had violated some young girls, and the villagers, justly indignant, were in a state of agitation and revolt, demanding that he should be punished. The case came up in the court to which I was assigned, and the Bench sentenced the guilty party to twelve years' imprisonment. Certainly it was an appalling business, since the degenerate had not even drawn the line at innocent children of four or five years of age, with grave danger to their young lives.

In Burgos, and, indeed, throughout the country, the matter received enormous publicity, which later, however, gave place— in the cathedral city—to an ominous silence on the subject. It was forbidden to discuss it either in the press or in public. And this absurd suppression of the truth led to the circulation of broadsheets written in rhyme, which were eagerly snatched from the hands of the persons selling them by those interested in the affair. The author and the distributor of these broadsheets were duly arrested and put into prison, to the general satisfaction of the Press and public opinion . . . except the *Burgos Gráfico,* which published an article expressing agreement, it is true, with the punishment imposed on the author of the offending verses, but at the same time claiming that their dissemination—indeed, the fact that they should ever have been composed—was due to the ridiculous hush-hush policy pursued by the reactionary newspapers and opinion.

I remember quite well that in the article in question the ecclesiastical and civil authorities came in for their share of blame for not having uttered a word of formal condemnation of that appalling crime which had tarnished the reputation of a whole village. "The fact that among the sons of the Church there should be such a monster"—the writer of the article went on to argue—"is no reflection on or condemnation of the whole calling, any more than the existence of a soldier who is a coward or a doctor who is a scoundrel brings discredit upon the whole profession. But what is scandalous and blameworthy is the way in which high society, the Church and the Press, have drawn a veil over the whole affair, when the newspapers devote columns to some petty theft committed by a poor working man. If only people had been told the truth and had been discreetly informed as to the punishment of the guilty party, as also the repugnance with which everyone regarded his deed, these obscene couplets concocted by some foolish pen-pusher, would never have been produced."

The article caused a sensation in Burgos and aroused such lively protests that the magazine had to cease publication. What actually happened was that the subscribers, readers and even the advertisers were "charitably" informed of the pernicious and mischievous character of the periodical in question and were told that no Catholic could give any kind of encouragement to it. . . . So, of course, the paper went under.

The military rebellion took place, and Antonio José was

arrested and put into prison. When I heard about this I was afraid of what might happen to him and made a point of mentioning the matter to a high official of the Falangist party. He assured me that his crowd had had nothing to do with Antonio José's arrest. I realized then whence the order had come.

A few days later, overcoming my fears, I went to try to see him at the city gaol, but . . . it was already too late. One of the prison staff, a kindly soul, with some diffidence and obviously feeling at heart as distressed as I was about it, related to me in detail what had happened. It seems that both he and other officials, all of whom were compelled to witness the whole affair, had done their best to prevent matters taking their course, but their efforts had been quite useless, and they were as indignant about it as I was. They understood perfectly well that he had never done anything to deserve the fate that had befallen him; besides, they had conceived quite an affection for him, with his friendly, childlike nature. But. . . .

Poor Antonio José! In his ingenuous way and in his ignorance of the state of affairs, he was always talking of his early release, enthusiastically discussing his plans, and referring to his new compositions. . . .

Two nights earlier he had been taken out of his cell, still half asleep, and put with the group of poor devils at the end of the corridor waiting for their grim marching orders. Then, and only then, did he realize what was happening. He saw the ghastly truth in the terror-stricken faces of his companions, some of them in tears, others being violently sick—and became for a moment like a frightened child. With tears running down his face, with anguished cries he made a vain appeal for some vestige of charity to those whose job it was to execute the criminal orders. With characteristic kindliness and humanity, even in that dread moment, he showed the artist's generosity and sense of the dramatic by asking to be allowed to meet his death tied to a poor boy, almost a child, who was an apprentice at the printers of the ill-fated *Burgos Gráfico*. The two of them bound, they left the prison together to get into the motor 'bus, and, together, brothers in a splendid cause in life as in their ghastly death, they were executed in the Llano de Estépar.

Llano de Estépar! . . . How often towards evening have I gone along to shed silent tears for Antonio José, lying there. I thought of him as I saw him, alone, helpless, terrified by the monsters who were responsible for his death.

And I made a solemn vow that one day a simple monument shall be erected on that spot to the memory of Antonio José and all the other martyrs at rest on that tragic soil. . . . And when that monument is unveiled there will be no military processions, no flag-waving speeches and fanfares . . . but only men and women of the people and a people's choir, composed of workmen and peasants like the one he had formed in Burgos: and with tearful eyes but steadfast hearts it shall chant that tune which used to stir his emotions so deeply:

> *Ya se van los pastores*
> *Ya se van marchando . . .*
> *Más de cuatro zagalas*
> *Quedan llorando. . . . !*

From Burgos Justice, *Knopf, New York, 1938;*
original title of chapter, "The Shooting
of the Poet-Musician, Antonio José"

Madrid

MANUEL ALTOLAGUIRRE

Horizon of war, whose lights,
whose unexpected sunrises, so brief,
whose fleeting dawns, promises, fires,
multiply the interminable death.
Here in Madrid, by night, solitary, sad,
the front and my frown are both synonymous
and above my gaze like a lament
the heroes crash, they fall submerged
in the green abyss of my face.
I know that I am deserted, that I am alone,
that the front parallel with my frown,
disdains my grief and me accompanies.
Before the glorious circle of fire
I can evoke nothing, nor anything from anyone.
There is no memory, pleasure, lived before,
which I can call back from my past.
There is no absence, no legend, no hope
to calm my agony with its illusion.

Here in Madrid, facing death,
my narrow heart keeps hidden
a love which grieves me which I cannot
even reveal to this night
before this immense field of heroism.

English version by Inez and Stephen Spender
From POEMS FOR SPAIN

Rather Be Widows of Heroes Than Wives of Cowards

DOLORES IBARRURI (*La Pasionaria*)

S PAIN WILL EITHER WIN as a free democratic country or will cease to exist altogether. The enemy cannot be defeated by enthusiasm alone, by faith in the justice of our cause alone. War is an art and a science and must be mastered. Despite the heroism of the anti-fascist fighters, the enemy has succeeded in dealing many blows because we lack organization, discipline and military science. These shortcomings must be made good, otherwise the enemy may pass. (*Voices: "He will not pass!"*)

He will not pass if we possess the will to victory, and that means the will to organize victory. We must establish order in the rear. Enough of street masquerades, enough of sham uniforms. The government has decided to militarize the people's militia. That is not enough; the whole nation must be militarized. A halt must be called to the inefficiency in the rear. In Madrid, houses are being built. Whom are they being built for, when the war is not yet over and the enemy has not been smashed? When we win, we shall build all the houses we want; but now labor power and funds are needed for the erection of fortifications and digging of trenches for the defense of Madrid.

Every working man who remains in the rear must become a watchful sentinel and keep a keen eye on the machinations of the enemy. The rebel generals boast that in launching four columns against Madrid they can count on the aid of a "fifth column," that is, the enemy in the rear, in the capital itself. We must never forget that the enemy "fifth column" exists and is active.

113

We must not conceal the fact that Madrid is in danger. The removal of this danger depends on the people of Madrid, and on them alone. The people of Madrid must remember the example of the Petrograd workers who in 1919 succeeded by their courage, endurance and discipline not only in repulsing but also in destroying the large enemy forces advancing on Petrograd. All the proletarians in Madrid, men and women, must learn the use of arms. International democracy is on the side of the Spanish people. The working people of the land of the Soviets are on their side.

They will not pass, the fascists will not pass! They will not pass because we are not alone!

The lives and future of our children are at stake. This is no time for hesitation; this is no time for timidity. We women must demand that our men be courageous. We must inspire them with the thought that a man must know how to die worthily. We prefer to be widows of heroes rather than wives of cowards!

Address at a People's Front meeting,
Madrid, October 14, 1936

114

"It Shall Not Be!"

FERNANDO VALERA

PEOPLE OF MADRID! History has presented you in this hour with the great mission of rising up before the world as the obelisk of Liberty. You will know how to be worthy of so exalted a destiny. You will tell the world how men defend themselves; how peoples fight; how Liberty triumphs. You will tell the world that only a people that knows how to die for Liberty can live for freedom.

People of Spain! Put your eyes, your will, your fists at the service of Madrid. Accompany your brothers with faith, with courage, send your possessions, and if you have nothing else, offer us your prayers. Here in Madrid is the universal frontier that separates Liberty and Slavery. It is here in Madrid that two incompatible civilizations undertake their great struggle: love against hate; peace against war; the fraternity of Christ against the tyranny of the Church. . . .

Citizens of Madrid! Each of you has here on this soil something that is ash; something that is soul. It cannot be! It shall not be that impious intruders trample the sacred tombs of our dead! The mercenaries shall not enter as heralds of dishonor into our homes! It cannot be. It shall not be that the sombre birds of intolerance beat their black wings over the human conscience. It cannot be! It shall not be that the Fatherland, torn, broken, entreat like a beggar before the throne of the tyrant. It cannot be! It shall not be! Today we fight. Tomorrow, we conquer. And on the pages of history, Man will engrave an immense heart. This is Madrid. It fought for Spain, for Humanity, for Justice, and with the mantle of its blood sheltered all the men of the world. Madrid! Madrid!

Excerpt from a radio address, November 8, 1936

The International Brigade Arrives at Madrid

PABLO NERUDA

The morning of a cold month,
of an agonizing month, soiled by mud and by smoke,
a month without knees, a sad month of siege and misfortune,
when across the wet windowpanes of my house the African jackals
    were heard
howling with their rifles and their teeth full of blood,
then,
when for hope we had only a dream of gunpowder, when we
    thought
that the world was full only of devouring monsters and furies,
then, breaking through the frost of Madrid's cold month, in the
    mist of the dawn,
I saw with these eyes that I have, with this heart that sees,
I saw the arrival of the staunch ones, the towering soldiers
of the thin and hard and ripe and ardent brigade of stone.

It was the grievous time when the women
bore absence like a terrible live coal,
and Spanish death, more acid and sharp than other deaths,
hovered over fields honored till then by wheat.

Along the streets the broken blood of men mixed
with the water gushing from the shattered heart of houses;
the bones of torn children, the heartrending
silence in mourning of the mothers, the eyes
of the defenseless closed forever,
were like the sadness and the lost, were like a garden spat on,
were the faith and the flower murdered forever.

Comrades,
then,
I saw you,
and my eyes are even now filled with pride
because I saw you across the misty morning coming to the pure
    forehead of Castile,
silent and firm,
like bells before dawn,
full of solemnity and with blue eyes coming from far away,
from your corners, from your lost lost countries, from your
    dreams
full of burnt sweetness and guns
to defend the Spanish city in which cornered liberty
might fall and die bitten by the beasts.

Brothers, from now on
may your purity and your strength, your solemn history,
be known to child and man, to woman and old man,
may it reach all beings devoid of hope, descend the mines
    corroded by sulphuric air,
ascend the inhuman stairs of the slave,
that all the stars, that all the ears of grain of Castile and
    of the world
may write your name and your bitter struggle
and your victory powerful and earthly like a red elm.

Because with your sacrifice you have caused to be reborn
the lost faith, the absent soul, confidence in the earth,
and through your abundance, through your nobility, through
    your dead,
as through a valley of hard rocks of blood
flows an immense river with doves of steel and hope.

Translated by Angel Flores
from RESIDENCE ON EARTH,
New Directions, New York, 1946

Arms In Spain

REX WARNER

So that men might remain slaves, and
    that the little good
they hoped for might be turned all bad
    and the iron lie
stamped and clamped on growing tender
    and vigorous truth,
 These machine-guns were despatched from Italy.

So that the drunken General and the
    Christian millionaire
might continue blindly to rule in complete darkness,
that on rape and ruin order might be
    founded firm,
these guns were sent to save civilization.

Lest the hand should be held at last more
    valuable than paper,
lest man's body and mind should be
    counted more than gold,
lest love should blossom, not shells, and
    break in the land
these machine-guns came from Christian Italy.

And to root out reason, lest hope be held in it,
to turn love inward into corroding hate,
lest men should be men, for the banknotes
    and the mystery
these guns, these tanks, these gentlemanly words.

From POEMS FOR SPAIN

Die Heimat ist weit,
doch wir sind bereit.
Wir kämpfen und siegen für dich:
Freiheit!

Fritz Giga

ALFRED KANTOROWICZ

AFTER THE SUCCESSFUL ADVANCE on the Spanish southern front, in the Pozoblanco sector, the Battalions of the XIII International Brigade found themselves in the Sierra Mulva hills above the city of Penarroya. The town, in the neighborhood of important metal and coal mines, was stubbornly defended by the Fascists.

For those members of the Brigade who came from the north of Europe, the Scandinavians, Dutch, Flemish, Swiss, Germans, Austrians, Czechs, Poles and Alsatians—the Brigade counted twenty-four nationalities—the summer climate of this southern part of Spain, the swamp and malaria district of Extremadura, was hard to bear. The daily ration of water was only a liter, and the food was scant and poor. We suffered from hunger and thirst, from heat and the prevalence of insects. Many took sick.

We looked forward to the evenings, which were a little cooler. After supper we sat on the grass or on stones around our quarters. One evening, we sat as usual, relaxed, because the moon had not yet come up and the sound of motors which we could hear were not those of airplanes, but of trucks. We could see their far off lights winding over the hills.

A few feet away the night watch were singing Spanish folk songs under their breath. The guards paced up and down. We could see their shadows in the last light of the long summer day. Then suddenly someone approached us from the right. The

119

guard called for his password: *Unidos,* he said, and the other answered as he was supposed to: *Valiente!*

It was an officer of the Spanish tank unit: three light tanks that had lain for weeks near us, ready for action. Every evening an officer came over to us to get the password of our sector for the next twenty-four hours. For the next day it was *Bilbao—No pasaran!* Then the officer would ask the General for news. The General would answer indifferently, in a deep voice, *Sin novedad* —"Nothing new," and with a mumbled *Salud* the officer would disappear into the darkness again. It would then be exactly 10 o'clock.

"*Sin novedad,*" repeated the intelligence officer of the Brigade, a man named Putzke, from Berlin, "it seems to me that the thing Giga pulled off last night is something new that might interest the Spanish tank officer."

"He knows of it long ago," Franz, the tall adjutant of the General, assured him. "The whole front section is talking about it."

Fritz Giga, leader of the reconnoitering unit of the Brigade, had put through an insanely dangerous mission the night before. The valley of Penarroya lay between the chain of the Sierra Mulva and the Sierra Noria hills, and there, on the left flank of our front line, rose a flat, rocky hill. A house with thick walls stood on this hill and was, we knew, the Fascist observation post. For weeks heavy machine-gun fire from this house had interrupted our communications with the neighboring VI Workers Brigade from Málaga. The Sixth Brigade was holding the Sierra Noria, and at night a company of their men joined a group of ours in the valley. During the day, however, the Company went up into the hills again and communication became very difficult because every move could be seen from the Fascist post. Also, fewer deserters had managed to get over to us during the night since the post had been established. This nest of machine guns had been getting on our nerves more and more.

One might think that we should have tried to destroy this nest with artillery fire. True, we had two cannon at our disposal, of 10.5 calibre and of the year 1913, and about fifty rounds of ammunition, or fifty-two, to be exact. But these had to be spared for more important undertakings.

The night before, Fritz Giga had reached this post and blown up the house with the thick walls. It was a hazardous feat. There were four men in his group, a Spanish worker from Penarroya, who knew the terrain and whose name was Julio; a young Austrian named Rudolf, who was a natural sharpshooter; a Polish miner, Antek, who had learned to handle dynamite as part of his profession, and Giga himself. Led by the Spaniard, they had slipped through the porous Fascist position and approached the house from the rear. With hardly a sound they overpowered the sleeping machine-gun crew, which consisted of only three men, and then Antek and Giga mined the house with professional speed, while Julio stood on watch and Rudolf guarded the three prisoners. Then, with the three Fascists, who had been warned to keep silent or be shot, they climbed down the rocks. At the foot of the hill Antek set off the fuse. They awaited the explosion in the shelter of the rocks; then made their way in and out of the Fascist lines and were back to their position in barely three hours.

Sergeant Kieper, a countryman of Fritz Giga's, said; "For Fritz everything comes out all right—he's immune to bullets!"

The General replied sourly: "No one is immune. Giga prepared the whole thing carefully, and that's why he was able to get back with all of them."

Putzke, the intelligence officer, remarked appreciatively: "It was good work! I studied the place of the explosion through my glasses this morning. The rocks are flat, as if they had been shaved—they won't be able to put any observers or machine-guns there anymore!"

"Giga always thinks out action like that—he's always on his toes," said Ludwig, the chief of the planning division of our Brigade.

Sergeant Kieper continued: "Nobody can hold that man back. How often have I warned him not to take such risks, but he always answers me, 'What risk is there for me? I've been dead a long time already.'"

"A dead man on leave," said Putzke.

"We are all dead men on leave," said the General. "All anti-fascists are dead men on leave."

That is true! We are all dead men on leave—all of us who have sworn to fight as long as there are Nazis or Fascists in the world.

Sometimes, on those evenings, someone tells stories from his own life. It is dark. We can't see the speaker, we can only hear his voice. He tells the story without pathos or sentimentality. Even though he is usually telling about an especially hard and dangerous bit of the hard and dangerous life of an anti-fascist fighter, somehow we laugh a lot. In looking back, dangers and terrors which have been survived and surmounted often have a comic aspect—indeed, don't we experience things daily which have a humorous side, even to the man who lives through them, provided he does live through them? That bomb, for instance, that should have blown you to bits, but didn't go off, is an excuse to laugh. Then we feel we have stolen a little more from death . . . but the story that Fritz Giga told us yesterday, the story of his murder, that was hardly something to laugh about. There was nothing humorous about it in any way, and yet the fact that he could tell it to us, sitting in our midst, made us glad—not exactly gay, but glad in a serious, thoughtful way that was good for our whole conscious being, for our faith in ourselves and in our cause.

We sat there, listening to the General. He was telling us about the struggles of the workers of the Rhineland more than seventeen years ago when they defended themselves against the lawless gangs which were the forerunners of Hitler's hoodlums. There were some among us who had participated in those early battles against Fascism and recalled that the General, a former officer in the Imperial Army, had been converted to Socialism during the First World War. When the young German Republic needed protection against uprisings organized by Kapp and

Ludendorff in the spring of 1920, he became one of the organizers of this first resistance against German counter-revolution.

"Fritz, my boy," interrupts the General, "Were you in Oberhausen during the Kapp riots?"

"Sure," replies Giga excitedly, "I was the leader of the group that occupied the City Hall there. We defended the town for a whole week, alone. Then we were relieved by the workers of Düsseldorf."

"Oh, you must have been the skinny one," remarks the General, adding after a short pause, "Don't you remember me, Fritz?"

"Were you in Oberhausen too?" Giga gets up and scrutinizes the General's face. The General laughs. "Look, Fritz, do you think that if you haven't recognized me in the Spanish daylight, you will now, in the moonlight?"

No gleam of recognition illuminates Fritz's face.

"Well, I remember you," the General continues. "When we met with the Oberhausen military leaders of the anti-fascist workers organization, you were there—as a unit leader." He pauses again. "Remember me now?"

"You—you were the captain! Why, that means that you—you are—"

"I am nobody," the General interrupts hastily. "I have no name, only nicknames. Now, as you all know, I am General Gomez. Who I was before—we both better forget."

Fritz Giga stutters inarticulately. In the moonlight we can see the outlines of his thin body, and sense the convulsive tremors that pass through his entire frame. We now know the origin of this nervous ailment, which starts at his left shoulder and distorts his face at regular intervals.

"You know," he says apologetically, "*since then* I can't always remember things exactly."

Since then, when the Nazi papers gleefully announced his "suicide" in prison. . . . We knew what he meant, because yesterday he had told us his story:

"After the Reichstag Fire, when terror began to spread

throughout the country, I was forced to leave my room. I dared not stay there any longer, because the Nazis had said often enough that I would be one of the very first they wanted to 'get' when they came to power. They knew I had struggled against them from the first appearance of the Nazi menace.

"I had no work. The fellow-workers from the mines, with whom I took shelter, were also without work. I didn't dare go out on the street in daylight. But after dark I went out to meet my friends, and we tried to organize opposition to the terror that was raging. Our group grew smaller and smaller. The Nazis arrested everybody of whom they had the slightest suspicion. And one evening they caught me, too. Just as I was going to a meeting at Max's . . . one of those gangsters saw me on the street and recognized me. He whistled, and immediately about half-a-dozen S.A. men ran out of a little tavern near by and surrounded me. 'So we've got the Red dog,' said one of them, and they took me to the S.A. headquarters.

"Upstairs was one of those lean dark-haired officers. I did not know him, nor he me. He was the Storm Troop leader. He asked me first if I could sing the Horst Wessel Song, and I said no. He said that soon the Devil in hell would whistle it for me and I could learn it then. The S.A. men standing around had a good laugh at that. They knew his witticism already, and he snapped his lips together like Goebbels, when he has spouted a phrase and expects a certain reaction. I thought to myself, here is someone who won't give up easily, but thinks up plenty to plague a person, and I said to myself, 'Fritz, even if you have to die here, they won't learn anything from you.'

"Then he began to question me. Somebody handed him a list, and he wanted to know where Heiner, of the miners union, was hiding himself, and where was Emil of the *Anti-Fascist Fighters?* I did not know where Emil was, but I knew where Heiner was, because we lived together. I said I had not seen Heiner and Emil for weeks. At that, they wanted to begin beating me at once, but the Storm Trooper leader waved them off, saying: 'So, we will show you where your friend Emil is.' An

S.A. man opened a door to an adjoining room, and there lay Emil, on the floor, making a most curious noise. He babbled, like a child that has not yet learned to speak. *Wah, wah, wah* . . . and the leader said: 'Go in and take a good look at the Red pig. He, too, didn't want to speak in the beginning.'

"I went to him and said: 'Emil, what have they done to you?' but he only babbled, and stared at me, and I could see what an effort he was making to say something to me, but he could not, because they had with a blow, probably with a black-jack, broken his jaw, and his chin was hanging down, straight down, so it was impossible for him to talk. He could only babble and look at me with his big eyes, and then he lost consciousness. I turned around and said: 'Please get a doctor for him.' The whole band broke out laughing and the leader said: 'We cure them here ourselves. He doesn't need any doctor.' I tried to go back to Emil, when the chief of the gang struck me from behind with his leather whip, just under the knees, so that I fell down."

One of us whistled through his teeth.

"Friends," said Giga, "when someone hits you just under the knees that way with a leather whip, you can't help falling, unless you're prepared for it."

"And Emil?" asked Sergeant Kieper.

"Emil? I never saw him again. They closed the door on him. He, also, was supposed to have 'committed suicide' in prison, as I was said to have done. He was a good fellow. You could trust him.

"I will never forget how he lay there and said *wah, wah, wah* with his broken jaw."

"At least they couldn't get any more out of him," said Karl Putzke in a matter-of-fact tone.

"That's just what I thought at the time. During the whole 'hearing' I always had to think of it. Several times, before I lost consciousness, I thought: 'If only they would break your jaw, so you couldn't speak at all—that would be the best thing that could happen.'"

"But they didn't do you that favor?"

"No," said Giga, and went on with his story:

" ' So you see,' the leader repeated, 'he did not want to speak either, your friend Emil—perhaps you will be more reasonable' and then he went on to ask me about a lot of names and addresses. He said that if I was not stubborn he would let me go again, and no one would do me any harm. I made no answer. 'You'll say something soon,' he said. 'Very well, you Red dog, if you don't do it with good-will, you'll do it with bad,' and, with that, he struck me across the face with his whip, while the others hit me with their sticks. I growled: 'You are heroes! Twenty against one,' and then one hit me so hard on the head that I lost consciousness and fell."

"Yes, twenty against one, that's their method. Then they were brave," remarked Putzke, who had also been in a concentration camp, in Oranienburg.

"When I came to, I was lying on a table in the middle of the room. They had thrown cold water over my head. I spit out blood and teeth. This amused them. The leader came up to me and said: 'Now, little friend, have you learned how to talk? Otherwise, we have a few kinds of special massage.' Then he became furious and shouted: 'Dog! We'll crack you yet. We've been able to get things out of much stronger bodies than that little shell of yours.'

"They threw me from the table and beat me again with the whips and leather straps and cartridge belts until I lost consciousness once more. This time it took longer, because they did not strike me with any hard objects, but only those which hurt most but do not knock you out. Finally, however, I did sink into oblivion.

"When I woke I was lying on the table again. They were all standing around me smoking cigarettes. One of them bent over me. He drew in on his cigarette and spat out quickly in my face, then threw his cigarette away and shouted: 'Damned it—it tastes like rotten pig, and they all laughed.

"I felt pain everywhere, but I could not move. Some of them held my arms, others my legs. I lay on the table just like a cross-

126

bound Christ," said Giga with a little laugh. None of us laughed with him, although we liked to laugh whenever we had a chance.

"Suddenly I had to cry out," continued Giga. "They started to burn holes in my flesh with their cigarettes, around the navel. It hurts terribly," he added, as if to make an excuse for what he seemed to think was weakness. "They bored into my skin with the glowing ends, then threw the cigarettes away and lit new ones. 'Don't get excited, my little friend,' said the leader, 'we only want to give you a visiting card to take with you on your way'—that was the kind of jokes they made. They were boys, perhaps eighteen years old, at least most of them, while I had fought in the World War and worked fifteen years in the mines. They kept on and it hurt so much that I flung myself from one side of the table to the other like a crazy man. They almost wrenched my arm and knee joints. One of them wanted to hit me over the head with the rubber club to keep me quiet, but the leader told him not to do it, so that I would feel everything properly.

"But I did not cry out again. I didn't want to give them that satisfaction. Above all, I was afraid that under the circumstances some name or address would escape my mouth. I bit my lower lip with my teeth, harder and harder till the blood came, and I did not feel the other pain so much. However, I finally lost consciousness again.

"I woke up once more from pain, and again fainted from pain. After the third time I was numbed against the pain. When they had finished the swastika on my belly, I fell off the table and lay on the floor. Then one of them stepped on my head with the heel of his boot and then I felt nothing more and I was happy, for I thought—now it's over Fritz and they didn't get anything out of you.

"I lay in a sort of trance on the floor and heard them talking. They said that they ought to finish off the pig since there was nothing more to get out of him. Several of them lifted me up and threw me, with a swing of their arms, out of the window, which was on the third floor, down to the sidewalk. Then what happened, I don't know."

What happened to Fritz Giga then he learned afterwards from other friends of his, who had been told the story by the anti-fascists of the town.

He lay on the sidewalk all night. Toward morning a passerby saw him. He was thought to be dead. They took him to the morgue. *Suicide in prison,* announced the Nazi evening papers in their evil jargon: "The notorious anti-fascist Fritz Giga during his examination jumped out of the third-story window and was crushed on the concrete pavement. Doctors who examined him pronounced him dead."

Meanwhile, Fritz Giga lay unconscious in the morgue. The doctor who was supposed to sign his death certificate came in late in the afternoon; in those days the doctors were very busy, and the dead could wait.

When he examined the bloody mass of flesh that lay before him, he detected signs of life. He could not make up his mind to fill out the death certificate as long as the mass still breathed. He would come by again later in the evening when the suicide would surely have breathed his last.

He said this to the Nazis who had "examined" Giga the night before. Some of them were standing around, waiting to get the death papers in their hands. They must be sure that "suicide" was written there, because "there must be order in everything." Hitler would want to say in some future speech that he could guarantee his "national revolution" had been completed "without a drop of blood being shed." If anti-fascist weaklings wanted to take their own lives, what can honest S.A. men do to prevent them? Hitler's word is Hitler's word, and a death certificate that reads *suicide* throws the word *murder* into the face of the insolent liars who dare criticize.

Everything must be in order. When the doctor came back later in the evening, the bloody mass was still breathing, the death rattle in his throat. The doctor also wore the brown Nazi uniform, but fortunately not all that wear the uniform are Nazis at heart. There are many who retain human feelings. Was it because the doctor was struggling with humanitarian considerations, or was it because of a professional sense of duty that he could not condemn a body to the category of the dead when there was still life in it? In any event, he ordered the body to be transferred to the hospital.

The next morning the doctor came to examine the mass of flesh and bones, which by this time had been cleaned up. He had not thought that the *suicide* would live through the night. But this astounding many-lived creature was still breathing. The doctor reported it to the head physician. It was an interesting case. Both doctors went over this phenomenon. They found five fractures of the skull, damaged kidneys, about a dozen other fractures, internal hemorrhages, and the swastika burnt around the navel. Still this broken human being continued to live.

Soon the S.A. men strode into the room with their heavy boots. They were led to the bed of the unconscious man and were asked to be patient. They would be informed when death occurred.

Then, with a feeling of professional sportsmanship, the doctors began to operate on Fritz Giga, trying to put him together again. He was really a most interesting subject for experiment and study for young internes, and his case was an exceptional test of skill for the master surgeons. Students of medicine, internes, medical professors' assistants, and even curious professors themselves stood around the table where Giga's "case" was being demonstrated. Fritz Giga had not yet regained consciousness six days later when the S.A. men came again. A week later, when they marched into the room once more, he had just relapsed into unconsciousness after a new operation.

The S.A. men grew impatient. They wanted to know if, and when, the pig would finally die. They had no understanding of this un-German talk about humanity, which the doctors used as an excuse. Was that carrying out the principles of the Führer, to waste so much time and medical skill on an inferior being that should by rights have been eaten by the worms long ago?

These and similar reflections of the new German spirit were

revealed by comrades who later escaped the Nazi hell. In Paris and Prague and Brussels, the story of Fritz Giga was told and re-told in anti-fascist circles. Through them, it was learned that the final attitude of the S.A. Storm Troopers of Oberhausen seemed to be that "if the pig was put together again, so that he really lived, he could be examined again." Indeed, this prospect excited the saviors of Germany; that would be a fine thing—to be able to torture to death someone that had *already been tortured to death!* A new sensation—one that Storm Troopers did not experience every day!

After that they took interest in the progress of Giga's recovery. After six weeks he was still not ready to be moved, much less to be examined. Two S.A. men came to make sure of it, and stood beside his bed. In these surroundings they were a bit circumspect, and, as is their manner, they wanted to pose as being very "resolute and manly." One of them, a Scharführer (sergeant of the S.A.), who had taken part in Giga's first "examination," put his arms on his hips in the approved Göring manner, and growled, half to Giga, and half to the doctor and the nurse who were standing on the other side of the bed: "We'll give him two weeks more; if he isn't dead by then we'll take him with us." He glanced angrily and slyly at the doctor and added: "We'll be able to cure him all right, and quicker and more thoroughly than you honorable doctors!" He dared to say this because this doctor was half-Jewish and was terrified at the possibility of losing his position.

The other S.A. man also wanted to have something to say. He laughed heartily, and added: "And cheaper than here, too. We have a few special massages that have brought all the sick men to their feet so far." He was a devoted pupil and follower of his Troop leader. He knew all his witticisms by heart, and never missed a chance of coming out with them. "Well, then, Doctor," ended the sergeant jovially, "it's understood—in two weeks—living or dead—" They stamped threateningly out, their high boots resounding through the hall.

The young nurse, who had developed a deep sympathy for her thin, broken patient during the last weeks, began to cry with indignation. "What outrageous talk," she sobbed.

"Hss, Sister Marta, how can you say such things?" the half-Jewish doctor whispered anxiously, and glanced around him to see if the patients in the neighboring beds had heard her.

"I must get out of here before they come back," he thought. to himself: "So I have two weeks," and then: "How can I get in touch with my friends?" He could see no way. Most of them would have changed addresses by this time anyway. And whom could he send to them? The young nurse?

"I must get out of here before they come back," he thought. He tried to raise himself up. He could only do it with the greatest effort, and it gave him great pain. He realized that he was too weak to make an escape. Perhaps in ten or twelve days' time he might manage it.

However, ten days later, another group of S.A. men came on a surprise visit and demanded Giga's custody, on the authority of orders from higher up. The doctor in charge took a hurried look at the orders, which seemed to be authentic, and shrugged his shoulders helplessly. Sister Marta turned white and could hardly hold back the tears.

There were four men in this group. "I looked at them," Giga told us, "and I did not believe I was seeing. For one of them was Otto and another was Karl. I had worked together with Otto in the same mine. Karl was a boyhood friend. I knew that many a good man had gone over or been converted to the Nazi cause—but Otto! Otto, who had been in the labor movement since 1918 and of whom I had always thought—there is a man you can trust! Otto in the brown uniform? I simply couldn't believe it!

"I couldn't stop looking at him, but he turned away, and growled: 'Make it snappy—we have more to do than stand around here.'

"I pulled on my trousers with the help of one of them. As I dressed I hardly thought about myself, because I could think of nothing but Otto, and how it was possible that they had really won him over.

"Only when I was finally ready, and two of them took hold of me, one on each side, because I could not walk alone, and as I looked at the face of the doctor and saw the nurse taking out a handkerchief and wiping away her tears, did it dawn upon me: 'Well, Fritz, now they have you again, and everything will begin all over.' Death no longer held any fear. I said to myself: 'You should have been dead a long time already, Fritz,' and I wished that I were really dead, and that they had not brought me back to life just so they could put me to death for the second time.

"Only one thing was easier this time. There was no danger of their finding out anything from me. More than two months had gone by since my first examination and I had not the slightest idea of the whereabouts of the people they wanted to find."

Down on the street stood an Opel car, a four-seater. The S. A. men whom Giga did not know were supporting him, and Karl and Otto walked behind so that he could not see them. A few passersby stopped to see what was going on.

"They dragged me rather than led me," said Giga, "I was still half a corpse. And soon everything would be over, I thought to myself. As I stood in front of the car and one of them opened the door, I thought: 'This is your last minute of freedom, Fritz, look around you, once more.' I trembled at the idea of stepping into the car and held back as they tried to push me in.

"One of the men whom I did not know took out his revolver and looked hard at me, saying: 'If you make any disturbance here, that's the end of you.' I answered: 'Here or there, what difference does it make?' But I was too weak to resist any longer.

"They raised me into the car. Otto and Karl took me between them in the back seat. The others got in front and off we went. The strain had been too much for me, and I lost consciousness.

"When I came to again, we were still riding in the car. It seemed to me that we had driven far away from the town. They had put me in one corner of the car, with my head resting on the back of the seat. I heard Karl say: 'He'll come out of it all right, otherwise we'll carry him.' I did not move, for I did not want to talk to them anymore. I was surprised that they had not brought me to the Storm Troop headquarters in Oberhausen. They drove quite fast. We whisked through several villages, but I could not see where we were going.

"I wondered to myself if I must go through as much suffering as the first time before I got so far that I didn't feel anything; I hoped that this time it would go quicker. . . . Then I wondered if Otto and Karl would be there when they tortured me. I could not quite imagine it, but still, if they had really become Nazis, anything could be expected of them.

"Suddenly the car stopped on a country road. I heard Karl call out: 'Turn off the light.' The driver switched off the headlights.

"Otto turned to the other Nazi: 'You change the license number,' and to Karl he said: 'Lift him out carefully!'

"They lifted me out of the car and noticed that I was no longer unconscious. Otto shook me gently and asked: 'Are you awake, Fritz?'

"I answered: 'I'm not going to talk anyway. Put an end to me as quickly as possible.'

"Otto put his arm around me: 'You old fool—did you really believe. . . . Here is the border, Fritz. We'll bring you safely over. It's only a few hundred meters. We have friends on the other side that are ready for you. They've been waiting for some time.'

"And the driver said: 'And give them our greetings, over there, Fritz.'

"And the other said: 'Do your best out there. We'll stay here at our posts. *Rot Front!*'

"Then Karl and Otto took me between them again. They wanted to brace me, but such joy went through me that I had the strength to take a few steps alone."

The friends who were waiting for him on the other side of the border took him to a place where he was well cared for. It took several months before Fritz Giga was really on his feet again. It was almost two years before he got back half his normal strength.

Then when the Fascists and Nazis began their attack on the

Spanish people, he volunteered as one of the first in the International Brigades of anti-fascists. It is understandable that at first they did not want to take this half-crippled, nerve-ridden man into the ranks where conditions were extremely difficult and dangerous. He had already fought and suffered enough, and they needed men like him in other positions of trust. But he had so much will and energy that he was finally able to persuade them to take him in. One must understand what it meant for him to be able to fight against his torturers, or men like them, with weapons in his hand.

He soon stood out, because of his bravery and energy, and was given leadership of a company, his beloved reconnoitering unit.

So now he stood in front of us, small, lean, but brimming over with vitality. He didn't look his thirty-eight years. Through his body ran this nervous twitch, from his left shoulder down, that distorts his face in almost regular rhythm. That was what remained with him of that night in the Storm Troop headquarters and in the morgue of Oberhausen.

But this man, who hardly had a sound place in his body, was held together by a holy hate. He didn't live his life anymore, it seemed to glow out of him, this second life, which served only to sublimate his revenge against the enemies of humanity.

He would be extinguished soon, we all knew it. But his life had found its fulfillment. Here, in his second life, he had revenged himself upon his own murderers.

From Germany: A Self-Portrait,
Edited by Harlan R. Crippen,
Oxford University Press,
New York, 1944

The Defenses

BEN MADDOW

White sky, and moonlight famous in our eyes;
locked by the tree, self-turning, kissed,
lost in our fierce imaginative love.

Then in morning heavenly the moon goes calm and transparent;
then we walk to our work, speaking subtly or smiling,

Writing in freedom, the thought moving among the papers
like a familiar bird; or looking, or asking;
the faces of everyone lighted almost with motives of love.

And then: but the cheerful radio ends in music,
the wrist-watch continues its simple seconds, and our hands
drop in the midst of lunch: —what was it?—
and feel the sick thrill of disaster.

Reading aloud in a room in the city and there came
extras at midnight like a violent heart-beat:
we too, some time, must, must

Set guns on the marble sills of the university;
our friends dead; the fascists controlling the insane asylum;

The pale eyes of our people; the bitter retreat;
defending the square of burned grass in the park;

And that night the open faces, the bandages black with wounds,
the alive going slowly back, entrenching by stones, by brook,
cursing the fatal moonlight that brings bombardment.

Yes by this tree we kissed, for which the shells are searching
minute by minute, may find and may destroy.

O cities across an ocean, Yenan, Chungking, with dark steel
guard yourselves! And you, capital of our world,

Madrid, Madrid!—since your great trenches hold

Death back from love; and if they hold, keep safe
our trees, our harbors, and our happiness.

From SALUD!
International, New York, 1938

non-intervention

(1937)

FALANGIST SPEAKER: "The Basques are anything but Spaniards. They don't even know our language!"

MIGUEL DE UNAMUNO: (rising) "As you all know, I am a Basque. But I have also had the pleasure of teaching some of the most distinguished inhabitants of Madrid the Spanish language."

GEN. MILLAN ASTRAY: (waving pistol) "Down with intelligence!"

MIGUEL DE UNAMUNO: "You will conquer but you will not convince!"

GEN. MILLAN ASTRAY: (pointing pistol at Unamuno) "Long live death!"

TRANSCRIPT FROM NATIONALIST MEETING held in Salamanca in 1937, in the presence of Franco's wife, Carmen, various church dignitaries, others.

I see and feel the People's Front fighters are making my war for me and for all of us, for all men, women and children. Spain's is the first opening battle of man for man—perhaps it is the most decisive battle. Anyway, it is ours, as they must know and we must know. I feel we do, and that we realize as they fight that we have to finish what they are starting.

The Spanish defenders are our world leaders.

STATEMENT FOUND IN LINCOLN STEFFENS' TYPEWRITER, *after his death on August 9, 1936.*

The World Will Be Ours

FRANCISCO GINER

We shall all be men
Facing a world that dies at end of day.
Love touching our temples, even as does the air,
Dwells in our open hearts.
Shouting and quarreling are futile: down by the river
The road that opens under the bright, full moon
Awaits our eyes and our thirst:
We shall all be men.
And because our brothers grimly fight in blood,
Because our hands shudder as with red roses,
The very stars promise new hope for tomorrow:
The world will be ours!

It does not matter that now the earth is moaning
With the foam of the fight on her lips,
Nor that the trees are blown by the winds of crime:
Love is already on her way through the air
With her hands outspread like a hundred wings,
Trembling in the song of a hundred seas.
They would cut short her flight over the world,
Hold back the night from embracing with her,
While they gnash their teeth at their own impotency.
Do not fear, brothers who fight with anxiety in your eyes:
It does not matter that their hands raise a thousand guns,
Nor that they sow the skies with assassin planes:
Our love will triumph!
We have raised shoulder-high our love for these lakes and hills,
We have our faith, ravishing our hearts

With hope and with life:
We have tomorrow flowing in our veins!

The War fires our woods and our meadows,
The bodies of a thousand brothers break like branches,
Our lips are sprayed with the blood of a thousand enemies.
But always we have Life with us,
And a world that awaits the warmth of our hands.
The light has died above our shattered houses,
And shines no longer on once lustrous silk.
But in our eyes nestles a glowing vision,
And our truth from the mouth shouts aloud to the world.

It does not matter that our hearts are grieving
For the dead on the plains:
To the New Tomorrow we speak
From the truth that burdens our souls,
From the sorrow that already fills the earth:
And the seeds that our fallen brothers have planted
Will spring from her.
We bring in our hands the strength of growing things,
And the love that floods our hearts shall water our fields.

English version by Ruth Lechlitner,
from AND SPAIN SINGS.

Not Valid For Travel in Spain

MIKE QUIN

THE OTHER DAY a friend of mine—a kindly old gentleman with pince-nez glasses and a long grey beard—applied for a passport. He was going to Holland and Switzerland to study cheese.

"You are not going to Spain, are you?" asked the man at the desk.

"Heavens, no," said the old gentleman. "I am going to Switzerland to study cheese. Why do you ask?"

"Oh, nothing—nothing," said the man. "I was just wondering."

After due formalities, the old man received his passport. Adjusting his glasses and opening it at random, he observed a paragraph rubber-stamped in red ink:

"This passport is not valid for travel to or in any foreign state in connection with entrance into or service in foreign military or naval forces."

And as if that were not enough, directly under it:

"This passport is not valid for travel in Spain."

And to make it completely emphatic:

"Este pasaporte no es valido para viajar en España."

And finally:

"Ce passeport n'est pas valable pour voyager en Espagne."

"Good gracious sakes," said the old gentleman, "what is happening to the world?"

"These are troublous times," sighed the clerk.

Clucking his tongue, the old man turned another page and read:

"This passport not valid for travel in or to China."

"Remarkable!" he exclaimed. "Remarkable!"

"The world grows smaller," said the clerk.

"Well, fortunately," said the old gentleman, "it is cheese and not pagodas that I am studying."

"I don't know," said the clerk. "I don't know what to think. No one who comes in here is going to Spain. Some of them are going to Paris to study art, some of them intend to photograph the cathedrals, some of them want to see the Sphinx—I even had one man who said he was going abroad to study spots on the moon." The clerk sighed. "But somehow, they all seem to end up in Spain in the Loyalist trenches."

"It's incredible," said the old gentleman.

"And you," said the clerk, "are going to Switzerland to study cheese. What am I to think?"

"Ah well," said the old man. "Ah well." He turned the passport upside down and a pink slip fell. Unfolding it carefully he read:

"You will note that the enclosed passport is endorsed 'Not valid for travel in Spain.' Accordingly, the use of the passport for that purpose without obtaining an appropriate amendment thereto by the Department or by an American consular or diplomatic officer will constitute a violation of Section 221 of Title 22 of the United States Code, which makes it unlawful to use a passport in violation of the conditions or restrictions contained therein."

"All this," said the old gentleman, "suggests to me that the tide of traffic toward Spain must be exceedingly great."

"It is the policy of America," said the clerk, "to encourage its citizens to take a neutral attitude toward foreign conflicts."

"Do you mean that the person should be indifferent to which side wins or loses?"

"That seems to be the idea," said the clerk.

"For a man to be indifferent about a vital issue the outcome of which will affect the whole world and everyone living, he would, of course," said the old gentleman, "have to be an absolute ass."

"Yes," said the clerk, "I believe that would be necessary."

From ON THE DRUMHEAD, *Pacific Publishing Foundation, San Francisco, 1948*

A Poem in Four Anguishes and One Hope

Spain

NICOLAS GUILLEN

ANGUISH NUMBER ONE: *Glances of Rock and Metal*

Now there is no Cortez nor Pizarro,
no Aztecs nor Incas to take the lash together;
now it would be better to have their hardy men
—hurdling the years—here with their shields;
here with their hands hard and calloused; here
at our feet with these remote militiamen, with their spurs
dug deep in their horses' leather; here with us in the end,
with these faraway soldiers, with these impassioned men,
    with
these close brothers bound and covered by blood.

With the stormy iron
of their bravest lances;
with swords that sink their points in dawns;
with their old ingenious impetuous rifles;
with spikes and horseshoes
of proud conquering feet;
with their skulls, their vizors,
their thick knee-guards,
with all the old imperialistic metal
that swirls and founders in these burning waters
where worker, soldier and artist
snatch bullets out of the air to use in their machineguns.

Now there is no Cortez nor Pizarro,

no Incas nor Aztecs to take the lash together;
now it would be better to have their hardy men
—hurdling the years—here with their shields
to look at this Spain, torn and broken;
to look at these birds circling these ruins;
and the long distorted boot of fascism,
and lightless lanterns on the corners,
and fists held high and breasts awakened,
and cannon trembling on the asphalt
over horses so still and dead;
to look at these sea-made tears,
salty, falling and splattering all these doors;
and the cries of terror out of all throats peering
with angry, wide-open eyes, with glances of rock and metal.

ANGUISH NUMBER TWO: *Your Veins, Root of All Our Trees*

Root of my tree, contorted, twisted;
root of your tree, comrade, of all our trees,
drinking blood, damp with blood,
root of my tree, of your tree, brother.
And I can feel it
—root of my tree, your tree,
of all our trees—
I can feel it
clutching the deepest earth of my land,
clinging there, clinging
down there and lifting me up and clutching
me tightly and talking to me,
weeping to me, this root of your tree, my tree.

In my land nailed
with nails now of iron,
of powder and stone,
and in burning tongues flowering

144

Nicolas Guillén

and feeding the branches where weary birds
make weary decorations; and flooding the veins
of branch and flower; our veins, your veins, root
of our many trees.

ANGUISH NUMBER THREE: *And My Bones Marching In Your
Soldiers*

Death dons the disguise of a monk;
oppressed by my tropical shirt
stuck to me by sweat, I kill my dance
and chase after death for your life.
Your two bloods, which in me are joined,
I return to you, since from you they came
and through your bright wounds they question me.

This is the people, against crown, against scepter
and mantle and sable, against cassock and I with you
and with my voice my heart speaks aloud to you:
I who am your friend, my friend; I who am your friend.
Tear my skin into strips to make your bandages
in the grey mountains and along red roads, along broken paths,
and my bones in your soldiers marching.

ANGUISH NUMBER FOUR: *Federico*

> *Federico García Lorca, poet of
> the gypsies, of Granada and
> Andalucía, greatest poet of
> modern Spain, died one August
> night before the fascist rifles.
> His crime: he was a people's
> poet . . .*

Now I knock upon the door of an old Spanish ballad:
"Does Federico live here?" A parrot answers:
"Gone. Federico's gone."

I beat against a door of crystal:
"Has Federico gone through here?" A hand
comes forth in answer: "In the river,
they've left him in the river."

And now I pound upon the door of a nameless gypsy:
"Is Federico here; tell me, is he here?"
There is no answer, no one speaks . . .
I cry in pain, "Oh, Federico! Federico!"

But the dark house is empty;
there is moisture on the walls;
the wooden well-bucket lies paralyzed in moss;
and the garden is running with little green lizards.

Over the weed-grown land
the small snails crawl slowly,
and July's red wind
pokes among the ruins.

Oh, Federico! Federico!
Where does a gypsy go to die?
Where do his eyes change to silver frost?
Where can this be, that he does not return?
Oh, Federico! Federico!

One Song

He left on Sunday, it was nine;
he left on Sunday, it was night;
he left on Sunday and won't be back!
In his hand was a stark blue iris,
in his eyes a burning fever;
the iris turned into blood,
the blood turned into death.

Nicolas Guillén

Another Song

Oh, where will Federico be,
where will he be that he won't be back?!
Oh, Federico, Federico!
Where will he be that he won't be back?!
Where will he be that he won't be back?!

Moment on García Lorca

Was dreaming Federico of spikenard and wax
and olive tree and pinks and white snow of moon.
This was Federico, Granada and Spring.

Like music flung beside a road,
like cutting solitude, he slept
within the ambiguous shade
of his ambiguous lemon tree.

High was the night, burning with stars,
dragging their lucid burrs
over all the highways of earth.

And the gypsies slowly passing
with sombre motionless hands
cried suddenly "Federico!" to the sombre night.

Such a voice from their bleeding veins!
Such ardor in their stiff numb bodies!
Such softness in their steps, their steps!

And my senses turned green, freshly darkened
on their hard invertebrate road were walking shoeless.

Arise, Federico, washed in light;
Federico, his Granada and Spring;
and with moon and pink and spikenard and wax
follow them over the perfumed mountain.

147

THE SONG OF HOPE: *A Joyous Song That Floats in the Distance*

We all know the road;
our rifles are oiled;
our arms are ready:
and now we march!
What does it matter if we die in the end,
for dying itself is no great victory;
much worse to be alive and bend
a slave's knee in the living.

There are those who die in bed
after twelve long months of suffering,
and there are those who die singing
with ten sharp bullets in their breasts.

But we all know the road;
and well oiled are our rifles;
our arms have been advised
and now we're marching!

And the forces have devised for us to leave like this,
walking, severely walking, walking cloaked in dawning
day; our bright new shoes will resound and say
to the tremulous forest: "We are the future passing!"

We know the road . . .
now all our rifles are ready . . .

Translated by Lloyd Mallan;
from WAR POEMS OF THE UNITED NATIONS

Tourists To Lyon

IRVING FAJANS

T HERE WERE PERHAPS thirty other Americans already seated
when Butch Johnson and I entered the room. We unfolded a
couple of chairs and sat down in the back near the door.

We were pretty jittery. Coming to Paris to volunteer for the
International Brigades, in the face of State Department opposition, had not been easy. Our passports had been stamped "Not
Valid for Travel in Spain or China," and the week's stop-over in
Paris, while the committee in the *Maison des Sindicats* arranged
the trip down to the closed French-Spanish border and over the
Pyrenees, had increased the danger of our being picked up as
"illegal volunteers," and either shipped back to the States or
thrown into a French jail.

We fidgeted around for a while in uneasy silence. "What's
holding up the works?" Butch whispered after a quarter of an
hour had passed.

"How should I know?" I replied. "Although there *is* a story
in the morning paper that the government won't open the frontier and will take additional precautions to prevent volunteers
from reaching the border."

"Precautions my eye," Butch said. "We could have crawled
down to the border on our hands and knees by this time."

Our conversation was interrupted by the appearance of the
chairman of the committee, who proceeded in careful English to
outline the difficulties which lay before us on our trip to the
Pyrenees.

"The French People," he said, "are overwhelmingly in sympathy with the Spanish Republic. Unfortunately, and for reasons
I will not go into, the government has seen fit to keep the frontier closed.

"Many Frenchmen have gone to Spain to fight and many others are coöperating in getting volunteers over the Pyrenees. However, France is filled with fascist agents who would desperately like to know how men are aided to join the Loyalists. Most are German and Italian, but some are French agents working for the *Croix de Feu*. It is for this reason that we must ask all of you to obey our instructions implicitly and conduct yourselves discreetly. Just last week, a group of Americans were arrested in Carcassonne and sentenced to forty days in jail.

"You are leaving for Lyon tonight. If you are questioned, you will say that you are American tourists who have come for the French Exposition and are traveling around the country waiting for it to open. One of your number, Comrade Johnson, will be given full instructions and he will be responsible for you during this part of the trip.

"You will be at the *Gare de Lyon* at seven-thirty. There will be many other volunteers of other nationalities taking the same train. Under no circumstances will you speak to anyone. If there should be any difficulty, look for Johnson and he will tell you what to do.

"Just a last few things before I give you your railroad tickets. It is an overnight trip and the train has no dining car, so I suggest you provide yourselves with some food. Your luggage should be sent home, but if you wish, you may bring it here and we will forward it to Spain when the border is opened. Also, it might be a good idea to buy a beret and discard the hats you are wearing as they identify you immediately as Americans.

"If there are no questions, I should like to close this meeting by wishing you the best of luck. Will Comrade Johnson please remain for a few minutes?"

Everyone felt better. At least, we were moving in the direction of Spain. The business-like instructions had quieted some of our uneasiness and the tourist story was certainly more plausible than any we had been able to devise for ourselves.

I got my ticket and some tags for the luggage and went out into the hall to wait for Butch, wondering what they could possibly be telling him. It would be pretty rough if we had to duck fascist agents and the *Garde Mobile* all the way down to the border.

In a few minutes Butch came out of the room. He scarcely saw me, so hard was he concentrating on the words he was repeating to himself.

"What are you mumbling about?" I asked, catching up to him.

"The password," he said. "I'm supposed to meet a guy in the station at Lyon and give him the password."

We returned to our hotel, stuffed some extra socks and toothpaste into our pockets, tagged our luggage and checked out. On the way back to the *Maison des Sindicats* with our bags, we stopped and bought two berets.

"How do I look?" Butch asked, pulling the beret down over his right eye.

"Stick a paint brush in your hand and you're a dead ringer for Picasso," I said.

"Well, you're not exactly my idea of Pepe le Moko," he said, with another yank at the beret.

We dumped the luggage and walked in a leisurely fashion to the *Gare de Lyon*, stopping for a couple of beers and to get some sandwiches put up.

The station was crowded. We made our way to the Lyons express and took a position close to the entrance of a third class coach. Soon little knots of two and three men gathered along the length of the train. All carried little paper packages of food. In addition, most had acquired bottles of wine and the corked tops peeked coyly out of their bulging pockets. And all, carrying out the instructions of the committee to the letter, had purchased berets.

Some secret stuff, I thought, looking at the clusters of blue-bereted heads. Any one mistaking us for tourists could also be convinced that Americans visited the Folies Bergère for cultural purposes.

"Not a weeping wife in sight," Butch said. "Let's get on the train before they trot out the band and play the 'Internationale.'"

We found a couple of seats in a compartment which was

already partially occupied. No one said a word. Men in berets tramped up and down in the corridor outside, looking for empty places.

Finally, the train pulled out of the station. Still no one spoke. I fixed my attention on the little tassle on Butch's beret. An hour passed. Every time I moved my head, my neck creaked like a wicker porch-chair after a day in the sun. Suddenly a man burst into our compartment.

"Which one of you is Johnson?"

"Me," said Butch.

"Then come on, we've got a fascist in our compartment."

"How do you know?"

"No beret. Besides he's been asking a lot of questions."

"Save my seat," Butch said. "I'll be right back."

What would Butch do, toss him off the train? I lit a cigarette and leaned back. Time passed. The train whistled for a curve . . . once . . . twice. On the third screech, Butch returned.

"What's the score?" I asked with a sidelong glance at our fellow travelers.

"Nothing to nothing," Butch said. "He's probably the only legitimate passenger on the train. He lives in Lyon and was only trying to be sociable."

There were no further alarms and after a while I dozed off. It was just growing light when the sudden braking of the train jerked me awake.

"We're coming into Lyon," Butch said.

We got off the train and Butch hurried away to make his contact. The station was soon crowded by the detraining volunteers. The baggage porters who had hurried to the steps of the coaches, backed away incredulously, as man after man stepped down without so much as an overnight bag in his hand. Other early risers gave dubious welcome to the foot stamping, face massaging, clothes brushing, invasion *des touristes.*

Soon groups of men were leaving the station. Where was Butch? Standing near the station master's office, two gendarmes regarded us suspiciously. Where was Butch? Soon, only our group of Americans was left on the platform. I debated with myself whether to show some initiative and get the men out of the station and into a café, but before I had time to make a decision, Butch appeared, trailed by a small, blonde-haired child, who couldn't have been more than six.

"This is Odette," he said. "She'll show us where to go."

"Are you kidding?" I said, studying the six-year-old Mata Hari.

"Don't worry, she's done this before. Her old man was the contact, but he's down with the grippe."

"Real conspiratorial stuff," I said.

We paired off at ten-yard intervals and trailed the child out of the station. At the end of the block, she turned down a narrow shop-lined street. We tagged behind, elaborately casual—tourists out for the morning air. I looked back. Stretching for a full block were pairs of blue berets.

Shopkeepers, raising their iron shutters, and black-shawled women with their market baskets, watched our curious procession pass. Tongues clucked and heads shook. As we neared the corner, a woman detached herself and asked the child if anything was wrong. Odette backed away frightened, and started to run.

"Come on!" Butch yelled. I turned my head. The whole line of berets started to bob up and down. Suddenly, she turned the corner. "Don't lose her!" Butch panted. I speeded up and rounded the corner. She was nowhere in sight. I ran a few more feet and stopped. Gasping for breath, the line accordioned up on me. We stood there for a moment at a loss as to our next move. The neighborhood, now fully aroused, eyed us with sympathetic amusement.

"*M'sieu*," the child's head appeared from behind a door to a stable, "*Ici*."

"Some secrecy," I said as we entered.

"Some tourists," said Butch, pulling his beret from his head and slapping it against the rump of a sad-faced horse.

The Battle of the Jarama

PABLO NERUDA

Between the earth and the drowned platinum
of olive groves and dead Spaniards,
Jarama, hard dagger, you have resisted
    the wave of the cruel ones.

From Madrid came men
with hearts gilded by gunpowder,
like bread of ash and resistance,
    they arrived.

Jarama, you lay between iron and smoke
like a branch of fallen crystal,
like a long line of medals
    for the victors.

Neither caves of burning substance,
nor choleric explosive flights,
nor artilleries of turbid darkness
    dominated your waters.

Your waters were drunk by those thirsty
for blood, water they drank face upward:
Spanish water and olive fields
    filled them with forgetfulness.

And ever it comes the rabid mist of sleeplessness
for a second of water and time the stream
of the blood of Moors and traitors
shimmered in your light like fishes
    in a bitter pool.

The rough flour of your people
bristled with metal and bones,
formidable and wheat-bearing like the noble
    land they defended.

Jarama, to talk about your regions
of splendor and dominion, my tongue is not
adequate, and my hand is pale:
    your dead remain there.

Your grievous sky remains there,
your peace like stone, your starry stream,
and the eternal eyes of your people
    keep vigil on your shores.

Translated by Angel Flores;
from RESIDENCE ON EARTH

Bringing in John Scott

JOE GORDON

IT WAS ALREADY dark, the First and Second Companies had advanced quite a distance, the firing was still heavy. One of our tanks had been hit, it was burning like all hell; it lit up a big area. Everything and everybody moved out of that area: the Fascists had expert snipers and besides we expected artillery bombardment. I was in a machine-gun group, but our gun had broken down. It was impossible to fix it. We were then told to move up with the infantry because there were no more machine-guns available.

No sooner had we reached the rear of the Second Company than a cry for volunteers came through, to bring shovels to the First Company. Four in our group volunteered; we were given two shovels apiece, told to find the First Company. No specific direction was given because nobody knew where they were exactly. They had advanced so far that they had lost all contact with everybody. Rumors were flying thick and heavy that the First Company was wiped out, that so-and-so was killed, etc. It was our first attack. Sweat was dripping from everyone even though it was cold.

The four of us started out together. We had to spread out, take all possible shelter we could find, and so in about three minutes we lost each other. I called their names, low as I could, but got no answer. Walking, running, flopping, the fire was hard. At last I saw somebody digging in. Running up to him, I flopped. "Say, where's the First Company?" "Don't know," he answered and kept on digging feverishly with his hands. I got up, kept on running, called out, passing other comrades on my way. Some answered, some didn't. The bullets were coming very close, and besides I didn't know where the Fascist lines were. At last I bumped into somebody. I knew he was in the First Company. He told me where the main body of men was. Advancing farther, I finally bumped into Bill Wheeler whom I gave the shovels to. He in turn gave the shovels to two Cubans and told them to start digging a trench.

I was pretty well out of breath by that time, so I took time out for a rest. Bill Wheeler then mentioned to me that Scott was wounded and where he was lying. I crawled about twenty yards farther and there I came upon Scott and Bill Henry who was now acting commander of the First Company. Scott was lying flat on his stomach with his right arm under him, his head twisted sideways. Bill Henry was pushing dirt in front of Scott's head to give him some protection. At every move he made, he drew fire. The fire coming from the Fascist guns was very visible. When I asked Henry how far the Fascists' lines were, he told me about sixty meters, and that all told we had advanced about five hundred to six hundred meters.

I moved over to Scott. "How do you feel?" I asked him. With his left hand he took hold of one of mine. No pressure. I could feel his strength slowly ebbing away. "I'm all right," he answered. He continued to hold my hand. I then told him I would go back and bring aid; he squeezed my hand hard for a few minutes and said, "Don't do it, it's a waste of time." "What the hell do you mean, waste of time?" I answered. "You're a human being, ain't you, and besides you're Captain Scott, see, and besides Joe Strysand will never talk to you again if you died." With all the suffering that he was going through, a smile came over his face; he loved Joe Strysand, his runner. I then told Henry that I was going to bring aid. I hated to break hands with Scott. It seemed as though I was giving him strength through my hand.

Instead of going back the way I came, I crawled to my left about one hundred and fifty yards. There was a road, but there was a high bank to get down. No sooner had I crawled down the bank than the Fascists opened up a burst of fire on me. Hugging the side of the embankment, I waited till the firing had ceased, then continued crawling on, passing a dead soldier in a very queer position. Knowing the ground a little, I knew the first-aid station was near.

I got up and sprinted a little, got down then, sprinted again until I finally burst right into the first-aid station. "Captain Scott's wounded, he's dying," I yelled at the first-aid men. "Where's a stretcher? Hurry up!" Nobody paid attention to me. I then realized that they were French and Hollanders. I tried the sign language and my twelve words of Spanish. They thought I had gone crazy. Finally a Hollander who could talk English came up to the station. I pounced on him, told him about Scott. "Look, comrade," he said, "I don't know what you're talking about. Sit down and collect yourself." So I cooled down and told him about Scott once more. He then called together two stretcher-bearers and we proceeded to go for Scott, with a white canvas stretcher, the only thing we could get.

The four of us went up the road about three hundred yards. I then suggested that we get off the road and start crawling on the dirt. This we did. We had crawled quite a bit and all the while it seemed they were firing right at us. Why not? A white stretcher in the black of night! One stretcher-bearer refused to go farther, whereupon the Hollander who spoke English drew a gun and threatened to shoot him. I guess he didn't like the idea of himself lying out there wounded, so he came. After what seemed hours we finally got to Scott. We then grabbed Scott, none too gently—we couldn't help it—put him on the stretcher or put the stretcher under him, I don't remember. He was groaning slightly; he couldn't groan any harder if he wanted to, he was so weak. We then called for some volunteers to help us. Paul Burns, Shapiro and one other helped along. What a target! But luckily no bull's-eye.

Now, the question of how to get back to the first-aid station: were we to crawl along the dirt and mud or go along the road? We decided to go by way of the road even though it was more dangerous. Four men then grabbed the handles, lying flat on their backs, counting three, then up and backward, then digging your feet in the dirt, pushing your way back to position. Poor Scott, what a target! It's a good thing he didn't know what was going on. After what seemed ages, one hundred and fifty yards all told, we finally reached close to the road. We pushed up to the embankment. I immediately hopped off the embankment, grabbed the two handles of the stretcher and gave a hard pull just as the Fascists opened up terrific fire right on us. Everyone was wounded except myself. Paul Burns, Shapiro, the first-aid men, everyone got close to the embankment. Scott also was placed close to the embankment. Being the only one who was not wounded, the first-aid man who spoke English told me to go back and bring help. This I started to do right away.

What a hell of a situation! You go after one wounded man and now look at the mess!

I started crawling on the side of the road. About three minutes later a terrific barrage of fire opened up, from left, right, the back and front of me. Not moving, lying flat on my face, I was hoping the fire would subside a little so I could move on, but it seemed to get heavier. Artillery and tanks started to bang away. But bullets were spattering close. I decided to push on, knowing that if I stood in the same spot, sooner or later I'd get it. Pushing myself with my feet and using my hands, not daring to raise my body, I moved forward slowly. I got a cramp in my left leg, also started to vomit. Resting a few minutes, then continuing onward, I finally came in sight of the dead soldier. Crawling up to him, I fixed his body so as to give me as much protection as possible. Soaked with his blood, which continued running, I don't know how long I lay. I'm sure he saved my life. I was almost afraid to breathe lest I sniff in a bullet.

The firing started to quiet down. I left the dead soldier all to himself, and began crawling on, hoping that one of our own men would not shoot at me. Finally I came into the first-aid station. I saw Cooperman, battalion secretary, told him what had happened. He told me to see Merriman. I went to Merriman and told him what had happened. He couldn't leave his post, but told me to do and use everything I could to bring back the wounded. Going down to the first-aid station I saw Cooperman again. There was an ambulance and one of our food trucks near by. I asked Cooperman whether or not we could drive down the road with the ambulance. He said yes. Both of us climbed into it. Just as we were about to start off, somebody came running up and told us to get the hell out of the ambulance, that it was pure suicide, that we didn't have one chance in a million. We got out, got together Toplianos, our first-aid man, Ralph Greenleaf and another man from the food truck, Tanz and myself. We took a stretcher with us, and started to go out again. Two of the first-aid men came in. Both were wounded in the legs; I don't know how they managed it. The firing was almost nil. We started walking up the road almost to the halfway mark, when we bumped into Paul Burns and Gomez, carrying in Scott. Telling the others to wait for us, Toplianos and I took the stretcher and carried Scott into the first-aid station. Scott was still alive. I felt very glad all our efforts had not been in vain.

Toplianos and I went up the road again and caught up with the others. We got off the road and started crawling, but not too far from the road because I knew if there was anybody left he would still be on the road. The Fascists opened up bursts of fire. Whenever they opened up, we would be still, and then continue. After a hard burst of fire at us had ended, I pushed the comrade next to me and said, "Let's go!" He didn't move. I looked at him, and found that Ralph Greenleaf had been shot right through the helmet. He died instantly, without a sign, a pool of blood forming quickly.

We continued pushing up. Hearing groans, we stopped, called softly, "Where are you?" No answer except the monotonous groans. We could tell by the sound that he was near by. Toplianos finally spied him. We climbed down the bank. When we got there Shapiro was lying in the middle of the road, groaning very loudly. He was in terrible pain. A bullet had struck his ankle. He had been bleeding hard, now it was already dried up. We grabbed hold of Shapiro, he was very heavy; we got him to the embankment where he was grabbed by the two comrades above. All together we lifted him off the road onto the dirt, where we got him on the stretcher. Again we started back in the same manner we had taken with Scott. After each yard we had to rest, he was very heavy, dead weight. His ankle or his foot kept turning around and around. All the while we were taking him in, he kept groaning terribly, drawing fire. After what seemed a lifetime, we finally got him into the first-aid station.

What a night! Killing can be a pleasure compared with the saving of life.

Cooperman told me to go to battalion HQ and take a rest. I was thoroughly soaked, as if I had jumped into a pool of water. At this moment Joe Strysand came dashing up to me, throwing his arms around me and kissing me, tears streaming down his eyes. We were sure Scott would live.

I walked up to the lines again, trying to find the members of my group. Food had already been brought up. All fire had stopped; all quiet. I took two pails of food, walked out into the fields, met Landetta, commissar of the Cubans, gave him the food. Just then word had come through to come back. We were amazed, stunned. After all the advance, and all the fighting, to get ordered back! Everybody, First and Second Company in one body, they all arose, stood up straight and dashed back to our trenches!

When it was all over, I walked back behind our lines, feeling punch-drunk, too tired even to see. My foot bumped into something soft, lying on the ground. It moved. I looked down, and it was X——, lying on the ground with a blanket over his head. His face was white. He asked, "What's up?" I didn't answer him, I just kept walking. I felt disgusted. He had been lying there, with the blanket over his head, all night.

FROM THE LINCOLN BATTALION, *by Edwin Rolfe*
Random House, New York, 1939

Poem

CHARLES DONNELLY

Between rebellion as a private study and the public
Defiance is simple action only which will flicker
Catlike, for spring. Whether at nerve-roots is secret
Iron, there's no diviner can tell, only the moment can show.
Simple and unclear moment, on a morning utterly different
And under circumstances different from what you'd expected.

Your flag is public over granite. Gulls fly above it.
Whatever the issue of the battle is, your memory
Is public, for them to pull awry with crooked hands,
Moist eyes. And villages' reputations will be built on
Inaccurate accounts of your campaigns. You're name for orators,
Figure stone-struck beneath damp Dublin sky.

In a delaying action, perhaps, on hillside in remote parish,
Outposts correctly placed, retreat secured to wood, bridge mined
Against pursuit, sniper may sight you carelessly contoured.
Or death may follow years in strait confinement, where diet
Is uniform as ceremony, lacking only fruit
Or on the barracks square before the sun casts shadow.

Name, subject of all considered words, praise and blame
Irrelevant, the public talk which sounds the same on hollow
Tongue as true, you'll be with Parnell and with Pearse.
Name alderman will raise a cheer with, teacher make reference
Oblique in class, and boys and women spin gum of sentiment
On qualities attributed in error.

Man, dweller in mountain huts, possessor of colored mice,
Skilful in minor manual turns, patron of obscure subjects, of
Gaelic swordsmanship and medieval armory,
The technique of the public man, the masked servilities are
Not for you, Master of military trade, you give
Like Raleigh, Lawrence, Childers, your services but not yourself.

From ROMANCEROS DE LOS VOLUNTARIOS
DE LA LIBERTAD, *Madrid, 1937*

Guadalajara

March-weather storms the house like shrapnel.
I hear the ice roar, and the guns.
And in the silent, sentry passes
the crazy dead stand to attention.

What did Napoleon see, who stared
at Moscow, as I watch the fire?
Frost climbed the window-pane for him,
but for his men the snow piled higher.

And Hannibal in the Alps, did he
rage at the cold and blame his luck?
The elephants and soldiers did
not listen when they froze to muck.
Caesar with Spanish slingers shivered
in Gaul; but knew the beds at home
would yet be warm. The slingers died.
And Caesar—Caesar whored in Rome.

In Libya the shaken sword
aches in the sun. The conquering boor
sweats and grows hoarse. But here his men
cough death beside the dying Moors.

What shall the rigid soldier say
who knows the cheat, yet cannot turn?
The ice builds bayonets in his veins
and the rough frost like anger burns,

and pity plucks him by the sleeve
and whispers in his ear that kings
will still be snug when water runs
the courses of his blood in spring.

What is my pity worth? I fret
no frozen body, but my mind;
and if I tremble, all my rage
weighs nothing in the bite of wind.

Forgive me, men at posts, who stiffen
for furies such as kings' or mine;
and suffer me no more than speak
the words your lips will never form,

the hope that hangs there like a breath
that fate shall break your frozen line,
break kings and break fanatic men;
that March shall break the world with storm.

From POEMS FOR SPAIN

"El Fantastico"

STEVE NELSON

E L FANTASTICO joined the Spanish company of the Lincoln Battalion at Jarama, and at once he was their hero, and they hung on his words. He told great tales of the 1934 revolt in his native Asturias.

"This is no fight here," he would say. "Ah, when you have to crawl on your belly all day like a snake, so they see nothing—and when night comes you are above them, the lovely Spanish officers smoking their cigars—you toss in one grenade—'*Arriba manos!*' you shout—and they walk out, those still alive, their faces white, their bodies shaking with terror, their snaky hips moving, so—educated gentlemen, white-livered dogs! Pah! I spit on them!"

He could throw a Russian bayonet to split a slender pole at fifteen paces. "I like these *Rusos*, they are long and heavy, they balance well." He showed the boys how to make an Asturian grenade of dynamite and bits of old wire cable, pieces of horse shoe, a few spikes. "And then, look out, fascist! You'd much better be home with your missus, or you're likely to leave a good-looking widow for *El Fantastico!*" He played the concertina well; he loved to sing the folk songs of Asturias. He loved living.

He was a fighting cock—vain, gaudy, flamboyant, with a heart of steel courage. For all his happy-go-lucky manner, he was deeply class conscious and he hated the fascists with a deep, blazing fury.

While the battalion was resting at Albarez, a call came from the government for each outfit long at the front to nominate men for the *guerrilleros,* the partisan fighters behind the fascist lines. *El Fantastico*—his real name was José—was an inevitable choice from the Lincolns.

When Steve told him of the new assignment, he thought the man was going to cry, so deeply moved was he by the honor that had come upon him; for every man knew that the guerrilla fighters were strictly chosen, from the fittest, ablest, most alert and most trustworthy of the Loyalist forces. "Comrade," he said, "this is no joke you are playing? You are not making fun?"

"No. This is no fun. This is the most serious work we have, and the most dangerous. Are you ready to undertake it?"

José smote his great chest. "You ask *El Fantastico* if he is ready? What must be done? Just tell me—what is necessary to be done?"

"You'll be told in Madrid. This American comrade is also assigned to the work; he will accompany you. You are not to say a word to anyone, your lips are sealed. . . . Goodbye, José. Good luck."

José departed, wrapped in deepest mystery and glorying in it. With him went the American, his "Comrade Yank," a boy from Brooklyn of Spanish descent, who spoke Spanish fluently, who had been an acrobat and was capable of amazing feats of physical prowess.

In Madrid a commission examined the men nominated by the various battalions. Of them all, twenty-two were selected. The twenty-two were told they might leave, to report back in an hour; José alone was told to remain at the office. He paced the corridor nervously, lighting cigarettes and grinding them out, sweating with fear that he was to be rejected.

He was called in. "Comrade José," the commissar said, "we think you are best qualified to be entrusted with the lives of these fighters, and as their leader to hold the confidence of the Republic."

"*Yo—comandante! Pero—pero—.*" He was overwhelmed and stammering. "I don't know why you comrades really think that I—but so be it. What do you want done?"

"First, see that your men fill in these forms. There is one for you, also. Then outfit your men with the type of clothing worn by peasants in Córdoba province. Get automatic pistols and underarm holsters. Here is a *bon* which will entitle you to draw

things you need from armories or quartermaster's depots. Tonight you will be given a sum of fascist money, and a truck will
take you to a post near Pozo Blanco. The commander in that
sector will give you detailed orders and supply horses and further equipment. . . . Now, can you repeat the order?"

José could and did. As a phonograph repeats, correct to the
last inflection. "José never writes anything down," he explained,
seeing the surprised stares of the officers. "He keeps everything
here."

Outside, the men had gathered. The commissar went with
José to meet them, announced that José had been chosen to lead
them. "As a son of Asturias, a veteran fighter for liberty experi-
enced in guerrilla warfare, we know he will live up to our expec-
tations and the glorious traditions of the people of Asturias."

The boys cheered. José, his face fiery red, wiggled uncom-
fortably and repressed an impulse to strut. "There is work to be
done, comrades. . . . First of all, I must have an assistant to take
care of the records and all details. Whom do you nominate,
chicos?"

Comrade Yank was elected. "Here, *chico;* first of all have
these questionnaires filled out. Check every sheet. All must be
perfect. Then to the armory, quickly, I will meet you there."

"Hey, José, wait! You didn't fill out yours."

José was furious. "*Madre de Dios,* are you not my adjutant?
José has no time! Fill it out for me. . . . And bring my concertina
with you to the armory."

"When you get near the bridge," said the commander of the
Pozo Blanco sector, "you will see a switchman's booth, No. 8.
Our comrade works the shift from noon to midnight. The comrade has a big gray mustache; he is short and fat, about fifty
years old.

"You will say, 'It's a wonderful day.' Two times you say that.
Then ask for a match. He will say, 'Certainly,' and pull out two
cigarettes, handing you one. He will not light his. You will say,
'Thank you, I have cigars, would you like one?' He'll say yes,
put the cigarette in his side pocket, and take your cigar. Then

he'll tell you his name, Montez, and you give him yours, with my name in the middle. After that, all will be clear. . . . Repeat the orders!"

The command waited two days, spending the time in equipping, in trying out horses, in target practice with the automatics and the two light machine guns, in learning to throw dynamite bombs in the Asturian fashion. In everything, José was the leader, the teacher. His manner was less swashbuckling, more subdued under the weight of responsibility upon him; he was patient and painstaking, with a wonderful eye for detail, and was satisfied with nothing short of perfection. They built a small rough model of the bridge they were to destroy, and rehearsed placing the dynamite charges. Each man was drilled in preparing charges, cutting the time fuse, and so on. Each was assigned his special task and drilled in it.

The nights, José spent with Comrade Yank in the town's best cafe, singing, drinking, making love to the girls, making friends with everyone present. He came away from the cafe with a detailed knowledge of the countryside, of the mountain passes, of alternative routes to and from the railroad bridge he was to destroy.

On the third day, the order came. José tossed the paper onto the table and bellowed for Comrade Yank. "The order. There on the table. Read it."

Comrade Yank read, and whistled.

"Will you remember everything? The paper must be burned, you know."

"I think I'll remember it."

"Thinking! That is no good. . . . Read it aloud! . . . Now again! . . . Now repeat it." Comrade Yank did his best and José corrected his slips. "Now bring along those peasant clothes and we will inform the *chicos.*"

José went out, carrying the order. Comrade Yank heard him summon the men. "*Chicos,* we have received orders which I will now read to you. As follows. . . ."

But the order still lay on the table. José had picked up the wrong piece of paper. Comrade Yank snatched it up and ran to the door, his mouth open to shout at *El Fantastico*.

". . . proceed to the railroad bridge twelve kilometers west of that town. The train to be destroyed will approach the bridge shortly before eleven o'clock on the night of—"

Comrade Yank stared dazedly at the paper in his hand. Word for word, José was repeating the order. The paper he held sternly before his eyes was a report Comrade Yank had been preparing.

Comrade Yank closed his mouth slowly. So *El Fantastico* could not read. But what need has a commander to read when he has a memory like a camera, and an able adjutant at his side?

Far away down the canyon, the train whistle sounded. José thrust the last stick of dynamite into place. "Now, the shovels. Cinders first, to keep it dry. . . . Now dirt. Plenty of dirt. Pour it on, *chicos*—the more weight on top, the higher she blows!"

The steel trestle was vibrating as the train came nearer, the supply train from Seville to the Madrid front. José picked up the fuse, followed it hand over hand to a clump of bushes. Forty yards, forty seconds. The end of his cigar glowed red. "Run! Run, Pedro!" The sharp hiss of the fuse sounded.

They all ran.

The engine and four cars were on the bridge when the charge let go, and the rest of the cars plummeted into the river. There were gasoline cars in the train. In a moment, the whole countryside was lit up as by a gigantic searchlight. It was necessary to crawl flat on your belly, like a snake. It was necessary to abandon the horses, to move by a long and circuitous route back to the Loyalist lines. A route of which José had learned while gossiping idly in the cafe.

He had lost his horses, his equipment. Above all, he had lost a man, a fine comrade. *El Fantastico* mourned his failure and would not be consoled. The duty of a commander was to take care of his men, and he had neglected to warn Pedro to be on the east side of the bridge when the train approached. Ah, that was bad, that was criminal, how could he have been so careless?

Even the praises heaped upon him by the command did not altogether console him.

"You have done the Republic a great service," said the commander.

"But we lost our horses," said José.

"We must expect these things."

"But we lost Pedro, and had I given Pedro the proper instructions, he would now be alive."

"We don't look at things that way, comrade," the commander said earnestly. "We expect you to take every precaution, to train yourself and your men; we treasure every man and do not take lightly the loss of a good comrade. But you did a fine piece of work, requiring courage, daring and initiative. We could not hope that we would have no losses. Keep up the good work, José, but profit from your experience."

That was the first exploit of *El Fantastico's* command. It was not the last.

Now, part of what follows was told by Comrade Yank and part was told, much later, by a Spanish comrade who, for a time and for a purpose, served in a fascist uniform as orderly for a certain fascist colonel.

The tale begins with an order to José, along these lines:

A number of very important leaders of the Republic were among those captured in Málaga when the city fell to the Italian invaders. By disguising themselves as common soldiers, they escaped the fate of the hundreds of captives who were executed.

Information came through that these men were held in prison near Córdoba, and that their lives were in danger.

"You are ordered, therefore, to organize a small band who will be dressed as fascist officers and men. You will approach the jail as though bringing prisoners to it. You will hold up the guard and release all prisoners, instructing them as to how they may reach our lines. You must see that horses are ready for the comrades whose names and pictures are sent you herewith, and you must see to it that they get through safely at all costs. You are to make all plans and arrangements necessary to accomplish this."

José and six other men drew fascist uniforms and fascist money, rehearsed the fascist salute, practiced fascist arrogance, learned a few fascist songs. They had all necessary information to pass themselves off as a fascist cavalry patrol.

Their swanky uniforms concealed canvas vests carrying fifteen clips each for the Mausers they wore. The Mausers swung in wooden holsters, and these holsters could be clipped to the butt of the gun, whereupon the pistol became a sub-machine gun. But the canvas vests were very hot. The men sweated, riding into Córdoba.

They lounged in front of a sidewalk cafe, ogling the women who passed. Late in the afternoon, José went to a place appointed, and said and did certain things, and from one there he learned that at about six-thirty, a few prisoners would be brought to the jail. He was also informed as to the number of guards on duty.

Toward sundown, José and his men strolled out of town along the road leading to the prison and waited on top of a hill.

A Fiat truck came crawling in low gear. José shouted, "Hey, *chico!* Stop!"

The chauffeur stopped and saluted. A sergeant rode in the seat beside him. "Yes, sir?"

"Our car has broken down. Give us a lift."

Two prisoners rode in the back of the truck. José growled at them: "Red dogs!" He offered the sergeant a cigarette. "What's the password for tonight, *chicos?*" José asked of no one in particular. "I forgot to ask."

"*Fusil,*" said the sergeant respectfully. "Rifle."

When the bodies of the sergeant and the chauffeur had been hidden at the roadside, Comrade Yank took the wheel while José himself instructed the prisoners as to what would happen at the jail. Just short of the prison, José dropped three of his boys to act as a sort of rear guard.

At the jail, José and the rest leaped out with drawn Mausers, cursing the *Rojos,* the Reds. José backed up the steps to the gate, his pistol threatening the two. The gate opened. A lieutenant stepped out.

"Desperate criminals, these," José told him. "Call the rest

of the guard. They made a break up the road. I had to shoot one of them."

The lieutenant blew his whistle. "This way, captain."

The prison had been an olive-oil refining plant. They entered the office. In the wall opposite the entrance was a steel door, newly hung; in one corner stood a desk and phone. The steel door opened and ten men, armed with rifles, entered. They lined up facing the prisoners. José moved to a position behind the desk.

"I want every man to get a good look at these dogs. Have you any more men in the place? All must be able to recognize them."

"No more men, sir."

"Put up your hands!"

Paralyzed, the fascists gaped at the guns held by *El Fantastico's* men, by the prisoners. They were quickly disarmed. José ripped out the telephone. "There are handcuffs!" he shouted. "Chain them to the steel door. All of them!"

He ran down the corridor leading to the cells. "Comrades! *El Fantastico* greets you in the name of the Republic! Come out! You are free! *Viva la República!* Down with Franco!"

There were some thirty men in the prison. José called out the names of the four men whose release was especially desired by the Republic. But only three responded. One explained: "Ricardo is dead. Ricardo died of the beating given him yesterday by the lieutenant you have chained up."

In the yard, Comrade Yank had smashed the distributor of the truck and slashed the tires. They were ready to leave. But José lingered. He addressed the soldiers: "You men, for you the Republic has sympathy. You are dupes of Franco, victims of these murderers. . . . But you, my brave lieutenant, who beat honest comrades to death—*El Fantastico* will decorate you for your valor!"

He raised his Mauser. But he was merciful to the lieutenant; he did not shoot him in the stomach. He shot him through the head.

If only they could get to the little mountain ravine where

their horses were hidden, the rest would be easy. But getting to that ravine was not easy. The prisoners were weak; they stumbled and fell continuously, and had to be helped, half carried along the steep, rocky trail. The night wore away. Gray streaks of dawn were appearing in the sky. In the ragged, black line of the mountain crests against the gray sky, José recognized a landmark. It was not much further. Another half hour.

The hoofbeats were very faint, far down the path behind them. But José heard. He called to Comrade Yank: "Cavalry coming! Quick, pull off your vest."

Yank said, "Wait. Let me help this comrade over to that bunch of trees." He thought the leader meant they would both stay to hold off the patrol. But José did not mean that. José cursed him angrily, calling him a woman. "You think *El Fantastico* needs help when there is but one patrol? Go! Get these comrades to the horses, and go on with them through our lines! That is an order. Obey it!"

When Comrade Yank had gone, José wiped tears from his eyes and snuggled down behind a big rock above the trail. He peered narrowly past the rock, watching for the first horseman to appear. He started to loosen the hand grenade strapped under his belt, against his stomach, but then he changed his mind and left the hand grenade in place. He laid out the clips of bullets neatly, his own and Comrade Yank's, and made sure the Mauser holster held the gun firmly, and that the pistol was set for automatic fire.

There were ten men in the patrol. Two of them went down in José's first burst of fire and he was quite sure he had winged another. The others took cover among the rocks. Chips began flying from the big boulder sheltering him.

For a long time, for an hour perhaps, nothing happened. There was only the intermittent stutter of gunfire, echoing through the canyon. There was only the wild whine of bullets glancing from the rocks around him, and the feel of the Mauser growing hot in his hands. There was only the dwindling pile of magazine clips beside him, the growing litter of empty shell cases under his elbows.

Two bullets hit the back of his shoulder and his right hand fell from the Mauser. A voice behind him yelled harshly, *"Manos arriba!"*

He staggered to his feet, one hand in the air, the other clasping his middle. The fascist officer came leaping over the rocks toward him. His fist smashed into José's face.

"Get up, dog of a Red! Where's your detachment?"

"El Fantastico ordered me to stay here."

"Where is he?"

"By now he's over the ridge—the bastard. He left me here all alone—to die—"

"How long have you been with him?"

"This is my first trip."

"Who gives him information? How does he get through?"

José grinned, the grin of a sly, stupid peasant. "Ha! If I tell you these things, then you will kill me."

Again the fist, and boots crashing into his side, his injured shoulder. He doubled up, groaned and yelled. The lieutenant said loudly, "Enough! Stop! Our orders are to bring in all *guerrilleros* alive."

José was yanked to his feet. The lieutenant smiled at him fatuously. "Never mind, old fellow. We'll take you to headquarters. You be good to the colonel and he'll be good to you, eh?"

The bullets had gone clear through his shoulder; he was weak from bleeding, his shirt and trousers were soaked with blood. "Bandage!" he gasped. "I bleed to death!" Grumbling, they produced a bandage and José snatched it and stuffed it under his shirt, into the wounds, and with his left hand he lifted his right arm and thrust it into the opening of his shirt, so his belt would act as a sling. "Can't move it—my arm," he explained. "It is dead."

He was too weak to walk. They loaded him onto the horse of one of the dead cavalrymen. With his good hand, he clung to the saddle, reeling.

The colonel's headquarters was in a beautiful country house, on a tree-shaded hill.

The lieutenant was proud of his capture. "Sir, we have one

of *El Fantastico's* men here."

"Ah! At last! About time, you blockheads." The colonel leaned forward across the carved oak table that served as his desk, staring at José. "What have you learned from him?"

"Very little, sir. He drives a hard bargain with us." He winked broadly at the colonel. "He insisted that he be brought to you, sir. He will be nice to you if you are nice to him. That is the arrangement."

José grinned dizzily at the colonel and let his knees buckle. That was easily done; they were made of jelly, his knees, and the room was full of colonels and aides and guards, madly spinning. A few minutes more, José. A very few minutes. "Water, excellency. God's mercy—water!"

The guard looked to the colonel, and the colonel nodded. José drank eagerly. "So," the colonel said slowly, "after all your crimes, you still wish to live. You ignorant, atheist dog! Talk, then. Your information had better be true and plentiful!"

"If I talk," said José, "how do I know you won't kill me then?"

"You question the word of a Spanish officer?" The colonel was on his feet; he strode forward, struck José across the face with his own hand. "Speak, damn you!"

The blow sent José reeling forward. His left arm clutched at the colonel, seeking support. His left arm was around the colonel's neck, clutching him tightly, straining his body against José's body; and José's right hand held the ring on the firing pin of the hand grenade strapped to his waist.

He tugged at the firing pin, felt it come away.

"I talk!" he cried. "I give you a message from *El Fantastico!* Listen!"

The grenade made very little noise, exploding. It was so tightly pressed between the bodies of the fascist colonel and *El Fantastico.*

From a book to be published by
Masses and Mainstream

Before Battle

JAMES NEUGASS

Long after the sun has gone down,
    long into the clockless hours of the
        night, the new Battalion waits at the roadside.

Knowing that the end of all waiting
    is to come the men sit quietly and talk
        light the darkness of their minds with cigarettes;

This was summer this was Spain and night
    late at night out in the countryside where
        only the howl of dogs marks the presence of men.

They have left all behind them but guns
    to defend their lives guns with which
        to take lives rifles to answer other rifles;

Here at the frontier of death five hundred
    men wait for the sound of trucks and listen
        for the droning of planes never never theirs.

Road and darkness are all they know
    the vein which will pump them like haemoglobin
        into the open festering moving wound of the Front.

No fire is lit but songs are sung,
    each man's heart is wrapped in the will
        he makes for himself "owning nothing but my rifle."

"Rich in bankruptcy, to the world
    I leave my heart to the Republic my gun
        to men's slow eyes my unvanishing footsteps":

No clock strikes when many trucks
    roll without lights out of the darkness:
        no order is given but the men come to their feet

In a clashing of iron load themselves
    solid into the steel boxes of the trucks
        many engines start and the convoy moves off.

Each minute is a passing kilometer
    how far is it to the Front how long?
        when will the sun rise when but not where

On the horizon the lights of a town appear
    they curse the village fools who make targets
        of the town and the road for night-flying bombers

When they come near they see that these
    are not street lights but many white stars
        hanging low on the hills in this southern sky:

All night long trucks carry them
    through the darkness they do not know where
        they are going but nevertheless understand;

With the passing of each kilometer
    the enormous certainty grows although
        they hear no cannon, they sense that the hour is near.

Still in darkness the trucks stop:
    they have stopped before but this time they know:
        no orders are given but the men drop to the ground

It is summer and the night air is heavy
    with the scent of grape leaves; the warm earth
        returns to the sun the heat it has taken up all day

If there are flowers in the villages
    each petal gives the night air its smell
        which blows cool on the lines of marching men

The smells of cooking and of woodsmoke
    hold the far memory of distant dreams:

the eyes of a cat seem like green gun-flashes:

Burdened with iron, travelling light
and carrying much metal they become tired
the singing and the talk fade and are gone

Each man walks alone with his thoughts
every ear listens for what it must soon hear
the men know that they are new, untried troops

The last crossroad lies far behind
the last backward step has been taken
the final decision made the last doubt thrown away:

Like a bridal procession and a
funeral parade they march to the altar,
the grave, the center of the worldwide stage

Too tired to speak or sing
quick to tire but long in strength
now too tired to curse, the men advance:

An order comes: they stop, fall:
the place is high rough treeless
false daylight has begun to lift

Cold as the echo of a magnesium flare:
color, purple yellow and poison-green
floats into the kindling fires of day

Down below in the valley is a village
"Villaneuva de la Cañada" the men whisper
this town is Theirs but must be, will be Ours:

A sleeping town clean of war,
every tree roof wall and window plant
exactly patterned, perfect, sweet and still

The men understand that by sunset
this town has to go, go up in blood-red
sheets of flame and black fountains of dust:

And the sun comes up violently
    sending its rays like bars of music
        from great brass instruments and there is no sound:

Behind us our cannon fire three times
    three cannon clap like iron fists on a pine door
        advance! it is daylight! forward! day has broken!

Advance! leaving night and death behind
    we advance into light and life! advance!
        leaving the old world behind us we march into the new!

No one hears the shot but our first man has fallen.

From WAR POEMS OF THE
UNITED NATIONS

Action At Brunete

HAROLD SMITH

H IS FIRST FEELING was outraged indignation. Those guys on the other side were actually shooting at him. As he trotted slowly up the hill, the air had bullet noises in it and the back of his mind said that this was absolutely ridiculous, people just didn't fire guns at you like that on a hot summer day. It just wasn't done. Then he saw that his squad which had been so nicely deployed when they started out over the treeless, wheat-stubbled ground was bunching up toward the left and the squad to the right was bunching up in the same way. That wasn't right. Over and over it had been drilled into him that when you came under fire, you spread out, you didn't bunch. "Spread out," he yelled to his squad. "Keep your distance."

Some of the fellows turned their faces toward him. Their faces were flat and calm but around their eyes they were deep, thoughtful and inward looking as if they were thinking of something far away. Something that concerned only themselves. He had the feeling that they resented the intrusion on their thoughts. But nobody said anything and without interrupting the clumsy jogging forward they spread out until the man on the extreme right bumped into a man from the next squad. Both were knocked a bit off balance but didn't say anything to each other, hardly turned their heads. They just ran a little faster to catch up with the other guys. By that time the first soldiers were getting to the top of the hill and somebody must have given them the order to lie down because they began taking positions below the crest. He came up then and lay down with his squad so that their heads were a little below the skyline. He looked around curiously at his squad. Everybody was there. Then he looked over the slope that they had just come up and it was clear except for a few

181

stragglers anxiously running to get up with the company. He thought, "Gee, we're lucky, all that shooting and nobody hit." Then immediately he realized that there wasn't so much shooting at all and that those bullets were passing way overhead. There weren't even any dust spurts on the slope. He had a funny little embarrassed feeling, a little disappointed too.

His company stayed on the hill long enough for his body to begin to feel again some of the dragging weariness that had weighed heavier and heavier during the long three-day hike up to the front. But not much because he was in battle at last and pretty keyed up about it. Some of the guys began kidding among themselves and wondering what was going to happen next. They knew the major objective of the campaign, that it was the first big really organized push and that they were supposed to play a big role. But so far it had been all marching for them and watching a few flights of their planes drop bombs up ahead. Their artillery had been firing too, but after the excitement of waiting for the opening of the big barrage it hadn't sounded like so much. Well, they knew they were pretty short on that stuff. They began to get restless. Why were they lying there? The sun was getting awfully hot and there was a lot of shooting going on over to their left. He was about to roll a cigarette when the order came to move.

There were no longer any strays or whatever they were in the air when they started forward. The battalion wasn't deployed for combat now. Instead they were marching in the open formation they had been taught back in the little village that had been their base during their three months of training. Since he was in the first squad of the First company, he was up at the head of one of the two stretched out parallel files into which the battalion was now divided. The outfit was moving steadily in the direction of the heavy firing. He had forgotten his weariness and was getting tight again inside. They walked for quite a while. The firing sounded nearer but it wasn't steady. It would burst out heavy for a while, then taper off. For the last few minutes there had been only a few scattered bursts. He smiled a little. The thought came to his mind that it reminded him of his mother. When she got mad. "Wow"—then it would peter out in little mutters of subsiding complaints. The files stopped moving and the men lay down for a short rest. The battalion staff were standing around a map that one of them was holding. Their heads were together like a football huddle. Well, that was their job. His attention wandered. Joe, the guy who set the training camp on its ear with his story that he had seen a fascist plane land nearby, had left the line to relieve himself. He looked very contented squatting there in the hot sun, resting his chin on one hand and using the other automatically to keep the flies away. Then Joe was on his face with his white behind sticking up.

Avión!!! He pressed himself against the ground. Where had they come from? He hadn't heard anything and now, right now the sky was full of their noise. JESUS H. CHERRIST! His stomach shrivelled as the bombs came down louder, louder and every muscle and bone crawled in anticipation. It's for me, he thought, it's for me. Then Whoomp Whoomp Whoomp WHOOMPWHOOMPWHOOMP and the ground jarred against his belly—hard. But nothing else happened except that he was alive and when he looked up the air was full of dark dust and instead of the bright brassy glare of sunlight everything was in strange beautiful colors as if a sudden, heavy summer thunderstorm were about to break and there was a lot of shouting further back in the file. He was on his feet now, running forward in obedience to the blast of the commander's whistle. At first he felt rather than saw that the rest of the file was running behind him. But then he looked back to be sure that his squad was keeping together, because that was his job. He held on to that thought. Things were getting mixed up and he didn't know where they were running to, but it was his squad and he knew that he had to keep it together.

He almost bumped into Detro, his company commander. Detro was standing up straight and tall waiting for them in front of a ditch. He looked good standing there grinning a little. He didn't know whether he grinned back, but he tried to. "Into the ditch, m'lad," Detro said, "and move way over to the left so the whole battalion can get in."

After they were all in the ditch, more *avión* came over. He heard them this time coming nearer. There were three of them, big bi-motor jobs, flying in V-formation. They went into a single file formation, circled once, then dropped their bombs. He could see the bombs coming down. He ducked but straightened out immediately. Those weren't coming anywhere near them. He watched them getting bigger and bigger then again the *Whoomps* that you felt in every part of your body and an upheaval of smoke, earth, flame and noise. All the guys in his squad, he too, began calling them bastards, sons of bitches and said the Spanish cursewords that they had picked up because Spanish is very expressive that way. He started to hate *avión* in a very special foot-soldier sort of a way.

The battalion started out again in the same direction but they were moving much faster now. The firing diagonally ahead had almost died out completely, but he felt as if he had eyes and ears all over his body and everybody kept looking up into the sky. Detro and his section leader came over to him and walked alongside. Detro said, "We're going to take up positions on that ridge there and when we get there report to me, your squad is going out front as an outpost." He asked Detro what the situation was, what was happening. Detro shrugged. All he knew was that the fascists were falling back but that we weren't where we were supposed to be according to the schedule, and that we had to be on our toes because you never could tell what was liable to happen. It seems things were a bit mixed up. Yes, a few guys were hit by those bombs. He said that he didn't know exactly how many or who.

When the battalion got to the ridge, he took his squad ahead and down into the valley and placed it along the forward lip of the ravine that had been pointed out to him. They were very careful when they went ahead. The whole squad walked on its toes. His mouth was too dry to spit. No sooner had they placed their Dikterov light machine gun in position than Rico yelled, "Cavalry!" They all scrambled into different positions because the horses were coming down the ravine itself. But before anything could happen they saw it was Republican cavalry. They were scared for a minute, too. Rico spoke pretty good Spanish, so he asked, *"Qué pasa?"* They didn't know anything much. They had just arrived themselves and hadn't seen anything. They had been told that there were lots of fascists around. They were a patrol from the such and such unit.

He sent that back in a message to Detro, feeling pretty good about it. "All information should be promptly forwarded to the next higher in command." This was his first message in combat. He felt that things were beginning to make a little more sense. The squad took up its positions again. They were very alert. Each one looked out over the particular sector that he had assigned to him. There was nothing much to see. The valley was full of small bushes that further off turned into stubby trees. There was another ridge some distance ahead. The valley itself broadened out diagonally to the left. Then it turned to the right and ran into some hills with one big hill that dominated everything. He didn't think much about that hill then.

Everything was quiet except for some artillery booming in the distance. They couldn't see any movement. Then shooting started. Lots of it, rifles and the stuttering rattle of machine guns and also a nasty cracking noise that he didn't know. It was over in the direction of the big hill. He looked hard over there and saw men running forward now, in the direction of the firing. Some tanks came into view and then were hidden by the ground. That's the noise, he figured, tank guns and anti-tank. He wondered what he should do. Detro had told him to stay there until further orders. He was just about to send a runner back for instructions when the Battalion commander appeared out of nowhere, all by himself, and began asking in a loud voice what the hell they were doing there and with a light machine gun too. He said that they were ordered to stay there until further orders and what should they do? The Battalion commander looked at him as if he were crazy and shouted, "Attack—attack" and waved his pistol toward the big hill.

He wasn't sure just what they were supposed to attack but he shouted to his squad, "*Adelante*—follow me," the same as they used to do in maneuvers. They all ran fast toward the firing. He didn't think much about anything except that he wanted to get to his company so that he would know what to do. Then he saw his company and some others up ahead and to the left. They were all widely deployed and running fast toward the firing. They were all hunched up. They weren't shooting or anything, they were just running.

Bullets whistled past him from the right and he knew they weren't going overhead. Dust began kicking up around him. Felix, who had the light machine gun, dropped behind a stump and began to fire in the direction that the shots came from. Felix yelled, "Over there," and "Johnny come here with those pans." He ran to Felix and dropped beside him. "Where are they?" Felix said, "There, they're coming from there." He couldn't see anything.

Johnny came running up holding his rifle in his left hand and a pan of bullets in his right. Then he dropped both of them and grabbed his shoulder. "I'm hit," he said. Then his voice slid all the way up. "What'll I *do?*" Felix just grunted as if it were none of his business. But he looked at Johnny kneeling there, eyes and mouth wide open and blood coming through his fingers, and said, "Go back." So Johnny began going back, holding his shoulder. Then he turned to Felix and said, "Let's go." He wanted to get to the company. The squad went forward again. The fire ahead was getting heavier and heavier but they were in a dip of ground now and nothing was coming near them. He couldn't see them now but he figured they were catching up with the company so his mind only held a moment of curiosity as to whether Felix had hit anything.

They caught up with the others where the valley broadened out, turned and sloped upwards to the hills. The big pointed ridge, obliquely ahead, loomed loweringly over everything.

A lot of guys were on the slope, struggling to get to the top. They were running in spasmodic dashes, throwing themselves to the ground behind a bush, in a furrow, any place, then they would get up and run forward again. Some didn't get up, they just lay there all shrunk up—still. Others were on the ground dragging themselves in different directions, awkwardly. It didn't mean anything to him. He wanted to catch up with his company. He saw Sam, a section leader, and shouted, "Where to?" Sam yelled back, "There," and pointed to the big hill. He turned to his squad and saw that they weren't all there. He waved his arm ahead and they left the shelter of the dip and started up the slope.

It was like going into a heavy storm. Bullets beat down and across the slope in sudden, vicious squalls. He no longer thought about his squad. He thought of nothing. It was not thought but a not-to-be-denied compulsion that forced him to go forward. Because his body didn't want to go forward. His body wanted to seek frantic shelter from the little slugs of lead that were seeking to tear its soft, unprotected parts to bits.

Every time he threw himself to the ground at the end of a short dash, his body wanted to claw itself deeper into the protecting earth. It was agony to leave the scanty shelter of even a little mound of dirt to make another spurt forward. Driven on, his body protested in sudden ways, with pounding heart roaring in his ears and grabbing at his throat, with roiling stomach and the hot dribble of uncontrolled urine running down his leg. There was nothing clear and formulated in his mind now that kept him going forward. The unanswerable logic that had brought him across the sea to Spain did not appear at this moment. The slogans which summed up reasoned argument in a compact bundle of powerful words and transformed it into action were not on his lips. When words came in occasional bursts, they were foul, filthy, gasping, repetitious, meaningless gutter words. There was no conscious decision but he knew he would not turn back. His decision had been made before. He had picked his way of life and this was it.

The Victory of Guernica

PAUL ELUARD

1

O lovely world of ruins
Of mines and meadows

2

Faces strong in fire faces strong in cold
In the face of night denial, in spite of
    curses, blows

3

Strong faces always
Here is the void that stares you in the face
Your death will serve as an example

4

The dead heart overturned

5

They make you pay for the bread
For heaven and earth, water and sleep
And the wretchedness of your lives

6

They said yearn for intelligence
They rationed the strong judged the insane
Begged for alms split a cent in half
They hailed the dead bodies
And overwhelmed themselves with courtesy

7

They persist they exaggerate they don't belong
    to our world

8

Women and children have the same treasure
Of green leaves spring and fresh milk
And time
In their pure eyes

9

Women and children have the same treasure
In their eyes
Which men defend as well as they are able

10

Women and children have the same red roses
In their eyes
Each displays his blood

11

The fear and the courage to live and die
Death so difficult death so easy

12

Men for whom this treasure was sung
Men for whom this treasure was spoiled

13

Real men for whom despair
Feeds the devouring fire of hope
Let us open together the last bud of the future

14

O! pariahs death earth and the hideousness
Of our enemies have the same
Monotonous color of our night
We will be proved right.

Translated by Alvah Bessie

Soldiers of the Republic

DOROTHY PARKER

T HAT SUNDAY AFTERNOON we sat with the Swedish girl in the
big café in Valencia. We had vermouth in thick globlets, each
with a cube of honeycombed gray ice in it. The waiter was so
proud of that ice he could hardly bear to leave the glasses on
the table, and thus part from it forever. He went to his duty—
all over the room they were clapping their hands and hissing to
draw his attention—but he looked back over his shoulder.

It was dark outside, the quick, new dark that leaps down
without dusk on the day; but, because there were no lights in
the streets, it seemed as set and as old as midnight. So you wondered that all the babies were still up. There were babies everywhere in the café, babies serious without solemnity and interested in a tolerant way in their surroundings.

At the table next to ours, there was a notably small one;
maybe six months old. Its father, a little man in a big uniform
that dragged his shoulders down, held it carefully on his knee.
It was doing nothing whatever, yet he and his thin young wife,
whose belly was already big again under her sleazy dress, sat
watching it in a sort of ecstasy of admiration, while their coffee
cooled in front of them. The baby was in Sunday white; its dress
patched so delicately that you would have thought the fabric
whole, had not the patches varied in their shades of whiteness.
In its hair was a bow of new blue ribbon, tied with absolute balance of loops and ends. The ribbon was of no use; there was not
enough hair to require restraint. The bow was sheerly an adornment, a calculated bit of dash.

"Oh for God's sake, stop that!" I said to myself. "All right,
so it's got a piece of blue ribbon on its hair. All right, so its
mother went without eating so it could look pretty when its father

came home on leave. All right, so it's her business and none of yours. All right, so what have you got to cry about?"

The big, dim room was crowded and lively. That morning there had been a bombing from the air, the more horrible for broad daylight. But nobody in the café sat tense and strained, nobody desperately forced forgetfulness. They drank coffee or bottled lemonade, in the pleasant, earned ease of Sunday afternoon, chatting of small, gay matters, all talking at once, all hearing and answering.

There were many soldiers in the room, in what appeared to be the uniforms of twenty different armies until you saw that the variety lay in the differing ways the cloth had worn or faded. Only a few of them had been wounded; here and there you saw one stepping gingerly, leaning on a crutch or two canes, but so far on toward recovery that his face had color. There were many men, too, in civilian clothes—some of them soldiers home on leave, some of them governmental workers, some of them anybody's guess. There were plump, comfortable wives, active with paper fans, and old women as quiet as their grandchildren. There were many pretty girls and some beauties, of whom you did not remark: "There's a charming Spanish type," but said, "What a beautiful girl!" The women's clothes were not new, and their material was too humble ever to have warranted skillful cutting.

"It's funny," I said to the Swedish girl, "how when nobody in a place is best-dressed, you don't notice that everybody isn't."

"Please?" the Swedish girl said.

No one, save an occasional soldier, wore a hat. When we had first come to Valencia, I lived in a state of puzzled pain as to why everybody on the streets laughed at me. It was not because "West End Avenue" was writ across my face as if left there by a customs officer's chalked scrawl. They like Americans in Valencia, where they have seen good ones—the doctors who left their practices and came to help, the calm young nurses, the men of the International Brigade. But when I walked forth, men and women courteously laid their hands across splitting faces, and little children, too innocent for dissembling, doubled with glee and pointed and cried, *"Olé!"* Then pretty late, I made my discovery, and left my hat off; and there was laughter no longer. It was not one of those comic hats, either; it was just a hat.

The café filled to overflow, and I left our table to speak to a friend across the room. When I came back to the table, six soldiers were sitting there. They were crowded in, and I scraped past them to my chair. They looked tired and dusty and little, the way that the newly dead look little, and the first things you saw about them were the tendons in their necks. I felt like a prize sow.

They were all in conversation with the Swedish girl. She has Spanish, French, German, anything in Scandinavian, Italian and English. When she has a moment for regret, she sighs that her Dutch is so rusty she can no longer speak it, only read it, and the same is true of her Rumanian.

They had told her, she told us, that they were at the end of forty-eight hours' leave from the trenches, and, for their holiday, they had pooled their money for cigarettes, and something had gone wrong, and the cigarettes had never come through to them. I had a pack of American cigarettes—in Spain rubies are as nothing to them—and I brought it out, and by nods and smiles and a sort of breast stroke, made it understood that I was offering it to those six men yearning for tobacco. When they saw what I meant, each one of them rose and shook my hand. Darling of me to share my cigarettes with the men on their way back to the trenches. Little Lady Bountiful. The prize sow.

Each one lit his cigarette with a contrivance of yellow rope that stank when afire and was also used, the Swedish girl translated, for igniting grenades. Each one received what he had ordered, a glass of coffee, and each one murmured appreciatively over the tiny cornucopia of coarse sugar that accompanied it. Then they talked.

They talked through the Swedish girl, but they did to us that thing we all do when we speak our own language to one who has no knowledge of it. They looked us square in the face and spoke slowly, and pronounced their words with elaborate movements of their lips. Then, as their stories came, they poured them at us so vehemently, so emphatically that they were sure we must understand. They were so convinced we would understand that we were ashamed for not understanding.

But the Swedish girl told us. They were all farmers and farmers' sons, from a district so poor that you try not to remember there is that kind of poverty. Their village was next to that one where the old men and the sick men and the women and children had gone, on a holiday, to the bullring; and the planes had come over and dropped bombs on the bullring, and the old men and the sick men and the women and the children were more than two hundred.

They had all, the six of them, been in the war for over a year, and most of that time they had been in the trenches. Four of them were married. One had one child, two had three children, one had five. They had not had word from their families since they had left for the front. There had been no communication; two of them had learned to write from men fighting next to them in the trench, but they had not dared to write home. They belonged to a union, and union men, of course, are put to death if taken. The village where their families lived had been captured, and if your wife gets a letter from a union man, who knows but they'll shoot her for the connection?

They told about how they had not heard from their families for more than a year. They did not tell it gallantly or whimsically or stoically. They told it as if—well, look. You have been in the trenches, fighting, for a year. You have heard nothing of your wife and your children. They do not know if you are dead or alive or blinded. You do not know where they are, or if they are. You must talk to somebody. That is the way they told about it.

One of them, some six months before, had heard of his wife and his three children—they had such beautiful eyes, he said—from a brother-in-law in France. They were all alive then, he was told, and had a bowl of beans a day. But his wife had not complained of the food, he heard. What had troubled her was that she had no thread to mend the children's ragged clothes. So that troubled him too.

"She has no thread," he kept telling us. "My wife has no thread to mend with. No thread."

We sat there and listened to what the Swedish girl told us they were saying. Suddenly one of them looked at the clock, and then there was excitement. They jumped up, as a man, and there were calls for the waiter and rapid talk with him, and each of them shook the hand of each of us. We went through more swimming motions to explain to them that they were to take the rest of the cigarettes—fourteen cigarettes for six soldiers to take to war—and they shook our hands again. Then all of us said "*Salud!*" as many times as could be for six of them, and three of us, and they filed out of the café, the six of them, tired and dusty and little, as men of a mighty horde are little.

Only the Swedish girl talked, after they had gone. The Swedish girl has been in Spain since the start of the war. She has nursed splintered men, and she has carried stretchers into the trenches and, heavier laden, back to the hospital. She has seen and heard too much to be knocked into silence.

Presently it was time to go, and the Swedish girl raised her hands above her head and clapped them twice together to summon the waiter. He came, but he only shook his head and his hand, and moved away.

The soldiers had paid for our drinks.

From The Portable Dorothy Parker
Copyright 1938, 1944 by Dorothy Parker
Reprinted by permission of The Viking Press, Inc., New York

194

Radio Seville

RAFAEL ALBERTI

Are you listening? Radio Seville!
This is Queipo de Llano barking,
bellowing, spitting,
braying on four legs.
Radio Seville!—"Ladies and gentlemen!
At the microphone: a savior of Spain.
Long live wine! Long live vomit!
Tonight I take Málaga;
Monday I take Jerez;
Tuesday, Montilla and Cazalla;
Wednesday, Chinchon, and Thursday
drunk. And in the morning
all the stables of Madrid, all the stalls
made soft by the over-piling of horseshit
shall give me a soft bed.
Oh, what a delight is sleep,
to have for a pillow
(in hiccuping distance)
two piles of alfalfa!
What an honor to go to the blacksmith
at the sign of the halter!
What a unique pleasure
to receive on my hoofs,
nailed with spikes,
the horseshoes that Franco
won by his venture in Africa!
Already my loins are straining,
already my rump is lifting,
already my ears are growing,

already my teeth are getting larger.
The cinch grows short for me,
the reins get out of control.
I gallop, gallop . . . on my way:
I shall be in Madrid tomorrow.
Let the colleges close,
let the taverns open.
Down with universities
and institutes—down, down!
Let wine flow to meet
a liberator of Spain."
—Are you listening?
Radio Seville!
The general of this military base,
a bleating fool,
Queipo de Llano,
is signing off.

English version by John Tisa from
THE VOLUNTEER FOR LIBERTY, *Madrid,*
August 9, 1937.

> *Every man is a people.*
> ANDALUSIAN PROVERB

The Denunciation

PRUDENCIO de PEREDA

THEY USED TO COME up in pairs, and only very seldom. Before the war they used to come up to the *pueblo* from the town only on very rare times, and the lone pair of them would come walking heavily and firmly along the white road, swinging their uncocked rifles and talking easily. Then when the people saw them go into the *pueblo*, they would come out to their doorways, talking in excitement and saying, "The Civil Guards! The Civil Guards are here! What can be the matter? I wonder what's the matter?"

And they kept looking after them; but they never stayed there looking long because they knew that nothing serious was the matter. Nothing serious was ever the matter in the *pueblo*. The guards were there probably to see if Luciano's permit to make and sell sausages was renewed and in good order, or to find out why Anastasio did not register his new ox-cart. And soon, in the night, long after the Guards had had a glass of wine in the tavern and gone back to town, the people in the *pueblo* found out that it had been some little thing like that, and that it was all over now.

But after the war came, they never walked up in pairs. They came often, now, and always in a body or with someone else. They came in groups of four or six and with their rifles on their shoulders and cocked. Quietly. Almost always a very quiet German officer dressed in plain clothes was with them when they came, and, once in the night, they came in a truck with Moors to take Blas away. They never stopped to drink now.

One Saturday afternoon when the war had been driving for a

year and a month Santos and Pedro, the two Guards who had been in Villarcayo for fourteen years, drove up to the *pueblo* in a car with the German officer. They stopped at the tavern and talked to Benito while the officer stayed in the car and watched them.

Santos, who was doing the talking, asked Benito to have his whole family at the tavern tomorrow morning after mass. The whole family? said Benito. He did not understand. He had no family. What whole family? The Varona family, Santos said. Your wife and you, Bernabe your brother-in-law, and the cousin from Bocos. What's the matter? Benito said. Is anything wrong with us? Nothing is wrong. No, nothing! Santos told him. It's just a formality. A formality! They want you to make a statement. A statement? said Benito. About loyalty? We've shown our loyalty very much. You know that! We've shown it. No, said Santos, not that. It isn't about that. It's nothing. We'll be here. We'll tell you what to do. We'll help you. Oh, said Benito. All right. All right!

Then, on Sunday, the mass at Bocos was celebrated an hour later than the masses at Mozares and Campo where Benito and his brother-in-law lived, and so Benito and his wife Felipa, and his brother Bernabe, had to wait a little while for the cousin from Bocos to come. They sat on the benches in Benito's tavern and talked a little. They talked about how the war against the Marxists was going, but they could not stay on that long. It made them all feel self-conscious to talk about it. They had been talking about it for so long! And all the little actual information that they had about it had been used up very long ago and they did not like to repeat themselves. They talked, then, about the crops and the livestock and then they did not say anything for a while. They tried to think only about what this thing that was going to happen to them could be, and no one thought of the right thing.

Soon, ten minutes before the cousin from Bocos would come, and while they were still silent, Santos and Pedro drove up with the same German officer in the same car. This time he got out. He got out first and then waited for Santos and Pedro and followed them into the tavern. He had a thin leather brief-case under his arm, and when they came into the room, Bernabe and Benito stood up. "Good days!" Santos and Pedro said together.

"Very good ones!" first Felipa and Benito, and then Bernabe said.

The German nodded his head silently and the Guards and he stood near the door awkwardly. "Did you advise the one in Bocos?" Santos asked Benito.

"Yes, but the mass is late there," Benito said to him.

"He won't come for a while then, eh?"

"No, I don't think that he will," Benito said. "You want a drink?"

"No. Thanks!" Santos said. "No drinks." Benito looked at Pedro. Pedro shook his head. The German was watching them.

When the three of them had come in, Bernabe had looked at them and suddenly felt uncomfortable. Without even trying to he had remembered suddenly that he wanted to plant some late August beans in the Villanueva *finca*, and now he wanted to go out and plant them right away. Quickly. The Bishop had given permission for work to be done on Sundays because of the big harvest. Now, Bernabe looked at the Guards and the German in the room and he wanted to be out of it. He felt cold and wanted the sun on him. He looked over at his sister. She seemed calm. Then he joined his hands between his open knees and began to move his thumbs one over the other and to watch them very seriously.

The Guards felt the tenseness that was growing up in there and they tried to make conversation, first with the others and then with themselves, but they could not do it. Felipa and Benito answered them in monosyllables and Bernabe kept his head down like that. They stood by the door with their guns held up and looked out the side window. What the hell is the matter with Bernabe? Santos thought. He always likes to talk and laugh so much. Especially on Sunday when everybody can sit around and talk and drink.

And then, five minutes had passed. The German pulled out his watch and looked at it. Benito, who was nervous and excited, went out into the yard and looked down the road into the *pueblo*. "He's not coming yet," he said when he came in. "He'll come," Felipa said.

They began to wait again in silence. Two men came in from the *pueblo* and had drinks. They left as soon as they had finished. Everyone watched them as they went out. How long minutes can be, Santos thought. He looked out the side window. A car sounded down in the *pueblo*. Let it be he, he hoped.

It was a car from Bocos. The driver got out and came inside. He had a note from the cousin for Benito. Benito took it quickly from him and his excitement over the note made him forget the disappointment he felt when it was not the cousin who had come. Now he read the note slowly to himself at first, and then out loud. Emilio, their cousin, could not be there. Some business had come up while he had been at mass, and he must go to attend to it at once. Let the officials contact him later in the day, if they would. With a kindly embrace, your cousin, Emilio.

Emilio, who had come back to Spain after making much money in Mexico, had property in all parts of the province and he was called many times to go to these places. To fix rents or rates. To survey a crop.

"Are these important things that he has to do?" the German asked out in clear, well-pronounced Spanish.

"He has a lot of business," Felipa said. "He has a lot of money to look after, Señor."

"It must be important," Benito said. "I told him that he had to be here."

Santos looked at the German. He made a sour face and shrugged his shoulders. The German nodded at him. All right! Santos cleared his throat. "*Señores!*" he said, "*y Señora!*" to Felipa. All of them turned to look at him. He got ready to say something.

"Please, *Señor*," the German said in the clear and well-pronounced Spanish. "May I?" Santos looked at him in surprise and then shrugged his shoulders again. The German turned his eyes to all the others.

"I am not sure that you all know why you are called together here," he said. He spoke as if he were reciting or reading carefully. "It is true that it is to go through a formality, but, at the same time, a very important formality. It is the spirit of it that makes it important. That counts. Now. . . ." He stopped and looked at Bernabe. "You have a brother in New York, no?"

"Yes, my brother Esteban lives in New York with his family."

"Right! He has many sons. Now, there is one among them also called 'Esteban' who was here in Spain at one time. Is that not correct?"

"It is correct," said Bernabe. "He was here with us three years ago. He did not stay long, though."

"A very good boy," Felipa, Bernabe's sister, said. "He lived here with us." They began to talk freely now. It was becoming definite. The thing was becoming definite and they were getting out of vagueness and mystery. They all began to think of Esteban.

"You all knew him, then?" the German asked. He looked around. They nodded their heads. "I should say that we did," Felipa said. "We knew him," Bernabe said. "Yes," Benito said slowly.

"All right, then," the German said. "That's all right. . . . This boy has become an active Marxist! He is now actively engaged in aiding the cause of the Madrid Marxist Government. We must ask you all to denounce him. In public!"

"How . . . ?" Benito said.

"Denounce him?" Felipa said. Bernabe did not say anything. The German looked at them all with a tense face.

"You have understood?" he asked them. He was growing a little excited. This was important. "You must publish this denunciation of him in the local paper. It will be copied in all Burgos. The importance of this is evident, of course."

"But how . . . ?" Benito began to say again.

"A formal denunciation," Santos said hurriedly. "A mere formal statement. You express your regret that he has been misguided and led into the Marxist camp."

The German looked at Santos. "This is not an order, Señor Santos," he said curtly. "The denunciation must be a spontaneous one, deriving immediately from the feelings of these people."

"What feelings?" Bernabe said.

"Your true feelings," the German said. "The only feelings that you can have in this case. . . . You must demonstrate that ties of family and blood are sacrificed in our work."

"What has he done?" Felipa said.

"What?"

"What has he done? How has he been active? You said that we must denounce him. Why do you want us to do this?"

"Oh," the German said, "I understand." He took a paper out of the thin case. He looked at it and then held it up for them to see. It was a mimeographed sheet with a crudely made newspaper head at the top of it. Bernabe stood up a little to look more closely. "It is written in English," the German said. "You can't read it." "No." said Bernabe, but he did no stop peering at it.

"But what is it?" Benito said. "Is it a paper?"

"This is the front page of a copy of the newspaper that your nephew, Estebán, edits and writes almost entirely alone," the German said. "It is issued daily under his supervision in the Marxist trenches for the American and English Communists who are aiding the Madrid Government. We have secured three copies of it. They are of three widely separated dates. So that it can be seen that he has put out many of them. His work has had volume."

"Estebán does this?" Benito asked him.

"Estebán Varona, your nephew, is almost the entire force behind this paper. We have proof of that."

"Where, though? Where does he do this?"

"He is working in Madrid. We believe he must go to the front many times."

"Estebán is in Madrid?" Felipa and Bernabe said together.

"Yes, he is in Madrid."

"Estebán is in Spain," Bernabe said as if he were telling himself a thing in a loud voice. "Our nephew is here in Spain."

"*Coño!*" said Benito.

"Not here, Señor," the German said to Bernabe. "In Madrid. In Marxist Spain!"

"Yes, I know that. But he's in Spain! He's here."

"He always said that he wanted to come back," Felipa said.

"Estebán in Spain," Bernabe said again. He could not get over it.

"Did you know about his work?" the German said abruptly. "Did he ever tell you anything about it?" He wanted to get on.

"We knew that he was making himself a writer," Benito said.

"He used to do some writing here," Felipa said. "Very innocent things. Once the cat peed on it," she said. She laughed nervously.

"Did he let you read it?" the German asked her.

"It was in English," Bernabe said. "He wrote in English."

"I see. Did he ever speak to you of radical and Marxist things?"

"No, never!" Bernabe and Felipa lied together.

"To you?" the German asked Benito.

"I didn't talk to him very often," he said. "We were not together many times. We spoke of other things. We spoke of the family."

"Were you not very interested in what was happening in the country at that time? In the new republic?"

"*Hombre,* we hated it," Benito said excitedly, trying to please, "but he was a visitor and we didn't want to worry him with what was happening here."

"It wasn't his business," Bernabe said.

"We wanted him to enjoy himself," Felipa said. "This was his first visit to his father's *pueblo.*"

"But you hated the republic, you say?" the German said.

"Yes," said Benito, "we hated it."

The German looked around then, watching every face. "I think you will be willing to sign this denunciation," he said. He said it very quietly.

No one said anything. Then Bernabe looked at him. "You want us to denounce him," he said. "If we denounce him we regret that he is our blood, eh?"

"You denounce him as a Marxist. You will completely deny him. Yes. He is an enemy! He must be negated."

"I won't denounce him," Bernabe said. The others listened to his voice and then watched the German's face. It twitched slightly. "Why will you not?" he said.

"He's my brother's son. I know him. I love him. He exists for me!"

"He's a good boy," Felipa said. "Truly he is. But the thing is that he's very young. He doesn't know about these things."

"He knows about them enough to work them against us."

"He isn't working against us," Bernabe said. "He wouldn't want to work against us. To hurt us. I know that!"

"We need calmness here," Benito said. "Let's be calm now."

"Is the denunciation a strong one?" Felipa said.

"Formal, merely formal," Santos said to her.

"Formal?"

"Please!" the German said. "Please! The language will be formal, but we must understand, and those who read it must understand, that a true spirit of denunciation exists and is sincerely felt there."

"But it isn't," Bernabe said.

"You say that, Bernabe," Santos said to him. "You're giving this too much importance."

"Señor Bernabe is perhaps in agreement with some of the ideas of his nephew," the German said very quietly. "Perhaps these things mean something to him."

"Señor Bernabe is a Catholic," Bernabe said, "and a Spaniard. I defend Spain and the Church against the people who I think are trying to destroy it."

"Like all of us," Felipa said.

204

"I don't understand," Benito said. "I don't understand all this."

"That's all right," the German said. "Please, now." He took another paper from the very thin brief-case and held it up in the air while he looked along the bar for a clean spot. When he found it, he laid the paper flat on it, and then took out a fountain pen and opened it and handed it to Benito who had been watching him and was nearest him. Benito took the pen and shrugged his shoulders. The German pointed to a spot at the bottom of the paper and Benito signed his name there with great effort. He handed the pen to his wife and slid the paper over a little. Felipa looked at Bernabe. "Do I sign it, Bernabe?" she said.

"If you think that you should," said Bernabe. She looked at him for a long minute. Then she turned and signed it. The German took the pen and held it out to Bernabe. His face was wet. He was finished with talking.

"Keep it," Bernabe said. "I won't sign."

"This is a serious matter, Señor."

"I believe it."

"You know what you're doing then?"

"I know it well."

"He has twenty-four hours before he signs," Santos said over the German's back.

"That is true," the German said.

"It doesn't matter," Bernabe said. "I won't change with the sun. I won't change." He got up from the bench and began to move towards the door. "*Adiós*," he said. "Until later." He walked past the Guards to the door. He was a big man and he moved a little awkwardly.

Bernabe walked along the white highway from Mozares to Campo. Campo was his *pueblo*. This was the *pueblo* that he had stayed in. Bernabe was the youngest of three brothers in the Varona family. The eldest had gone first to Madrid and then to Vigo and made a fortune there before he died in middle age, and the second had gone to Madrid and then to Cuba and New York and made a fortune before he lost it in the depression of 1929. Bernabe had stayed in their *pueblo* and worked the old lands and raised a family of thirteen children. There were only six of them left living, but they were beautiful children and this was a beautiful country.

Bernabe was a fool for staying in that hole, his brothers had said. You had to go out of there to get someplace. He loved his brothers very much and tried hard to understand about what they meant, but he could not do this. He just stayed there working and sweating, and being happy when a boy came, and when the crop was good, and when the pigs grew big and fat; and waiting always for the letters from his brothers and the rare, very rare visits. Once, after twenty-five years, Estabán had come from New York. The brother who had been his chum in youth, and then, ten years after that, the little Esteban had come to Spain, but he was not little, but tall and handsome and bright, and clean.

Bernabe had been surprised then. It had been a very pleasant surprise. This kid had been from New York, the greatest city in the world, but he talked to you and went along with you as if you were his equal and he was very happy to be with you. He had said, too, that he wanted to try everything that his father had done. So he minded the oxen, milked the cow, plowed and wrestled hay, and even cleaned out the stable and the pig-sty with that smell there that choked you.

Bernabe remembered now how he had always liked to stay in Campo. He didn't like Benito because Benito thought too much about business. He wanted to stay at Bernabe's house with Bernabe and the wife that he loved so much and that anyone could see that he loved so much.

I should denounce him, they say. I must deny him, now. He is not my own blood and a typical Varona, the way I hoped Varonas would always be. No! No, no, no! Not I! I don't deny him. He is of the blood. He is truly! In New York there are many Marxists and they must have told him many things. They always have things to tell. We ought to know as much about our part of this. Why don't they tell us more so that we can talk, too, and tell others?

He could not think that side of it out. He only shook his head and went home. After dinner he went out to the Villanueva *finca* with the beans.

In the night he sat around the open fire in the small kitchen of his home and listened to his wife and two daughters talk about the other daughter who was out "serving" in Burgos. He was waiting for his little son Angel to come in from a visit to a friend's house.

Bernabe did not want to talk. He sat and watched the coals of the supper fire grow first gray and then black, and sat and listened to the voices of his wife and daughters. When Angelito came in he went over and stood by the bench his father was sitting on and leaned his shoulder against the side. Bernabe put his arm around him.

"Angel," his father said, "Estebán is here."

"Papa!" Angel said. He turned to look at his father.

"What?" the others said. "Estebán is here?"

"He's in Spain. He's in Madrid."

"In Madrid?" Bernabe's wife said. "There in Madrid. Oh, Bernabe!"

"He's been here a long time."

"But Papa," one of the daughters said, "in Madrid! That's no good." The disappointment showed all around.

"But he's here in Spain," Bernabe said. "He's here."

The next morning at ten o'clock Santos and Pedro came up along the highway from the town, walking slowly in front of a car that the German was driving. Two Moors on horseback rode behind the car. Santos and Pedro kept looking at the faces of the people working in the fields that lined the highway. Then Santos saw Bernabe cutting wheat in his *finca* on the highway just before it turned into Campo. Santos broke away and walked through the cut stalks up to where Bernabe was bent over cutting.

"Bernabe," he said.

"Hello, Santos," Bernabe said. He did not get up.

"Are you going to sign it, Bernabe?"

"No, Sir!"

"Think it over, Bernabe. You're getting too serious about it."

"It's a very serious thing," Bernabe said. He stood up with the cut wheat in one hand and the sickle held in the other. He looked at Santos and then over at the car and the Moors.

"Do you want me to go into town with you?"

"Sign it, Bernabe. Don't you want to sign it?"

"No, Santos. Thanks for the consideration."

"They want you to come in to town, then."

"All right," Bernabe said. Santos turned around and began to walk back to the car. Bernabe tied the stalks in his hand together. He used one of the stalks as a cord. Then he laid them on the pile of stalks and put the sickle down beside the pile. He walked after Santos.

When he had seen them start to come over, the German had turned the car around and now they were ready to go. Bernabe was to ride in the back seat of the car with Santos. He came up to the road and stopped and stood looking at them all. Santos was standing at the door with his hand on the knob and waiting for him to come and get in. Pedro was in the front seat already. He stared straight ahead.

Bernabe looked at Santos and then down the road to where the car was pointed. The car was pointed down towards town. It would go riding fast into town. He did not like to go to town since the war had begun. They had changed the buildings and there were many people there that he did not know. There was darkness down there now. Dark places and dark spots on the streets. They might do things to you there in the dark.

While here he was in Campo. The beautiful earth with the beautiful children on it and the wife that he loved very much and that anyone could see that he loved very much. Would they do anything here?

He turned around and began to walk slowly back across the field. "Bernabe!" Santos yelled. "Bernabe!"

He heard him, but he did not stop. Here! They could do it here, if they wanted to. "Bernabe!" Santos was growing excited. "Varona! Bernabe!"

Bernabe walked slowly, slowly on the earth at Campo. Here! Here! He could not see that one of the Moors had turned his horse to the side and was taking careful aim at his slowly moving back. He went on and on slowly over the stalks he had just clipped and heard Santos yell only once more in the voice growing hoarse with excitement before the first bullet came, and then the second in quick succession.

The second crashed through the base of his skull just before he fell. He was dead when they turned him over and the blood began to flow freely into the earth.

From SALUD! *International, New York, 1938*

For Milton Wolff

City of Anguish

EDWIN ROLFE

I

At midnight they roused us. In the distance we heard
verberations of thunder. "To the cellar," they ordered.
"It's safest under the stairway." Pointing,
a veteran led us. The children, whimpering,
followed the silent women who would never
sing again strolling in the *Paseo* on Sunday evenings.
In the candle-light their faces were granite.

"Artillery," muttered Enrico, cursing.
Together we turned at the lowest stair.
"Come on," he said. "It's better on the rooftop.
More fireworks, better view." Slowly we ascended
past the stalled lift, felt through the roof door,
squinted in moonless darkness.

We counted the flashes, divided the horizon,
90 degrees for Enrico, 90 for me.
"Four?" "No, five!" We spotted the big guns where
the sounds came crashing, split-seconds after light.
Felt the slight earthquake tremor when shells fell
square on the Gran Via; heard high above our heads
the masculine shriek of the shell descending—
the single sharp rifle-crack, the inevitable dogs
barking, angry, roused from midsummer sleep.
The lulls grew fewer: soon talking subsided
as the cannonade quickened. Each flash in darkness
created horizon, outlined huge buildings.

Off a few blocks to the north, the *Telefónica*
reared its massive shoulders, its great symbol profile
in dignity, like the statue of Moses pointing,
aged but ageless, to the Promised Land.

II

Deafening now, the sky is aflame with
unnatural lightning. The ear—
like the scout's on patrol—gauges each explosion.
The mind—neither ear nor eye is aware of it—
calculates destruction, paints the dark pictures
of beams fallen, ribs crushed beneath them; beds
blown with their innocent sleepers to agonized
death.
  And the great gaping craters in streets
yawn, hypnotic to the terrified madman,
sane a mere hour ago.
       The headless body
stands strangely, totters for a second, falls.
The girl speeds screaming through wreckage: her hair is
wilder than torture.
      The solitary foot,
deep-arched, is perfect on the cobbles, naked,
strong, ridged with strong veins, upright, complete. . . .

The city weeps. The city shudders, weeping.

The city weeps: for the moment is silent—
the pause in the idiot's symphony, prolonged
beyond the awaited crashing of cymbals, but
the hands are in mid-air, the instruments gleaming:
the swastika'd baton falls! and the clatter of
thunder begins again.
      Enrico beckons me.
Fires there. Where? Toward the *Casa del Campo.*
And closer. There. The *Puerta del Sol* exudes
submarine glow in the darkness, alive with
strange twisting shapes, skyfish of stars,

fireworks of death, mangled lives, silent lips.
In thousands of beds now the muscles of men are
aroused, flexed for springing, quivering, tense,
that moments ago were relaxed, asleep.

III

It is too late for sleep now.
Few hours are left before dawn. We **wait for**
the sun's coming. . . . And it rises, sulphurous
through smoke. It is too late for sleep.

The city weeps. The city wakens, weeping.

And the Madrileños rise from wreckage, emerge
from shattered doorways. . . .
                              But always the wanderer,
the old woman searching, digging among debris.
In the morning light her crazed face is granite.

And the beggar sings among the ruins:

> All night, all night
> flared in my city the bright
> cruel explosion of bombs.
> All night, all night
> there, where the soil and stone
> spilled like brains from the sandbag's head,
> the bodiless head lay staring;
> while the anti-aircraft barked,
> barked at the droning plane,
> and the dogs of war, awakened,
> howled at the hidden moon.
> And a star fell, omen of ill,
> and a man fell, lifeless,
> and my wife fell, childless,
> and, friendless, my friend.
> And I stumbled away from them, crying
> from eyeless lids, blinded.

Trees became torches
lighting the avenues
where lovers huddled in horror
who would be lovers no longer.

All night, all night
flared in my city the bright
cruel explosion of hope—
all night
all night . . .

IV

Come for a joyride in Madrid: the August morning
is cleared of smoke and cloud now; the journalists
dip their hard bread in the *Florida* coffee,
no longer distasteful after sour waking.
Listen to Ryan, fresh from the lines, talking
    (Behind you the memory of bombs beats
    the blood in the brain's vessels—the dream broken,
    sleep pounded to bits by the unending roar of
    shells in air, the silvery bombs descending,
    mad spit of machine guns and the carnival flare
    of fire in the sky):
                "Why is it, why?
when I'm here in the trenches, half-sunk in mud,
blanket drenched, hungry, I dream of Dublin,
of home, of the girls? But give me a safe spot,
clean linen, bed and all, sleep becomes nightmare
of shrapnel hurtling, bombs falling, the screaming of bullets,
their thud on the brain's parapet. Why? Why?"

Exit the hotel. The morning constitutional.
Stroll down the avenues. Did Alfonso's car
detour past barricades? Did broken mains splatter him?
Here's the bellyless building: four walls, no guts.
But the biggest disaster's the wrecking of power:
thirty-six hours and no power: electric

213

sources are severed. The printer is frantic:
how print the leaflet, the poster, or set
the type for the bulletin?
                              After his food
a soldier needs cigarettes, something to read,
something to think about: words to pull
the war-weary brain back to life from forgetfulness:
spirited words, the gestures of Dolores,
majestic Pasionaría speaking—
mother to men, mother of revolutions,
winner of battles, comforter of defenders;
her figure magnificent as any monument
constructed for heroes; her voice a symphony,
consoling, urging, declaiming in prophecy,
her forehead the wide plateaus of her country,
her eyes constant witnesses of her words' truth.

                    V

Needless to catalogue heroes. No man
weighted with rifle, digging with nails in earth,
quickens at the name. Hero's a word for
peacetime. Battle
knows only three realities: enemy, rifle, life.

No man knows war or its meaning who has not
stumbled from tree to tree, desperate for cover,
or dug his face deep in earth, felt the ground pulse with
the ear-breaking fall of death. No man knows war
who never has crouched in his foxhole, hearing
the bullets an inch from his head, nor the zoom of
planes like a Ferris wheel strafing the trenches . . .

War is your comrade struck dead beside you,
his shared cigarette still alive in your lips.

From First Love, *Larry Edmunds Bookshop,
Los Angeles, 1951*

"I Hope It Doesn't Bore You..."

DAVID McKELVY WHITE

SRI, Albacete, Spain

DEAR ——————:
 I suppose that almost all of us in the Battalion have had the experience of reading in letters something like the following: "So and so has done such and such, and—but how can you, who are living through such momentous events, be interested in such trivial things." After that, we are generally due for a solemn harangue of some sort. Is it any wonder that, grateful as we are for letters, we are tempted to consign such writers to a lifetime of reading nothing but propaganda?

Not long ago, however, it struck me that you in the States might be feeling the same way, for I have noticed in your letters appeals to be told the little, obvious, trivial things about our life here. And it occurred to me that very likely my letters have been getting duller and duller as I have become more and more accustomed to Spain, and ever more inclined to take small local events and customs for granted. Let's try it, then—a collection of disconnected trivialities, the sort of things a writer finds so useful for spots of local color and that I have grown too accustomed to notice without a special effort.

All the towns in which we have been quartered at various times have been supplied with electricity, but none of them have had any plumbing system. The water supply has invariably been a stone fountain, almost always in the square before the west façade of a church that towers over the town. Here water flows from pipes into a great stone trough. Here the women come all day long to fill their beautifully shaped clay jugs and here, morning and evening, the sturdy and stubborn little burros are watered. These admirable animals, with their big ears and strong slender

215

legs, and the larger mules of the somewhat more prosperous are so necessary to the farming peasants that no family appears to be without one. They are capable of carrying remarkably heavy loads and have given us a good deal of assistance with machine guns and ammunition. Beginning about 5 or 5:30 in the morning the square is alive as these animals are led or sometimes dragged to the water, often by very small children. Morning gossip is exchanged as the women wait in line to fill their jugs—generally stepping aside to insist at the sight of us that we step in and fill our canteens. The animals are watered and usually loaded with 4 jars fitting into a saddle arrangement they have, and back they go through the hard baked clay streets that in most towns are carefully watered and swept by the women of the houses.

The houses are much alike, all whitewashed, with few windows and those small, and completely blank and self-contained. The walls are very thick to keep out the heat—which they do—and the only decoration is an occasional coat of arms in stone over the door or bits of ancient and interesting iron or woodwork at the windows. Yet as with the brown stone fronts of New York the interiors are surprisingly varied in arrangement and design. Usually a court of some sort, open or covered, sometimes more of a biggish hall. Off this, perhaps, a stable and maybe chickens on one side or at the back and often very beautiful heavy wooden doors leading off to the living quarters and a strong, simple stairway. This space is much used, too, as general living quarters. There are squat chairs about and here meals are served. We soldiers feel naturally an obligation and a still stronger desire to be on the best terms with the local people. They are very friendly and have been genuinely and demonstrably sorry to see us leave.

The other day, at the barbershop, a friend and I were invited to stay for dinner. A difficult decision: we wanted the food, the experience, and the company. Yet many of the food stuffs—meat and sugar, especially—are rationed and anything we ate the family would be doing without. Well, we stayed and were served with, first, a sort of soup, made of bread and cheese and doubtless many other delicious but indeterminable things. We, indignantly waving aside plates and formality, this dish like the others was simply placed in the center of the table and we all pitched in with spoons. The next course was beans, the large squarish sort they have here, boiled (I think) in a little olive oil; then a bit of meat, lamb, very little of it and much palaver about our helping ourselves generously. Finally a swell salad, in the most delicious dressing, of tomatoes and cucumbers, and coffee, made especially for us. With this water and good red wine in jugs. These jugs have two spouts, a small one from which you pour into your mouth (if you are lucky or practiced) without touching it, the other a larger one for filling and as an air hole. Conversation during this meal is sketchy, but enthusiastic and at the end the mother offered to cook some eggs for us on the following evening, an offer we accepted on condition that we be allowed to pay her. Then farewell, with many saluds.

There are other things about the people which once struck me as curious and interesting. The fact, for instance, that, contrary to my expectation, the Spanish people are not tall and slender but in the main short and small. To the despair of the Quartermasters of the International Brigades, for nothing supplied to the regular army is of any use for these tall husky Americans and some other nationalities have difficulties, too. Shirts rip, trousers split at the seams at the first hint of activity, and shoes often have to be made to order. Another thing is the rather depressing but I suppose eminently practical custom the women have of almost always wearing only black clothes. One doesn't expect much smartness in poor peasants—and are they poor!—but after one's lifelong picture of "colorful" Spain. . . .

And the country itself does not encourage such an adjective, so far as I could tell from the parts I have seen. I had no idea Spain was so mountainous nor so bleak. I have not, of course, seen the more beautiful (in the conventional sense) and fertile parts. Our action at the front, for instance, took place on a plateau of some 3,000 feet and in a countryside so bleak and bare that, in moments of discouragement and fatigue I have half-wondered why it wouldn't be more sensible to let the fascists have the place and see what *they* could do with it.

Yet Spain has a grandeur of scenery all its own, somewhat stark and bold, sharply outlined in the crystal air and with wide and noble mountain distances. In this setting the occasional color is emphasized and a field thick and bright with poppies takes your breath away. Earlier in the summer at one of our training places we were, as a matter of fact, engulfed in field flowers. On maneuvers or wandering during free time in the fields it was very easy to pick up the national colors—poppies, a thistle-like weed (or maybe they are thistles), and some sort of flower resembling a largish buttercup. . . .

This letter turned out very differently from what I intended or expected. But it's too late to do anything about it now. I hope it doesn't bore you. Thanks for the dictionary, which arrived at last.

Salud!

David

Albacete, August 13, 1937

Looking at a Map of Spain on the Devon Coast

JACK LINDSAY

The waves that break and rumble on the sands
gleaming outside my window, break on Spain.
Southward I look and only the quick waves stretch
between my eyes and ravaged Santander moaning
with many winds of death, great blackening blasts
of devastation and little alley-whispers
where forgotten children lie.

        The map of Spain
bleeds under my fingers, cracked with rivers
of unceasing tears, and scraped with desolation,
and valleyed with these moaning winds of death.
Aragon I touch, Castilla, and Asturias.
The printed words black on the small white page
waver like mountains on the expanse of day.
They ring me round, sierras of history
granite above time's stream with human meanings
that make the stars a tinsel and the thundering
waves on the rattled beach a trivial echo
of their tremendous wars.
I lean towards Spain over the sundering waters.

The brittle mask has broken, the money-mask
that hid the jackal-jaws, the mask of fear
that twisted the tender face of love; and eyes
now look on naked eyes. The map of Spain
seethes with the truth of things, no longer closed

in greed's geography, an abstract space
of imports, exports, capitalist statistics,
the jargon record of a tyrannous bargain.
The scroll of injustice, the sheet of paper is torn,
and behind the demolished surface of the lie
the Spanish people are seen with resolute faces.
They break the dark grilles
on custom's stuccoed wall
and come into the open.

In the city-square the rags of bodies lie
like refuse after death's careless fiesta.
Sandbags are piled across
the tramlines of routine.
A bullet has gone through the town hall clock,
the hands of official time are stopped.
New clocks for the Spanish people:
New springs and cogwheels for the Time of Freedom.
The garrotting machines are snatched
out of the chests of old darkness
and strung between lamp-post and balcony
in the streets of sunlight in Barcelona.
My friend is holding the cartridge-belt, the gun
is trained on the corner, the turn in the dark street,
round which the Fascists will come.
The noticeboard of the People's University
is nailed above the church's door of stone
over the face of the Virgin in the shrine.
New clocks for the Spanish people:
New springs and cogwheels for the Time of Freedom.

These images slip through the mesh. They flush
the superficial map with hints
of what the tumult means.
You girl in overalls with young breasts of pride
bearing the great banner down the street,

your pulse accords with the day's terrific cymbals.
You militiaman leaning
beside the soup-cauldrons on the ridge of stones
and bushes flickering with heat, your hands
speak of the sickle and hammer, and the rifle
you hold in such a way
breaks to a cornsheaf in your dreaming hour
deep-rooted in Spanish earth, because you love
that girl with flower-eyes and breasts of milk
lifted with promise on the day of work
like olive-trees tousled silver under the wind.
The old man choking among the thistles
by the peaked windmill with the lattice-wings
has spoken a curse. The child blindly crying
down lanes of terror in the endless night
of bursting faces, and the mother riddled
with rape on the dungheap, and the friend
who smiled at you yesterday
now crucified on the garden-wall,
litter these names. Oh, watch the map of Spain
and you can see the sodden earth of pain,
the least blood-trickle on the broken face,
and hear the clutter of the trucks that bring
the Moorish firing-squad along the village street,
and through the frantic storm of shattering guns
the child's small wail. You hear it in your heart,
louder than all the roaring. An accusation
that shall be answered.

And louder too than all the hell of war
clanging over the tiles or the hilltops hoarse
with raiding planes, there sounds the pulse of work,
the hum of factories in communal day.
The girl with the cap of liberty at the loom
weaves the fate of Spain,
the web of brotherhood on the warp of courage.

The factory-windows crimson with the sunset
flash signals to the fields of toil;
the slow echelon of sickles
advance upon the wheat. Now in the battle
the Spanish workers ride
the horses of the year, wild mountain-horses,
tamed to draw the plough of man.
Hear the confederate engines throb
the belts whirr and the hammers of power leap thudding,
to bring about at last the generous hour
when man and nature mate in plenty's bed.

Oh, Map of Spain creviced with countless graves,
even now, even now, the storm of murder comes.
The burning face of day is blind with tears.
I stand at the Atlantic edge and look
southwards and raise my hand to Spain. Salute.

From POEMS FOR SPAIN

Doran At Belchite

T HE SITUATION WAS tense. The crisis was rapidly approaching. Days of bitter street-fighting, unceasing attacks against positions heavily fortified by machine-guns and snipers' nests were exhausting the Brigade. The Fascists in Belchite put up a desperate resistance. The Brigade had to fight its way into the town, house by house, taking every inch of ground by assault.

The main Fascist forces, superior in number, were still behind a barricaded area. The well-planned military campaign had brought the Brigade within sight of victory. But the casualties were mounting and, worse still, the men were dropping right and left completely spent, unable to keep their eyes open any longer. The clinching of the victory required another assault.

But time was pressing. Every additional day of siege wearied the attacking troops and gave the enemy time to organize relieving columns. Already there were heavy counter-attacks at Mediana. Radio messages were broadcast to the besieged Fascists from Saragossa stating that reinforcements were on the way. Fascist airplanes dropped food and the radio was trying to bolster up the morale of the Belchite garrison by boasting that they had recaptured Quinto and were now approaching with a strong force from the rear, while a strong army from Saragossa was about to launch an attack from the North.

It was precisely at this stage that the political leadership swung into action. Dave Doran, youthful Brigade Commissar, who had been urgently petitioning the Division for a propaganda truck, suddenly spied one belonging to the Army Corps passing by the road. He commandeered the truck, got hold of a Spanish interpreter, wrote out a short speech, brought the truck up to the Church and with the Fascists only a half block away he launched his political attack.

Doran's speech was brief but terrifying in its directness. It stripped the political issues involved to their barest elements until every word became a sledgehammer smashing through sandbags, barbed wire fortifications, battering away on the barricades. It was the heavy artillery of the science of politics, employed to its fullest in a war fundamentally political, and it laid down a psychological barrage on the most vital centers of resistance.

The guns of Fascist propaganda were silenced by his opening sentence. He told the Fascists that their radio was lying. Quinto was safely in Republican hands. Instead of Fascist reinforcements it was the Republican Army that was steadily pressing on to victory. Next, he contrasted the status of the enemy rank and file with that of the men in the Republican Army:

"The Fascists have taken your land. They have oppressed and exploited you and kept you in poverty. The Republic is distributing land. It has brought freedom and democracy.

"The Fascists are the enemy of the people. When you are on their side you are fighting against your own brothers, against the people of Spain.

"If you remain on the Fascist side you are condemned to death. If you keep fighting for them you will be killed, every single one of you.

"But we don't want you to die. You are our brothers and we want you to live. Come over to the people's side where you will have freedom and democracy, where a new life is awaiting you.

"Take your choice!

"Further resistance means death. Death for each and every one of you.

"Come over to us and live. If you don't you will all be killed in our first assault at dawn. We have you surrounded on all sides so none of you can escape. Our guns are trained on you this minute, to blow you to a million pieces at the first streak of the dawn.

"Drop your arms and come over the barricades one by one.

"All who come over to us will live.

224

"Come over the barricades one by one. If you don't come over you will all be killed in the morning."

The speech ended right there. Deathly silence followed from behind the Fascist lines. Their machine-guns had ceased firing; the voice had silenced them all. There was an unearthly hush. The word "Death" seemed to have taken on a shape, a living form, stark and grim, ghastly and enormous, pressing down with ever-increasing, monster weight on the Fascist lines. Hours seemed to have passed in ever mounting tension. Then the break came.

A Fascist soldier, a former student, wounded in the shoulder, who spoke a little English, came over the barricades asking for medical aid. They were about to take him to the First Aid Post. Doran grasped the situation and pounced on it in a flash. He instructed the prisoner to go back to his comrades and persuade them to surrender, promising him that none of them would be harmed.

The prisoner was reluctant, but Doran gave him no alternative. He made his way back over the barricades and remained there. There was another half-hour of mounting suspense, then suddenly—

The street behind the Fascist barricades began swarming with men, Fascist soldiers shouting *"Viva la República"* and *"Viva el Frente Popular,"* came over the barricades, without arms—one by one.

The surrender of the rank and file of the Fascists was complete. They gave themselves up to a force inferior in numbers. Force of arms had been supplemented with politics, and the costly attack planned for the morrow was not needed any more. The officers, seeing that the men were deserting them, made a desperate sortie under cover of women and children, trying to get away under a shower of hand-grenades but were subdued in a fierce hand-to-hand combat. Next day was spent in cleaning-up the rest of the houses. Belchite was again in Republican hands.

From THE BOOK OF THE XVTH BRIGADE, *Madrid, 1937*

Benicasim

SYLVIA TOWNSEND WARNER

Here for a little we pause.
The air is heavy with sun and salt and color.
On palm and lemon-tree, on cactus and oleander
A dust of dust and salt and pollen lies.
And the bright villas
Sit in a row like perched macaws,
And rigid and immediate yonder
The mountains rise.

And it seems to me we have come
Into a bright-painted landscape of Acheron.
For along the strand
In bleached cotton pyjamas, on rope-soled tread,
Wander the risen-from-the-dead,
The wounded, the maimed, the halt:
Or they lay bare their hazarded flesh to the salt
Air, the recaptured sun,
Or bathe in the tideless sea, or sit fingering the sand.

But narrow is this place, narrow is this space
Of garlanded sun and leisure and color, of return
To life and release from living. Turn
(Turn not!) sight inland:
There, rigid as death and unforgiving, stand
The mountains—and close at hand.

From POEMS FOR SPAIN

"The Little War"

LILLIAN HELLMAN

A T TWELVE O'CLOCK on an October day in Valencia it is usually
warm and sunny. I stopped at the flower market and bought
a bunch of flowers and some green leaves I had never seen before.
I went around the corner and down the street and felt good walking in the hot sunshine. Ahead of me was a cat and I don't
think I paid any attention to what had happened until I saw
the cat suddenly sit down in the middle of the street. While I
stood there looking at him, I began to hear the sirens. A woman
with a pushcart suddenly picked up a little girl, threw the child
on the cart, and wheeled it swiftly away. I think a few people
began to run, but most people stopped, suddenly, and then
moved on again more swiftly. I knew afterwards, by the way
my jaw felt, that I had been pressing my teeth together too hard.
I turned, too, and began to walk, and told myself over and over
again that as long as the sirens sounded the planes had not yet
arrived. I didn't really believe that, but people were standing
quietly in the open square, looking up. I went through the square
quickly and towards my hotel and when I first heard the noise
of the motors I didn't want to turn to see where they were. I
thought: in that hotel room is a toothbrush, a clean nightgown,
a cake of soap, an old coat and a box of lousy candy. Yet I am
hurrying to it, it is where I am trying to go, it is the place where
I have what belongs to me. And I knew, suddenly, why even
the poorest women in Madrid wanted to stay with what was
theirs.

But when I got to the corner of the hotel, the noise of the
planes was close. I stopped at the corner and leaned against
the wall. The planes were high in the east and flying fast. Next
to me were two soldiers. One of them had a bunch of grapes in

his hand. In a minute he said something to his friend and pointed in another direction. From the south four planes were flying towards us. They came up, swung around. Suddenly the soldier touched my arm and shouted, "They are ours." "There go ours." Then he pulled off some grapes, wiped them clean on his coat, and handed them to me. He said, "Our planes are up. It's all right, now." It wasn't all right. In the section around the port, three minutes later, the Italian bombers killed sixty-three people. But as we ate the grapes and smiled at each other, we didn't know that.

I drove up to the base hospital at Benicasim with Gustav Regler. Regler, who is a Jesuit-trained Catholic, was a fairly well-known novelist until Hitler came in. He was a captain in the World War and had been badly injured in this, the "little war," when his car was bombed to pieces going up to the front lines. Driving fast towards Benicasim, we talked about writers and writing and got excited and argued and had fun. We got to Benicasim at dinner time, and the Germans and the Americans were eating at one large table. Some of their wives were there with them and I thought what good-looking people they all were and how generous they were with their food and cigarettes. (There wasn't much food and it was very bad.)

The next morning the American, Dr. Busch, Regler, the political commissar and I went on a round of visits. In the third room we visited, there were two men. One was a Canadian. One was a New York boy with that small, pinched, pale face that is so common among poor people in New York. The Canadian had lost his foot and didn't know it yet. The American boy was lying on his left side, his face twitching with pain. He was so bad that I couldn't look at him and, as Busch went over to the bed to examine him, I moved away. The political commissar was a fat little man who had just recovered from a bad spine wound. I heard the New York boy cry out in pain and I said to the political commissar, "What's the matter with him?" He said, "He was shot through the kidneys and through the thigh.

The thigh wound is open." I said, "Can't you give him dope? Listen to him scream." The commissar nodded, "Sure. Busch will give him something. But don't mind the boy too much: he's a bad hypochondriac."

In the courtyard of the press office in Madrid, somebody has put a great many big statues. Nobody is very clear about how they got there, or what they are, or why they are there, but everybody agrees they are very bad statues indeed. Wednesday night, at about seven o'clock, a newspaper man said to me, "They're pretty awful. If they've got to shell, why can't they ever hit these things?" We reached the door to the street. "Can you find your way in the dark?" and I laughed and said sure, I was old enough not to be afraid of the dark. But when I opened the door and came out on the sidewalk, I knew that it was a foolish thing to have said.

Without meaning to, I gasped. It is a terrible thing to see a city in complete darkness. A modern city is not meant to be without light at night: the buildings meet at the top in distorted triangles, and the sky seems too close to the earth. I went down the street, trying not to stumble, trying to find the curb of the sidewalks, trying not to step in holes. Twice I got lost, and once I turned my ankle and fell, and when I got up I was crying, and thought I was crying because my ankle hurt. But when I finally got to the hotel, I ran through it, feeling safe again. That was at seven o'clock. At eight-fifteen there was a sudden, whistling noise and then a far-off, muffled crash. A few minutes later, an English girl who worked in the Blood Transfusion Institute opened my door and came in to ask what I had done that day, did I like Madrid, did I want a drink, couldn't she—and stopped to listen and then to talk again quickly.

They were dropping forty shells a minute into Madrid and the whistling noise was growing very close. She turned to me, "Do you know what that is?" "Yes," I said, "shelling." "All right," she said. "I came up because I knew it was your first time. Come in the bathroom and you'll be able to tell how close it is." We

229

went into the bathroom and she sat on the tub and watched me. In a few minutes the whistling went straight by the corner window and the crash this time was heavy, not sharp, and very close. She got up. "I'll go see if I can do anything. Go down to the dining room. It's in the center of the building." I said, "What good does that do?" She laughed, "Not much," and went out. I stood there looking out into the darkness. There were no sounds but the whistling, the flight of the shell and then a sharp or a dull crash. Suddenly there was a long heavy sound in the darkness—I think it was from a man—and through it a second sound. When the sound from the man ceased, the second sound came clear: a child was screaming, shrilly. In the hour and a half that Madrid was shelled that night there were many other sounds. Some of those sounds have no name in English.

This was the damage done that night: eighty people had been killed, two hotels had been hit, one grocery store and some houses in the poorest section of the town were gone, the press office had three shells in it, and the gentleman who didn't like the statues had been there to see two of the statues get two shells. In a kitchen back of my hotel, a blind woman was holding the bowl of soup that she came to get each night. She was killed eating the bowl of soup. Afterwards an Englishman said to me, "Not much sense to this kind of killing. They don't even try for military objectives any more, or for men. When I was on the Franco side, a few months ago, I heard the German technicians call this 'the little war.' They're practising. They're testing, testing the guns. They're finding the accuracy of the guns, they're finding the range." Finding the range on a blind woman eating a bowl of soup is a fine job for a man.

From The New Republic, *April 13, 1938.*
Original title: A Day In Spain.

For Those With Investments in Spain: 1937

BRIAN HOWARD

I ask your patience, half of them cannot read,
Your forbearance if, for a while, they cannot pay,
Forgive them, it is disgusting to watch them bleed,
I beg you to excuse, they have no time to pray.
Here is a people, you know it as well as he does,
Franco, you can see it as plain as they do,
Who are forced to fight, for the simplest rights, foes
Richer, stupider, stronger than you, or I, or they, too.
So, while the German bombs burst in their wombs,
And poor Moors are loosed on the unhappy,
And Italian bayonets go through their towns like combs,
Spare a thought, a thought for all these Spanish tombs,
And for a people in danger, grieving in breaking rooms,
For a people in danger, shooting from falling homes.

From POEMS FOR SPAIN

The Road to Los Olmos

EDWARD K. BARSKY, M.D.

ONCE MORE OUR motorcade, a chain made up of most uneven links, took the road. It was colder, rougher and steeper than anyone had imagined. We were menaced by the speeding lorries rushing down the mountains to get fresh troops to take back to the front. Our radiators boiled and we had to keep melting snow to put into our radiators. Our cars and ambulances were of many makes, of many nationalities, and spare parts were almost unknown; spare tires more precious than gold. One of the travesties of our situation was that here as almost everywhere else during our service in Spain we had plenty of money. It can be very useless stuff.

We climbed but our speed was conditioned by the imperative necessity of keeping together; that meant that we were no faster than the slowest link in our motor chain. With everybody's brakes screaming and with a skid like the gnashing of teeth, my car just barely managed to avoid collision with a lorry, empty, tearing downhill full speed. I got out to do a little old-fashioned American bawling out but somehow my conversation with the driver got off to another tune.

"How are things further up?" I asked him.

"If you mean the road, you will never get up it; if you mean at the front, it is the most furious fighting of this war." As he climbed back to his seat I acknowledged his salute.

"*Salud,*" we said, both together.

The cold day began to fade and I wondered if any of us would know our destination, Los Olmos, when we had come upon it. I had been told it was a small place but I do not think my informant had ever seen the town himself. We were always finding ourselves in places in Spain where the inhabitants had never before seen a foreigner. The Spanish themselves do not travel into the more remote regions of their country—and why, I asked myself, would anyone on wheels want to attempt this road? At last we were told by an old peasant that Los Olmos was above us—"*arriba*"—how far he could not say for kilometres meant nothing to him. We must just ascend. This, in spite of boiling radiators and tires exploding on jagged stones, we managed to do.

Mountain mist covering our windshields like a sheet had now made it necessary for my chauffeur to proceed by reports which I made to him by looking sideways out of my window. In this way I saw that we had come to a place where the road forked. We got out and saw through the mist a little plaster house hunched under a craggy bluff. The snow piled on the potsherd roof and drifted against the plaster walls looked as if a mistake had been made on a cheap Christmas card. The little house which we saw under snow and mist ought to have been set amid palms against a bright blue lake, and the snow should have been that bright tinsel stuff they use on such things.

We knocked, loud and soldierly, and an old man opened the door as cautiously as he dared.

"Señor, por favor, a dónde está Los Olmos?"

"Los Olmos, mi Comandante, está aquí."

In other words, we had arrived.

Downstairs the little house contained just one room with its fireplace built under an arch, Spanish fashion. Around it hung polished long handled copper pans and dippers. The old woman was stirring a very few *garbanzos* over a stingy little fire. The whole thing looked like a group in a museum and only the little mess of chick-peas which the old woman never forgot to stir gave the scene a sad reality.

We crowded in and the old people had more company than they had ever seen before in their *casa* which, according to the Spanish form, they insisted belonged to us. We tried to tell them about the war, to make them understand that we were doing our best to help, and yet before we had left them we had burned up their entire supply of wood! We took turns at warming ourselves before the biggest fire that poor hearth had ever seen.

I thought of the quartering on the shield of Spain during the reign of Ferdinand and Isabella, the proud lilies which were the symbol of Ferdinand's Aragón. But were not these two, both broken and old, peasants of the lowliest degree, yet full of Spanish dignity and Spanish courtesy, were they not the real symbols of Aragón?

We took our turns getting warmed up by the fire; took turns getting in wood. Though none of us knew where they would get more wood, the old couple never suggested that we stint ourselves.

Only three days before the old ones had seen their first tank. Life which had up to this time been a bitter fight with unrelieved poverty was changing for them. We told them that the army of the Republic was defending their home, we told them that better things were ahead. God help us we believed what we said.

Suddenly breaking the frozen quiet outside the house there was the sound of heavy motors coming up the mountain. It was a detachment of the International Brigade. The commander himself leading it as it turned out; Bob Merriman came into the crowded room and looked around.

"What are you waiting for?" he asked.

"Orders," and I explained that at this point I was to meet Major Chrome who was in command of the Sanitary Service of the International Brigade, and concert plans with him. He was to bring my orders and his own to this point.

During the ten minutes or so Major Merriman had been with us, his troops, our own American boys, had been passing on the road outside, troops, lorries and tanks going up to the front. The sounds of their motor difficulties which we so well understood came in to us. But it was much worse when these sounds had died away.

"You will be needed!" Bob Merriman had said as he left us.

There was no conversation in the little *casa* now. We had, I think, only one unspoken thought. The troops were going into

234

severe action, Spaniards and Americans with them, men we knew and men we might never know, but they were going into action *without medical aid.* Each one of us knew, by remembering things we might wish to forget, exactly what that might mean.

An officer must obey orders always but an army doctor must be there when the wounded depend on him and his equipment for the relief of their agony. Calling Chrome choice names under my breath did not relieve me much. We had all seen the hazards of the road. At ten o'clock I found continued inaction impossible. I got into my car with my chauffeur and we headed up into the Sierras. Perhaps I might find out something, at least I would be able to examine the state of the road.

It was much worse than any we had yet been over, winding up at a grade which was possible to a burro but all but impossible to an automobile. It was cut into by jagged promontories and full of hair-pin turns, at each one of which we seemed to avoid the abyss beneath the precipice by good luck alone. My car had no chains, no windshield wiper. It was snowing and appeared to us to be getting much colder. My old radiator leak was especially troublesome as the radiator heated up under the strain. We tried various methods for melting snow as the water in our system of pitchers and containers became used up. At first we had been menaced by the lorries like those we had seen in the afternoon rolling down the mountain like marbles down a chute, engines shut off coasting to save fuel, but for a long time we had been alone on the road. Was it after all the right one, I kept wondering?

"Do you see what I see?" asked George.

"You mean that black thing ahead off the road? Looks like a stalled car."

The car was careened in a gully and it was being snowed under. I took my flash-light and saw a man fallen over the wheel.

"Is he dead, Doctor?" asked Jim.

My flash-light played on his face. He wasn't dead. The flash-light had revealed something else; the man at the wheel was Major Chrome!

We shook him awake for he was drowsy with cold. He had, he said, sent his chauffeur down the mountain on foot for help. He had my orders all right. They read, as we had known they would read, to proceed at once to the front and to choose a situation for a front-line hospital, "as near Teruel as Dr. Barsky may deem expedient."

There were some entrenching tools in our car and somehow the three of us got Chrome's car headed down hill. When that was done Chrome wasn't sleepy any more.

Now it was our turn to roll down mountains like marbles. Back at Los Olmos we stirred up the outfit. The wait had been better for the men than for the motors. One vehicle, a combination truck and ambulance, was frozen. We had to tow it with the good old douche-wagon. Many of the other cars were almost impossible to start but in the big sterilizer we boiled water to pour over frozen manifold pipes and before long we were on the road again with the douche-wagon bumping along with the big truck-ambulance lurching behind. Presently on a little downhill stretch when the big truck was dangerously close to the rear wheels of its foster-mother, there was the welcome sputtering sound as the truck came to life.

The road had been all but impassable for my car alone; now it was naturally very much harder for all of us. One stalled car halted us all. At such times even the nurses would get out and push. I could not help seeing that the snow was getting deeper and the going tougher all the time. Somehow, each intolerable halt called for a brand new type of creative mechanics to get us started again, somehow we went higher into the mountains during the black hours of darkness. Many times I had thought I saw dawn breaking and when at last we were moving in a kind of half light I maintained a kind of protective skepticism. But it was the dawn, no mistake about it.

We had been going, with the exception of the break at the little house, since this time yesterday. I could not believe that the inanimate members of our party would stand the strain much longer. Those thirty-two vehicles, many with a piece of smart mechanical thinking inside of them where there should have been a spare part, how long would they all last? One auto-chir bounced and rolled up the mountain with a certain elegant disregard of its expensive vital organs. In the dawn where the snow had blown off I could see the gleam of its chromium trim. She was like a fleshy duchess, sparkling with diamonds, dressed for a court function gone alpine climbing instead.

Leading in my car, every time I sent a man back to report I dreaded his return. I seemed to have seen the whole thing before when at a bend, a very sharp one, we saw a ten-ton Mack truck half on, half off a narrow bridge over a chasm, abandoned. It would be necessary to stop our rear immediately. Directly back of me was one of our most practical units, the small Ford ambulance which carried four stretchers. I instructed the driver to go down and give my orders to the rest to halt while we worked on the stranded truck. In the darkness we had gone through a small town. I tried to estimate how many kilometres back. I hoped that we could turn everything back to that spot so that there we might prevent men and motors from freezing.

We pushed the Mack on the bridge—the bridge was sagging under its weight—over just far enough so that my car could squeeze by. The snow which had been falling all night was swirling down faster and a cruel wind was cutting through our clothing, chilling us where we had wet our clothes with sweat getting that truck moved. I remembered that a friend of mine, who is an arctic explorer, had said, "There is one rule in the North: Don't sweat!"

We crossed the bridge without breaking through and slowly climbed another impossible half mile when we ran into a real obstacle. Another great truck had been in a head-on collision with something else—we couldn't tell what, for the other party was an indistinguishable mass of wreckage. It must have been a mighty smash-up. There was a pile of tangled steel twelve feet high right across our road. It would take many men hours to clean up this mess. It was now imperative that we get the whole outfit

back to that town. Even in Romeral I had amputated frozen feet.

We got out and did what had become a matter of course on this march; we got out and lifted the car around so that it faced down hill; turning had been impossible from the start. We went down as fast as we could past the truck on the bridge. There was a blot ahead. Nearer I saw that it was my mobile little Ford ambulance off the road hopelessly stuck. No message had gone to the rear.

I told the boys in the Ford to keep on working. In my car, besides the chauffeur, were only Chrome and myself. Our progress going down the mountains seemed now more difficult than coming up had been; no doubt it was. We kept skidding off the road. Finally, I decided no matter how good a driver my chauffeur was that I was a better one myself. I took the wheel. He walked ahead in the snow trying to show me the road. Just remember that we had no chains, no windshield wiper. For a while things seemed to go a little better. Then twice we skidded, once nearly to kingdom come. The third time we were careened at a dangerous angle. While we were working to right ourselves we were almost run down by a big thing which loomed suddenly out of the snow: the Harvard ambulance with some of our personnel. The heaviest of all the ambulances, loaded down with everybody's baggage but chauffeured by an expert who didn't know when he was beaten. We could not have seen a worse sight. This meant that the whole unit would be stuck in those mountains during this storm.

We lifted the heavy Harvard around. No one had any faith that it would be done but no one said so, and in the end somehow she was headed down hill.

I got into the ambulance with Chrome, my chauffeur following in my car. We looked back pretty soon and it was evident that it was not following any more. We walked back and found my car as we knew it would be, off the road, this for the last time. I left my chauffeur with it and Chrome and I got into the big ambulance . . . felt the skid as I had felt so many skids before, the engine raced and we were careened in a ditch almost covered with snow. Hopeless this time.

It was mid-afternoon. A night on those roads and no one would be left to tell the tale. Chrome and I would walk back to the town. I wondered how far it was and whether we would ever get there?

We had no boots, just shoes. We were not heavily dressed and our clothes were dirty and cold and sweaty. We had been fighting to get up those mountains now for over thirty hours.

At times as we walked we were not even sure we were on the right road. We stumbled without words, each trying by turns to walk in the other's footsteps. I tried not to notice how Chrome swayed as he walked. We both knew that if we once stopped we would never go on. I wondered who ought to shoot who. It would not be the thing to leave a buddy to freeze; those boys up the road had at least a bit of shelter in their wrecked cars. Ought I to talk over with Chrome this somewhat delicate matter? I did not want to be left to freeze so no doubt he did not want to any more than I did. I decided finally that I would let the matter settle itself. If I gave out or if he did, it would be time enough to make the decision. Our revolvers were still dry. I could not feel my feet, and the declining day had already made it definitely colder. Was I then to end it all in a way none could have imagined back in New York? Was I to freeze to death in Spain? Not even a soldier's death.

At that minute, about five-thirty, Chrome was walking in my footsteps. That was the way I liked it best because I could not see him stagger. I took a malicious pleasure in staggering myself. I knew that scared him as it did me. A swirl of snow was blown upward. One of us fell. The other kicked him to his feet.

"It can't be far, now," said one.

"The hell, you say!" said the other.

Was this perhaps the time to settle that recondite social point? Keep stumbling along and think it over thoroughly.

"Do you see something?"

"Yes, or I think I do."

"Well, come on, that much further anyway."

The thing we saw was a big snow drift, but out of this snow drift came smoke. You could have said we smiled frozen smiles. It was the auto-chir. We cleared a spot on the glass window and looked in. The nurses never got tired of talking about the anxiousness in our dirty bearded faces. We looked like the heads out of two El Greco crucifixions, they said. Well, why not? For inside the auto-chir those nurses were making tea!

The town which had been the star of our pilgrimage was Aleaga, that natural fortress. It is situated in the small level space enclosed by three great cliffs. Only a narrow road leads into the town between the steep unclimbable defiles. After that cup of tea I trudged over this narrow pass and routed out the Alcalde. He listened to my story: our whole outfit caught and frozen on the mountain, ours the only medical units being sent to the front. The mayor acted at once. Due to his initiative the mayors of all the surrounding towns turned out crews and snow plows and a large force worked all night on the roads. In the morning we were again going up, this time in winter sunlight.

We went ahead with all speed possible, tormented by the thought of what our delay might have meant at the front. That night we were all together and all safe at Mesquita, a town only a few kilometres from Teruel. We were having a meal but we did not finish it. Open trucks rolled into the town plaza—open trucks which had come forty kilometres over the sort of road we ourselves knew so well—open trucks in that weather, filled with wounded men.

We all went to work in an operating room which was hastily set up. I think that for us we established a record. We operated for fifty hours.

Two Poems

To Margot Heinemann:

Heart of the heartless world,
Dear heart, the thought of you
Is the pain at my side,
The shadow that chills my view.

The wind rises in the evening,
Reminds that autumn is near.
I am afraid to lose you,
I am afraid of my fear.

On the last mile to Huesca,
The last fence for our pride,
Think so kindly, dear, that I
Sense you at my side.

And if bad luck should lay my strength
Into the shallow grave,
Remember all the good you can;
Don't forget my love.

JOHN CORNFORD

Grieve in a New Way for New Losses:

And after the first sense "He will not come again"
Fearing still the images of corruption,
To think he lies out there, and changes
In the process of the earth from what I knew,
Decays and even there in the grave, shut close
In the dark, away from me, speechless and cold,
Is in no way left the same that I have known.

All this is not more than we can deal with.

The horror of the nightmare is that it evades
Your steady look, steals past the corner of the eye,
Lurks in the sides of pictures. Death
Is fearful for the fifth part of a second,
A fear that shakes the heart: and that fear lost
As soon, yet leaves a sickness and a chill,
Heavy hands and the weight of another day.

All this is not more than we can deal with.

If we have said we'd face the dungeon dark
And gallows grim, and have not meant to face
The thin time, meals alone, in every eye
The comfortless kindness of a stranger—then
We have expected a privileged treatment,
And were out of luck. Death has many ways
To get at us: in every loving heart
In which a comrade dies he strikes his dart.

All this is not more than we can deal with.

In our long nights the honest tormentor speaks
And in our casual conversations:
"He was so live and young—need he have died,
Who had the wisest head, who worked so hard,
Led by his own sheer strength: whom I so loved?"
Yes, you'd like an army all of Sidney Cartons,
The best world made conveniently by wasters, second rates,
Someone that we could spare,
And not the way it has to be made,
By the loss of our best and bravest everywhere.

All this is not more than we can deal with.

MARGOT HEINEMANN

From POEMS FOR SPAIN

dress rehearsal

(1938)

He says, "My reign is peace," so slays
    A thousand in the dead of night.
"Are you happy now?" he says,
    And those he leaves behind cry, "Quite."

He swears he will have no contention,
    And sets all nations by the ears;
He shouts aloud, "No intervention!"
    Invades, and drowns them all in tears.

WALTER SAVAGE LANDOR (1775-1864)

"*Christ said, 'Father, forgive them, for they know not what they do.' In this case they shall not be forgiven, for they know very well what they are doing.*"

LOUIS DELAPRE
Paris journalist, shot down flying over Madrid.

Instead of being sulkily ostracized she (Spain) should be welcomed as the nation which, first among the nations of the world, had the foresight to understand the Communist menace,

and the courage to conquer it. So, in spite of any criticism I have felt bound to make, I must end by joining with all lovers of Spain in the cry, "Arriba España"; and, as long as the Communist menace remains, even in the cry "Viva Franco!"

RT. REV. MONSIGNOR ARTHUR H. RYAN,
in a pamphlet published by The Paulist Press (N. Y.) under the imprimatur of Francis Cardinal Spellman, Archbishop of New York,, 1948.

"*We have more than two million persons, card-indexed with proofs of their crimes, names, and witnesses. Those who are granted an amnesty are demoralized . . . the epoch of the Liberal regime is over. The State must intervene directly in the national life.*"

FRANCISCO FRANCO,
in an interview granted the British United Press, July 11, 1938.

Journey Into Spain

ESLANDA GOODE ROBESON

Tuesday, January 25, 1938. Arrived at Benicasim about noon, a gorgeous sunny noon. The village is right on the sea front; a protected bit of coast and the calm lapping of the waves on the sand and the lovely vista of flat calm sea is very soothing and restful, and must be marvelous for the nerves of these war veterans.

The place used to be a summer resort for the rich Spaniards. There are lovely villas on the sea front, which are now used as hospitals. The place rather reminds me of Sochi. Palms, red earth, the stretch of sea and the white villas. The roads thronged with soldiers, wounded and convalescent. As our car came to a standstill I noticed a young Negro soldier. He saw Paul and stopped dead and stared. When we got out of the car, he gazed, astonished, and Paul went up and spoke to him. He said he recognized Paul at once but simply could not believe his eyes.

He is a Spanish Negro from Harlem and his name is Roderigo. He has been here eleven months, fighting, and was wounded at Teruel last week, but is much better now. He was delighted to talk about Harlem and Negroes. Is quite young, about twenty-two or twenty-three, I should guess. Speaks Spanish fluently.

Many English and American soldiers, white, immediately surrounded Paul and began talking all at once. They too were astonished, all had read about him, many had seen his films, one Canadian soldier from Toronto had heard him sing at Massey Hall, Toronto, several years before.

Then another Negro joined us. His name was Gibbs and he comes from Chicago. Also young, rather Indian cheek bones—quiet, serious—he too knew Paul and knew about him and was astonished to see him here. Still another young Negro, Clark

Bringle, of Bellaire, Ohio, joined us. He had been wounded at Teruel by a bullet from the tower of the Church. He was much better now and had only a gauze dressing on the wound just below his collarbone. He showed us the bullet which had been taken out of the wound—steel, bright, wicked-looking—about an inch and a half long.

A young English girl, daughter of a well known English woman, joined us and showed us around. The men call her "Angel." Paul sang at the big meeting place where the cultural program is carried out, and where many could congregate. He had to sing without accompaniment and the soldiers crowded round and were wildly enthusiastic and grateful. He sang in a hospital where many seriously wounded were lying, right in the central ward. Also in another hospital. So here in Benicasim he sang in three different places, all within an hour. The men were enormously grateful and appreciative and applauded wildly. All asked for "Old Man River." . . .

Everywhere soldiers recognized Paul and appeared astonished to see him—English, American, Canadian.

Benicasim used to be the convalescent place, but is now the base hospital, nearest the front line. . . .

At Benicasim the men told us that even there they had been bombed in an air raid. It seems the Fascists are especially interested in a railroad cut near the shore and had been bombing it for several days. It happened that a very lovely villa was near the cut, right on the sea, and was used for a hospital, but they had to evacuate it finally because of the bombing.

Wednesday, January 26. Back at Albacete . . . in our so-called Grand Hotel. Off to Tarazona, the training camp for the International Brigade. Arrived about twelve, had a good lunch with the men.

Saw lots of Negro comrades, Andrew Mitchell of Oklahoma, Oliver Ross of Baltimore, Frank Warfield of St. Louis. All were thrilled to see us and talked at length with Paul. All the white Americans, Canadians and English troops were also thrilled to see Paul.

A Major Johnson—a West Pointer—had charge of training.

The officers arranged a meeting in the church and all the Brigade gathered there at 2:30 sharp, simply packing the church. But before they filed in, they passed in review in the square for us, saluting us with *Salud!* as they passed.

Major Johnson told the men that they are to go up to the front line tomorrow. The men applauded uproariously at that news. . . .

Then Paul sang, the men shouting for the songs they wanted: "Water Boy" "Old Man River," "Lonesome Road," "Fatherland." They stomped and applauded each song and continued to shout requests. It was altogether a huge success. Paul loved doing it. Afterwards we had twenty minutes with the men and took messages for their families.

We visited the First Aid building which they are gradually converting into a hospital. Met a fine young American lad who has to do the diets, and promised him a good layman's book on dietetics.

Drove out to the edge of the town and looked down on it. Passed the stream where the women of the village were doing their washing along the banks. Up on the hill, could get a good view of the town with its characteristically dominating enormous church, so typical of every Spanish town and village.

Monday, January 31. Interviews and more interviews. The delegates for the Cortes are all arriving today and tomorrow. The opening of the Cortes, the Parliament, is tomorrow, February 1st. The coast is being heavily patrolled by planes for protection.

We had a good talk over lunch and afterwards over coffee in the lounge, and then we went off to the border. Fernando, in civilian dress, accompanied us, and Lt. K., armed in full uniform, was our official escort.

We found K. most interesting. Fernando had told us that the Spanish people loved him as a Spaniard, that he was sympathetic and worked untiringly for them. He had been working very hard the day before, helping in the rescue of the victims of the bombardment.

As we drove along, K. got talking and told us the story of Oliver Law. It seems he was a Negro—about 33—who was a former Army man from Chicago. He had risen to be a corporal in the U.S. Army. Quiet, dark brown, dignified, strongly built. All the men liked him. He began here as a corporal, soon rose to sergeant, lieutenant, captain and finally was commander of the Battalion—the Lincoln-Washington Battalion. K. said warmly that many officers and men here in Spain considered him the best battalion commander in Spain. The men all liked him, trusted him, respected him and served him with confidence and willingly.

K. tells of an incident when the battalion was visited by an old Colonel, Southern, of the U.S. Army. He said to Law—"Er, I see you are in a Captain's uniform?" Law replied with dignity, "Yes, I am, because I *am* a Captain. In America, in *your* army, I could only rise as high as corporal, but here people feel differently about race and I can rise according to my worth, not according to my color!" Whereupon the Colonel hemmed and hawed and finally came out with: "I'm sure your people must be proud of you, my boy." "Yes," said Law. "I'm sure they are!"

K. says that Law rose from rank to rank on sheer merit. He kept up the morale of his men. He always had a big smile when they won their objectives and an encouraging smile when they lost. He never said very much.

Law led his men in charge after charge at Brunete, and was finally wounded seriously by a sniper. K. brought him in from the field and loaded him onto a stretcher when he found how seriously wounded he was. K. and another soldier were carrying him up the hill to the first aid camp.

On the way up the hill another sniper shot Law, on the stretcher; the sniper's bullet landed in his groin and he began to lose blood rapidly. They did what they could to stop the blood, hurriedly putting down the stretcher. But in a few minutes the loss of blood was so great that Law died.

Captain Bernardi's Cannons

JAMES NORMAN

For fourteen months we've been firing these same cannons. We've fired an endless chain of sound and concussion.

I don't remember how many times. There is no counter telling how many shells slipped into the breeches. Or how many thousand projectiles rushed from their mouths into the sky, cutting hollow invisible sounds there. But it's a long time and eventually one begins to feel a part of the cannons.

No one thinks of these things when he's firing. I never had a chance to consider them until today when we had trouble with ammunition and Number 1 blew up.

Even then, it was only after Captain Bernardi fired the cannon no man dared shoot that I realized there was more to knowing cannons than merely being part of them like a fleshy piece of mechanism attached to a lanyard. Bernardi didn't explain it in so many words. In fact, he didn't use words at all. Everything that came together at one moment explained why Bernardi was the best anti-aircraft artillery man in the whole war.

All this morning we waited for new ammunition. While waiting we watched the sun rise from behind the last ridge of mountains and stab division camions that rumbled up the road toward the front loaded with men and supplies. Some of the soldiers in the trucks had bayonets and no guns while some had no ammunition. It's that kind of a war, where one never has two things together at one time.

"It's bad," said Albert, our battery commander, and he shook his sour, box-like face. "Bad, bad. They're late. The sun is up too high and the planes will catch them on the road."

He didn't have to tell us there was going to be another battle and the soldiers were late for it. No one had to tell us

249

the lines would break again. We always knew it—they've been breaking, re-forming and breaking two months now. Pretty soon we'll be back to the sea.

Jolting camions on the road raised a yellow tunnel of dust that stretched back for miles like a long bloated caterpillar. Some of the dust drifted up to our battery position where we waited.

Our cannons had been placed in a bunch of scorched scrub oak on a knoll above the road. Some of the trees were broken from yesterday's bombing, but none of the cannons had been touched. They were silent and camouflaged with branches. It doesn't mean much to put branches on a gun, but it's nice to imagine the birds don't know there are cannons under the branches they perch on.

"That's what camouflage is for," Bernardi used to tell me. "It doesn't make any difference to the planes. They always find you."

Bernardi could say things like that. He was strange and cool. He never seemed to need courage to face a war.

At nine o'clock the first of our two munition trucks, big six-wheel Whites, nosed out of the yellow dust caterpillar on the road, turned and backed toward us. The second truck followed a short distance behind. At the same moment a squadron of planes filled a corner of the sky. Enemy planes!

The drone of their motors, like angry swarms of bees, paralyzed everything on earth. On the road, camion after camion stopped as if someone had pulled a switch cutting off an entire conveyor belt. Then the soldiers poured from the trucks, running for cover among the bronze rocks on each side of the road.

A second flight of planes rode on the tails of the first. They brought bombs and laced them along the road.

I could hear the drop and the explosion of the bombs, they were so close. They make a continuous relentless sound like a big funnel of escaping air which abruptly expands within a hollow drum. SsswoosshHHHOOOOMB! Geysers of pepper dirt bloomed along the road and in the rust fields. The sunlight seemed to rock and reverberate with each blast as if daylight were made of bricks and windows.

A truck up the road flopped over on its back with the look of a dented turtle. Its wheels, visible through the dust, spun helplessly.

The men around me, the sixty gunners, waited in little groups at each cannon. Five of us crouched near Number 3, watching the explosions, when suddenly the planes swung our way. We began feeling weak and very brittle. We wanted to run, but we couldn't. A man can always run into bombs for there's no telling where the next one will land.

Had we been firing we wouldn't have felt like that. It's not good to be without ammunition; to stand by, seeing planes sail overhead, while your cannons gape silently at the sky. It's like getting clipped on the jaw—one, two, three times—while your hands are tied down so you can't hit back.

When hitting back, you never notice how much you might get hurt. And when you're firing it gets so that you set fuses, feed shells and jerk lanyards as if nothing else in the world matters. You fire twenty-eight a minute. How many minutes?

The planes fly over for hours. They tire you out like a cautious fighter. They curve over in bow-bends, sometimes high enough to look like silver minnows when the sun strikes. The archies puff about them in creamy cotton balls. Sometimes you see the bombs fall toward you. Mostly you don't. But you hear them, just before and after, if you're not hit.

Suddenly a bomb exploded near our munition trucks. I watched the driver of the first truck get out. He stood with a foot on the running board, indecisively—wondering whether he should run or duck beneath the truck. He crawled under.

"*Conyo!* Why not drive right up here?" I swore. "We gotta have ammo. We can't wait all day."

"We'll go get it," said Marcel.

"Wait!" Albert ordered.

Albert's face was tilted like a shoe box. His eyes were glued upon the planes. They were so close now the motors no longer sounded like motors and the black bands on the wing-tips stood out clearly, looking like the paint on women's fingernails.

"Two thousand meters up," Albert said. "They'll drop them

now! They've seen us."

"They're off course," Marcel cut in.

"They'll drop them now, I tell you," Albert repeated. "They'll be right on us—down!"

It didn't matter what was said or who was right. War is not politics. Either the bombs hit one or they don't. Knowing the height and course of the planes, one can tell exactly where they have to be to bomb one. If they aren't there, most men are still sure they're going to be hit. It makes for a better feeling when the smoke blows away and one is not bleeding.

"Down," Albert bellowed again.

I dropped on my face beside the other men. The roar of the planes swelled as the earth began rocking with explosions. I dug my nails into the ground, clutching and hoping that if one landed near, the concussion wouldn't bounce me so that the shrapnel from a second bomb would clip me in mid-air. I once saw a man die that way.

SsswoosshHHOMMB! SsswoosshHHOMMB! The ground quaked like jelly.

A bomb exploded with bursts of red flame just below me on the road. A direct hit! Our first munition truck leaped above the dust and gnarled smoke like some prehistoric monster. It turned over on its side. The chauffeur underneath became part of the thick dust that flowered above the twisted steel frame. They'd have a time re-assembling him on Judgment Day.

The fire licked through the smoke. The cases of shells flopped around the truck, cracking open, spilling shells, burning and exploding.

"In the trenches!" Albert shouted. He crawled around on his hands and knees shouting orders. "In the trenches. What's the matter with you men? You want to get killed?"

I skidded into the waist-high ditch we had dug around the base of our cannon. Albert followed and held a spade over his head in place of a tin hat.

Shrapnel from the burning munition truck began whistling and swooshing overhead, shredding the leaves on the trees and ricocheting off the cannon barrels. Flame colored dust spurted all over the area between the guns while shells, our precious anti-aircraft shells, shrieked off every which way, paying no heed to the airplanes that skated across the sky until they were distant droning dots.

Behind me, Frico began crying. It seemed pretty useless to cry in the face of so much noise, but it was understandable. Frico was an artificer, which means wiping grease off 76.2 shells. Normally this would keep a man who is as thin and excitable as Frico occupied. But this morning we couldn't fire. It was like getting clipped on the jaw, hard. One could see it by the look in Frico's soft eyes.

I kept my head down and began wondering when Bernardi would show up. He always walked in, just when a battery was under fire. He walked through shrapnel as if it couldn't hurt him.

But he didn't always come. There were two other batteries along with ours which he belonged to. That was a big job, taking over the command of three battery and staff headquarters when the staff was too poor to afford a car. He usually rode from one battery to the other, spinning down the dry roads on the rear of a motorcycle, holding his hat on with one hand and gripping a briefcase full of topographical maps with the other.

Then I forgot Bernardi and found myself listening to the explosions from the munition truck. The noise was tremendous, not like ordinary explosions.

"*Rompedores*," I told Albert. "My God, listen to them!"

Albert nodded. "Sure. Now we get good ammunition and we can't use it."

We hadn't used *rompedores* in the cannons yet. The enemy was using it, but we could never lay our hands on any. They were high explosives and could rock a plane like a leaf at a hundred meters with concussion alone. They threw solid chunks of shell-covering instead of the triple-edged, ladyfinger strips of shrapnel packed in the regular shells.

"Can you see the other truck?" Albert asked.

"Yeah," I said. The second truck hadn't been touched off. "When's this gonna stop?"

The sun grew hotter as it climbed toward the western part

of the sky and we waited for the fire and explosions on the road to burn out. Every so often a blast shook the ground. It shook the heat and was followed by silence. Then the silence would be punctured by the distant chatter of machine-guns and less distant booming of artillery. The fighting was moving our way.

Gradually the men began leaving the trenches around the guns in two's and three's, always keeping well below the rim of the knoll. We began watching for signs of retreat.

"All right! Hurry!" Albert was bawling. "Unload that second White. *Artificiers! Marche vite!*"

Men went down to the road's edge, cautiously. They returned, bending under creosoted wooden cases of shells. We unlatched the boxes and stared at the shells packed neatly in slots, four to a slot like eggs. They were the same as the old ones—trim, but without the lethal look of five-inch shells.

For a while there was nothing to do but watch the *artificiers* wipe grease and screw on the shiny alloy time-caps. Then we cleared the camouflage from the guns and waited. No planes came over. They were up ahead, strafing the lines beyond San Mateo and the river.

It wasn't until late afternoon that we fired a shell. And that was because the lines broke again.

Camions on the road no longer went forward. They began coming back, driving over the dust covered road as if they were afraid of something behind them. After a little while there were no more camions, only armored cars. Soon men began straggling over the hills.

Their faces were haggard and sweaty, burnt to a kind of copper crisp in the light of the ruddy sun melting in the sky west of San Mateo. Some stopped by the battery to ask us for water. Then they went on again while the hunted look in their eyes told of the desire to rest—a desire defeated by fear.

A half hour later the road behind us was being shelled by enemy artillery. It meant our flank had been broken also. It meant that we might be surrounded.

The battery telephonist was ringing our observers and staff headquarters every five minutes on his little box. *Allo? Allo Bat-*

terie Française? Allo! Estado Mayor! Allo?

Albert and the men waited around the telephone. It was as if the telephone plugged in on a direct line with God. That was how much we depended on Bernardi. Finally the telephonist stopped the incessant *Allo's* and listened.

"We withdraw?" Albert questioned.

The telephonist's chin sagged. "*Tout à fait.*" He turned to Albert. "The enemy has broken through on the left. The Fourteenth Brigade is withdrawing to the river. They'll attempt to hold the enemy there. Bernardi says we must destroy the bridge by San Mateo. Then withdraw to kilometer nineteen. The bridge isn't mined."

"Is Bernardi coming?" I interrupted. He didn't say.

"Contact the observers," snapped Albert. He turned to the cannon crew of Number 1: "Prepare to fire."

Men scattered to their guns and became parts of them again; waiting there as the breech waits to receive a shell or the lanyard waits for the sudden jerk. Number 1 prepared to fire a test shell for range. It was like a new game. Only once before, at Mora, had we used the anti-aircraft guns as field artillery.

Albert figured out the trajectory of fire and gave the figures to the gunners. Then he sat himself on a stack of munition boxes behind the gun. The crew loaded: Bizotte set the time-fuse; Marcel coordinated the cannon, watching the dial on the left side while the rifled barrel leveled its mouth with the land. Gerome waited to pull the lanyard.

"*Coördonnée,*" Marcel announced.

"Ready," Gerome repeated, satisfied. He looked toward Albert.

We watched Albert's field glasses sweep the rust and green swells that filled the seven kilometer gap between ourselves and the iron bridge by San Mateo. Without glasses we couldn't see the bridge clearly, but we'd see the explosion. We'd know if it fell true or wide.

"Fire!" Albert called. Gerome jerked the lanyard pole.

The cannon trembled, tearing at its ground moorings. Suddenly brilliant flame arched from the breech and a dozen arms of blue light lashed out. The barrel sleeve backfired, plowed out the blown breech and shot past Albert's startled face.

Three men on the cannon platform blew into the air, thrown twenty feet like limp rags. Chunks of cannon metal shrieked overhead and the air echoed the concussion of the explosion. Trees snapped and the grass bent over the sweep of wind.

Confusion spread through the battery. It was a private view of hell for a moment with men blasted down by concussion, others running about wide-eyed, some screaming.

"I'm dead!" someone yelled.

"Put the fire out," I shouted. "Put it out, there's munitions!"

A gunner raised himself from the ground, glared at his torn shoulder and began searching for his arm. It was a dozen feet behind him, lying crooked and crimson, resembling a length of sausage. He shook his other fist angrily at the stump of the shattered cannon, took a step toward it and collapsed.

Before the smoke had cleared we began taking inventory: four men hurt badly, three dead. *Medico* took care of the wounded. The rest of us gathered the parts of the dead that we could find and put them in an orderly pile, covering it with canvas.

It wasn't pretty. Explosions are never pretty, nor are they horrible after you get used to them. Gerome's head had been sliced away and had rolled into the trench beside the gun. We couldn't find his body, but the head looked like his. There was also a part of a torso: some shreds of legs, bones and boots slammed against Number 2 cannon. They had belonged to Marcel.

Bizotte was less hurt, but he was dead. It was just as good that he was dead. The blast had taken something which would have left him less a man had he lived.

The telephonist's voice rang across the battery. "Albert! Estado Mayor calling to say we should not fire the new *rompedores*. A cannon exploded at the Czech battery. Nobody touched but the cannon bellied."

Albert's face turned the color of drab enamel. His solid, box-like head seemed to puff slightly. Suddenly he dashed toward the wrecked cannon, howling madly and pounding his fists upon the jagged metal. "It can't do that! It can't!" he cried.

"Cut it, Albert," I snapped.

It took four men to drag him back and hold him. He continued ranting and cursing until his voice finally wore down. Then he began chuckling foolishly.

Right then and there Albert was through as an artillery man. He'd never be able to look a gun in the face, peace or war. No one had to tell me that. It happens when cannons you've been working with and you think you're part of suddenly go off on their own like a live thing, and do things you don't expect them to do.

Either a man comes out of it knowing cannons and having something that's more than courage, like Bernardi, or he's through, like Albert. It doesn't happen often.

Once, when our battery was first formed and Albert and I hadn't joined yet, the cannons went berserk the same as today. At that time the cannons came in boxes with instructions, so they had an interpreter—a woman—to help put them together piece by piece. In this kind of a war men couldn't be spared for that kind of a job. When the guns were together the men trained under Bernardi for a week; observing, ballistics, the planchette, telemeters and firing.

Then every man thought he knew his cannon until the planes came over and the cannons took things in their own hands.

One gun aimed sixty degrees away from the planes. The other pointed in the opposite direction. Number 3 cannon leveled its dark mouth directly at the first, ready to blast the entire crew and cannon to kingdom come.

The order to fire barked out. The cannons roared in the wildest salvo ever aimed at nothing. But Number 3 never fired. There were still five live men at the first gun and a woman interpreter without a left hand. She had blocked the breech with her hand.

After she had been taken away, Bernardi had the cannon cleaned and made the men fire it so they wouldn't lose their nerve.

Of course, the war was young in those days. It was a little

more heroic and a little less grim than now. Lines weren't folding up as easily; men weren't dying as hard. Perhaps that might explain Albert's collapse.

When Albert didn't stop chuckling we knew we were without a commander. Someone had to make decisions. Behind us the road was still under shell fire and ahead of us there was a bridge to be blown. A lot depended on that bridge.

"We'll never get out," I told Frico. "We'll never save the guns unless that bridge is blown. We can't move fast enough."

"You'll take Albert's place, won't you?" said Frico. "What are you going to do?"

"I don't know," I grinned.

"Let's plug the cannons and go over the hills. The lines won't hold even if we blow the bridge. We're going to lose the war. Why should we die for something we're going to lose?"

"Why don't you bury Bizotte and Marcel?" I said.

"Why don't you?" Frico answered.

It was clear that the men wouldn't touch the dead any more than they'd touch the cannons now. It would be that way for a little while at least. They waited around the telephonist who tried to contact staff headquarters.

I sat with Albert on a munition box, but pretty soon I couldn't stand hearing him chuckle. It wasn't only Albert, however.

The color of the declining sun, the eerie whistle of shells falling on the deserted road behind us, the flash and sudden boom and the bloom of copper dust lent an unreal air to the rocky landscape. It was as if we were fighting a war in another world.

Suddenly an ambulance appeared at the far rim of the road. A shell exploded fifty meters ahead of it. The ambulance swerved, keeled along the shoulder of the road, and raced there with its tires grabbing the dirt as if to keep it from toppling over.

They were mad in that ambulance. There's always a madman driving an ambulance.

The wheels regained the road and at the same instant shells exploded to the left and right. Earth spurted up in fountains, arching over the ambulance like two great trees.

The sun glare caught on the windshield like the flash of an explosion. Then the machine vanished. It plunged into view again, rocking crazily from side to side, growing larger.

I held my breath for the men in that ambulance, wondering if they'd hold the road or shoot off among the rocks. Boom! Boom! Two, three more shells flared in the dust—one on the side, a second a bit behind and the third in front. The machine rocked wildly. It must have been going eighty kilometers an hour.

The battery gunners crowded on the knoll and fastened their eyes upon the ambulance, almost as if they themselves were pulling it through by sheer Will or Wanting.

Then they began cheering when the ambulance hurtled beyond shell range and rushed by us, stopping a short way up the road. They were cheering, not only for an ambulance which had plunged through a curtain of flying steel, but because they themselves felt rescued. Captain Bernardi climbed from the ambulance cab.

It is always that way. Bernardi always coming when men think they need him most. There is something in the manner in which he *does not* look like an officer that inspires confidence. One forgets the twinkle in his blue eyes and the boyishness of his face.

"Ça va?" he smiled.

He handed me his map-case and signalled Lieutenant Murrat to follow to the battery position. Then he ignored Murrat because the man was a fashion-plate officer, afraid of the war and afraid of fighting.

We looked at the wounded men and Bernardi had them carried down to the ambulance. "I'll take them back," he said. Then we went over to the smashed cannon. Finally we walked past the canvas under which Gerome, Marcel and Bizotte waited patiently and went to cannon Number 3.

"The grooving in the sleeves is worn," I said. "Perhaps the shells are a fraction of an inch too big."

Bernardi nodded and turned to Albert who had tagged along behind us like a puppy waiting to be scratched behind the ears. "Albert," said Bernardi, "the bridge?"

Albert glanced up anxiously and began chuckling again. Bernardi seemed to understand. Without saying a word he made it very clear that the bridge by San Mateo had to be destroyed. The men understood at the same time; a few hesitated, then took their places at the gun.

"Get back over the hill," Bernardi ordered them. "You don't want to have it happen twice."

The men hesitated again but finally followed the others beyond the rim of the hill, leaving the battery area almost deserted. I didn't want to stand near gun Number 3 either. No one wants to stand near a cannon that's going to explode. Still, there are some things a man will do in Bernardi's company that he won't do alone.

"Should I?" I asked.

"You get in the trench," Bernardi smiled. "I'll tell you when."

He sat himself on the gun platform and held a *rompedore* between his knees. He hummed some little French song about sunshine in the windows and a sparrow on the sill in a musette voice while tampering with the time-cap.

Murrat watched, and the longer it took, the more his knees quaked. He turned white when Bernardi asked me for the range figures and finally jammed the shell into the cannon breech. He glanced hesitantly at the canvas covering the dead men and started to move.

"I think I will go now," he gasped. "*Je m'en vais.*"

"Wait a minute," Bernardi interrupted. He unclipped the brown Red Cross pack from his belt and tossed it to Murrat. "Take it. You'll need it soon."

Murrat squeezed the sack until the bandages almost bulged out of the ends.

"Take it," Bernardi repeated softly. "You'll need it if you run—I'm going to shoot you. The men don't like to see their officers run."

Lieutenant Murrat shrugged. "On the other hand, I think I'll stay," he said.

"That's right," Bernardi grinned. "If you have to die, do it like a hero. You're an officer now, though God only knows why."

The lieutenant's legs swayed like those of a marionette and sagged beneath his weight. His face grew mottled green when Bernardi's hand dropped upon the lanyard.

"*Bien!* Look out!" Bernardi warned.

I dropped into the trench behind the gun and waited for the explosion.

Somewhere beyond the rim of the knoll sixty pairs of eyes held cannon Number 3 within their frames. Sixty men felt their hearts stop. Everything stood still. The shelling on the road paused. The air and fading sun became pensile. Perhaps even the war waited to see what would happen to Bernardi and the lieutenant.

A minute passed. Then seconds. Abruptly—a flash of angry light, the explosion a split second behind it, then gusts of wind sweeping dust over the ground. Finally there was a metallic click, the shell released from the breech. That's how it always is when a cannon shoots as it should shoot.

"Stay back," Bernardi ordered. "Missed the bridge. We'll shoot another."

"It's insane," Murrat cried, wanting to get away.

"Sit still. We fire another," repeated Bernardi.

I scrambled out of my trench. "I'll give you a hand," I said.

"Get back," Bernardi warned me.

The third shell, which finally found the range and blew the bridge by San Mateo so that it buckled and caved into the river, took as long to fire as the first and second. However, only Murrat worried about it. Then, when the firing was over and the men returned to the battery he strutted about like a peacock.

The men ignored him and crowded around cannon Number 3.

"Don't fire the shells," Bernardi told us quietly. "They'll still blow up—perhaps the next one, perhaps not for five or ten more. But they'll blow up. They don't fit."

"You fired them," I said.

"That was a chance," Bernardi shrugged. Then he smiled and straightened his pancake hat and went off.

From THE CLIPPER, *Los Angeles California, March 1941*

How Do You Sleep, Franco?

HEYWOOD BROUN

Francisco Franco, Generalissimo, how do you sleep of nights? Possibly you are not sensitive to sounds. But a scream can be distracting. Even a moan may murder sleep. To some there is a nightmare quality in the curious rhythm made by the feet of hundreds running for their lives. And the cry of a child in anguish seems poignant to many people.

And so, Francisco Franco, your lot is not a happy one. You must live on until the day of your death with this savage symphony ringing in your ears. Even a Generalissimo may discover that it is impossible to stay the thing he has begun. Bombs loosed in the night may set up a succession of waves as pebbles tossed into a pond. Franco, you cannot evermore issue an effective order for firing to cease. You are doomed to carry to the grave the din of bombardment and those noises which men and women and children make when they die.

Our own Mr. Ellery Sedgwick, an ornament to that New England culture which gave us Lowell and Thayer and Grant, has bestowed a blessing upon you. He has written that after you have prevailed by "peremptory methods" you will "work out Spanish salvation in a thoroughly Spanish way." I assume that Editor Sedgwick in his impulsive Puritan way, intends to compliment you. Poking about among the ruins, he seems to say, "neat work, old fellow."

But, Francisco Franco, you will err if you take the Brahmin blessing too closely to your heart. I trust I labor under no misapprehension. Before salvation can be attained there must be absolution. Ellery Sedgwick is a thoroughly respectable member of a highly respectable community, and I do not mean to belittle him when I say that the *Atlantic Monthly* is neither broad nor deep enough to wash all your sins away.

Indeed, it seems to me that there is no one this side of the Judgment Seat who could possibly say, "Francisco Franco, Generalissimo, you may walk forth into God's sunlight a man pure of heart and stainless."

It has been said of those who injure children that it were better to have a millstone hung about your neck. Have you noticed, Franco, that you can no longer hold up your head? And so it is and will be.

Some have bestowed the title, "Defender of the Faith." What faith can that possibly be? Surely there is no coherent connection between the raids on Barcelona and the Church of Christ. The song of the herald angels cannot be scored in such a way as to admit the dissonances of those who cry out in agony.

But it has been said that you are a liberator who took to the sword only because Spain was Red. It is redder now. Barcelona is drenched in the blood of men, women and subversive babies.

Francisco Franco, Generalissimo, how do you sleep of nights?

From New York HERALD-TRIBUNE,
March 21, 1938

It Is Not a Fact

LAWRENCE A. FERNSWORTH

To the Editor of the New York *Times*:

May I refer to a letter from Albert Whelan appearing in your issue of March 2? As a reporter I am not interested in controversy but in fact, and so, perhaps, I may be excused in noticing the controversial as well as the personal aspects of that letter.

I think there exist no fuller reports on the 1936 Barcelona church burnings than my own, for I was through them all at a time when no other foreign correspondent could get in—or out. While those events were in the news I wrote about them as faithfully as possible, striving to place them in their right setting. But, being a reporter of present-day events and not a transcriber of ancient history, I could not—as my critic would have desired—reiterate what had been repeatedly and fully stated in its own good day.

It is not a fact, as it is stated to be, that there remain no churches in Barcelona fit for worship. I could name various churches, beginning with the cathedral. One was the Church of San Felipe Neri, which was rendered unfit when a bomb from a Franco plane tore through a roof and killed 150 children in the basement. There is another, the Pompeya Church, two blocks from my home. On July 19, 1936, the Capuchin fathers opened its doors to the wounded and dying of that terrible day —and the people respected it. No doubt many of those wounded and dying had been hit by the bullets that for two days—as I heard and saw and barely escaped feeling—poured from the fortified church know as the Carmelitas, which stands on the corner of my own block. The people did not respect it.

It is not a fact, as it is stated to be, that my story was "a release to impress the American public" and "a publicity stunt."

The restoration of religious worship has been going on quietly, without any attempt to impress any one. I dug this story up without hint or suggestion from any source. It surprised the censor, who was not cognizant of the facts.

It is not a fact, as it is stated to be, that the government "liquidated the clergy." It is a fact that the government, through numerous officials, often at great danger to themselves, helped hundreds, if not thousands, of clergy and nuns to leave the country or find a haven.

It is not a fact, as it is stated to be, that "the Bishop of Barcelona was executed some months after the beginning of the present war." It is a fact that he was saved through the instrumentality of the Catalan Government. This is likewise true of the Cardinal Archbishop of Tarragona, Vidal and Barraquer and others.

It is not, therefore, a fact, as it is stated to be, that "the office of vicar general automatically ceased."

Nor is it a fact that any prelate was executed or otherwise put to death in Barcelona. The Auxiliary Bishop of Tarragona and the Bishop of Lerida I understand to have been killed by mobs in those first days of chaos in which the church had a role. All the remainder of the nine Catalan Bishops got away; in most instances, if indeed not all, helped to safety by the government.

May I now refer to a comment on my story made in your issue of February 28 by the Rev. Francis X. Talbot?

It is not a fact, as it is stated to be, that all the Spanish Bishops signed the Bishops' pastoral. Neither the Cardinal Archbishop of Tarragona nor the Bishop of Vitoria, who was a virtual prisoner in rebel hands for his refusal to bow to their dictates, nor the Bishop of Orihuela, now in London, would sign it.

It is not, therefore, a fact, as it is stated to be, that there remains no Bishop not implicated in that pastoral to try the Bishop of Teruel should he be brought before an ecclesiastical court.

Catholic clergy and laymen here do not understand it to be a fact, as it is stated to be, that the Pope approved the pastoral letter.

It is not a fact, as it is stated to be, that in Barcelona "all the priests are in hiding or in close surveillance." They live as freely as any other men. Indeed I should judge, after a conversation with police officials, including Don Paulino Romero, the General Commissioner of Public Order, that they are even less likely to molestation precisely because the government does not wish to appear as embarrassing the clergy.

It may be a fact, as it is stated to be, that the Bishop of Teruel is an old man. But in Spain today there are thousands of men and women much older, and there are children and babes, who literally have not a stone whereon to lay their heads, whom these past few weeks I have seen fleeing terror-stricken through the streets of Barcelona, not knowing whither, who are all victims of the rebellion which the signers of that Bishops' pastoral, including the Bishop of Teruel, and my critics as well, so openly support. And the Bishop of Teruel is comfortably housed and treated with special consideration.

It is a fact, for so I have observed, that certain Catholic spokesmen and organs, including the journal published by my critics, which I regularly receive through the ordinary mails, notwithstanding that it so openly gives "aid and comfort to the enemy" and apologizes for rebellion, have been perturbed because a supposed "anti-God" government refused to sanction religious worship.

Can it also be a fact—for on that point I confess to misgivings—that they are likewise perturbed to learn that the government is not "anti-God" and insists, even in the midst of Franco's terror, on sanctioning and protecting religious worship?

From New York TIMES,
April 10, 1938

266

Breakthrough

HERBERT L. MATTHEWS

Barcelona, Spain, April 4—

T HE INSURGENTS were approaching Tortosa today, being apparently somewhere around Cherta, about five miles north, this afternoon when this correspondent visited the ruined town at the mouth of the Ebro River. It was learned that the bridge over the River Segre leading into Lerida had been blown up and the Loyalists had taken up positions just outside that city.

Driven before the Insurgents' mechanized steam roller, scattered by its shattering power or caught behind in the machinery were the remnants of the Loyalists' Fifteenth Brigade. We learned more about them today and about the tragic fate that befell the Lincoln-Washington Battalion, but it is a confused and still very incomplete story gleaned from a few survivors.

They all knew last week that the drive was coming and foresaw the possibility that this brigade might be broken up. Chief of Staff Robert Merriman showed every man what he had to do and where he had to head if Insurgent tanks and cavalry filtered in.

Then came the smash through at Villalba. The Lincoln-Washington got the brunt of it, for it was on the right wing. Soon it was split in two. One brigade commissar, John Gates,[*] a veteran of the Cordoba campaign last spring, took command of one company, which fought and twisted its way through to Gandesa, losing men as it went along. He and five other survivors of that group—Joseph Hecht,[**] George Watt, Alvah Bessie,

---

[*] After his return, John Gates became a member of the National Committee of the Communist Party of the U.S.A. See p. 478.

[**] See Joe Hecht, by Alvah Bessie, p. 444.

Simon Le Nof and Felix Kusman—told us the story this afternoon just outside Rasquera (about twelve miles north and slightly east of Tortosa), where they sat shivering on the ground in the warm sunlight. Three of them—Messrs. Gates, Hecht and Watt—escaped only by swimming the Ebro River.

They were behind the Insurgent lines for three days and two nights, sometimes deliberately following the Insurgents, for they knew this would take them to the front lines. At other times they tumbled on the Insurgents in error.

Last night they went through an Insurgent encampment without recognition. When challenged, they answered in Spanish. Some of the Insurgents cursed them for stepping on their legs or faces as they went through. The three Americans did not know who the other soldiers were. One asked and, he related, got the answer in German, "Eighth Division." They knew what that meant, but none of them lost his head and all trudged calmly on.

For many hours Saturday they were "sniped at," as they put it, by Insurgent artillery, a striking example of the wealth of material the Insurgents possess. An observation plane hovered above them, and every time they made a move the place and direction were radioed back to artillery headquarters and a rain of shells would come over.

The group gradually scattered, some getting across the Ebro in boats. But the peasants of the vicinity had been ordered to burn all boats to delay the Insurgent advance, so there were precious few to be found.

The group had been reduced to nine, partly by casualties but also through various components becoming lost or scattered. They were trapped and they knew it. Some of the men were wounded.

The Ebro is deep near Rasquera and flows swiftly, but none had any doubt that death awaited him if he was caught. All preferred to die trying to escape. So all took a few hours rest to recover their strength and then stripped and entered the chilly water. Of the nine, only three got across.

All morning they lay around and then trudged for hours, unclothed, until they met some Spanish comrades who were able to give them everything but shoes. When we met them they were waiting for trucks to come along and take them with about 300 other International Brigade survivors back for recuperation. They were gaunt and shivering with the cold, but they could still joke about their experiences. They said they wanted another chance at the Insurgents.

We found the three other Lincoln-Washington Battalion survivors—Messrs. Bessie, Le Nof and Kusman—with them.

A supply of food had been brought up, and everybody was waiting for a column of 300 to march back. A good hundred of them, they thought, would be Lincoln-Washington Battalion members and others Canadians from the MacKenzie-Papineau Battalion and British. Those were men for the most part who had fought the rear-guard action back from Gandesa.

Then there was a group that included commanders. There were about thirty-five in that group when it got together finally on a hill overlooking Gandesa, including Chief of Staff Merriman, Brigade Commissar Dave Doran, Battalion Commissar Fred Keller, Leonard Lamb, Milton Wolff and Chief Scout Ivan, whose last name nobody ever seems to know. It was from them that we got the story of what had happened.

The group held that hill against all attacks and artillery fire during the whole of Saturday morning. They were under heavy fire from two angles, while Moorish cavalry kept trying to cut them off. So they decided to move.

Their idea was to get around Gandesa somehow and reach the main road. However, they soon ran into an impossible fire in which they lost some men, so they set about struggling back to the old positions. This they succeeded in doing, and all afternoon they held the hill against repeated cavalry charges. It was a small group but composed of determined fighters who had plenty of ammunition.

Nevertheless, theirs was an untenable position in the long run, and they knew it. As the sun was sinking they decided on a last desperate break for safety. Their scout went ahead with a rank and file man known as Joe, closely followed by Messrs. Merriman, Doran and Keller. The last-named was wounded in the hip, but only slightly.

The main part of the group lagged about a thousand yards behind and in the growing darkness lost their direction slightly. So instead of passing between Corbera and Gandesa, as they intended, they struck Corbera itself. The scout recognized it, for some headquarters used to be there; but before they could retreat he and Joe were challenged.

Of course they could not be sure Corbera was in Insurgent hands, so Ivan just said, "*Qué hay?*" ("What do you want?"), keeping his hand on his pistol.

The answer was an abrupt, "*Manos arriba!*" ("Hands up!") Then the soldiers shouted to the sergeant of the guard, "Reds, Reds!"

When Mr. Merriman and the group behind him heard that instead of running away they rushed toward the Insurgents. The scout, who knew the terrain, dashed to the left with Joe at his heels, shouting to the others to follow. Instead he heard shots behind, and finally a business-like "*Manos arriba!*" shouted in such a way that he decided the men must have been cornered.

He and Joe got up over the hill and circled Gandesa, getting clear. But they have heard nothing more of the others. Some of them may have broken clear. Yesterday when we went to Mora and spoke behind the lines to Brigade Commander Vladimir Copic, who had with him Eli Biegelman and Alvin Cohen, he also had heard nothing about the Lincoln-Washington Battalion survivors.

So all in all one can say about 150 out of the original 450 can be accounted for today. Almost certainly more of them will turn up in the coming days, and some may be prisoners. But lots of very fine men are not going to be seen again. . . .

From New York TIMES,
April 4, 1938

The Thirteen Points*

1. *Independence*. To ensure the absolute independence and complete integrity of Spain. A Spain entirely free from all foreign interference, whatever its character and origin, with her peninsular and insular territory and her possessions untouched and safe from any attempt at dismemberment, alienation or mortgage, and retaining the protectorate zones assigned to her by international agreements, unless such agreements should be modified on Spain's own intervention and with her assent. Fully conscious of her historical and traditional obligations, Spain will draw more closely together the links forged by a common origin and sense of universality —a traditional characteristic of her people—which bind her to the other Spanish-speaking countries.

2. *Liberation of Spain*. The liberation of our territory from the foreign military forces that have invaded it, as well as from those who have entered Spain since July, 1936, and who, under the pretext of technical collaboration, are intervening or attempting to dominate the juridical life of Spain in their own interests.

3. *Democratic Republic*. A People's Republic, represented by a virile state based on principles of pure democracy, ruling by means of a government endowed with the full authority conferred by universal suffrage, and symbolizing a strong executive power dependent at all times on the will of the Spanish people.

---

* The Thirteen Points were proclaimed by the Republic on May 1, 1938. They constitute a statement of the aims for which the Spanish people were fighting, but in point of fact are merely a recapitulation of long-established domestic and international policy.

4. *A Plebiscite.* The legal and social structure of the Republic shall be the work of the national will, freely expressed by means of a plebiscite to be held as soon as the war is over, one to be held without restrictions or limitations and with full guarantees to assure those taking part against every possible reprisal.

5. *Regional Liberties.* Respect for regional liberties without prejudice to Spanish unity. Protection and development of the personality and individuality of the various regions of Spain, as imposed by historic law and fact; this, far from signifying disintegration, is the best means of welding together the various elements of the nation.

6. *Rights of the Citizen.* The Spanish State shall guarantee the citizen full rights in civil and social life with liberty of conscience, and will assure the free exercise of religious belief and practice.

7. *Guarantee of Property.* The State shall guarantee property legally and legitimately acquired within the limits proposed by the supreme interests of the nation and the protection of producing elements. Without prejudice to individual initiative, it will prevent the exploitation of the citizen and the subjugation of collective effort by the accumulation of wealth, which weakens the controlling action of the State in the economic and social life. To this end it will encourage the development of small properties, guarantee family patrimony, and foster every measure leading to the economic, moral, and racial improvement of the producing classes.

   The property and legitimate interests of foreigners who have not assisted the rebellion will be respected, and the damage caused involuntarily during the course of the war will be examined with a view to granting corresponding indemnities. For this purpose the Government of the Republic has already appointed a commission for foreign claims.

8. *Democracy and Land Ownership.* A radical agrarian reform to abolish the former aristocratic semi-feudal system of ownership, which, lacking as it did every human, national, and

patriotic sentiment, has always been the greatest obstacle to the development of the country's great resources. The establishment of the new Spain on the basis of a wide and solid peasant democratic ownership of the land it cultivates.

9. *Social Legislation.* The State shall guarantee the rights of the worker by means of an advanced social legislation, in accordance with the specific necessities of Spanish life and economy.

10. *Improvement of the Race.* One of the primary and basic concerns of the State will be the cultural, physical, and moral improvement of the race.

11. *The Army.* The Spanish Army, at the service of the nation itself, shall be free of all leadership depending upon bias or party, and the people must be able to see in it the certain instrument for the defense of their liberties and independence.

12. *Renunciation of War.* The Spanish State reaffirms the constitutional doctrine of renouncing war as an instrument of national policy. Spain, loyal to agreements and treaties, will support the policy represented by the League of Nations. She claims and maintains the rights of the Spanish State, and demands, as a Mediterranean Power, a place in the concert of nations, being always ready to collaborate in the support of collective security and the general defense of peace.

13. *Amnesty.* Amnesty for all Spaniards who wish to co-operate in the tremendous work of reconstructing Spain and making her a great nation. After the cruel struggle which is laying waste the country, and which has reawakened the classic racial virtues of heroism and idealistic fervor, it would be an act of treason to the country's destiny not to yield up all thought of vengeance and reprisals on the altars of a common mission of work and sacrifice which, in the interests of Spain's future, all her sons must fulfill.

Notebook From Spain

JOSEPH NORTH

The Haberdasher Goes to War

Barcelona, May 2, 1938

WHEN THE BOMBERS came, we went down in the subway on the Plaza Catalunya, Barcelona's Times Square. Seven flew overhead, and the anti-aircraft worried them. Loyalist Spain was down below; refugees from Aragón and Lerida sitting on their mattresses with babes in arms, Barcelona workingmen hastening to supper, Catalan businessmen in Parisian-cut suits, all jammed down on the lower landing. The fellow in front of me, with a little bay window and baldish head said, "They won't stay long; our anti-aircraft is a lot better now, since March 17." Others who heard him hoped he was right, but they didn't say anything.

I got to talking with the fellow. He gave me his card: "Felipe Alvarez Rega, Haberdasher, 27 Cortes." He told me that his class, 1927, was to go up tomorrow, and showed me his *carnet* —identification card—which said that he had given eight blood transfusions. "I am husky," he said, "I've a lot of blood to give." No heroics about him; he talked calmly, as if about last week's receipts. Now he's going to handle a gun instead of a cash register.

"We can't afford"—he said "afford"—"to let Franco win. We little business men will be squeezed to the wall if fascism wins. The government protects the little fellow," he said. "Franco is big business. *Claro!*" (*Claro* is Spanish for "sure"; they seem to say it every other sentence.)

When the all-clear alarm sounded and the planes went back to Majorca, he invited me to his store and I went with him. It was a nice store and I bought a bright necktie for May Day.

274

"Everybody buys bright merchandise nowadays," he said cheerfully. "Business is good. Nobody wants to save money nowadays because you never know. . . ." He wanted me to come around and have dinner with him when he came back from the war. I shook hands with him. What party are you in?" I asked. "Left Republican," he told me. "I'm Communist," I said. "I'm no extremist," he replied, "I'm middle of the road. But bombs," he said with sly Catalan humor, "bounce as hard off Republican heads as off Communists." I shook hands all around again, with him, his chic wife and his aging clerk, and he told me to come around any time and I'd get good service.

When I left that store, I thought how splendid a political instrument the People's Front was. To win against totalitarian warfare you need the totality of the people with you, you need every man and his wife in the rearguard as well as at the front to work for victory.

You think of trenches when you think of war; no-man's land, machine guns, artillery, going over the top. But the wars of 1938 aren't won by military men alone; they're the vanguard but you can't win without the rearguard. Politics has the last word.

Last night I went to a conference of the *Juventudes Socialistas Unificadas*, of Catalonia's youth. Six hundred delegates from Barcelona to Port Bou sat in darkness to save current for war industries, and held their meeting. Twenty-year old Secretary Wenceslao Colomer stood in complete darkness on the platform and made his report lasting an hour. He laced into lads none older than himself, most of them between fifteen and twenty, for not having "spread their work sufficiently to all strata of the population." "We must bring the Popular Front program to everybody," he said. He was hard and spared no one, including himself. They took it, these kid brothers of men at the front. They sat with Sam Browne belts and revolvers. They brought candles and took notes in the feeble glare. When we said that we were from the *Estados Unidos* and had come to help them in their fight, the kids got up cheering, and shouted "*Viva La Solidaridad Internaçional!*" They sang *Joven Guardia* ("Young

275

Guard"). They were very happy that the *extranjeros* had come to help their fight. And they cheered away there in the dark.

ALLAH IN MADRID

Madrid, June 2, 1938

IT'S EIGHTEEN MONTHS NOW, a long time in wartime. The enemy has been inside the gates, the Moors have been praying to Allah in Caso del Campo for a year and a half now. I got to town the night the German electrical battery rained four hundred shells into the city. There were funeral processions the next day, white coffins for the young and black for the old. And the living went on in the life I never imagined possible. Pilgrimages should be made to this beleaguered city to learn how to live.

I have never seen a more serene folk, stout-hearted and confident. And Madrid differs only in degree from the rest of Central Spain, where some eight million Spaniards live. Hemmed in on three sides, their only outlet to the world is the Mediterranean coastline. And Italian ships hide in the coves.

Madrid has but one roadway, veritably its lifeline, to the lush subtropical fields of Valencia, and Franco is pressing hard to come down the Teruel highway into that province and cut Castellon away from Loyalist Spain. That is the picture, and is it any wonder Mussolini scans his maps in the *palazzio* and storms around with his chin stuck out? By all canons and clauses in military text books and by the heritage of von Ludendorff, this war should be over. I have just returned from this area and can tell you the normality of life here is staggering. The morale of the people in Central Spain is matchless. Consider Madrid: I picked up a song from an urchin in the street the other day, which might well be the theme song of this Spanish drama. It was a popular Madrileno ditty, which says, *"Quieren pasar los Moros, Quieren pasar los Moros, mamita mia. No pasa nadie, no pasa nadie."* Literally it means, "Those Moors want to pass. Those Moors want to pass, baby, but nobody's passing, baby, nobody's passing." They sing it clapping their hands in Andalusian fashion when they get off those dizzying *flamencos* that sound a thousand years old.

Mayor Rafael Henche told me the city's difficulties: only half a pint of milk daily to Madrid's 63,000 children under the age of five. That worried him more than anything else—that and the traffic problem. He talked about stop and go lights and one-way streets while machine guns could be heard hammering away at University City, less than a mile from His Honor's offices.

In the face of omnipresent danger the trivialities of ordinary life strike you as peculiarly heroic. The fact that twenty theaters and forty-six movies stay open and have been open every day since the Moors crossed the Manzanares; the fact that schools haven't shut down a single day, and that girls skip rope in shell-pocked streets. *Con pan o sin pan*—with bread or without bread —they resist. There is a minimum of food, yet enough to keep the Castilian alert and even spry. He has never lost the pride in personal appearance so typically Spanish. You can't get your shoes shined without waiting half an hour in line. Bookshops are crowded all day from the moment the doors open, and you can get any classic you wish in Spanish, including Mike Gold's *Judios Sin Dinero*. That's right, *Jews Without Money*. And it sells very well, *compañero,* a salesgirl told me.

COUNTRY OF THE BIG UPSET

Levante Front, June 7, 1938

THIS IS THE COUNTRY of the big upset. The Levante Front runs, roughly, from the Mediterranean to the mountains of Teruel. It reaches from Tortosa at the mouth of the Ebro to just below Alcala de Chivert on the coast. The battlegrounds run through the mountains and glens of Castellon and Teruel Provinces, rich lands coveted since olden times by Moors and Romans.

We examined three prisoners taken a few hours ago near Albocacer, as hang-dog a trio as I have ever seen. A young political commissar with his hand in a sling questioned them. They answered with averted eyes, evidently thinking their last minute was here and by rights they should be saying their prayers. The prisoners confessed they couldn't understand it. "We expected the war to be finished when we reached Viñaroz," the Navarrese said. And many of the parents waiting at home will never again see their sons in Franco's forces who wrote these cards. For losses of the fascists along the coast of Levante have been tremendous.

The political commissar of the division was young, his arm in a sling, but he was one of the most active men I have met in Spain. He took us to his room in a villa occupied by the commissariat, overlooking rolling hills that sloped off to the Mediterranean. He showed us positions on maps and made crosses to indicate where the enemy is and where we are. His manner was rapid-fire, as though impatient to get done with the business. Then he pulled a drawer out of his desk and handed us his work of love: a copy of the division's paper, *Lucha*—"Struggle." It appears daily and has fine engravings and drawings by artists who fight in the trenches and take time off to draw scenes near to the men. The commissar kept repeating, "Our men have complete faith in the democratic peoples of the world." I shall never forget how he said it. *"El Soldado Español lucha y lucha con gusto"*—"The Spanish soldiers fight and fight with gusto—not only for their own freedom but for the freedom of the entire world," he said. "And we're sure the world will send us aid. We're absolutely sure the world will send us aid."

Wherever we went we found leaflets, posters, newspapers carrying Negrin's Thirteen Points, summarizing the ideals for which Loyalists fight. Publication of this program has produced enthusiasm among the troops. One can't imagine how much until he talks to them. The bulk of the army are peasants, and peasants are suspicious people. Bilked and picked clean so often, they want to be shown—and shown often. The Thirteen Points reiterated the government's goals—goals of the fighting men. This declaration further cemented their ties with the Negrin government, for it showed them that the government, more than ever, was theirs, spoke their language, had their ideas, fought their fight. Peasants, they hungered for land. One of the Thirteen Points promised land, aid and security to the farmer. Many are religious even though anti-hierarchical, and the declaration assured them religious freedom. The Thirteen Points summarized all their aspirations, and they were happy. The young political commissar showed us a headline in the latest edition of *Lucha: There's Only One Barrier to the March of Aggressors—the Resistance of Those People Who Are Unafraid to Defend Their Independence.* These men are unafraid to defend their independence.

"Resistance," the commissar said, "has become part of our nature, so to speak." And he showed us the leading story in the edition that day: There was an Italian attack on the Teruel sector. It passed over the first and second-line trenches of the Loyalists. The Republicans stuck to their guns and fought so hard Italian infantrymen feared to follow their tanks. As a result, the whippets were captured.

That's just one day's story. Every day brings its budget of heroism to the soldier-editor's office. That's the way things go down here on the Levante Front; it is the reason why Chamberlain and Mussolini feel so embarrassed these days. It's the reason why these upsets keep on happening when there are so many handsome, made-in-Milan whippet tanks in the hills. Mr. Chamberlain and the military experts had better take another whiskey and try to figure it out.

Barcelona, July 19, 1938

AT THE MINISTRY OF EDUCATION, they get thousands of postcards from men in the army daily. They showed me some—results of the Milicias of Culture, the front line schools. One soldier wrote, "Thanks to the new government I can read and write. Now I am a man."

To comprehend the Spanish people's resistance during these two years, you must understand these postcards. *El soldado* who wrote "Now I am a man," is not afraid to die for that privilege.

Two years of war. Premier Negrin's adjuration to resist is heeded; resistance breeds victory in today's world, where the aggressors are 60 percent bluff. This is no military axiom discovered yesterday. Spain has known it for years, over a century. In the war of 1808, Napoleon had whittled away until Spain retained only a small slice of the Levantine coast and a patch in southern Extremadura. Napoleon couldn't win because the Spanish people wouldn't stop fighting. Thomas Babington Macaulay, shrewd observer of European history, wrote in 1833, "There is no country in Europe which it is so easy to overrun as Spain; there is no country in Europe which it is more difficult to conquer." And Macaulay was wise when he said, "War in Spain has, from the days of the Romans, had a character of its own; it is a fire which cannot be raked out; it burns fiercely under the embers; and long after it has, to all seeming, been extinguished, bursts forth more violently than ever."

There is, of course, historical basis for all this. The old Iberian Peninsula was inhabited by different peoples, separated by steep mountains and differing tradeways. They spoke different languages, their armies presented disunity to the invader. But the commoners were unusually hardy and able. They harried the life out of the invader until he was glad to return home with a few regiments left. Today's picture is different; Republican Spain, under a government of national unity, presents a people and an army united as no Spanish people ever was.

Again: in addition to the war for independence, the Spanish Republican war is for a better economic system. Never have the people benefited by social laws as today. Wages are double and triple—the average Spaniard today makes between twenty-five and thirty-five pesetas daily. The popular restaurants feed him well at five pesetas a meal. Rent is one-third that of pre-war days. The schools are open for his children, he himself has learned to read and write. Four hundred thousand in Barcelona eat two good meals a day for ten pesetas—one-third their daily wage. They get beans or lentils, potatoes or rice, in the first plate; meat and potatoes or two fried eggs or salt fish in the second. There is always some fruit for dessert. Never even in peace have they lived so well in that country whose riches were gobbled up by feudal landowners and the Juan Marches.

Joseph North

The Ebro Crossed

Falset, by courier to Barcelona, July 30, 1938

WHEN I GOT TO CORBERA, the enemy was shelling the ghost town from Gandesa, whose spires are visible from the hilltop. First the snarl and then the thud and then the cascade of bricks tumbling down. I met an ancient peasant, with black headkerchief and cane, clambering over the ruins on the Street of Dr. D. Jaime Ferran. This main street of the rural center is the one with all the Franco pictures painted on the buildings and the Falangist arrows and crossbow by every doorway.

"*Buenos dias*," the peasant said. I said good-day to him as another shell landed up the same street a few hundred yards off. "*Malo*," he said. "Bad." I shook my head in agreement.

"*Si, Señor*," he said, looking at the ruins. "The work of many years is being undone now." "*Si*," I said. He clambered to the top of the ruins, looked inside the building where a cock still stood in the wreckage, and went on.

The old man spoke more truth than he knew. Franco's shells and Il Duce's bombers were undoing the work of centuries. They are shattering buildings with their own Falangist abracadabra painted on them.

The lands which the Popular Front has taken back in last week's drive are among the richest in Spain. The splendidly cultivated fields roll up to the top of the Barrancos. Potatoes big as both your fists grow in the rich soil. But the tillers are happy that the Republicans came back. One, a gnarled fellow in tight breeches, kissed the Catalonian red and gold flag when the troops came marching in again. The terror of the Moors and blackshirts, of Franco and the Falangists, had been too much. And now; heartless barrage and aerial bombardments hourly. These are the folk Franco admitted in his Burgos communique had "helped the enemy cross the Ebro."

This offensive ranks with Guadalajara; in some ways it is a greater achievement. It happened that Peter Kerrigan of the

281

London *Daily Worker* and your correspondent crossed, accompanied the Republicans and saw what a job it was. They crossed with astounding ease, exhibited a meticulous planfulness that amazed Europe's military experts.

Friday the Republic had been bringing up trucks loaded with quaint fishermen's boats. The highways from Port Bou to the Ebro were crowded with them: green, red, yellow, blue. Planes carrying spotters notified Franco; yet he was unprepared when the blow came. He doubtless thought the preparations would take much longer. For he was preparing the same action. I could see that on the outskirts of Corbera, where I counted some seventeen Franco boats lying sixteen kilometers from the Ebro. The Republic beat him to the punch.

The boats, oarlocks muffled, crossed before dawn Monday, July 25. Volunteers rowed them over, among them many Americans who had been seamen or lifeguards, and those who had done a "stretch" in the United States Navy. Once across, along the Western bank of the Ebro from Amposte to Maquinenza, the engineers threw bridges over for the heavy stuff—tanks, artillery, truck-loads of ammunition. The bewildered fascists fled in disorder practically all along the line—a distance of over a hundred miles. They ran wildly for the first forty-eight hours.

Now it is *Schrecklicheit à la* Hitler. The Messerschmitts glided into view by threes, sixes, twelves, up to thirty. They strafe in patrols of three or six, circle about their prey while one swoops down with its rat-tat-tat of machine-gun bullets. Then it rises and the second comes down, and so on. All with the grace of a condor. The action is hatefully deliberate, maddeningly scientific.

But the government pushes on. Men hide under trees or in ditches; small-town guardsmen fire two rifleshots in the air and the people take to the *refugios*. Hundreds of lovely old buildings crumble in a rush of bricks and plaster. But the toll of human life and materials is relatively small. The advance continues. The entire action came as a complete surprise. London, Paris, Berlin, and Rome thought that the fate of the Republic was sealed. Then came the lightning counter-stroke.

Joseph North

I had the opportunity of observing the Republican troops more closely in this action than ever before—excellent infantry-men. I saw them during several actions about Corbera. Victory was on their faces, and zeal for freedom. They came through disheveled, bearded, dirty—but glorious.

From a work in progress to be published by MASSES AND MAINSTREAM, *New York*

Somos la joven guardia
que va forjando el porvenir;
nos templó la miseria
sabremos vencer o morir . . .

By the Banks of the Ebro

DAVID GUEST

IT IS A SPRING NIGHT, an hour after sunset. A pale and sickly new moon swims through the clouds. Only here and there are the brighter stars to be seen.

I am lying in the reeds by the water-side, concealed as far as possible, watching, listening, waiting. Over on the other side, invisible and silent, except for occasional confused noises, about two hundred yards away are the trenches of the enemy. Presently the noises grow louder until at last the semi-silence is broken by a clear voice ringing out in authoritative, confident tones, *"Oyez, Oyez, Rojos! Rojos!"* "Listen, you Reds," repeated several times, but only being met with silence on the Republican side.

"And who is going to win the war now?" "We are!"—a chorus of shouts from our side of the river. (Cynical, brutal, coarse laughter and shouts from the fascists.)

"Listen, you Reds," says the voice, "we have got the guns, the tanks, the airplanes—how can you fight us without losing? Don't be fools, come over and join the troops of General Franco, who must win."

From our side a din of more shouts, angry, confused, but suddenly these cease and give place to another voice. "How can you win, when the whole Spanish people are against you? Traitors—who have brought in Italians and Germans to bomb our Spanish cities!"

Loud cries greet this sally and for an instant their voice is

284

disconcerted, but then it replies, "General Franco is saving Spain from Russian Bolsheviks, and besides, he is protecting the Church." Next voice, "Then why does he need the Moors? Since when have they become good Christians? And there are no Russians in Spain anyway." So the debate goes on, a continuous wrangle—point by point, sometimes developing almost like an academic discussion, sometimes interrupted by cries and shouts.

Listening in the reeds, with head closely pressed to the ground, it seems almost incredible that I am on one of the battle-fronts of Fascism and Democracy. Memories come back of street corners, oh, so familiar, in London, where rival meetings, Fascist and Anti-Fascist, were held. The same arguments tossed to and fro; the same efforts of Fascism, using all the methods of terror-ism, enticement, corruption, bluff to win over some support from backward people. The same indignant exposure of the Fascist lies by Democrats; it seems as though the two voices, our voice and their voice, have become symbols of the world struggle that is taking place.

Just then their voice makes a particularly sneering reference to the "Red scum" and says that the young weaklings in the Republican army dare not stand up to real men. The Spanish youth who have volunteered in thousands to make up the cream of the Republican army cannot bear this insult; an excited young lad, shouting in reply, pokes his head just over the parapet of the trenches on the left—a shot rings out, followed by a cry. For a very short interval there is silence. But then, the magnifi-cent song of the Spanish youth, the "Joven Guardia," gets taken up and rolls from one section to another of the line of trenches.

Presently this song, fervently coming from several hundred throats, fills the air with youthful faith in victory and reduces all other voices to silence. Only the intermittent crackling of Fascist rifle fire tells us the final answer of the dark, old world to the claims of the new.

700 Calendar Days

O. H. HUNTER

HE WAS THE ONLY SOUL hurrying along under the plane trees that shaded the promenade of the Ramblas. The street was closed down and silent as if an air raid were about to begin. When the young Negro reached the Plaza de Catalunya, his cadence slowed to a halt. The Ingersoll wrist watch read: 5:45 A.M.

Above the wide white space of the spacious Plaza, a Mediterranean blue sky was delicately patterned with long wisps of white clouds which were just becoming suffused with a pink let-down from the red sun still hidden behind the city's bastion of high hills. Jay remembered that:

> Mackerel scales and mares' tails
> Make lofty ships carry low sails.

At home, he thought, shifting his knapsack, those clouds would promise a storm. I'd better trim my sails anyhow on this June 6, six to six, 1938. Christ, only seven years ago a trade school class was being whipped into shape for graduation in Virginia, U.S.A. Tidewater campus, the quiet of the soft clean Chesapeake air was disturbed only by the passionate songs of birds making love in the veridian sanctuary of every tree, so far and long gone.

Yesterday had been one hellish day of rushing about for Political Delegate Jay. Things had really jumped-off. In the morning he had been abruptly relieved of his work in the Central Garage of the *Ayuda Medica Extranjera* (the Foreign Medical Aid Section of the Spanish Republican Army). "Prepare to leave Barcelona at once for a new post," the message read. A postscript invited him to a reception given that evening for a delegation from the States. He had attended the reception. Now was not the time, but he damn well had to go over the disturbing conversation he had with the prominent Negro liberal member of the delegation. Rushing across Barcelona to meet his commanding officer, destination unknown, pushed everything else into the background.

As he approached *Rambla de Catalunya* 126, he saw a camouflaged Renault with the circle and five pointed star of the *Comisariado* parked in front. A chauffeur was at the wheel. The door of the *Jefatura* opened. Commissar Carlus, immaculately uniformed as always, ran down the broad white steps.

"*Buenos dias, Camarada* Jay." He looked tired and irritated. "Is everything in order? Ready?"

"*Buenos, Camarada* Carlus. Everything is OK." Jay opened the car door, but Carlus beckoned him in.

"You turned everything over to the *responsable* at the garage?" he asked, lighting an American cigarette after Jay had refused one.

As Jay explained details to his commander, a canvas covered Matford pulled up to the curb behind the Renault. Carlus signaled the truck, gave a quick command in Catalan to his chauffeur, and the two cars moved up the *Rambla* toward the Barcelona suburbs.

"I saw you talking to a man of your people last night," Carlus said unexpectedly. "Did you enjoy the talk?"

Last night! Jay grimaced with inward discomfort. Enjoy? He said, "I found him an *analfabeto* — understands nothing — about Spain."

"An *analfabeto*?" Carlus was irritated. "Is he a sincere antifascist? He'll learn to understand from us. No?"

"Yes, yes, only there were things. . . ."

"*Je ne te comprends pas*," Carlus said.

"It is hard for me to make you understand. We did not agree about—about the Negro. I guess that is the best way to put it."

"Did you know him in America?"

"*Camarada* Carlus, I worked in a factory. He is a *big* man among my people. A spokesman. I know his work, it doesn't move me."

"What factory?"

"Stock yards in Chicago."

"Yes, Packingtown," Carlus said, "The American writer, Upton Sinclair. *'The Jungle.'*" He lit another cigarette.

There was silence in the speeding Renault for a short distance. Traffic was increasing as the sun mounted into the high flat sky. A military convoy was making the going tough when Carlus broke the silence.

"Well, *Camarada* Factory Worker, in '36 could we have thought that so soon we would come to a place where so much would be demanded from us? Who could have dreamed of the International Brigade?"

Jay's body tightened. Here it comes, he surmised.

"*Comandante* Minkow, the *camaradas* from the Murcia hospitals say your work was good. I do not know. You have not been with me long; we have talked little. They are the ones who recommend. I accept. Where we go the work is *muy duro* —very hard. Minkow says you are the *camarada* for it."

"He is a great teacher," Jay said. His tightness loosened on the slack. If Minkow had a hand in this—it had to be OK.

"You must be a good student. The American *camaradas* believe in you, too. I heard only lately of the hospital train you Americans brought through in the northern evacuation. Then your work was good, also, no?"

"There were mistakes, but everyone gave the best he had."

For a second there was a smile on the elongated El Greco face: "Where we go now there have been more than enough mistakes. I am afraid those who have been before you used up even your share." He extracted a sealed envelope from his brief case. "Put this away."

Jay hefted the twin envelope, he reluctantly slipped it into a pocket. Carlus was napping. And Carlus asleep amused Jay. This man who when awake couldn't stand or sit quietly; couldn't walk below a dog trot; who carried on his work with a driving restless immediacy, and demanded as much from others; this small-boned, nervous body asleep was relaxed as a becalmed banner.

They entered Badalona. The going was tough—most of the thoroughfare was blocked off after last night's bombing. Some fires still smouldered. Since the first days Jay had seen bomb devastation, but today the battered agony of Badalona caught his throat with extra cruelty. It was the wanton destruction. It was the children. In the narrow streets, in and out of the heavy traffic, emaciated youngsters played games so important to all children. The Renault passed a group using the gutted skeleton of a house as a sort of grotesque jungle gym. In a crazy way it was like his neighborhood on the Chicago Southside. There the kids played in wrecked houses. Houses torn down by landlords. If relief clients can't pay rent—evict; if you can't evict—wreck. All he needed were the railroad tracks and it could be home.

Outside Callella the road began its ascent. To the right the sea was a wide curvilinear bowl, sun-glazed a brilliant ultramarine. The tile roofs of fishing villages began to appear in each inlet. Salt-bleached blue and green fishing boats were beached, and fishing nets draped on poles were exquisite festoons of lace in the bright distance. Here was sea land that recalled his mommer's home in the North Carolina-Virginia Tidewater. Pine trees were trimmed stark naked excepting for a clump of glistening foliage at the top. Every patch of fertile space had a crop going. Where were the oyster boats? Did they catch porgies or tread clams here? Again the small canker formed the previous night began to ache.

"*Costa Brava!*" the driver said above the laboring motor and the shrill screeching of circling gulls.

"*Olé! Olé*" interjected Jay loudly.

Carlus was awakened by the noise. And he was ready for work. "Have you opened your orders?" Jay was startled to attention. "*Vaya! hombre!* go on, open! It is not a Christmas present." Jay meticulously tore the envelope.

"Read," Carlus said.

There it was. Signed, sealed, with the five pointed star of the *Comisariado de Guerra de Ayuda Medica Extranjera.* A promotion! *"El camarada Jay con esta fecha ha sido afectado como Comisario Politico del Hospital de S'Agaro. . . ."* Promoted from political delegate to Commissar.

"But S'Agaro?" Jay asked stupidly.

"You know about S'Agaro?"

"Yes, *Camarada* Carlus, it's where *les inutiles—*"

His short dry laugh sounded more grim than mocking. "Who are *les inutiles?*"

"The crippled, the wounded, the chronically ill *camaradas,* passed by the Medical Commission, are going home through S'Agaro."

"Oh! ye-s-s-s?" The row of sharp needles in the commissar's voice pricked the wind out of Jay's schoolboyish recital. Jay hesitated. Why the needle? Then it hit him. *Nobody* from the Brigade could cross the French border legally. It was closed.

"You understand? Border locked tight. *Les inutiles* do not go through S'Agaro. They stop there. In Paris they said—yes. Our organizations made ready. Then the 'conditions' commenced; among many, *camaradas* from the democracies may enter, but no one from a fascist country. Only those with *papier.*"

"Some day they will choke on their *papier* and protocol," Jay said.

"You are wise, *hombre.* There are many more 'conditions.' In S'Agaro, *les inutiles* cannot believe the French government locked them out."

"How many are waiting?" Jay asked quietly.

"Five hundred and fifty." His voice was bitter with accusation. "Five hundred and fifty men, some of our best people and a few of the worst. *We* dismissed them from the Army with honors. We said, 'A *bientôt, camarades.* Until we meet in a victorious world.' But they are still there."

"They blame the Brigade?" Jay asked.

"I come to that. Are they still soldiers? Their papers say no. *Et la discipline de la Brigade est partie.* Gone."

Carlus was off in high now. The sleep *had* recharged his batteries. "The Quai d'Orsay wants trouble, and there are those in the hospital who know how to make it for them. Since Madrid, at the front, in the hospitals, they lived active anti-fascist lives. Every day we kept their understanding alert. Now they think they are stranded! The work is stopped. They eat, sleep, wait. As if that is not enough, they wait in fear. There is great danger of bombing. To have survived this far as soldiers only to die on the day they should be in France. Every day now is that day. Men of iron would rot living so.

"If *permiso* came tomorrow? A train of grumbling individuals would arrive in France, overflowing with complaints and false information about the Republic. Gone our precious unity. That is what those (and we know them) who sow the lies, gossip, rumors—plan. When they leave, all will be unified antifascists again—our plan! *Comprendez?*"

"I understand," Jay said. "You want the last training base of the International Brigade at S'Agaro. They must go home soldiers as at Madrid, Jarama, Teruel and on the Ebro."

"*Bravo! hombre!* First study carefully, quietly. *Mais attention!* If you do not like something in the administration—wait. Start at once a grand enthusiasm for digging *refugios*. There are none. Much talk about them but no work."

Carlus outlined other steps for pushing the rehabilitation work. Words formed sentences into paragraphs, into anxieties heavy as concrete slabs which stacked to an oppressive tonnage atop Jay's mind. His attention slipped.

Up to a minute before the reception last night, these instructions would have taken form in his mind as one simple image: There's a hell of a hard job ahead. But that was Spain. It was the Internationals every day. If one believed—one could expect little else. He believed. Spain was the place to fight them. They were everywhere. But today—Spain! Not for a moment had he offered a waiver on this. There was *one track* to run on. Last night this was questioned by one of his own people. Not questioned — challenged. He pulled himself back to his commander's words.

Carlus was easing up on his pitch. There was tenderness in his tone. Jay began to separate out two words. Again and again. Gone the *"camarada,"* gone *"hombre."* Now he was encouraging with the Hispano-Americano: 'boy,' and the familiar Spanish: *muchacho!*

"Boy, you have the *faculté.* . . . Boy, you have the *capacité* . . . *muchacho,* listen to me. . . . *Muchacho,* you must be strong. . . ." Boy: *muchacho.*

White man call me "boy" back home! anywhere up North, Jay remembered smiling, I'd say damn fast: "How big do men grow where you come from, cracker?" And be ready to nub. Might as well say "Sambo" or the universal "George." But get the meaning here. My, how a word can shift. It wasn't hard to understand Carlus. He was being *muy simpático*—a real homey. This was a pal sounding off up on Lenox or in the Hundreds on Madison Avenue. If he knew, he'd be saying: "pops," "old man," or "buddy boy."

Back home below the "Line" where a colored man from womb to grave is a "boy"; back home a Christmas in '27. In Virginia "my home by the sea." Most of the campus had cut out for home. Long empty days. If the shops weren't closed perhaps one could have worked off the clinging homesickness. But relief came in the festive form of a trip to Norfolk for the school dance. Three roommates, Sippie, Baby Lloyd, Monk Gray, and Jay pressed-up and took the ferry. And it was a ball!

About 2:30 A.M. they walked to the edge of the white section to catch the last ferry car. The town was dripping from a cold wet wind. They decided to kill the half hour wait in the Argos lunchroom across from the car stop. The counterman gave them a big welcome. Excepting for a small shriveled man crouched over a cup of java, they were the only customers. Seeing one of their people sitting there, dressed for July in a hand-me-down long-gone linen coat, made them want to do something. Sippie invited him to chili . . . He said, "Thanks, don't mind if I do."

The chili was going down hot and fine. The door opened

hard and mean. Three burly cops. Heavy, evil cracker cops stomped in bringing the chill with them.

"Hello, Charlie," they said to the owner. "Stan' up nahgers. Git back agin the wall!" Real rough.

Sippie, Monk and Baby understood. But first to jump was their friend.

"What you, a smart nahger?" Officer Hog Maw was hollering at frozen me. Thawed me out, and I got up, too.

Sippie wasn't waiting: "We's all right, officer; we's from de Institute." He was putting on a real down home accent for the damn crackers.

"What you good nahger boys doing out. Where's yo home boy?" Boy: me, me: boy. "Cleveland, sir." A big joke.

"Well, looka hyare! A nahger boy from up no'th." He noticed the elderly man. "Well, goddam! What de hell you doin' in hyare boy? Ain't you John Paul Jones?"

"Henry Johnson, please sah," the little man said.

Here it comes. Hog Maw moved hard.

"Git de hell—! Come on run! Run nahger!" Mr. Johnson staggered out, booted through the door by a pair of size fourteens. "Catch yo black ass on this side a town agin! Ah'll whip yo haid to a blood puddin'."

That was back there where a mule cost more than a colored man.

Here, right now, Jay heard the coarse screeching of the Matford's brake bands. They were descending. Carlus was busy with a sheaf of official papers. Soon the highway reached sea level and was absorbed into the narrow streets of Quixols.

They parked along the promenade bordering the sheltered harbor. Carlus pointed across the transparent crystal blue air; towards land's end, his finger remained fixed. "S'Agaro." The series of stucco chalets with red tile roofs were strung like a shell necklace along the high cliff.

As they took a side road to S'Agaro, Carlus said simply, "There are a few here who will return to Barcelona in the *camion*."

The dining room was packed to capacity. As Carlus, Jay and the chauffeur entered the large barn-like room an uproar of male voices and food sounds greeted them. Red banners were hung around the room:

Viva El Glorioso Nombre De Las Brigadas!
Viva La Victoria Definitiva!
Luchar Y Resistir!

Carlus led them at a slow pace past the closely arranged tables of eating men. Their presence was discovered and a sudden deafening silence exploded in the room. In the wake of its echo the only sound: three pairs of boots on the bare wooden floor.

Far back against the wall came a single rasping voice: *"Permiso?"* Carlus did not break his slow sedate stride. Still the silence.

Again the voice. Rasping and anguished: *"Permiso?"*

The hall reacted violently. The silence got sharp as a knife made in Albacete. Carlus continued to walk past the rows of graven men. Abruptly he changed his mind. He slowly mounted an empty chair and raised his right fist:

"Camaradas," he said softly. Then the small body arched like a bantam rooster's. *"Salud! camaradas!"* he shouted.

From his audience came the sullen response, almost a groan, *"Salud."* After a pause, Carlus continued translating for himself into French, German, English, and Russian for the Slav section.

"Permiso. Did I bring the *Permiso?* We in Barcelona have not received them from Paris. Spain's *Frente Popular* government has given you consent. The French government has not deigned to keep *its* promises. This you must believe. There are liars and rumor-mongers among you whispering like hissing snakes: 'They do not let you go home those bureaucrats in Barcelona!' Why? They do not know! but it is the truth they say. "See, are we not still here?" Or they hiss the terrible lie of disunity: 'The English, French, and Americans could go home tomorrow—if it were not for the others from the fascist countries.'

"Liars! Saboteurs! Silence them. You are not children. Read the news from Europe. The problem is more complex. You must understand Europe and America need you—the leading anti-fascists of the world. Comrade Marty, and the *Front Populaire* is doing everything to move the government on your behalf. Evacuation will come. But until that day you have much work to accomplish in S'Agaro. Some of the trouble here we could expect. But much is unworthy coming from veterans of the *Brigadas*. Those who are responsible are known. We know what has to be done. Heroic fighters against fascism! rally to the program which will be presented to you. *Y nada mas.*"

When the three men arrived at the table shared by *Comandante* Fredericka and her staff, Carlus introduced Jay as the new commissar. There was a brief flutter of surprise. Only the *Comandante's* face remained immobile. Her blue eyes, framed with colorless lashes, gave her the deceptive appearance of being blind. The three men joined the staff and had a quick lunch.

Jay watched the Renault and *camion* with its return load pull away. They were leaving him with a hell of a job, and for the first time in Spain he was lonely, stalled. It was time to plunge. Yet, he felt as useless as a Maxim without a firing pin. Since Murcia he had hoped for work in another hospital. Then why the sinking stomach, this lassitude? He refused to believe it was fear. Murcia, before Minkow, had been as disorganized. He recalled Jarama in February and March. . . . Was it because of last night? Was it going to be true? Should he have stayed home in the Stock Yards and worked? An elderly Polish *camarada* walked up and saluted.

"*Camarada* Commissar, please ask Barcelona for my *carte d'identité*. It must be in the *Jefatura*. . . ." Here and now—this was his work.

Word spread among the men once hospitalized at Murcia. The new *politico* was one of *Comandante* Minkow's cadres. The remainder of the afternoon there was a steady stream of these men. Jay sat in the office of the commissariat and listened to them all.

They told of bad medical organization, the lack of reading material, the tobacco shortage. But no one complained directly about the evacuation. Late in the afternoon, a young English nurse asked that something be done about the political isolation of the hospital personnel from the men. One *camarada* complained bitterly about sanitary conditions in the hospital wards and the filthy condition of the grounds. All agreed to organize squads in the chalets to dig *refugios*.

During supper Jay reviewed the past hours. Again, the old familiar story of the Brigade, the *activistas* are always there. All they ever need is leadership they can believe in.

He left the dining hall with Ernie, a Californian, whose fluent German made him invaluable for work with the German group. A slender gray-haired woman in a nurse's uniform stood waiting for Jay. When the American walked away, she introduced herself. "I am Comrade Mary." She knew his name. "What can I help you with?" he asked.

"Well, it isn't for me," she said, "it is for a comrade in Villa 13. He heard about you and wants to see you."

"What is his name?" Jay took out a notebook.

"I don't remember his full name but we call him Comrade Willie." Jay promised to visit all the Villas soon. Mary hesitated. "Yes, Comrade Mary?"

"Well," she said shyly, "I do hope you see him soon." Again he promised.

During the next several days he didn't get around to the Villas. He did, with the aid of the *responsables* from the various language groups, get the *refugios* started. The hard red Catalan soil was next in kin to shale; digging into it would have been bitter even for the healthy.

The fourth morning, Mary approached him. Had he forgotten Villa 13? Every day Willie asks for the commissar. Jay said as a matter of fact he intended to visit all the Villas the next day. Again she seemed to be withholding something. "What's up, Mary?"

"Well, eh . . . a . . . perhaps I should tell you he is a colored man. . . ."

"Colored?" Jay looked at her for a long moment. His face

296

clouded up. He was aware that time was overdue for his visit to the bedridden. But why did she feel he should go to a colored comrade sooner than the others?

Part of her reason became clear when she said, "He is quite ill. The doctors think he is dying. Terrible tuberculosis."

"I'll go now," Jay said quietly. She seemed gratified.

Villa 13 was perched on a promontory high above the sea. Jay imagined a middle class family summering in this Catalan "Salt Box." Inside he formed an image: sickness. The smell of illness permeated the air of the low ceilinged room. Empty cots lined the walls. He looked for Willie. He could hear him. From the upper floors came a distant harsh barking. All he had to do was follow the sound.

Jay climbed up three flights of narrow steps.

The room was in a cold grey shadow, there was no sun shining into the small deep casement windows. One bed was against the far wall. "Comrade Williams?"

A hoarse voice answered, "Hello, home."

The old familiar name made Jay feel real beat. He thought, standing there looking at him, "Home." Not *Salud*, but for the first time in a long spell, "Home."

"Hello, homey."

"I'm here," answered the man in the cool grey shadow. "Come in, man. I've been wanting to see you."

"I know, home," Jay explained apologetically, "but you know I'm new up here and there's a gang of work. I had to straighten out a few deals. You know how it is."

"Come on, man, grab a chair and sit awhile."

Jay looked at the ill man. His face was as deeply grained and worn as the handle of a shovel used in a silica pit. He must have been a big man once. The grey blanket drawn up to his ashen brown face showed the wasted outline of a large frame.

"Glad you got here in time. Did the steps beat you?"

"No."

"They have to put me away up here. The comrades downstairs just did get through the war. They can't see chancing

297

nothing now. Those boys want to get out bad, don't they?"

"So they tell me, but do you mind being way up here alone?"

"It ain't bad. I might as well be up high now cause they tell me it's low where I'm going," he chuckled.

"What's your story," Jay said. "In a couple of weeks you'll be riding in a lower berth on your way back to the States and a good sanitorium."

"Not me," he began to cough again, a spiteful thorax-wracking spasm. When he quieted down, he tried to smile. Then he repeated, "Not me. I've been in Spain 700 calendar days. From now on I will not and I won't. Will not worry about home; won't fool myself 'bout getting there.

"I'm home."

"How did you get—get hurt?" Jay felt awkward about the question.

"To hell with all that, home. I didn't call you up here to talk about such things. But I know how I brought it on. I was up at Teruel driving a Division truck. Snow, wet, sleeping out, caught me a cough. . . ."

"Why didn't you climb down and see a doctor?"

"Why? I'll tell you what happened. When the hell cooled down a little I figured reporting sick. Could a used a bath and bed. I got down to the evacuation hospital. I saw some of the comrades from the XVth who got their feet froze up in the trenches. Did you know David Stein or Fred Mowbray? I come across the mountains with both of them.

"First time I ever saw frozen feet. David was laying there waiting to go somewheres for an amputation. He didn't tell me. A nurse let me in on it. Now what in the hell is a chest cold when you see good people. . . ."

"I get what you mean," Jay didn't know what else to say.

"I never been hit. But a bullet can't be worse," Comrade Williams was breathing more regularly now. "Back home," he continued, "I never buddied around with white people. But when we got to the mountains and they paired us up in deuces for that long walk, they didn't pick us by matching color. I

298

guess I would a got to know white people back home. But it happened quick here in Spain. When you eat, sleep and take the same beatings with somebody, you get to know them."

Jay remembered. "I wish you were with me my last night in Barcelona. Met one of our people from home. A big big shot. Come to see what it's all about. We had quite a session about colored matters. He asked me how many of our folks were over here in the Republican army. I gave him a number."

" 'Well, tell me two things,' young man,' " Jay was unconsciously imitating the ministerial manners of the man. " 'First, how many of you went or tried to go to Ethiopia; second, what would have happened if Ethiopia had had some of this help and enthusiasm?' "

"What did you tell that skull?"

"Well, you know, man, he was a guest. But I tried to straighten him out. I told him the invasion of Ethiopia hit me harder than the news in July '36 from Madrid. Hell, I didn't have enough 'jack' to hide in my mouth. I couldn't get from State Street and 47th to South Chicago if somebody told me I'd find a bag of gold out there. I helped picket the Italian Consulate on Michigan Blvd. We had a protest parade out South. The cops broke it up and put some fine people in the hospital."

Jay had hit something in the memory of the sick man. "Ethiopia," he said. "I wanted to go to Ethiopia and fight Mussolini. Couldn't get there. I guess your pal didn't know they wasn't running boats from West Street. I was around New York there on the PWA raking grass seeds and listening to them nights at the corner meetings talking about what we got to do about our blood brothers. I heard them. I got to Spain. This ain't Ethiopia, but it'll do."

"I know what you mean. Well, I told him Spain was the only way I could answer for Addis Ababa! I tried to tell what it meant to us Negroes in the original Lincolns. Being part of the first mixed American Battalion of black and white men to go into battle together. Told him that if a black man had it in Spain the comrades here could and would use it."

"Are you telling me? Look at you. What did he say to that?"

"This time he capped me. 'Yes,' he said rearing back, 'we've read about the Negro who became a commander and others in responsible posts. But tell me, don't you think,' his big comfortable face broke into a slick smile, 'aside from the little you can contribute, that you have found personal salvation, not a universal one?' Whatever the hell that means. He said our people were still suffering at home and will be when we get back. Said that most of our people didn't even know we were here. Said our place, if we had ability, was back there."

"Man," Willie said, "he's talking Jim Crow. And he'll go right back there and eat crow. If nothing else happened to the American Negro, for once some of us learned to be men in a place where there ain't a speck of Jim Crow."

"That's it!" Jay said. "If it did show its head—it got stomped damned quick."

"Yes, and ain't I got a brother in the Army back home and ain't he Jim Crowed as possible. If you look at my papers you see they say, William Williams. Country: North America. Nationality: North American. That's the last time, and I could say the first time, a piece of paper called me anything but 'colored,' 'black,' 'Negro,' or just plain mean: 'nigger.' If I find my deep six here, could I do better? When you get back and somebody asks about me, Willie Willie? Buried some place where white and black march, eat, sleep, fight and love, side by side." He seemed to be resting. "Tell them I didn't die on Welfare Island."

"You know something, Comrade Williams, I'm thirty years old. The first time in my natural life I ever sat down in the dining room of a big hotel with the rest of the guests was here in Spain. That's not much, but it's more than ever happened to me back home."

"My deep six will be dug here," said Williams, "but you and the others will go back some day. You and the white comrades will take all you learned and give those crackers hell." His cough came up out of his throat. The long ebony hand held a stained handkerchief to stifle the eruption.

300

"We'll *all* go back and give 'em hell. They'll never dig a deep six here for you, daddy," Jay tried to pass over the spell. "When I came here I used to tell 'em all, I come with nothing to lose but them goddam chains we've been wearing from the day our mommers dropped us. I know we ain't going back and put them on again. No, daddy, when that train starts up the north road to Port Bou it'll be taking you home first."

"You say the road north, huh? I took a road north once. I was in a big hurry, too, just like some of the comrades here in S'Agaro. A different reason, of course, I was trying to get the hell out of Georgia before some cracker shot the hell out of me. I was running but when I got north, I found those crackers waiting for me."

The nurse came up the steps with warm milk. She gave him a powder dissolved in water. She said it would quiet his cough.

After the milk and the medicine, and obviously under the influence of the warm exchange which he had been looking forward to intently since he heard the gossip around Jay's arrival, Williams became expansive. They talked about Spain, where each had been, what they had seen, of the dead and the living. He questioned Jay about many of the white comrades he had come to know on the various fronts. They talked about food, and about what they liked to drink. Williams talked about a woman, his wife, who died the year before he came to Spain, and about the wonderful women of Spain. Jay listened. As the sick man talked on, Jay could feel an expanding sense of relief replacing his four day depression.

"Talking about women, reminds me," Comrade Williams said suddenly, "I'd like you to read a letter from my sister in Georgia." He sounded proud. "You know, all my folks sharecrop cotton. Not my sister. She got to Normal School somehow, and got to be a teacher.

Sylvania, Ga.

Dear Brother Willie,

We received your letter. And I know I do not have to tell you how surprised everybody was when I read it to the family.

We are all glad to hear that you got work, even if it is so far from home. You did not say much in your letter about what you are doing. But whatever it is I hope and trust it is honest. Save your money, brother, for you will need it when you return. Things are still bad everywhere. Cotton crop still does not bring a price to those who farm it, and everybody owes the Commissary. And I hear things are not any better up north. No need my telling you to behave, you always did that. Before I close I would like to say if you can send mama a little something it would sure help out. . . .

A deep agonized roar shattered the room's quietude. At first it seemed to come up from the sea. It was like the cry of some mythological sea monster in distress.

Jay leaped to the window. Far below, the Mediterranean was at peace, playfully tossing small white-capped waves against the narrow strip of pebbled beach. Down the side of steep rock a tenacious mountain pine's heavily waxed needles glistened brilliantly in the morning sun.

The roar settled into a repetitious mournful moaning. It was coming from Quixols. An air raid! Jay thought appalled. Noonday raid! Carlus said so, Carlus said so, he droned, as he ran stumbling and falling down the narrow funnel of the staircase. Had he shouted to the nurse on the way out to get Williams downstairs? Later he couldn't recall clearly.

The sun blinded him as he ran. A quarter mile, it was a quarter of a thousand miles to the dining hall. As he raced, the morning space so quiet moments before became glutted with the ominous drone of tripled motors. Once heard, never forgotten—Savoias from Mallorca.

As his leaden feet fought the distance, his eyes helplessly devoured the unending strip of red road over which he ran. At first he was a wingless fly scrambling along a ragged length of red ribbon, powerless against the fingers about to squash it. At first. Then the training of the past months and years welled up to command his flashing thoughts. This was no ribbon! *This was his single track!* Whatever happened now—he was way back beyond the hour of that Barcelona reception. Now, one demanding need: get to the men assembled for lunch!

Jay was too late. They were overhead. He heard the first two begin their careening, eerie, screaming descent. He fell face forward into a ditch. The shaking earth made him know that they were big ones. The shrill tinny howling of incendiaries followed in rapid succession. Down in the direction of Quixols an anti-aircraft gun began to crack rapidly. Before the motors' beat faded into the distance, leaving a corpse-like silence behind, he was up running down the road sobbing with anxiety, "Jesus, Jesus, I'm late, too late."

From the hill above the dining hall he could see the men climbing out of partially dug *refugios*. Some were returning slowly from the fields around the building. Jay couldn't see any damage, there were no bomb craters in sight. A reprieve. The sensation of relief made him want to shout.

A Canadian from the XIIIth, using his new crutches with difficulty, hobbled up to meet him. Jay had known him in the hospitals at Murcia. He'd lost his leg at Huesca.

"*Salud*, Comrade Jay," he was trembling with emotion, "where are those damn *refugios*. If the bastards weren't such lousy marksmen there would have been hell around here! Who's sabotaging the *refugios?*"

"No one now, Paul," Jay forced reassurance into his voice. "Did any land nearby?" The Canadian pointed unsteadily with his crutch to a garden across from the base.

"I'm going over there," Jay said. "Go have your dinner."

"I'll come with you." As they walked toward the field the Canadian spoke. "I want to volunteer to work on the shelters. I won't be able to do much. But I'll try to learn to use a shovel again."

"That's what every man able to walk has to say and do," Jay answered. "All the wounded comrades must learn all over again. Paul, enough time has been lost here in S'Agaro. This is the place to start rebuilding. You'll need to use more than a shovel but that's a good start. Help get the chalets mobilized.

Speak to your political *responsable,* he'll need you."

Jay helped Paul across a shallow ditch into the garden. The bomb's crater had destroyed the geometric orderliness of the planted rows. Paul bent awkwardly and picked up the shattered handle of a hoe. The other part was near the one who had been working with it. A Catalan *campesina* lay crumpled in a small pitiful heap close to the edge of the crater. There was a jagged line of death where the coarse grey hair grew back from the forehead. Jay absent-mindedly picked up the other part of the hoe. The two men stood silently, each busy with his own thoughts. Jay reflected: Where can you go on this earth where people work the land, that you cannot find a hoe?

"Come, Paul. I'll send the ambulance." Paul was rubbing his stump and crying. "Paul," Jay said gently, "the bastards will get what's coming to them yet."

"I know, but look at me. How much good will I be able to do about it when I get back home?"

"There are many ways to fight. You'll find your place along with the others," Jay said insistently.

"Come on, Paul, I'm going to call a meeting right after lunch. I want you to speak. . . ."

Jay rubbed a clod of clinging dirt from the blade of the hoe and remembered: ". . . *cotton crop still does not bring a price to those who farm it . . . if you can send mama a little something it would sure help out. . . .*"

The New Offensive, Elbro, 1938

MARGOT HEINEMANN

This new offensive drugs our old despair,
Though, distant from the battle-line,
We miss that grave indifference to fear
That has so often now saved Spain.

Let fools and children dream that victory
Drifts lightly on the waves of chance,
And all that riveted and smooth-tooled army
Should melt before this proud advance.

Not this war's weathercock, brave when things go well,
Afraid to think of a retreat,
By turns all singing and all sorrowful:
We've not to watch, but win this fight.

Offensives must be paid for like defeats,
And cost as dear before they end.
Already the first counter-raids
Take no positions but they kill our friends.

A miracle is not what we can hope for
To end this war we vainly hate.
We shan't just read it in the evening paper
And have a drink to celebrate.

For two long years now when you sighed for peace
To slip from heaven as an angel drops,
You were confronted with your own sad face,
And once again time holds the mirror up.

It was not a few fields they fought to gain,
But months and maybe years of war.
Time's on their side: by time we mean
The heirs of time they thought worth dying for.

This narrow ridge of time their valor won,
Time for us to unite, time to discover
This new offensive is your life and mine,
One nation cannot save the world for ever.

From POEMS FOR SPAIN

Si me quieres escribir
Ya sabes me paradero
En el frente de Gandesa
Primera linea de fuego . . .

Hill 666   For Aaron Lopoff, who died there

ALVAH BESSIE

THERE WAS STILL some light in the sky as we moved out of the rest-camp under the olive trees, along the narrow trail leading over the low hills toward Gandesa. We followed this trail for quite a time, then emerged onto a well-travelled highway. Ahead, muffled by distance, was the sound of artillery in the night—always more terrifying than it is by day, though less effective. We marched, in all, for twelve kilometers, reaching and passing through the small town of Pinell, and then the road wound steeply uphill, bounded on one side by a precipitous gorge out of which came the sudden sickly smell of the dead, and on the other by towering peaks and crags that would have been fantastic even in the day-time. There was one rock-peak shaped like the prow of a great ocean liner, steep and sheared to a point, that menaced the road with its bulk and its shadow, and the men toiling up the grade. Then we turned off the main road onto a goat-path that led into the hills.

For two and a half hours we bent to the forty-degree angle, twisting and turning, slipping and stumbling up the almost impassable way. There was one thought in our minds: it's going to be hell getting food, water and munitions up this hill; it's going to be tough for the wounded; it would all have to be done by mules, and mules were only flesh and blood. There was a moon, and the smell of burnt wood; half-way up the mountain, the sudden, incongruous sight of a soldier sitting on a rock by the path (it was past three a.m.), reading a letter as though it were the last chance he would have in the world to read that letter. It was unreal. And as we progressed up the slippery broken stone the unreality augmented it until it all seemed part of a bad dream. For God never made a more desolate stretch of territory, and man never contributed more to its further desolation. We sweated and groaned under the weight of our equipment, our guns. Rock walls bordered the goat-trail that led to the wind-torn summits, and near the crest we came upon terrain that had been fought over, lost and recaptured by the famous XIth Division, Lister's men. Here they had withstood heavy shelling; here the Fascist planes had rained incendiary bombs and, temporarily, driven our men off. It looked like a landscape on the moon—tumbled, crumbled rock, black and slippery; burnt-off shrubbery that caught our trouser-legs and tripped us up. We slipped and fell, stumbled and cursed; there was a bitter wind and the smell of wood-smoke.

Even before dawn it was possible to see that there was no cover here; there were no trees; there were no bushes; there were no natural cavities in the rock; the earth itself was stone—you could not dig in it. And there were no fortifications facing the enemy. Lister's men had done the best they could; they had scraped shallow trenches into the crest of the hill, and they had erected stone parapets topped with a few sandbags. These were the lines we had to hold, and they were important for if the enemy could retake this hill (number 666 on our military maps), and hold it, he could dominate our main bridgehead at Mora and the entire sector would become untenable. There is no way to understand why the Lincoln Battalion, in fighting strength the weakest in the XVth Brigade, had been detailed to hold this position, but these things sometimes happen.

Before dawn, Aaron Lopoff, our company commander, established the men in the lines; moved the *plana mayor* back down the central crest about a hundred meters, against a relatively low stone bluff. Here the company staff was to be in the direct line of fire, and here it was to stay, for there was no other place to put it. The position was heart-breaking; there was no food, no water on the hill, and if we could escape the fire, there would be the sun. Sam Spiller, Antonio Antón, Rafael the youngster whose clipped head looked like a cocoanut, the other runners and the observers, Virgili and Albareda, the barber Angel, the *furiel,* Lara, the American secretary Curtis and the Spanish secretary, Sans, the stretcher-bearers and the *practicante,* Lee got to work constructing what looked like modern bathtubs, cradles of loose stone against the wall of the low cliff. And when the dawn came we climbed into them with the field-telephone and the Battalion telephonist detailed to us. Aaron went up into the lines, where the men were already cursing the impossible fortifications and the lack of cover against anything the Fascists cared to throw at us.

With the dawn we could really see what we had to work with; a bare mountainside thrust into the empty sky, facing a concealed enemy slightly below. Gandesa was a kilometer or so below us. Corbera was to the right of the Battalion sector, on the road below; Pinell was behind us and to the left. On our left flank was the Canadian Battalion, the Mac-Paps; behind us somewhere were the British, in reserve. On our right flank there was nothing but the steep slope of the hills, falling away to the valley through which the road ran to Gandesa. The mountainside was pitted with shell-holes, strewn with splinters and casings. (We used some of the larger pieces of shrapnel to construct our parapets.) The back side of our hill was folded; our company staff was on one grade; no men were stationed on the other but stretcher-bearers were to pass across the opposite slope on their way toward the *sanidad* behind the right-hand hill.

All day we waited in the heat; there was no water. Then some water came up—water disinfected with iodine and mixed with Spanish cognac; it was warm to drink and rotten to the taste. A squadron of Fascist planes came over and unloaded upon the Mac-Paps, on our left. We waited patiently for our turn, but they ignored us.

They came and they ignored us, but Curtis would say, "Christ, here they come! Christ, we're gonna get it now!" To which we said nothing.

"This is a hell of a place to be," he said.

"You're right." He was lying low in the "bathtub" next to mine, with the telephonist.

"What?"

"I said, You're right."

"This is a hell of a spot—*look* at 'em!" he said. "Thirty-two of 'em. Jesus, are we gonna get it now!"

"Shut up!"

"Why?" he said. "I didn't say anything. I was just saying look how many there are—"

"We can count."

"Well, I didn't mean anything; I was just saying—Holy Christ!" he said.

There was a meeting of company commanders going on, back of the hill at the *estado-mayor,* and we lay baking in the unbroken sun, our mouths dry with the heat, the thirst, the tension. Aaron finally came back, near dusk, with Archie Brown the new commissar and Dick Rusciano, and he told us an attack would be made that night to capture an isolated peak of our hill that was held by the enemy. "It'll be a cinch," he said. "A handful of men could do it." He stayed up in the line that night, sending occasional messages to me, telling me to stay near the telephone and send one of the runners when an order came. I lay in the little niche we had constructed for him, hard as only rock can be hard, waiting. Late that night there was a flurry of hand grenades and machine-gun fire, which lasted ten or fifteen minutes, but no order came down from the line, and I was nailed there anyhow. In the morning we were told that our Company 4 had captured the isolated point without firing a shot, without a casualty; there had been nobody there when they arrived, but the Fascists on other hills, thinking we were attacking, had cut loose with hundreds of grenades, mortars and even artillery, and then later sang in triumph at having repulsed our attack!

Word therefore came that that day or the next one our Battalion, Brigade and Division were attacking in force, our particular objective the capture of a series of hills to the south of Gandesa. There was fog early that morning, but before noon the sun began to burn it up and the sound of airplanes filled the air. All the night before food had been coming up at intervals of an hour, and we woke the men each time it arrived; there was coffee (fairly warm), a sort of vegetable imitation hamburger cooked in olive oil, sardines, bread, fruit, cookies and wine. Some mail came too, with cigarettes from Carnovsky and Brand of the Group Theater, and from my flying club. We looked at ourselves in the morning; we were black from head to foot, from scrambling among burnt rocks and the shrubbery.

"Christ!" said Curtis. "Here they come!"

At three we moved up, by order, to the back side of the main crest, where we were to wait till the attack began. Artillery support and aviation had been promised, and now there were about three hundred men sitting and lying on that slope, in plain sight of the sky, waiting. We sat, our backs to the hill, looking down the long *barranco* that led, eventually, to the road, and waiting. We streamed with sweat and lay snuggled among the hot broken rocks, flattening ourselves to the earth as much as possible. We did not talk much; some men ate their sardines and bread, others merely stared at their toes. Promptly at three-thirty our artillery awoke, and we enjoyed the sound of it coming over our heads tearing through the air like ripping silk. The sound tapered off and then, from the distance, came the report of the explosions, one-two-three. Shell after shell came over; no heavy barrage, but enough to keep them busy and uncomfortable. Then the shelling stopped and all of five of our *Chatos* appeared over the lines, diving across us and opening their machine-guns at the Fascist entrenchments across the way. It was good to see them, though they were so few, but they stayed for only about five minutes, and then they too were gone. No order came, and so we merely sat. I looked at Nat Gross, who was lying next to me, his Czech machine-gun wrapped in a piece of blanket. The lines in his hard young face seemed deeper, harder than usual, but he smiled. "This is a hell of a way from Wall Street," he said.

Then he said, "I knew it," for the Fascist artillery, stung and annoyed by us, had opened up in its turn, and was throwing its stuff over our lines. At first it was far over, and we watched the shells with a speculative interest, bursting far below us down the mountain side. "That's where the British are, in reserve," said Nat, and we both laughed. We flattened, perhaps unconsciously, a little closer to the broken rock on which we were lying, and we found a tin of sardines and began to eat it. But even as we concentrated on the food, we were aware of the fact that the Fascists had lifted their guns (there was an observation plane far above us) and we watched, since we had not been told to move, as the shell bursts came closer to us, crawling slowly up the slopes. We looked around for a runner, who should have come up about that time and told us to scatter, but no runner was in sight. We looked around at the hundreds of other men, calmly lying there as the fire crept slowly back up the mountainside toward us; they did not move, they were cleaning their guns or eating or lying on their sides talking, or trying to catch a few winks of sleep. It was getting too close for comfort, and now we were as flat as we could be. They were falling a few hundred meters below us; I was watching two men carrying a stretcher (it was empty); I just happened to be watching them, and then they were not there. The shrapnel whined viciously over our heads, slapping against the stone of the hillside, whirring away into the middle distance. I heard a brief conversation between two men I knew belonged to the Mac-Paps (I don't know what they were doing in our lines).

"Jim's gone," one said.

"How?"

"Bumped himself off; I tried to take his gun away."

"Why?"

"His leg was off; he said, 'Kill me,' but I couldn't, so he reached for his pistol."

"That's shit," the other said.

All the time we expected their planes; we listened for them, but they did not come. We could not understand why they did not come, for the enemy must have known by our barrage, by our planes, that we were planning an attack; they must have known we were lying there naked on the hillside, exposed to anything that came along. But no planes came, and it was getting dark, and no word came from the lines, from the Battalion headquarters. And so we stayed there.

Then Aaron sent Antonio for me, and I crawled up onto the crest of the hill. "Get in here, Poppa," Aaron said from behind the parapets, and I crawled over and dropped in, where the men were crowded against each other, arm to arm, waiting. "Listen," he said. "We're going over when it gets dark. We didn't take that point last night; we're going to take it tonight."

"What do you want me to do?"

"Stay here with Curtis and Sans, and when we take the point, come over with ammo."

"How will we know when you've taken it?"

"Well, it will be quiet for awhile, then you'll hear a lot of hand grenades and rifles going off, and a lot of yelling, and when it quiets down, come over."

"I'd better go with you, hadn't I?"

"You'd better stay here; I won't need you. I'll take Sam and Rafael. There won't be anything to the job." He was smiling, standing in the trench, his head about level with the stone parapets. Rafael, the young runner, was sitting up on the parapet, firing a rifle, grinning like a Cheshire cat. "Get down from there, you dope," said Aaron, and pulled his leg. The shelling had died down with the growing dark, and only a few rifle bullets were coming over now and then.

Aaron took the rifle from Rafael, and climbing halfway up the parapet, began to fire. He looked back at me, and said, grinning, "It's so long since I've had a rifle in my hands, I've forgotten what it feels like." He smiled, taking careful aim with his Mauser, and fired conscientiously for a time. He was a good shot; I remembered from the practice maneuvers, when he had always taken his place in the line, either with a rifle or a light machine-gun. He looked younger than ever, younger than his twenty-four

313

years, standing there, firing over the parapet. The men near by stood or crouched in the shallow trench, watching him, smiling....

. . . The dark forms moved silently over the parapets into the darkness, moving off to the right into the greater darkness that lay in the pocket between our hill and the little point that was to be taken; and for a long time Curtis and Sans and I kept our heads raised above the stones and watched and listened. The silence was absolute; it was suspicious. We felt that either they did not know what we were doing, or they knew too well. It was difficult to breathe, to swallow. It was difficult to watch, for there was nothing to see, and we strained our ears with listening. We crouched in the trench; then we climbed out and began to assemble ammo boxes, carrying them by their handles to a central point, from which it would be easy to bring them to the men.

For fifteen minutes it was absolutely silent, and we wondered how our men could move so quietly; then it began. Curtis ducked behind the stones, but Ramón Sans and I watched (I could see his scholarly face with the horn-rimmed spectacles, occasionally lit by the flashing lights)—in the distance, toward the point, there was noise; the spectacular pink roman-candles of the hand grenades going off; the hysterical chatter of the machine-guns going full blast, taken by surprise, confused shouting and yelling. Then it stopped. "Do you think we have the hill?" I asked, and Ramón said, "I don't know." Then it started again, and the echoes multiplied and reverberated among the peaks; it seemed miles away, though it was only a few hundred meters at best. There would be a sudden, heavy explosion and a bright flower-pot of bursting flame as a mortar exploded; silence, the shouting and the subdued murmur; a few bullets cracked near by and it was quiet. Alternately, every few minutes, this went on, then silence. Then it was silent for a long time and suddenly we were aware that there were men near us, coming by us silently, not very many men at first, but soon more and more of them, filling the emptiness around us with heavy breathing. Some one was sobbing. Some one said, "Help me, I'm wounded."

Antonio was in front of me, he saluted and said, "*La pistola del Comandante*," and thrust the automatic into my hand. I grasped it; it was sticky, and I held it up and could see it was wet with something. "*El Comandante?*" I said, but Antonio was gone, and Sam was in front of me, breathing rapidly.

"Aaron's hurt," he said. "In the head. It's nothing. Don't get excited; take it easy; he'll be all right."

"Are you sure? Where is he?"

"They took him out; they got him out. Did you get his pistol? He said to give it to you to keep."

"Yes."

"Christ it was shit up there," the kid said. "They had machine-guns; they had barbed wire; why didn't they tell us they had barbed wire? How were we to know they had barbed wire?—" He was out of breath.

"Where's Dick? Where's Archie?"

"I don't know. They wouldn't go ahead; they lay down in the woods—"

"Who?"

"Who do you think? The same guys; the bastards, the cowards."

I could see in the pale light that filtered from behind the streaming clouds that he was crying. I remembered that Aaron had told me about that day on the first hill, when Sam had finally found him, after thinking him lost in the attack, and had become hysterical.

"Take it easy," I said.

"Aaron's all right," he said. "I helped him walk a little way back. Did we take the hill? he said; I told him Yes; How's the company? he said; I told him Fine. He'll be all right," he said. "*He'll be all right.*"

"Go lie down," I said. "Get some rest."

"Oh, Jesus," he said. "The bastards."

Dick appeared, and Archie, and we rounded up what men we could find and posted them in the line and behind the parapets. We distributed the hand grenades and the munitions as far as they would go, and sent back for more, in the event of a counter-attack. It was bitter cold and we lay on the bare rocks, waiting, waiting for what we did not know. They were singing over on their hills, a weird Moorish song that curdled your blood and made your spine run cold. We listened to them singing, and we watched the sudden moon come from behind the wet clouds, and then disappear again. The wind came up and blew the clouds away, and we lay strewn all over the hilltop like the dead, waiting. Seeing the men in these grotesque positions I remembered a play that I had seen, "Johnny Johnson," and it occurred to me that this was life imitating art again, or was it that the play had been so accurate a mirror of this life? I couldn't make up my mind.

Wolff was up on the hill with us, and Lamb and some of the Brigade staff, consulting in a sandbag dugout, lit with a candle, over maps and possibilities. He asked for a report, and we did the best we could; one known dead, fifteen known wounded, many missing, a rout and a retreat without orders; that was all we could determine. You couldn't find anyone in the dark anyhow. Stretcher-bearers had disappeared; the men were all mixed by squads and *pelotóns* and companies; the wrong companies had gone first, misunderstood the orders; the wrong information, or worse, no information at all as to the extent of the enemy fortifications. So we hung around and the British were brought up from reserve, and with all our men in position in the lines, the British went through just before dawn and attacked in turn, and the same thing happened to them. The Mac-Paps, who had come up to hold our positions when we jumped off, returned to their original position on the left flank; we returned to ours; the *plana mayor* of the company which was now commanded by Rusciano, retreated to its stone *refugios* alongside the cliff face, and dawn came up through the heavy fog.

Fog meant no airplanes, so we could relax. Yesterday they had been active all day, bombing Pinell behind us, Corbera and the road to Gandesa on our right, Mora and our lines of communication. We could see them from the hilltop, cruising slowly in formidable array and with damnable slowness over the terrain, sowing their seed up and down, back and forth over large square areas, and for hours the air was full of smoke and dust and trembling with the constant drumming of the explosive. Our "pom-pom" guns sniped at them pitiably. This is a long, light anti-aircraft gun that was fairly effective, but we had so few that they paid no attention to them. Seventy-five planes merely sailed with exasperating ease through their sparse fire; then when ten of ours appeared they had to run a gauntlet of fire that blackened the sky for hundreds of acres. It was heartbreaking, and you could thank France for that; you could thank England and its Non-Intervention Committee; you could thank Italy and Germany, and last but not least you could thank the good old U.S.A. and its "Neutrality" act, that permitted the sale of American-made munitions to Italy and Germany for transshipment to Franco.

By ten in the morning we could hear them, however, above the fog, and Curtis, flat in the next hole, said, "Here they come!" "Don't worry," I said, "they can't see through the fog," and so we remained silent and listened to them droning and droning overhead. Then I thought, Hurray, the bastards are lost and trying to find their way downstairs, and I began to hope passionately that they would misjudge their altitude and crash into one of the jagged peaks, but they kept on droning overhead, invisible to us through the heavy blanket of the fog, moving back and forth across the range, fading into the distance and returning. And then, suddenly, there was the familiar whistling and a load fell directly into the *barranco* behind the hill, across the way from us, and the earth rose under us and threw us off and we fell back again, our hands clasped over our heads, hearing the falling rocks and dirt, waiting to be hit, our ears ringing.

Later that day the ceiling was unlimited but there were no further planes; the afternoon grew deathly quiet and the heat grew intense, but nothing happened. No rifle fired; there was no shelling; no mortars came sailing in their high parabola over the hill. "*Qué pasa?*" I said to Ramón Sans, the intellectual secretary, and he said, correctly, *"Nada."* That was the end of our third day in that hole. Earlier there had been mail with cigarettes, and I had sent two of them in an envelope to Ed Rolfe, who I thought must be back from Barcelona now, with the Battalion *estado-mayor. Still here and in one piece,* I wrote, *Enclosed please find. Hope you are the same.* I could not say, For Christ's sake hurry up and get me out of this hole; for Christ's sake *do* something; Lister's men were here for twenty days and this is only the end of our third. . . .

. . . For a change there were plenty of cigarettes, that had come from my kids, from Carnovsky and Brand in London, from others, and I had them stuffed into the pockets of my leather jacket, my shirt (where they got soaked with sweat, but tasted just as good), everywhere. We were crouched in the shallow *refugios* alongside the cliff; I was lying on my back and Dick was catching a little sleep at my feet, with Archie behind him with Sans. It had just passed noon when they opened up, and from the start they had our range. We could count about seven batteries at work, all of them concentrated on our sector, that was no more than five hundred yards wide. They began coming over, and we stayed down; they came, you heard them from the start to the end, the three low harmless thumps of the faraway guns, then a brief silence, then a low, hissing, growing crescendo into a riffling whistle (a scream if they were coming close) and then a deafening crash that reverberated between the two slopes that enclosed the *barranco* behind the hill. We stuck our heads up to see where they had landed, saw the brown and white smoke drifting away, the rocks falling as though in slow motion, possibly a couple men running. Then they were coming again and we ducked again.

"That was close," Curtis said. "They've got us spotted."

He was in the next hole with the telephonist, Felix. I turned onto my back, saw Aaron's automatic pistol tucked between the two rocks where I had put it, still streaked with his dried blood. (Doc Simon had sent word that he would be all right.) I heard them coming again, and closed my eyes, put my arms

318

over my face and waited. You felt nothing at such moments except a tightening of the belly, and you drew up your legs instinctively and then it was all over. There were occasional duds; occasionally a shell whistling close overhead would suddenly lose its twirling motion and, turning end over end, go scuffling through the air making a noise like a small boy blowing air between his lips. You wanted to laugh when you heard those.

"Oh, Christ," said Curtis, "this is awful!"

"Shut up!"

"Why, what's the matter?"

"Nobody likes it any more than you do."

From where I was lying, if I lifted my head, I could see the built-up parapets of the other men in the *plana mayor*, the stretcher-bearers, the barber, the quartermaster Lara. When the shells were coming they were nowhere to be seen; after they had landed and the shrapnel had stopped screeching and smacking at the stone, they all sat up, sticking their heads over the parapet as though they were puppets in a Punch and Judy show. It was funny. Dick was crouched in front of me, with Archie behind him and Sans lying on his face the other way. "What about it?" Archie yelled, and Dick shouted, "What about what?" "We ought to be up in the line," the commissar said; then they both ducked and the thing went off and deafened us and the stones fell in on us from where the shrapnel and concussion had chipped away the cliff.

There was a terrific tearing smash and everything was black and a voice was screaming, screaming. I went out for a moment and came to, and put my hand on top of my head and looked at my hand, but there was no blood on it. It was difficult to see, the air was clogged with rock dust and smoke and the ringing was continuous and the voice kept screaming on a high note. Far away, I heard Dick say, "Who got it? You, Bess?" and I said, "I don't think so," and sat up. The screaming came from behind me, so I got up and looked, and there was Curtis, lying on his belly, his buttocks torn away, holding them with his hands, his face turned to me, dead white and powdered with rock dust, and his mouth open, his eyes looking at me, his mouth open screaming. I could not take my eyes away from his.

"Come on!" Archie shouted, and he and Dick ducked out and up the hill.

Felix lay behind Curtis, his legs bloody and his face still, and I climbed over the few stones that remained standing between us, and Felix said. "Take him first, he's worse." Curtis kept screaming although his mouth did not move, looking at me with his eyes wide open and staring, and I was saying, "Take it easy, take it easy, take it easy," and suddenly it was *good* to be moving, good to be doing something instead of just lying there waiting for something to happen. I yelled for the *practicante*, but he was in the lines; I yelled for a bandage, and was handed a small one-inch roll that was worthless. I called the stretcher-bearers, who came and we lifted Curtis out under the arms and knees (he was not screaming now) and they went away with him through the fire that was falling before us, behind us (Rafael was looking up over a near-by parapet, his mouth open), the noise was terrific and the shrapnel whining and slapping around.

Felix's legs were badly torn and his foot was broken to bits, the bones stuck through the torn leather of his shoes. I gave him a cigarette (like in the movies) and tried with my wet red hands to light it for him, succeeding after a time. Rafael threw over a canteen of wine, and he took a slug or two. There was a pool of rapidly congealing blood, like half-stiffened *Jello* on the floor of the *refugio*, and I threw a blanket over it, spread the other over Felix and climbed back into my own hole. Dick and Archie had gone, but Sans looked at me and asked for a cigarette, and we both lit them and laid low.

They were pounding the shallow lines on the hill-crest; with artillery and anti-tank shells they were hammering away from left to right and back again, and it hurt to watch; it hurt in much the same way that a sore knee hurts when you clumsily bang it again and again. "God damn the bastards," I said to myself. "God damn the lousy c—— s—— sons-of-bitches," but that didn't do much good. They hammered at the lines and the men ran out from behind the parapets, seeking shelter on the bare back of the hill; then they came back to the lines again. They pounded at the same place time and time again, and you would see forms that looked like moving-picture dummies rise slowly in the air and fall back again. You knew that they were men.

The telephone was dead; the telephonist had become unconscious, the cigarette dead between his thin white lips, and he moaned in his stupor, over and over and over. The blood on the earth stank in the heat, turning your stomach, and I moved to look at Sans. He was calmly smoking the butt I had given him, lying on his belly, facing me. He did not smile when I smiled at him. They were coming over all the time, on top of the little cliff, in front of us, behind, and I thought, it's only a question of time before another lands right in this place. I had sent a runner to headquarters for another telephonist; the *camilleros* had not yet returned, for they had to run the gauntlet of that fire with Curtis's dead weight (dead?), down the slope and up the opposite, around the hill to the *sanidad*, where the men must have been arriving every minute. I saw the little barber's head and little beard, and he saw me and said, "Bess-ee, this is a bad place."

"I know," I said.

"We ought to go some place else," he said. Then he ducked and when he reappeared I said, "*Chico*, this is the company command-post; *El Teniente* Rusciano needs us here."

"It's a bad place," he said, and then the shells came again, and I saw Lara, the middle-aged quartermaster, run out of his hole and down the hill. I grasped Aaron's pistol, expecting that his example would provoke a panic among the others in the hole, but they obeyed my order to get down and that was a relief, for I knew I could not have shot one of them for running away. I could not even have fired after one.

All day, hour after hour they kept it up. They covered our parapets and every inch of the back side of the hill. They wanted, by the sheer weight of their steel, to blow us off that hill. Hour in and out they kept it up, and the body was utterly exhausted and indifferent to conscious fear, but straining to the snapping point. There was sweat, and there was internal pain; the word "waiting" came to mean something more than it had meant before, for you were definitely waiting for them to find you and to finish you. It was impersonal; it had nothing to do with men or with machines; the steel and the noise that filled the air—they came from nowhere, but you knew they were directed at you by some agency with more than human guile. The boys in the trenches were hammered, their rock parapets smashed down; there were many wounded, many killed, many missing. There was no connection with the Battalion, and you twisted the handle of the field-set just the same, knowing that you would not get an answer. Planes came over, but they withheld their bombs, possibly because our lines were so close to theirs; you did not care. Time stood still—but absolutely. What do you think? What do you feel? Everything and nothing . . . invoking the names of your children, over and over, "Dan and Dave stick with me now, and all the days to come, stick with me now." And it was astonishing how you could not hold their image in your mind. Talking in a rational tone of voice to Ramón Sans, to Joe Riehl, the new telephonist who arrived a couple of hours after it started, but who could not go out to repair the line. Listening to him say, "Boy, I never knew before today what a good Catholic I was," you laughed, and he laughed with you. (He had been to Spain earlier, gone home and then returned.) Talking rationally, remaining where you were, when everything in you said, Run for your life and scream out loud!

The pauses were worse than the shelling, before and after, waiting for them to cool their guns. When they are dropping the mind is impersonal even if the body is not, but waiting for them to begin again. . . . A fly is attracted to your bloody hands and clothes; you shake it off. A louse is crawling in your groin and you think, At least you're safe, you louse, and laugh. Dry lips, rising gorge, sweat and shaking limbs. You look at your hands, filthy and covered with the blood of two men who have finally been taken where? you lie and insanely cover your face with your leather jacket when you hear them coming, as though it offered any protection. You throw it angrily from you, knowing yourself a fool, but grasp it again instinctively when the whistling is growing louder and your mind tells you *this* one will be close. Hour after hour, waiting for them to find you and finish you, waiting like a rat in a trap, chained to the command post by the commander's simple words, "I'll need you here." And chained by more—for you cannot run away from this struggle: it is everywhere; you could not look yourself in the face again. For six hours, no word from the Battalion, no connection, and then, coming through the fire there are two men, one of them bent with the weight of a spool of wire on his back, reeling it out across the bare *barranco*. Orders. You speak calmly, trying to keep your voice even and level. "What's happening up there?" "They're throwing the shit all around." "Keep a few men in the lines and let the others seek what cover they can find; the Mac-Paps are extending their lines toward your left flank; the British are coming up with reinforcements. In the event of an attack, put all the men back in the line; get up munitions now." That is Wolff's voice speaking, a young man who is not here.

It all seems very far away and meaningless although you know the meaning or you would not be there; there is no immediate reality in this. You can think of Times Square with all its cars and all its people, and the focus narrows down and you can see their faces, ordinary commonplace faces like the faces you have known all your life, like the faces of the Spanish men and women and children you have seen in the cities and the small towns and the country, who are waiting back of the lines now, maybe reading a newspaper: Our forces in the Sector of X . . . repulsed, with heavy casualties, a violent enemy attack and withdrew to predetermined positions on Hill Z. . . . And what does that mean, tell me, do you know? Faces. Do they care about us over there? and do they even think of us with love? The women and the children and the men; do they know we are so far away from them and dying for them? Do they know this is *their* struggle too? There is no connection between the fact of war and people; not when you are in it. It seems to be something taking place upon another, insulated plane of existence that does not, while you live it, touch the people whom it really touches. You think of love.

Yes, you can think of love. The love you have never had and could not give; the love that does not need words to create itself, but exists as a bond between the man and the woman who can look at each other and say inside their minds, I love and I am loved. The body is precious to you; the body wants to live. It wants to live to touch again those tender parts of a woman's body that are so much of woman (her symbol and her essence), those parts you only need to touch so lightly with your hand to know again that you are a man and she is a woman and that there *is* a meaning to the world and to the life we try to live, but which they are trying to steal from us. For it is love alone that can, for even a moment of our time, give you the illusion that you are not alone, penetrate your loneliness and separate it from you for that moment. And you are afraid that you will die without that love; you are not just afraid to *die*. And this is the meaning of it all (the people's war); these men behind these fragile rocks, these men whose tender flesh is torn to pieces by the hot and ragged steel; they could not accept their death with such good grace if they did not love so deeply and so well—were not determined that love must come alive into the world. What other reason could there be for dying? What other reason for this blood upon your hands?

From MEN IN BATTLE, *Scribners, New York, 1939;*
excerpted from Part III, The Offensive

Two Poems

LANGSTON HUGHES

TOMORROW'S SEED:

> Proud banners of death,
> I see them waving
> There against the sky,
> Struck deep in Spanish earth
> Where your dark bodies lie
> Inert and helpless—
> So they think
> Who do not know
> That from your death
> New life will grow.
> For there are those who cannot see
> The mighty roots of liberty
> Push upward in the dark
> To burst in flame—
> A million stars—
> And one your name:
> > Man
> Who fell in Spanish earth:
> Human seed
> For freedom's birth.

HERO—INTERNATIONAL BRIGADE:

> Blood,
> Or a flag,
> Or a flame
> Or life itself
> Are they the same:
> Our dream?
> > I came.
> An ocean in-between

And half a continent.
Frontiers,
And mountains skyline tall,
And governments that told me NO,
YOU CANNOT GO!
   I came.
On tomorrow's bright frontiers
I placed the strength and wisdom
Of my years.
Not much,
For I am young.
(*Was* young,
Perhaps it's better said—
For now I'm dead.)

But had I lived four score and ten
Life could not've had
A better end.
I've given what I wished
And what I had to give
That others live.
And when the bullets
Cut my heart away,
And the blood
Gushed to my throat
I wondered if it were blood
Gushing there.
Or a red flame?
Or just my death
Turned into life?
They're all the same:
Our dream!
   My death!
   Your life!
   Our blood!
   One flame!
They're all the same!

The Life and Death of James Lardner

Somebody Had to Do Something

RING LARDNER, JR.

J IM WASN'T A VERY GOOD newspaperman. You could say he was
if you wanted to—I suppose it makes a more dramatic picture
to think of the expert reporter suddenly deciding that just observing wasn't enough. But it wouldn't be Jim. You see, he more
or less drifted into newspaper work and he never did quite take
hold. He left Harvard because it didn't seem to be doing very
much for him and that raised the problem of getting a job. The
likeliest spot was the *New York Herald-Tribune,* where his older
brother, John, had done pretty well and where the family name
served as a valuable introduction. But it was in the main a stop-
gap where he could earn a living while he was finding his bear-
ings. His heart was never in the monotonous routine of banquets
and funerals and minor suicides and interviews with moneyed
morons that is the lot of the young reporter on the city staff
of a metropolitan daily, and he was much too shy and reserved
to make a success of it.

He passed his time with rambling mental excursions into
Proust, Nietzsche, higher mathematics, cryptography and contract bridge; with gambling, drinking, all-night arguments, prize
fights and baseball. Politics was a game; he prided himself on
his prediction of the exact number of electoral votes for Roosevelt in 1936.

Three years was enough of that; the chance of a job on the
dreary Paris offshoot of the *Herald-Tribune* offered a diversion
at least and a wider field in which to find a starting-point for life.
It was routine stuff, too—translating, re-writing, waiting outside
a *chateau* in Southern France to hear whether Wallis Simpson
would be married on a Wednesday or a Friday.

But the world struggle was closer there. You couldn't work

in Paris without being exposed to French politics and you couldn't watch French politics without observing the betrayals and the sell-outs of men who thought of their investments first and France second. He wrote me a long letter in January, 1938, about the downfall of the government, expressing the theory that Bonnet had manufactured the crisis to further his own ambitions. He mentioned that a friend of his had been fired by the United Press for predicting *Anschluss* in March, followed by a Nazi-engineered uprising in Czechoslovakia. It seems the U.P. had lost its only two customers in Berlin as a result of the story. Things like that make you wonder—if you have something to wonder with.

And Jim's mind was in many ways the finest I have ever known. It was a mechanical instrument almost completely divorced from his emotions, such as they were. A few people were actually frightened by the coldness of his logic and by his contempt for irrationalism in any form. Not many though, because he rarely opened up except when he felt himself among fairly compatible spirits. His complete lack of visible emotion was an amazing phenomenon; he and I were very close, since I was only fifteen months younger than he, yet I never once saw him lose his composure, display temper, or for that matter enthusiasm, to any obvious extent.

Spain was the beginning of his life and the end of it. Anti-Fascism derived from a simple process of logic; it only remained to get close enough to the conflict in order to see the necessity of taking an active part in it, of engaging, for the first time in his life, in purposeful, directed effort toward a tangible goal. Pacifism, evolved by a previous mental process, was abandoned because its logic no longer obtained.

Jim went to Barcelona on his vacation rather than as a correspondent. He managed to get his paper's permission to send them a feature story or two and he also secured credentials from the *Copenhagen Politiken* to help him get close to the front but he went on his own time and money. He wrote me about the proposed trip, saying that his main purpose was to gather material for a short book on the Lincoln-Washington Battalion.

He went down from Paris on April 1, 1938, in a compartment with Ernest Hemingway and Vincent Sheean. He made a couple of trips to the front lines, observed the tragic plight of the decimated American forces and wrote one long dispatch which appeared in the Paris *Herald-Tribune* in characteristically mutilated form. Then he announced to his friends in Barcelona that he had decided to volunteer. I am told they all tried to dissuade him but I don't think their hearts were in it. You couldn't know Jim and expect to win an argument like that.

Their influence and pressure from home had an effect, not on Jim but on the army authorities; they assigned him to an artillery battery in training, which, because of the lack of guns, meant that he would be kept in the rear for many months. Jim demurred, and they sent him to the training base in Catalonia, which was also good for weeks or months away from the front. There he made another decision: he "deserted"—from the rear to the front.

It was early in May, just before his twenty-fourth birthday, that he showed up on foot at the battalion headquarters near the village of Darmos on the east side of the Ebro River. A correspondent there described him as "neat, clean, his khaki clothes almost spotless, with a brand new rucksack in which he carried, among other things, a French grammar, a Spanish grammar and a copy of 'Red Star Over China.' "

On July 13th he wrote me: "Life here is surprisingly peaceful. Since I joined the Lincoln-Washington Battalion, 15th Brigade, more than two months ago, we have not been near a trench nor put in a single day's fighting. This in spite of the fact that we are supposed to be shock troops. A lot of planes have passed overhead but none has condescended to notice our presence.

"Nevertheless I am kept pretty busy learning and practicing infantry technique. There is more to it than you might think, though not so much that I am not getting a little bored and anxious to see some action. Two or three times we have set off

329

with full equipment, presumably headed for the front, but each time it has been a false alarm for one reason or another.

"I suppose that you expect me to give you the inside dope on the war, but it is really harder to follow it from here than from California. It looks as if it would drag on here until some big change in the international situation decides the outcome. Fortunately, almost any change would favor us."

Before I received that letter I had heard the news that Jim had been wounded in the Ebro offensive. He had omitted to mention the fact that Commander Milton Wolff had chosen him as one of the soldiers to be sent to a short-term non-com officers' school from which he had emerged with the rank of corporal.

The story of his first action he told in a letter to his mother: "I don't know whether you are aware of the sad fact that I was wounded six days ago and am taking it easy at a popular Mediterranean hospital. I didn't have the money or facilities to cable. Anyway, it is nothing serious, just enough to keep me out of action for a couple of weeks.

"It seems that after a couple of days of forced marching and patrolling on the far side of the Ebro River we encountered the enemy and rapidly took 200 prisoners. I was one of those sent back with them as a guard. We reached the river in the afternoon of the 27th very tired and hungry, and were ferried across.

"I heard a rumor that there was an orchard 200 yards away and not having eaten all day, got excused and headed for it. There were some unripe pears and apples and peaches, which were better than nothing, but my attention was soon distracted by one of the frequent duels between anti-aircraft guns and bombing planes. The small round white puffs of smoke where the shells explode keep appearing all around the bombers until either one of them lands and a plane comes down or, much more often, the planes fly away after dropping their loads.

"This time the bombers were coming directly overhead. I began to wonder what were the chances of my being hit by one of the anti-aircraft shell fragments. It didn't occur to me that there was any danger of being bombed all by myself until a munition truck 300 yards away burst into flames with the explosion of a bomb.

"I was lying on my stomach when the plane passed over, but the bomb was a little too close. The explosion and the concussion were terrific, but I didn't discover I was hit right away. In fact, I walked over to where my rifle, munition belt and canteen of water were lying, picked them up and started back. Then I began to notice that my left calf and the left side of my behind were hurting. I felt them and found my trousers were covered with blood. A little further on I found several soldiers waiting in a trench for all the planes to go. I joined them and one, a Negro friend of mine, went for a stretcher. The stretcher-bearer dressed my wounds and took me to an ambulance. Since entering the trench I haven't been able to put any weight on my left leg. It seems the flying shrapnel hit me in the flesh and muscle, picking very soft and fortunate spots. It will be about ten days more, I think, before I shall be considered cured. I hope to get a few days in Barcelona before returning to the front.

"This hospital is clean and sunny, but nothing to read."

A few days later he sent me a postal card illustrating the department of hydro-therapy in the hospital. I had cabled him the news of the birth of my son and he wrote: "While you are doing your best to increase the tribe of Lardners there seems to be a counter-revolutionary plot here to thwart your work. They missed me this time, fortunately for the People's Army, although I did stop a little flying iron in my eagerness to pick up the bomb and throw it back at the pilot. . . . Expect to be out of this joint in about a week. On the reverse side you see one of the many methods that are not being employed in my cure."

He left the hospital with the wound still raw, not completely healed. It took him two weeks to win his insistent fight to return to the battalion; it was September 6 before he was sent back to the front, in charge of his squad.

On September 21, Premier Juan Negrín announced at Geneva the Spanish Government's decision to withdraw all volunteers from action immediately. On the 22nd the Americans, knowing that a Spanish Brigade was coming to relieve them, moved up to help hold the weakening lines against a deadly artillery barrage by the fascists. That night was their last in action.

Jim was sent out in charge of a three-man patrol into no-man's land to locate a missing platoon. They heard the sound of men digging; Jim stopped and challenged, not knowing whether it was the outpost they were seeking or the enemy's first lines. He started ahead by himself; rifle and machine-gun fire burst out and hand grenades exploded around them. One of his comrades, a Spaniard, was killed. The other, Anthony Nowakowski, an American, returned alone.

Weeks later Ernest Hemingway, seeking definite confirmation of Jim's death, learned through a correspondent with the fascists that a corpse had been found on that battlefield with press credentials. We never received any more definite confirmation than that. He was among the last losses, perhaps the very last, of the American forces in Spain.

There is only one recorded statement of his reason for joining in that fateful struggle. He had seen the Spanish people in what remained of their country, he explained to other newspapermen; he had visited the front and seen the situation there; and he had reached the conclusion that "somebody had to do something."

Published by the James Lardner Memorial Fund, Los Angeles, California, 1939

Spain 1938

H. B. MALLALIEU

Pity and love are no more adequate:
They have not saved ten thousand who are dead
Nor brought relief to peasants who in dread
Gaze at that sky which held their hope of late:
They have not stifled horror nor killed hate.
Europe is not impatient of her guilt,
But those on whom her tyranny is built,
By love deserted, have grown desperate.

Tears are no use, the suffering mind is mad.
Let sanity have strength and men unite
Who in their individual lives are glad
That what remains of peace may yet prove strong.
We have the will, then let us show the might,
Who have forborne and pitied far too long.

From POEMS FOR SPAIN

Spain Will Not Forget

MR. PRESIDENT:

IN THE NAME OF the Spanish delegation permit me to make a
declaration and formulate a petition to this assembly.

The Spanish Government has followed with profound anxiety the crisis which is threatening the peace at present. The
hidden insinuations according to which we are desirous to see a
general conflagration as a solution to the fight we are engaged
in, are so impertinent that they merit nothing but contempt
on our part.

We are interested in the maintenance of peace for reasons
of principle. The interests of a country must never come into
conflict with the universal and humane interests of the community of nations. And we are only interested in defending the
legitimate interests of our own country. But we are desirous
of avoiding a general conflagration not for the sake of principle alone. We are guided in this by our national egoism
also. After more than two years of war we know very well
the significance of preventing a world conflict.

It is not necessary for us to provoke catastrophies to solve
our problems. It would have been sufficient and it will be
sufficient to recognize our rights and re-establish our international rights that have been violated to assure a rapid solution to the Spanish problem.

The elimination of foreign intervention in Spain would
assure a policy of national conciliation under the firm and
energetic direction of an authoritative government, enabling
all Spaniards to forget these years of suffering and cruelties
and to re-establish rapidly interior peace.

Then the great tribulation suffered by our country might be considered as a baptism by fire, as a form of ransom that had to be paid for the renovation of Spain and for the rebirth of a national spirit the decline of which, in the past generations, was in a great measure the cause and origin of the tragedy we are suffering.

And now, Mr. President, I am coming to the concrete point which is the motive of my declaration.

In her desire to contribute to the pacification and "restraint" which we all desire, and in order to eliminate all pretexts and possible doubts about the genuinely national character of the cause for which the Republican Army is fighting, the Spanish Government has decided to withdraw immediately and completely all the non-Spanish combatants who are participating in the fight in Spain on the side of the Government; it is to be well understood that this withdrawal is to be applied to all foreigners without distinction as to their nationality, including all those who have acquired Spanish citizenship since July 5, 1936.

Here is, then, my petition: The Spanish Government has decided to solicit the Assembly of the League of Nations to constitute immediately an International Commission with the mandate of doing all the investigation and verifications necessary to guarantee to the League of Nations, their member States and to world opinion that the decision to retire the foreign volunteers will be carried out in its totality. Furthermore, the Spanish Government pledges itself to concede to this Commission all guarantees, all facilities and all collaboration that they deem necessary to fulfill their mission.

It is with a feeling of great sorrow that we regard the idea of separating ourselves from this group of brave and self-sacrificing men who, led by a generous impulse that will never be forgotten by the people of Spain, came to our aid in the most critical moments in our history. I want to proclaim here the heroism and the high moral value of the sacrifice they have voluntarily undertaken, not to safeguard petty selfish interests, but

335

solely to serve and defend the purest ideals of justice and liberty. We are absolutely certain that they will readily undertake this new and painful sacrifice which we are asking at present in order to benefit the cause for which they were ready to give their lives.

Spain will not forget those who have fallen on her battle-fields nor those who are still fighting on her soil; but I feel safe in saying without equivocation that their own countries will feel proud of them and this is the highest moral recompense they can receive.

I have the honor to submit to the Assembly the following resolution:

"The Assembly, informed of the decision of the Spanish Government to proceed to retire immediately and completely all non-Spanish combatants who are participating in the Spanish war on the side of the Government, decides to accept the petition of the Spanish Government soliciting the naming of an International Commission with the aim of giving the League of Nations and their member States the guaranty that the withdrawal will be executed in its totality as stated in the declaration of the Spanish Government, along with the promise that this Commission will be given all guarantees, facilities and collaboration necessary to the fulfillment of its mission.

"It is decided to accede to the demand of the Spanish Government to recommend to the Council, without loss of time, the formation of such International Commission as requested by the Spanish Government, and to work out in accordance with this, all necessary practical details that will enable the Commission to complete its mission as soon as possible."

Speech before League of Nations,
September 21, 1938

Spanish Sequence

NORMAN ROSTEN

I

He stands against the brick wall,
or in the open field, and ten rifles
converge upon the liquid beating heart.

He waits behind the blindfold of his eyes,
shouts at the onrushing dark
as he falls, and his blood slowly dies.

Such is the man we now come upon.
Such is the verdict we have yet to meet,
and many of us are still young.

Now, with fire controlling their cities,
and sky controlled by accurate planes,
honor, like a sun, dawns over the Pyrenees.

Now, when runners arrive stunned
from their coast's bombardment:
now, beginning this intimate season

when Spring with its punctual grass
prepares an arbor for lovers; today,
at last, we meet the shape of our years.

Turn, dreamer, to the burnt fields
where they wait calmly in trenches,
those who are first to fall, and least famous.
Turn where your own life may hold or fail.

II

Spain, the body,
and in its center
calmly beating
the great heart, Madrid.

Weep, women, for the children are gone
the houses are gone
but the heart
still beats.

Listen:
over the roar of planes
above the wail of death
feeding its defenders
the heart beats.

Madrid!
Burning in the night
bleeding in the night
but still standing.

They have thrust all year
at the center of this man.
The heart of a people can bleed
but not to death
never to death.

III

Were there stars in the sky, Federico,
when the fascist rifles struck you down
without even a sheet to cover your body?

    (in the evening, the dark evening)

Were there dancers in your brain, Federico,
when you faced the singing of the fields
and the cold fanatic faces of the Moors?

    (in the evening, the murderous evening)

Lorca, friend, did you smile perhaps

when death appeared in that poised moment
and called you by your first name?

(in the evening, that terrible evening)

Evening, the warm loam of earth;
and beyond, the waters of Málaga
slowly turned red with his blood.

Who would have said it were true?
Who would have said that his great body,
ringed with poems, could so swiftly be broken?

Federico, did you wish it a silver thing,
the dagger of the moon, a luminous death?
Did you wish it to come as a horseman,
or sleep, or the failure of sunlight?

Or death as a woman, white and wonderful,
whose breasts at your mouth were grapes?
It was the bullet, Federico.
It was the bullet made of lead.

Did you think of the bullfighter Mejías
who died with a horn in his heart,
while you were caught in the arm of afternoon
without robe or stance or sword?

Ask the stones of Granada to shield you!
Command that the air become armor!
Call down the stars to blind them
for their rifles are raised, Federico!

Sky, be blue over his hill.
Earth, turn more gently now.
For Lorca is gone, and his wisdom.
He fell with the roar of pistols in his head.

He lies on no slab of stone,
nor are there pennies on his eyes;
he sleeps in the alkaline dust
and worms destroy his sacred lips.

He is in the great arena of silence
where heavenly bulls pierce the matador

with their bloodless horns, and angels
weep in the stands like little children.

His poems are frozen in the skull
and no Spring shall ever thaw them.
How shall we find his voice again,
and his guitar, which the wind now plays?

IV

In Guernica the dead children
were laid out in order upon the sidewalk,
in their white starched dresses,
in their pitiful white dresses.

On their foreheads and breasts
are the little holes where death came in
as thunder, while they were playing
their important summer games.

Do not weep for them, *madre*.
They are gone forever, the little ones,
straight to heaven to the saints,
and God will fill the bullet-holes with candy.

V

Ben Leider,
appointed to the flame,
rider of the same air we breathe,
who fought in the sky, which has no country. . . .

One motor, miracle of metal,
took the plane off the ground
and once in the air, she hung on,
her pistons pounding. He could feel
the heavy pull of the earth upon her:
she lacked the lightness of soaring.
Ben smiled,
                    Pegasus old girl
you're way past pension time. Even horsepower
gets old, but Spanish horsepower sure dies
with its sparkplugs on, if it's got sparkplugs.

Slowly, with the immaculate lovely lift
of all flying things, the plane rose
and soon the landscape was a toy below,
his city to protect, his people now.
He was their *Americano*, their great cowboy
who could fly the Atlantic on a kite,
make love to Greta Garbo, shoot to kill
straight from the hip, leap over Niagara,
swing from the saddle to the soaring plane.
Yes, he was Tom Mix: they believed it.
They believed, they trusted. . . .

Above the earth, he has a wisdom
only height can give: height and love
and knowledge of action. This brown land
accepting its endless toll of blood
was the road all peoples walked:
it was bread and growth and loneliness,
it was the warm place for giving birth,
it was the cold place that received the body
after death.
        He rides alone, companion to air;
he lives in relation to the earth's curve.
Suspended between sky and grass
the airman will not die as an ordinary man.
His heart beats as all men
but his blood refuels from wind and stars
and death can claim him only as he lies
finally smashed upon the ground.

He sees them coming, the bright row
of armored assassins, the cold Heinkels,
their motors tight and thundering.
He pulls the stick back sharply:
the plane jolts, takes the climb hard,
hovers high, waits. . . .
           Ben talks to her:
"All I ask Peggy is that you hold together

because we're going down a lot faster
than we came up. Let's hear your guns
and don't shoot the damn prop off
while you're bragging!"

                    The guns tested fine.
One of the cylinders started to kick
but it didn't seem to matter now.
He looked around the blue enamel sky,
his most intimate home, his heaven,
and smiled, pushed the stick forward
thinking, This is a hell of a dive-bomber
but here goes
          and down down
down the bright wide roadway of the sky,
Ben Leider, alone, smiling and calm,
making the air beautiful with his honor.

He felt blood in his mouth. . . .
Time to go home . . . straighten out,
this is too good a crate to lose,
we need every one, every one,
pull her up, pull her out,
lead her home, Ben, easy, easy, home. . . .

Turn, pilot, and look the other way!
Look at your sky and sun and dazzling air,
for their bullets are closing in.
O strike his heart quickly, be sudden,
make him lifeless there in the swinging tomb
that he may be spared suffering!

Airman,
cheered so often from below
by the good people of Madrid,
the earth pulls you homeward now,
and their hands will take you tenderly.

We watch you fall like a flag.
All the suns dip to the horizon.

O Icarus, welcome him,
wingless now, and a wanderer.

VI

Generalissimo Franco,
the man of God, the pope's choice,
voted most likely to succeed. . . .

Approach, friend, and be recognized!
Greetings! We rejoice with you!
The State Department on this occasion
of your victory takes your bloody hand
in most fraternal greetings! Welcome
into the christian brotherhood of nations!
May you be blessed with crops and obedience.
May your reign be long and prosperous
and overflowing O with great goodness
and charity holy in the name of holiness. . . .

We assume the German and Italian troops
will leave as quietly as possible.
Let everything take place quietly.
Let the political prisoners be shot quietly
and the bleeding be as internal as possible.
Let the firing squads perform with silencers.
Let the barbed-wire camps be quiet.
Let Guernica sleep, and the children there.
Let darkness come down like a robe
to cover this infamous year.

To die, and die, and yet to lose;
to bleed, to give life freely as water
and still lose! How bitter the day is!
Let this day be bordered in black forever.

                    Man's heart
takes on the definition of iridium,
and he spits upon this whore, Justice,
and tears the cloth from her eyes

and casts her out as a leper.

Remember this, betrayer;
remember this, you who feared;
you the sleeper, the doubter,
the diplomat with white gloves,
all who struck with the same knife.

The earth turns and turns.
History has written it down.
Time will not forgive.

VII

After the defeat, remorse of the delicate,
and the intellectual's lingering neurosis,
remember how those durable in spirit,
knowing ultimately of Time's wisdom,
consolidated behind the shattered wall
and grew strong, and would not forget.

While others withdrew their names,
left no forwarding address.
These have retired secretly
in the cynic's tradition of the doomed.
They fought without losing blood,
grieved publicly for a while, and
returned to the ease of earlier causes.

Heroes at home, in small rooms
or in their fabulous summer houses,
they took the cure, became penitent,
spoke to no one without an appointment,
would not answer the telephone,
preferred to live quietly and alone.

Their sleep is poor and they age quickly.
They condemn their own sons to death.

From The Fourth Decade.

Goodbye, Brothers, Till Our Speedy Reunion

DOLORES IBARRURI (*La Pasionaría*)

I<small>T IS HARD TO SAY</small> a few words in farewell to the heroes of the International Brigades, both because of what they are and what they represent.

A feeling of sorrow, an infinite grief catches our throats ... sorrow for those who are going away, for the soldiers of the highest ideal of human redemption, exiles from their countries, persecuted by the tyrants of all peoples ... grief for those who will stay here forever, mingling with the Spanish soil or in the very depths of our hearts, bathed in the light of our gratitude.

You came to us from all peoples, from all races. You came like brothers of ours, like sons of undying Spain; and in the hardest days of the war, when the capital of the Spanish Republic was threatened, it was you, gallant comrades of the International Brigades, who helped to save the city with your fighting enthusiasm, your heroism and your spirit of sacrifice.

In deathless verses Jarama and Guadalajara, Brunete and Belchite, Levante and the Ebro sing the courage, the sacrifice, the daring, the discipline of the men of the International Brigades.

For the first time in the history of the peoples' struggles, there has been the spectacle, breath-taking in its grandeur, of the formation of International Brigades to help to save a threatened country's freedom and independence, the freedom and independence of our Spanish land.

Communists, Socialists, Anarchists, Republicans — men of different views and different religions, yet all of them fired with a deep love for liberty and justice. And they came and offered themselves to us unconditionally.

They gave us everything: their youth or their maturity;

345

their science or their experience; their blood and their lives, their hopes and aspirations—and they asked us for nothing at all. That is to say, they *did* want a post in the struggle, they did aspire to the honor of dying for us. . . .

Banners of Spain! Salute these many heroes! Lower Spain's banners in honor of so many martyrs! . . .

Mothers! Women! When the years pass by and the wounds of the war are being stanched; when the cloudy memory of the sorrowful, bloody days returns in a present of freedom, peace and well-being; when the feelings of rancor are dying away and when pride in a free country is felt equally by all Spaniards, then speak to your children. Tell them of these men of the International Brigades.

Tell them how, coming over seas and mountains, crossing frontiers bristling with bayonets, watched for by raving dogs thirsting to tear at their flesh, these men reached our country as crusaders for freedom, to fight and die for Spain's liberty and independence which were threatened by German and Italian fascism. They gave up everything: their loves, their countries, home and fortune; fathers, mothers, wives, brothers, sisters and children, and they came and told us: "We are here. Your cause, Spain's cause, is ours—it is the cause of all advanced and progressive mankind."

Today they are going away. Many of them, thousands of them, are staying here with the Spanish earth for their shroud, and all Spaniards remember them with the deepest feeling.

Comrades of the International Brigade: Political reasons, reasons of State, the welfare of that same cause for which you offered your blood with boundless generosity, are sending you back, some of you to your own countries and others to forced exile. You can go proudly. You are history. You are legend. You are the heroic example of democracy's solidarity and universality, in face of the shameful, "accommodating" spirit of those who interpret democratic principles with their eyes on hoards of wealth or the industrial shares which they want to preserve from any risk.

346

Dolores Ibarrúri (La Pasionaría)

We shall not forget you, and when the olive tree of peace puts forth its leaves again, entwined with the laurels of the Spanish Republic's victory—come back! . . .

Come back to us. With us those of you who have no country will find one, those of you who have to live deprived of friendship will find friends, and all of you will find the love and gratitude of the whole Spanish people who, now and in the future, will cry out with all their hearts:

"*Long live the heroes of the International Brigades!*"

Farewell speech to the International Brigades,
Barcelona, September 1938

Spain

DON GORDON

Then we could not praise them: they
    were prone
On the burning hills with their guns,
    and thermite
Drenched their houses. The battle was
    the pulse of beaten lands.

The year has flattened the unmarked graves,
    the bones
Are white under the invisible flowers
    in the thoughts
Of distant strangers, nourished by workers
    in their bleak gardens.

They did not die for flowers, nor memories
    to be pressed
In the archives of another war. They wanted
    to end indignity,
They fought for life and its continuance. We
    are that life.

We do not praise the valor of these fathers.
    We respect
That time and place: there was light in men,
    their women were beautiful.
Respect is not enough: we are the sons they
    could not have,
The daughters they did not see. We inherit
    graves and guns.

the conscience of the world

(1939)

"The Holy See does not consider it necessary to make any appeal to Generalissimo Francisco Franco for clemency."

VATICAN NEWS SERVICE,
special communiqué of Jan. 28, 1939, in reply to plea to Pius XI by prominent Catholic laymen in France, England and Spain.

He cerrado mi balcón
porque no quiero oír el llanto,
pero por detrás de los grises muros
no se oye otra cosa que el llanto.

Hay muy pocos ángeles que canten,
hay muy pocos perros que ladren,
mil violines caben en la palma
    de la mano:
pero el llanto es un ángel inmenso,
las lágrimas amordazan al viento,
y no se oye otra cosa que el llanto.

FEDERICO GARCIA LORCA

INDIGNATION OF A HIGH-MINDED SPANIARD

We can endure that He should waste our land.
Despoil our temples, and by sword and flame
Return us to the dust from which we came;
Such food a Tyrant's appetite demands:
And we can brook the thought that by his hand
Spain may be overpowered, and he possess,
For his delight, a solemn wilderness
Where all the brave lie dead. But, when of band
Which he will break for us he dares to speak,
Of benefits, and of a future day
When our enlightened minds shall bless his sway
Then, the strained heart of fortitude proves weak
Our groans, our blushes, our pale cheeks declare
That he has power to inflict
    what we lack strength to bear.

WILLIAM WORDSWORTH

They Fly Through the Air With the Greatest of Ease

NORMAN CORWIN

NARRATOR   Assume it is morning.
You know what mornings are.
You have seen thousands of them:
They rise out of the East, huge as the universe
And stand in the sky till noon.
Oh, you've seen all kinds of them.
Some come up dirty-faced, as though they had
      spent the night in a gutter between two
      stars;
Some bluster, brandishing big winds;
Some, at dawn, are like a streak of blood across
      where night met doom;
Some are all innocence, surprised to be playing
      morning to such a little earth.
You know what mornings are:
Their coming and their going is cosmic busi-
      ness,
Yet casual and common and taken all for
      granted,
Having to do with milk trains,
And cockcrows, and street lamps going out,
And alarm clocks.

All right; so it is morning.
It is morning on a level field, still wet with dew;
A field once used for haying, flown over at one
      time by birds going north or birds going
      south to build homes;
A meadow mowed upon by men, buzzed in by

351

bees, and lingered on by lovers in the
moonlight.

Here, where last year stood the windrows of
the hay,
Is now an aviary of such birds as God had
never dreamed of when He made the skies.
Look close, and you will see one now.
They are wheeling it out of the hangar,
Carefully.

Oh, do be careful, gentlemen.
It is so dumbly delicate:
Its fabrics and its metals, its gears, its cylinders,
its dials,
The million dervishes ready to whirl in its
motors,
The guns fore and aft,
The sights, the fins, the fuselage,
The bomb racks and the bombs.
Do not jar them; do not jar them, please.
Be gentle, gentlemen.
This bomber is an instrument of much pre-
cision,
A mathematic miracle
As cold and clean and noble as a theorem.
See here: Have you no eye for beauty?
Mark how its nose, be-chromed and tilting
toward the heavens
Reflects the morning sun and sniffs the lucent
air.

VOICES   (*Coming on, ad-libbing, during preceding
line.*)

NARRATOR   These voices?
We were expecting them, for they it is who

> guide this big blind bat
> And who will take her soaring soon.
> They are fliers;
> They are officers;
> They are gentlemen;
> And they are yours to listen to.

PILOT   You couldn't ask for a better day. Not a ripple in the air.

RADIOMAN   A peach, all right.

GUNNER   With this bright sun there'll be no trouble picking up objectives.

MECHANIC   (*coming on*) Bomb racks loaded, sir.

PILOT   Have you turned up the engines?

MECHANIC   Yes, sir, they're all warmed up. Both engines showed 2100 r.p.m. at full gun.

RADIOMAN   Did you tighten up that loose fair-lead I reported yesterday?

MECHANIC   Yes, sir, everything's secured.

PILOT   Top off the gas tanks and check the oil?

MECHANIC   Yes sir. You have capacity load.

PILOT   Checked your bomb load? Are the releases working okay?

MECHANIC   Like a clock.

PILOT   Well, gentlemen, let's get aboard.
Sound of climbing aboard. Door slams.

PILOT   (*projecting*) Wind 'em up!

MECHANIC   (*well off mike*) Switch off? Gas on?

PILOT   Switch off. Gas on.
Inertia starter; over it, sound of wobble pump
    worked by hand.

MECHANIC   All clear!

PILOT   Contact!
Motor up.

PILOT   Pull the chocks!

MECHANIC   Chocks clear!

PILOT   (*lower*) All set, back there?

RADIOMAN   All set.

GUNNER   Okay here.
Take off. Level out. Sound of motors as heard
    within cockpit is cross-faded to exterior
    perspective and held under.

NARRATOR   So you are off the ground and in your element,
O fighting men!
And are you comfortable now?
You do not mind this rolling on the billows of
    the air?
Are you as snug within your cockpits as your
    bomb load in the racks?

Look below, boys.
Behold the moving carpet rolled out over the
    edges of the world;
The earth, your home;

The earth, in which you were a million ages
    coming,
Your home for all the balance of eternity.

This is a temporary thing, your being off the
    earth—
You will come down, of course.
Whatever leaves the earth is only lent to air,
Including birds and vapors and ten-ton
    machines.
You'll home again.

The earth is venerable stuff, believe me, sirs.
It's seen ten million seasons crossing overhead,
And all those mornings that we spoke about,
And mists and clouds and lightnings,
And moons enough to burst the oceans bubble-
    like,
And galaxies slow-wheeling in the boundless
    skies,
And meteors, auroras, rainbows, nimbuses. . . .
All these the earth has seen, but never, until
    now,
A bombing plane.

How looks the morning to you, gentlemen?
You there, gunner in the turning tip-up seat,
Were you admiring the sunlight on that river
    to the north?
And you with earphones on, what thoughts
    think you between them?
Of life? Of death? Of poker hands?
Of breasts? Of thighs? Of furbelows?
Spaghetti? Of your leader? Of the enemy?
Oh, yes, the enemy.
Why, one would think that on so fair a day
    as this,

Hostility should scatter like breath upon the
air.
Surely this sweet and fertile land can bear no
hate?
Yet you must have an enemy below,
Else why a belly full of bombs, and gun belts
stuffed with cartridges?
Of course, the enemy.

We wonder what your foeman's doing now
where you will strike him down?
What monstrous machinations?
What menacings, what vicious villainies ap-
point you to his punishment
And rouse the indignation of your bombs?

Excuse us; we'll go on ahead to see.
Start fading motors.

NARRATOR   Allow us to precede you.
We flash ahead
As fast as thought anticipates a deed.
Motors out.

NARRATOR   And here we are: the city:
Blinking in the sun
With sleep still skulking in the shadows of its
streets.

This is the encampment of the enemy:
These hostile roofs and threat'ning chimneys,
These trees, like bayonets upraised along the
avenues,
These churches sticking steeple-swords into the
sky,
This is the enemy.

What do they plot
So early in the morning?

Let us investigate downtown,
In that apartment building near the park.

Pick you at random:
Shall we say the base of war
Is tenement 3B?
We take you through the wall
While still it stands upright.
See how the enemy is girt for war.
*Breakfast table sounds faded in with conver-
sation:*

FATHER   Just the same, you had no business telling him
he could take the car.

MOTHER   Oh, he's old enough to be treated like an adult.

For Heaven's sake, think of the time when
you . . .

DAUGHTER   That's right, Dad. Jack's . . .

FATHER   Nobody asked your opinion, Elly. Pass the
toast, please.

DAUGHTER   I don't know what's the matter with this
toaster. Look, the toast isn't done, after all
this time.

MOTHER   There's some coffee left in the percolator.

FATHER   (*between mouthfuls*) It isn't the fact that he's
driving the car, it's the principle of the
thing!

MOTHER   What principle of what thing?

FATHER   Well, that Jack should ask *you* for the car, instead of coming to me. What's the matter, is he so positive I'll refuse him that he's afraid to ask my permission? Why, you'd think I was a tyrant, the way he avoids making an issue of things with me.

MOTHER
You're the one that's making an issue, not he.

FATHER
You're deliberately misconstruing the whole business. Now look: Who owns the car?

MOTHER
You, obviously.
    (*Fading.*)

FATHER
Who pays the repair bills?

MOTHER
Get to the point.

FATHER
Who pays the garage bill? Who buys gas and oil? Who pays for the tires when Jack has a blowout? I do! And therefore when he wants to take out the car he should ask me not you.

NARRATOR

There is dissension in the foeman's ranks.

This house that is divided cannot stand,

And fall it will, with beams and timbers heaped upon the breakfast table—

Plaster in the coffee.

Leave off this argument, conspirators,

For Jack will sell the car to bury you.

And let us quit these quarrelers and go

To tenement 5A.

Music: As the quarrel at the breakfast table fades out, fade in piano music. Some moments elapse after the music is fully established before the Narrator speaks:

NARRATOR   (*over music*)

Are these your drums and trumpets, enemy?
Is this your war song, coming from a baby
  grand?
Is this your reveille, your charge, your anthem?
Music: Continues.

NARRATOR   What kind of soldier trains
             By practicing an étude in the morning?
             Music: Continues.

NARRATOR   Play on:
             The movement ends before it's meant to end.
             A great fortissimo
             Will twist your hands
             Inextricably in the strings.
             Music: Begin cross-fade to crying of baby.
             Over both:

NARRATOR   And here,
             Cross-fading in,
             Is tenement 8F.
             Music: Piano out.
             Crying up.

SECOND MOTHER   (*wearily.*) I give up. You take her now.

SECOND FATHER   I should think after crying all night, she'd get
                  tired and fall off to sleep.

SECOND MOTHER   Her teeth are bothering her, poor lamb.

SECOND FATHER   I'll bet if I rubbed paregoric on her gums she'd
                  go to sleep.

SECOND MOTHER   No, dear, I tried that. Didn't work. Just walk
                  her up and down; she'll drop off.

SECOND FATHER   *Goes on and off mike chanting "Ah, ah,
                  ba-by", while crying of child follows in*

359

relatively same perspective. Bring down for:

NARRATOR   (*over effect*)
Be patient;
The little enemy will enter soon her longest
    sleep.
And you will enter with her.

A matter but of minutes,
For even now the Sandman hums his level
    tune
Within the city's limits.
Exterior motors in slowly.

NARRATOR   We are caught up with; the plane is fast.
The crew is taut and eager,
Silent and intent,
Like pointers in a hunt.
Cross to interior. Motors under:

NARRATOR   And now they speak the jargon of the kill.

PILOT   All right! This is bombing altitude. You can set
up your bomb sights.

GUNNER   Okay, sir. I'm going to use that church steeple
as a marker. Will you steer close so as to
pass over it?

PILOT   Okay. (*Pause.*) All set with that bomb sight?

GUNNER   All set now, sir. Got the steeple traveling right
down the groove.

PILOT   That's fine. You can count on the same wind when we reach the downtown area. (*Pause.*) Put your sights on that apartment building near the park; that's the first objective.

GUNNER   A little more to the left. (*Pause.*)

PILOT   How's it now? (*Pause.*)

GUNNER   We're right on, sir. (*Pause; then quickening.*) Hold that heading!
Clanking sound as bomb is released.

GUNNER   First demolition bomb gone. (*five-second pause.*) *Dull boom, not too clearly audible over motor.*

PILOT   Nice work, fella. Right on the nose.

GUNNER   Interesting pattern, the way that wreckage is flying outward.

RADIOMAN   See how deep that crater is. Must have been soft earth under the house.

PILOT   All right, Carlo, put your sights on that red warehouse. We bomb the market place now.

GUNNER   Steer about ten degrees to the right. (*Pause.*)

PILOT   How is she now?

GUNNER   Just a touch more to the right. (*Pause.*) Okay, we're on.

PILOT   Let go four incendiaries this time.
Sound of bomb release.

GUNNER   Salvo released! (*Five-second pause.*)
*Series of booms, not far apart but not evenly
spaced, as bombs strike.*

PILOT   Beautiful! You're sure hot today, kid.

GUNNER   Thanks.

PILOT   Alec, notify headquarters we've bombed the
objectives successfully.

RADIOMAN   (*perfunctorily.*) Plane No. 6 calling Headquarters 9th Bombardment Group. We
have bombed both objectives successfully.
Proceeding with attack. No enemy planes
in sight. Acknowledge, please.

FILTER VOICE   Headquarters to Plane No. 6. Your Message
No. 1 acknowledged. (*Pause.*)
Cross to exterior motors.

NARRATOR   It is acknowledged that the baby sleeps.
It is acknowledged that the toast is burned.
It is acknowledged that the piano's out of tune.

O wingéd Victory!
The Spartans would have coveted
The courage of your combat!
Just think:
Ten thousand savage rooftops, tarred and tiled,
Against a single plane!

There is a ratio to Valor.
Heroes are made by odds:
The lad who slew the giant with the slingshot,
    he was one;

Horatio, outnumbered at the bridge;
And you, three men and half a dozen bombs
Against the regiments of tenements, arrayed
     between the banners of their wet wash,
The bed sheets and the shirts and pillow slips
Snapping defiance in the fresh-sprung breeze.
Not even these bold oriflammes can daunt
Your purpose and your cause.
Your Message No. 1 has been acknowledged,
     gentlemen,
Your heroism noted and approved and filed
     away,
Next week to be submitted to the Ministry of
     War
With other matters of routine.
The State is pleased.
Proceed with the attack, O Bomber No. 6!
What new scents do you pick up in the traces
     of the air?
Cross to interior motors.

PILOT   Say, there are an awful lot of people on that
        road, aren't there?

GUNNER   Looks like some more refugees. We sure got
        'em on the run this morning.

PILOT   Okay. Set up your sight. Pick the center of the
        mob.

GUNNER   All right. Just keep her over the road. (*Pause.*)
        Hold that heading. (*Pause.*) Stand by.
        (*Pause.*)
        Sound of bomb release.

GUNNER   Well, there she goes. (*Pause.*)
        Dull boom.

PILOT   Gee, that's fascinating! What a spread! Looks just like a budding rose unfolding!

RADIOMAN   Must have been two-three hundred in that crowd.

PILOT   Okay, man the guns. No point letting any of the rest get away.
Plane dives suddenly. Machine-gun fire in. Two guns in four-second bursts; hold at least twelve seconds. Plane climbs and levels out.

PILOT   Well, that's that.

GUNNER   Yeah.

PILOT   Let's call it a day. Getting on toward lunchtime anyway.

GUNNER   Yeah. I'm getting kinda hungry.

RADIOMAN   Chicken Tetrazzini today.

PILOT   Come to think of it, that was a pretty thorough job of strafing. That work always reminds me of mowing wheat—as though some invisible mower were cutting across the field.

RADIOMAN   Nice symmetrical pattern, isn't it?
Cross to exterior motors.

NARRATOR   It is. It is.
A symmetry of unborn generations,
Of canceled seed.
The dead below, spread fanlike in their blood,
Will bear no more.

The pattern is symmetrical indeed—
Of ciphers linked, repeating down infinity.

How can we justly celebrate the odysseys
Of demigods who finger destinies upon their
    trigger tips?
With wreaths of laurel?
    Laurel withers fast.
By sculpturing in bronze?
      Too cold; too passive;
      Also, in emergencies, it may be melted to
        make other things.
Rechristen with your names a public square?
      That's vulgar;
      Furthermore, no single square is big
        enough.
A poem, perhaps?
Aha, that's it! A poem!
A verse or two that will contract no rust,
A bombproof ode, whose strophes will stand
    stout
Against all flood and famine, epidemic war,
And pox and plague and general decay.
Yes, poetry's the thing.
It has served soldiers far beyond their shields.
Where would Achilles be without a Homer?
Hector? Agamemnon?
Why, no more numbered in the lists of im-
    mortality
Than those immobile refugees whose bodies
    stiffen as we speak.
We're right; we're right;
An ode's the only vessel fit to bear so much of
    honor.
But we must get away to think:
The music of the motors is monotonous;

Our meter will be influenced. . . .
So you continue home, now, bombing plane—
Give us a while to mint a metaphor.
We'll overtake you later.

Let us withdraw to some precinct of peace
To meditate, for poems are materials of mood.
Motors fade out.

NARRATOR   Yes, this is better;
It is silent here.
The cogwheels of the brain turn quietly.
Let's think this out. . . .
Let's see, now. . . .
Where shall we begin?
Mm.
It's harder than it seemed, a moment back,
To conjure up conceits.
What words can compass glories such as we
     have seen today?

Our language beats against its limitations.

Some things defy description. This you know.
Do you contend it? Well, has beauty ever been
     described by "beautiful"?
Can phrases tailored to a patch of earth
Be stretched to fit the sky?

Our rhythms jangle at the very start,
Our similes concede defeat,
For there is nothing that can be compared to
     that which lies beyond compare.
You see? We are reduced already to tautolo-
     gies.

It's awe does that.
The wonder of it all has set us stammering.

Compare these men to whom?
Olympians?
No, that won't do; these Jupiters could blast
The peak right off Olympus.
To Icarus?
Worse yet.
These gentlemen know how to navigate.

That settles it!
We cannot undertake this ode.
Let's drop this random dreaming and return
  to things we're sure about—
To the familiarity of Bomber No. 6.
Exterior motors in.

NARRATOR   Yes, here it is, as we expected we should find
                it:
              Unswerving in its homeward course.
              Its fuselage impeccable, its tail raised proud.
              The sun is higher now.
              It spills its benison
              Upon the curving earth
              And down the edges of the hemispheres.
              But here the morning is mature.
              It smiles a slow seraphic smile
              And spangles the propellers with its gold.
              Far to the south
              Some clouds are having traffic with a current
                of warm air.
              There is a tendency toward noon.

              Bear home, bear home, O Conquerors!
              Fly by your spellbound compass

To the midday meal. It's in the ovens now.
A toast awaits you,
Pledged with rich red wine
To him who leads you.
Then comes the soup and then the meat
And after that the fruits and cheeses.

Tonight there will be music in the quarters;
Books to read;
Perhaps a letter to the folks:

> All prospers well upon the farm, you'll
> want to know?
> No trouble with the bugs raiding the vines
> again this year?
> Are Father's cows giving more butter to
> the hungry state?
> Has Mary seen her husband since he vol-
> unteered?

And then to sleep
Between clean sheets
The deep, untroubled sleep
Of tranquil consciences;
The mind released, the eye unfocused, and
the—
Cross to interior motors.

NARRATOR   What bothers you, O gunner in the turning
tip-up seat?
Why do you peer behind?
What is it you're about to say?

GUNNER   There's a fighting plane on the right side. Distance about one mile, heading this way.

PILOT   (*concerned*) Where?

GUNNER   Right over there. Just over the wing tip now.

RADIOMAN   (*hopefully*) Maybe we're getting an escort.

PILOT   (*alarmed and excited*) We're not getting any
         escort! That's an enemy plane! Man the
         guns! We'll run for it!
     *Interior motors pick up to maximum speed,
     then cross to exteriors.*

NARRATOR   No, no.
     There must be some mistake here.
     It is the victor who pursues;
     The vanquished breaks for safety.

     One moment:
     Let us get this straight:
     Is this a sparrow rushing down upon a fright-
         ened hawk?
     Or is this some maneuver
     Leading up to ambush?

     And yet the pilot said to run for it.
     Can we have heard correctly the command?
     To flee this antic rooftop, coming to avenge
     The market place?
     What frenzied, wild delusion beats the wings
         of the pursuer?
     Has he not heard, does he not know
     That you are armored with invincibility?
     That you are of a race of warriors above all
         others and imperishable?
     Does he not know you are equipped with
         slender guns and coiling cartridge belts
     Spitting two thousand mortal venoms in a
         minute?
     Leave well enough alone, O lonely wasp, or
         you will lose your sting,
     And all else with it.

No: I see Death sucks you down the skies as
    flame intoxicates a moth.
Oh, well, there'll be a churning of the air
    when you engage.
Cross to interior motors.

GUNNER   (*anxiously*) He's gaining on us!

PILOT   (*coldly*) Stand by to open fire!
Cross to exterior motors.

NARRATOR   Stand by? . . .
Your only adversary up to now
Has been the force, invisible, anonymous,
Of gravity.
Now you must reck with some upstarting fool
Of no especial lineage;
A driver of a truck, perhaps, in lesser times.
Stand by to open fire, gentlemen,
For even now he closes range.
*With perspective always on the bomber (in-
    cluding interior motors), open fire with
    on-mike guns.*

*Bring in sound of attacker's motor quickly up
    and down to indicate passage close to
    bomber during the fighting. At height of
    this effect, open fire with attacker's guns
    through filter, to distinguish from guns of
    bomber. Overlap both of bomber's guns
    in random pattern, always being sure to
    maintain short bursts of fire.*
Bring whole effect down and continue behind:

NARRATOR   Only in lists of love and war
Is there such burning concentration.
The warriors in Bomber No. 6
Now lack the luxury of time to contemplate

the patterns of the banking foe:
They watch his loops, his climbing and his
dives,
With little eye to form.
The free and flowing curves of his maneuver-
ing
Are not felicitous—so far from this,
That prickles stand upon the pilot's nape.
The tenement's avenger flies too close;
He must be brushed away.
Combat effect up.

PILOT   (*very excited*) Get him! Get him! *Get him!*
He's getting on us! Watch your tracer,
Carlo, you're . . .

*Sharp burst of filter gun. Scream of pain, as
from Pilot mortally hit by fire. Gunfire
out. Motors begin to cough.*

*Effect of uncontrolled spinning, which builds
into a long, slow crescendo until the crash
at the conclusion of the following speech
of the Narrator:*

NARRATOR   This is humiliating, gentlemen,
To reel so drunkenly
In sight of all the sober earth:
There's apoplexy in your motors now
And they will not recover.
Sirs, I speak to you:
Be calm!
Compose yourselves!
Keep down your sudden nausea!
Unclutch your frantic hands!
Be calm, for there is beauty all about you:
The sun, the air, the earth,
They're all the same.
It's only you have undergone a change;

Be calm:
Sit back:
There still is time
To see
A final symmetry:
The spiral of your spinning
Is a corkscrew in the sky.

Be hopeful, gentlemen;
Perhaps the government will help you now;
The ministry of war will buoy you up;
Your press will warn the earth against this act;
Perhaps your Leader, thundering a threat,
Will terrify all gravity.
Be hopeful, boys . . .
Your people are supreme in war!
Tremendous crash; then absolute silence—several seconds of it.

NARRATOR   That's all.
That's all the fighting they will care to do.
They have a treaty with the earth
That never will be broken.
They are unbeautiful in death,
Their bodies scattered and bestrewn
Amid the shattered theorem.
There is a little oil and blood
Slow draining in the ground.
The metal still is hot, but it will cool.
You need not bother picking up the parts.

The sun has reached meridian.
The day is warm.
There's not a ripple in the air.

Radio play first produced on
Columbia Broadcasting System,
February 19, 1939

The Winds of the People

MIGUEL HERNANDEZ

The winds of the people sustain me,
spreading within my heart.
The winds of the people impel me,
and roar in my very throat.
Oxen may bow their heads
gentle and impotent
before their punishment;
but lions lift their heads
and with their strident claws
they punish in return.
I come not from a people of oxen,
my people are they who enthuse
over the lion's leap,
the eagle's rigid swoop,
and the strong charge of the bull
whose pride is in his horns.
Oxen were never bred
On the bleak uplands of Spain.
Who speaks of setting a yoke
on the shoulders of such a race?
Who has set yoke or shackle
on the rigorous hurricane,
or held the thunderbolt
a prisoner in a cage?

You Basques of armoured stone,
you brave Asturians,
lively Valencianos
and tempered Castillians,

worked-over like the soil
yet as airy as wings,
Andalusians like lightning,
born amidst guitars
and forged in torrential
smithies of tears,
rye-field Estremadurans,
Galicians of calm rain,
dour trustful Catalans,
pure-born of Aragón,
dynamiting Murcians
so fruitful in your race,
men of Navarre and León, masters
of hunger, sweat, and the axe,
kings of the mineral kingdom
and lords of the work of tillage,
you who amidst roots,
like noble roots yourselves,
go from life to death,
go from nothing to nothing:
you men of the scant grasslands,
they would set on you a yoke,
a yoke that you must shatter
in two across *their* backs!
The twilight of the oxen
heralds a sparkling dawn.
The oxen are dying, clad
in the humble smell of the barn.
But the eagles and the lions,
and behind them the sky,
and the arrogant bulls
are calm, will not die.

The agony of oxen
is of little countenance.
That of the virile animal

travels the universe.
If I must die, then may I
with my head high at last.
Dead and twenty times dead,
my mouth in the coarse grass.
My teeth shall remain clenched
and my beard bristling.
Singing, I wait for death,
for there are nightingales that sing
above the rifles' voice
and in the battles' midst.

Translated by A. L. Lloyd from
POEMS FOR SPAIN

Departure

HOWARD FAST

IN A WAY, it was like I had become old overnight, and I woke
up heavy; I woke up like a man suddenly with a family, two
kids and a wife, and rent to pay, but I had none of those things,
only a feeling that this, for me, was the end of a lot of things,
crazy drinking sprees and whoring and foolish bats of one kind or
another, all the things that made them grin at me and put up
with it, too, whatever it was, the way you put up with a clown.
"Clowning," they would say, "that sonovabitch is always clowning." But they didn't mind.

I shaved carefully and thoroughly, and Laurençon, who had
a four-year-old girl at home, made some crack about how she did
as well but without a blade, just a time-worn inept crack, but an
indication that it was nobody's lark, nobody's day of grace. "Go
to hell," I told him.

"No offense, sonny."

"To hell with you, pop. You can't offend me. My mind to
me a kingdom is. Age is no achievement; it's just a passage of
time."

The trucks were waiting, but I still dressed slowly and deliberately. For some reason I didn't fully understand, I had a rela-
tionship with my clothes, the boots I had won at the bandage
raffle, the heavy brown pants, the blue ski jacket, the black
beret. I had never liked my clothes before, but I liked them
now; they seemed to be unusual clothes, and I felt foolish but
sticky and sentimental toward them. I even borrowed a clothes
brush from Cohen and brushed them off. It was good for a
laugh from everyone who saw me, but I didn't do it for a laugh.

The whole battery was like that. To see them offhand, you
wouldn't have known, but as I was with my clothes, so each of

them was with one thing or another; and in the thick soup of dawn, they moved with measure and deliberation, as if they were counting out steps to a prearranged dance. I try to think of some of the things that were said, but it was so long ago and I was young. Words don't stick as well as the scent of the damp earth, the sound of the truck motors idling, the pale flash of a spotlight that had overstayed the darkness. These things made a pattern for memory; I suppose Lossowski was telling us to step lively and get moving, but I don't remember for sure. I do remember that the truck we got into was already half-full of Croats, big, sleepy-eyed, blond men, who grinned at us and pushed together to give us plenty of room.

Our truck roared into life, and we drove out of the hospital compound.

"Goodby, Denia," Mac Goldstein said thoughtfully and respectfully. Then he handed me one across the behind, and told me, "Nice to go home, huh, kid?"

"Home is where you make it." Parker, an Englishman, used to say that, and I picked it up. I would pick up a lot of words and phrases then; maybe that's the way speech grows when you're a kid. Sometimes, I used them right, but mostly wrong, I suppose, and it may be that they stand out across all that bridge of time for that reason. A word, a phrase, or a sentence is flung away, and how are you supposed to remember, even if you have taken an oath and are up before a formal court of the law? If I were under oath and answering, I don't know but that I'd perjure myself anyway.

How old were you?

I don't know—twenty or twenty-one.

You don't know? Surely you know. Surely you can think back and calculate. You are an intelligent and thoughtful human being.

Am I?

What date was it?

It was the fourteenth of January, or the fifteenth, or the sixteenth. They don't figure a date by a date, you know; the way they figure—when my first born saw the light, or when I threw a fistful of dirt on the grave of my blessed mother, or when the cow calved, only there were no more cows then, or when the shadow of the church was ragged instead of straight and heat lightning of four colors flashed in the east; but not by a calendar. So I can remember that before we went into the barracks at Valencia, where they all were, the men of all nations, French and Slavs and Croats and Serbs and Germans and yellow-haired Northmen and dark-haired men of the South, the Italians and the Greeks and the Crete men—before we went into the great barracks there, I saw a Spanish girl who was more beautiful than any other girl that lived, slim and with a lissom stride, and she walked past and was gone, but I remember her and that was the day it was, and I have been in love with her ever since but never saw her again.

I remember too the color of the Mediterranean sky that evening when we went down to the boats.

It was the same day?

Well, I think so. It seems to me that it was the same day. You see, I was in love with the girl, and thinking about her, and it seems that I was only in the barracks for a while, because all I remember, aside from the fact that there were many thousands of men there, was that the Greeks were singing a song. I remember that because I always thought what strange people the Greeks were, not like us or the British or the Germans, either, more like the Spaniards, maybe, and they never seemed to grow tired; it was always beginning for them; wherever they were, it was beginning, a very hopeful people. I remember the song because it was a song of love, and I was in love, in a way of speaking, and the sky over the harbor was like that, pink that turned violet and made me want to cry. You know the way guys are; they kept ribbing me because I had stopped clowning; it wasn't fair to them, I should have kept on clowning, but I couldn't; and then when we marched onto the boat, I began to cry; but it was almost dark and nobody noticed.

It was an excellent operation, smooth and without a hitch,

378

just the way the League of Nations and the Congress of the United States and the Reichstag wanted it to be, except that the boats were old and dirty and rusty and nobody was very sure about what kept them afloat. We marched onto our boat and down the steps into the hold. Before we went down into the hold, I looked back at the beautiful city, Valencia, the jewel, the ancient one. How do I recall what I thought then? I was a kid, a tough, hard-boiled, wise-cracking kid who would live forever, but I was tenderly in love and my face was wet with tears, and I must have thought profoundly and deeply. Or perhaps I thought of nothing but goodby.

If I thought goodby, it was the way you do when you are very young, and every place you are you will be back again, so dry your tears of sorrow. The French have a good word for it, but there is no word in English that is just right. There was a Welsh miner there from Pittsburgh, who was a captain with the 129th Brigade, who were Yugoslavs, and a hand grenade had torn open his loin, his testicles, his stomach and his legs, yet he was able to walk; and he stood at the edge of the hold, watching the darkening city, the jewel city, the bereaved one, but said nothing. I don't know what his goodby was. There were thirty-five or forty of us who were Americans, and we went down into the cargo hold, a big, empty place at the bottom of the ship, and all around us there was warmth and odor from the men of many nations, the sick, the wounded, the stretcher cases too, and they clamped on the hatches so that not an ounce of light shone through, and the ship put out to sea.

I can tell it as a dream, but not really as a memory. When I lie at night and I am afraid to die, as all men are, except now and then when there is a thing worth dying for, I think of it, and it's like a balm for a troubled soul. But what is memory as against the facts? And, believe it or not, there is no memory for terror, for there in that hold men couldn't breathe or sleep or move, but I do not remember that anyone was afraid. But maybe my memory is poor and because I was a kid, they were good to me, asking me:

"How's it going, kid?"

"Good enough."

"Well, take it easy. Easy does it."

"Look, lay off me. I'm all right."

"Sure, you're all right, kid, you're all right."

But where do you stow your thoughts when your thoughts tell you that the fascists must know, and they will come out in a fat-bellied German battleship and pick off the old tubs like a hunter picks off ducks? The Slavs made a song; they are the loneliest people in the world, and yet they are never lonely the way we are lonely, and when they sing a song there is a memory of all the hurts they knew and their fathers and their grandfathers. I like our songs better. We sang *Digging Our Way to China*. Then we sang *There's a Long, Long Trail a-Winding*, which is the most beautiful song in the world, and the saddest, too, as I remember, for someone in love and lost of his love. I don't remember anything else of particular importance, and I suppose we slept.

It was seven o'clock in the sunny morning when we arrived at Barcelona, and for some strange reason our arrival there is confused in my mind with all the old newsreel pictures I have seen before then and since of troops coming home by ship and departing too; but really I don't suppose it was too much like that. But there were people on the dock, and I learned afterwards that Negrín was there. I don't remember him, but I remember André Marty; it was the first time I had seen him, and the guys pointed him out.

They had let us up on deck with the sunrise. A submarine was escorting us, and after I saw it, I felt a lot better. I don't remember us talking about anything else but the submarine, even when we entered the bomb-wracked harbor and saw the sunken ships. And the bigness of Barcelona was different from the loveliness of Valencia. We hold Barcelona, so I told it to the nameless girl who had walked past me with such a lissom stride. We hold Barcelona, and, by God, we will hurl the fascist back into the hills of Portugal, and there will be a victory parade in Madrid, and as I march down the Avenue, I will see her and she will recognize me.

You remember well, and you remember badly?

It's that way, I'm sorry, some little things you remember and some big things you forget. I remember a melon rind floating in the water.

By eight o'clock we were all of us disembarked. The trucks for us were drawn right up to the docks, and we climbed into them. They took us to the barracks, which were on top of a hill outside of Barcelona. I don't know what the hill was called, or what was the name of the barracks, but it was a barracks in the old Spanish style, four square, with a compound in the center, and there were balconies all around four or five stories high, a place big enough to hold all of us, and we were thousands. There were all the Internationals who were left; there were the men of the nations. Someone—I don't know who it was—but someone said to me:

"Put it in your memory, kid, put it in your heart."

"My heart is full," I said, speaking in Spanish. "My heart is full and flowing over. I don't want to go home. I have no home, I am the homeless one." You say things in another tongue, and they do not sound foolish, as they would in English. Whoever he was, he answered so softly, "*Vamos juntos, vamos juntos* ——." And I thought of the thousand and one times I had wanted to go home, whimpered to go home, pleaded to go home, wept to go home, a frightened kid and no soldier, but now I was a soldier and no land to fight for, no people to give me arms and say: Stand here, stand and no further.

They called us out and we filled the balconies and listened to Marty speak. Then Negrín spoke. Then the whole place broke into the *Internationale*, in fifteen tongues, and that is a memory, for when had it happened before and when would it happen again? And we were going away; we were leaving Spain, who is like a beautiful woman you love, and we were going away.

It could have only been a day or two later when the thing happened. The fascists had reached Barcelona, you understand,

and we had moved up to a place called Casa de la Selva. It was the way out; it was the end already, and there were only the Cubans and the Mexicans with us, and we had stayed too long; we were guests departed but lingering, and we had given away to the Spaniards left behind our guns, our leather belts, our boots, and whatever else was of value. We ate and we slept and we waited, and rumors filled the air; but the strongest of all the rumors was to the effect of Barcelona being handed over to the enemy, the pig with a voice, the dog without even a dog's soul, the fascist; given up and no struggle; handed over and no struggle; a gift for the devil. I lay in the sun, and my love lay beside me. I told someone then that I was in love. With whom? With a Spanish girl whose eyes are like black olives and whose lips are like poppies. They would have been fools to believe me, but we believed anything then. It was my first love and my last.

You remember what you want to remember; a man's past is part of all the past, and everywhere little gates are carefully closed. Only when it is all finished, our way, will we open all the gates. It was two or three or four days after we were there that the big meeting was called in the one theater the town boasted. Seven or eight hundred of us crowded in there, full and over-filled and cloudy with the smoke of our brown-paper cigarettes.

This is it, kid, someone who knew and was on the inside.

He spoke in Spanish, "You men of the Internationals, *amigos de corazón,* you men of the Internationals who are my comrades, my brothers-in-arms, listen to me! We will defend Barcelona to the death. We go back!"

That is also a memory. I cried again; I put my hands over my face and wept, but I haven't wept since then. Through all the rest, I was dry-eyed. No more clowning, and the kid was not a kid anymore. Sitting and listening to the speakers, one after another, telling how Barcelona could be held and made a bridge-head for all free men, I made a disposition of myself. Then we went outside into the dry sunlight of Spain.

The people from our land, America of the lovely name, the

382

free land over the mountains and over the sea, went to a carpentry shop, and there some volunteered and others said they
would go home. The volunteers would not go home anymore.
They stayed together, talking and making arrangements for the
battery; I didn't have anything to say, and someone asked me:

"What is it, kid, worried?"

"No."

"Take it easy, kid. Nobody is brave."

"I'm not brave," I said. My childhood was over, youth and
adolescence and the sprouting of the weed as juices run through
its stem, and the wonderful, beautiful conviction that you will
live forever while all other mortals die, manhood is a benediction
as well as a curse, and the calm inside of me was life's repayment. It was a fair exchange. "I'm not brave," I said. "I want
to stay here."

You see, it was to defend Barcelona to the death, if necessary, and most likely necessary, and you made your own choice.
The great bulk of the Internationals were gone, but you had
stayed with the leavetaking. You had overstayed; then sleep,
and tomorrow we will break bread again.

What else do you remember?

Well, then, I also remember these things: the children who
played in the streets, they the inheritors, and I was grown now
and saw them as children. The fresh baked bread we had for
our dinner, oh, honored guests. We shared our bread with the
children, who made us at home as you do with a guest who is no
longer a stranger. There were also things to be done, arrangements for the new guns, which were coming down from France,
arrangements for officers and for a table of organization, arrangements into the sunset, the sweet cool night. I was bedded with
a cobbler's family, and we sat before bed with a glass of wine
and a piece of sausage.

Partake, oh cousin, and tell us about how it goes in the
South. Is there death in the South? Will there be victory or defeat? Will the fascists be driven back?

A su tiempo.

Cunning words from an old fighter. You are one of the new

383

ones, a machine gunner?

An artilleryman.

Drink the wine and don't spare the sausage. When will Spain see better men? A glass of wine makes the couch easy.

And then I slept until a whistle wakened me, and this was it, was it not? We formed into ranks and then onto the train, and nobody really knew except rumors; but after a while we understood. The train was going north, not south. Barcelona would not be held; the last of the Internationals were going away. This was a night train for the border, salute and farewell. Somewhere, men were afraid; somewhere men lost heart and hope, and they had opened the doors and said: Take this maiden for yourself, she with the lips as red as poppies and the lissom stride. I had only hatred and contempt for those whose eyes were wet now.

"What is it, kid?"

"To hell with you! To hell with you!"

And when the train stopped in the morning, we were in France.

From DEPARTURE AND OTHER STORIES
by Howard Fast, by permission of the author.

The Last Days

HERBERT L. MATTHEWS

THE LAST PERIOD of the Catalan offensive, which centered around Figueras and which I covered by daily trips from Perpignan, was one of the most baffling and significant of my career. I often think about it and wonder whether I made a fool of myself, and to what extent I harmed my reputation. After it was over my publisher reproached me with having misled readers of *The New York Times* into believing that the situation was consistently better than it proved to be. From the professional point of view, I had to acknowledge the justice of the reproof. And yet. . . .

Negrín's idea to move straight from Barcelona to Madrid, rather than Figueras, was more feasible and nobler, but the other members of the Government, with a few exceptions, were made of weaker stuff. Figueras was the only other possibility, after it became obvious that Gerona would soon be on the battle front. But there had been two much delay, too much preparation in Figueras, and a complete disorganization in all the services, with those thousands of refugees acting as an incubus that could not be shaken off.

Yet there were moments when it seemed as though Negrín could handle the matter, at least to the extent of restoring order and hanging on for a month or so. The two weeks that elapsed before the Rebels cleaned up Catalonia and reached the French frontier seem brief in retrospect—as, indeed, any two weeks must be in the life of a nation—but to those who lived through them day after day they were interminable. There was a great deal of Spanish—and, for that matter, European—history packed into those days, and the session of the Cortes which was held in the Castle of Figueras on February 1, 1939, will be a symbol as glorious in its way as that of Cadiz in 1811, when Napoleon's Army had overrun the Peninsula. Those are the pages of a nation's history which never fade. Figueras was not the last agony of an ancient order. A live and enduring force was evoked there, something essentially and eternally Spanish, and it will rise again.

Negrín was, as always, the rallying point for whatever strength there was in the resistance. I saw him in the Castle of Figueras on January 27. The Castle had been a fortress, prison, barracks, but never in its long history had it been the seat of government. It was built on a hill dominating the town—a huge, rambling structure, with outer and inner walls, a drawbridge and deep cellars. Safe and powerful it certainly was, but completely devoid of any facilities for being the seat of government. Pieces of paper had been pasted up on various doors: "*Ministerio de Estado,*" "*Presidencia de Consejo,*" and the like, and inside were bare rooms with plain tables and chairs. In contrast with the luxurious buildings in Barcelona, nothing could have been more depressing.

Indeed, every physical aspect of the whole situation was depressing. Figueras was a madhouse of bewildered officials and soldiers, struggling desperately, not only with their own work, but with those thousands of swarming refugees who filled every house and doorway and covered almost every inch of the streets where men, women and children slept through the bitterly cold nights with almost no food, and certainly no place to go.

The inevitable drift was toward the frontier, and there the refugees found the French *Gardes Mobiles.* My guess that day was that there were no fewer than 250,000 unfortunates strung out all along the road and in every village from Mataró to the frontier. That proved approximately right, but I never thought that virtually all of them would end up in French concentration camps. . . .

But, in spite of everything, there was that high, indomitable resolve which somehow gave a feeling of hope, despite the evidence of one's eyes. Negrín was so positive about it, and I knew the man too well to think that he was bluffing.

"The war will continue; the Army is establishing new lines; the rearguard is being reorganized," he told me. "This is where we stay as long as we can, and we hope it will be indeed long —that is, until we can get back to Barcelona and Madrid."

Foolish words, you might say, but the spirit that prompted them was the same as that which had saved Spain before. You cannot speak with contempt of people who do not know when they are beaten. At worst, they had the foolhardiness of Don Quixote.

However, there was no loss of authority, except in so far as the difficulties of communication hindered the transmission of orders. There were no mutinies or rioting or usurpations of power. The chaos did not come from that. The customs and police authorities were doing their duties as usual. The Army was taking orders from the Government. There was still plenty of money available. A recovery seemed possible, but only on one condition—and this everyone realized—that new materiél be allowed in. For a few days the Spaniards nourished the hope, despite all disappointments, that France would relent. . . .

When I went back to Figueras [from twenty-four hours in Perpignan] the hopes rose again. There had been a lull at the front and a line—a very weak one, but still a line—had been established, with the troops actually counter-attacking in some places. Communications, although still bad, had improved. To Figueras had been given a new life, and one with genuine order. Traffic was being routed through with reasonable speed; the refugees were being cleared out slowly but steadily, and those who remained were being fed free at the popular restaurants, where they received one dish per meal, of rice or beans and meat. . . .

A reorganization of the Army staff had taken place. Sarabia had been removed and General Jurado named to succeed him. The stories we heard in Perpignan of wholesale desertions or the flight of the Army were false. There had been some desertions, but relatively few in the circumstances, and I saw more soldiers returning toward their units than straggling toward the frontier.

Above all, there was the fact that the Cortes were to meet the following day, February 1. For those who had fought so hard and so vainly, that was somehow a symbol of hope and promise. It meant that the Second Spanish Republic still existed—against Franco and the whole world. The constitution was to be obeyed; the framework of democratic government, however weakened, was to be supported once more. A gesture was to be made, as truly Spanish as any ever made in the tragic and glorious history of the country of Don Quixote.

To go through Junquera alone was a matter of a full hour in a car, crawling by inches through swarming humanity, and often having to stop because of jammed traffic. Fires were springing up all alongside the road, in the fields and back in the hills. The scene was an unending gypsy camp, as those thousands of pathetic individuals, who had nothing to do with that war except to suffer in it, settled down for another cold night.

We were back in Figueras early the next morning, for the meeting of the Cortes. No time had been set, because the Government did not want to send an invitation to the Rebels to bomb them. It was a day of tension, because everyone expected Figueras to be badly bombed. As we drove in, the trucks bearing the artistic treasures of Spain which the Government had so carefully packed and preserved throughout the war were lined up along the road, ready to be driven to safety. The weather was springlike, and the Government's protecting planes, working in relays from the airfield near Vilajuiga, were able to keep up a fairly constant patrol. . . .

Not even at Cadiz had the Cortes been held in so strange and picturesque a setting—down in the dungeon-like vaults of the old castle on the hill. At one time the place had been used for stables, and the stalls were still there, on one side of the low-ceilinged hall. The night was chilly, and some of the ministers and deputies kept their overcoats on throughout the session. The twelve ministers were squeezed together on a plain bench too short for them. Other benches and chairs had been placed facing them, and at right angles on their right, while on the left a dais and a rude tribune had been fixed up for Martinez Barrio, the President of the Cortes. . . .

Azaña, to his eternal disgrace, had refused to take the risk of being present. Some others, like La Pasionaría, were in Madrid and could not get there; others, like Portela Valladares, who had rallied to the Government when it seemed likely to win, had thought better of their loyalty; still others, like Caballero and Araquistain, were nursing their bitterness in other places. In all, there were present less than seventy of the full Cortes of four hundred and seventy-three deputies.

It was in this setting, with the Republican flag displayed for the last time at a Cortes of the Second Republic, with its tribune covered with red brocade, with cheap carpets on the stone floor and plain wooden seats, that Martinez Barrio tapped his gavel at 10:25 on the night of February 1, 1939, and the session began.

"You are meeting in difficult circumstances," he said. "You are the legitimate and authentic representation of the people. Keep your passions in check. This session will probably be historic in the life of Spain. You are writing a page of honor for the future of the Spanish fatherland."

Negrín was the first speaker, and the only one who mattered. Those of us who knew his state of physical exhaustion and discouragement wondered whether he would be able to keep on talking. Several times he had to stop to pull himself together, and sometimes he seemed almost too dazed to express his thoughts coherently, especially after his notes gave out when he was half way through, and he had to speak extemporaneously. I do not believe any text of his speech has ever been published, and I only have my disjointed notes to go by.

He spoke of the "severe atmosphere of war" through which they were passing, but said that now "spirits were tranquilized and fears calmed." There could have been "a definite disaster," but it had been avoided. For a while "a wave of panic had almost asphyxiated the rearguard, paralyzed the Army, destroyed the Republic." There had been "a lack of communication between the Government and its people, and an exploitation of that panic by the enemy, but there had been no rising against the Government. In fact, the contrary was true."

He then went on to explain why there had been a panic. There were "too many people in Loyalist Spain. Millions had fled before the Fascists, and that is the best proof of the feeling of our people. The massacre of Santa Coloma de Queralt demoralized the rearguard. It was no surprise, and the Government was prepared. After the fall of Tarragona it had asked the French Government to accept 100,000 to 120,000 old people, women and children, but had been refused.

"Public order has been maintained by public will, and not by force. The Government's energy is national. In three days it had solved the refugee problem, thanks to the French Government."

Again he spoke of the panic, which had affected many soldiers as well as civilians. They were taking "strong measures," but "the morale of the Army was good." There had been "a panic organized by provocateurs, by lies, which undermined morale. Those were our worst enemies, and we could not combat them for lack of means. There are few examples of an army that fought so long against such odds. Many were without arms, waiting for their comrades to die so that they could pick up their rifles. The lack was not their fault, nor the Government's." (This was the only time in his speech that he showed emotion, and for a moment it seemed as though he would break down.)

"Our terrible and tremendous problem," he continued, "has always been the lack of arms. We, a legitimate Government, had to buy arms clandestinely, as contraband, even in Germany and Italy! We managed to make some, and scrape along."

Fixing his eyes steadily on us of the foreign press, he told of the Government's loyalty and how it had kept all its promises, hoping thereby that the democracies would change their attitude and give the Government a chance. With deep bitterness the Premier spoke next of "the farce of 'Non-Intervention' and 'the Italian withdrawal [of 10,000 men] followed by new shipments of men and materiél.'"

Before the last offensive he had said that "we would lose ground, but must save the Army, so that if materiél came through we could thus save the situation. We could have brought matériel in if we had kept our nerves, if the rearguard had conserved its unity."

"The Army has reformed," he claimed. "If we can hold on to a part of Catalonia, it would mean the prolongation of the war, with all its consequences."

Negrín's only attack on the British followed. He picked a little thing, the treatment of the Government destroyer *José Luis Diez* at Gibraltar, but from the significant way in which he looked at us, it was clear that he wanted the major point to be driven home. He told how the repairs in Gibraltar harbor were made by the Government at its own expense; how the British had announced the date of departure; how the Rebels were allowed to attack the *José Luis Diez* in British waters, damaging it badly. Finally, he told how the crew was arrested by the British authorities who, ignoring the Government's protests, asked each member separately whether he wanted to go back to Loyalist Spain or into Franco Spain. Every man voted to return to the Government side.

In this protest against a relatively unimportant injustice, Negrín was diplomatically but clearly condemning the whole British system of favoring the Rebels against the Loyalists.

"We are fighting for the independence of our country," he went on, "and also for democracy. This is a struggle of two civilizations, of Christianity against Hellenism. We are defending other countries—which are not only not helping us, but are causing us our greatest difficulties.

"To save the peace of Europe they let Austria go, and cut up Czechoslovakia. If the time came when Spain would provide one more sacrifice, would they be in a stronger position to meet the aggressors, to defend themselves? Here is where the answer will come to the question of whether a few totalitarian powers will control the world, or whether it will continue divided. Hitler and Mussolini are wrong in placing their support behind Franco, because the people are not with him, and because the fruits of victory will never be gained."

The Premier then offered three points which would be accepted by the Loyalists as conditions of a just peace: First, a guarantee of the independence of the country; second, a guarantee that the Spanish people would decide on its regime and its destiny; third, that when the war was over all persecutions and reprisals would end.

"We will fight to save Catalonia," he concluded, "and if we lose it we will continue to fight in the central zone. Countries do not live only by victories, but by the examples which their people have known how to give in tragic times."

It was on that noble theme that the long speech ended. No one could call it an oratorical masterpiece; it was disjointed, and badly delivered, by a man so exhausted that he could hardly stand, yet it should take its place with the great documents of Spanish history.

Representatives of each of the major parties then followed, with brief addresses. Martinez Barrio asked for an explicit vote of confidence in the Government, which was passed unanimously, by acclamation. . . .

So ended the last Cortes of the Second Spanish Republic. . . .

Whether or not the Spaniards were in a panic, the French were certainly becoming panicky. They had tried from the beginning to wash their hands of the war; now it was coming toward them in the form of 250,000 civilian refugees and about 150,000 soldiers, and much as the French wanted to keep the Spaniards out, it was being realized gradually that the only way to do so would be to line up the French Army along the frontier and shoot the Spaniards down as they tried to come over—which was unthinkable even to the Frenchmen who were handling the situation. In spite of all warnings, no preparations had been made to care for the huge mass of men, women and children. The French at first wanted none of them; then they thought they would take the women and children. Next, they saw that the wounded would have to be let in, and finally, that the border would have to be thrown open to all. When that happened, the results were appalling—for the refugees.

The Loyalist soldiers were fighting now only with the primitive instinct of protecting their women and children, their wounded and the old people who were trekking desperately toward the inhospitable frontier while Rebel planes swept along the roads in raid after raid of bombing and strafing. The soldiers had but one task left—to "cover" the refugees until they could get to safety—and then to go down fighting to the end. No other action of the Loyalists did them more honor than that last despairing stand of men so fatigued they could scarcely hold their rifles, with virtually no ammunition, and still facing fearful odds.

During the night the Government had gone to the village of La Bajol, just inside the frontier opposite Las Illas. We could not even find them that day, because nobody at Figueras seemed to know where they were. We tried Agullana, which was very near, and actually saw Rebel planes bombing La Bajol without realizing why they were doing it.

The evacuation had been forced by the long-expected destruction of Figueras from the air. Gerona had been bombed sixteen times the day before and an equal number of times on the 2nd. The bombing of Figueras never stopped for five hours on the afternoon of February 3. No one knew why the Rebels did it, since they were advancing as fast as they could go, and it made little difference whether the Government left there on the 3rd or a day or two later. Perhaps it was merely an automatic reaction of the military mind.

Figueras was half deserted when we arrived, and trucks were taking out what civilians remained. Up in the Castle, preparations were under way to clear everything out. Huge piles of documents were being burned. We asked a high staff officer whether we could drive on to Gerona, and he quickly disabused us of the idea. At the end he made a bitter remark which I had heard only a few times during the war: "If we had only fought as the totalitarian powers did, bombing, killing, working on the rear-guard as they have on ours, treating prisoners as they did ours, we would not be in this fix." . . .

The next morning a report got about that Figueras had fallen. Who spread it, or why, will never be known, but the effect was electrical. For the French it meant that the Loyalist Army was almost on the border, and they could no longer postpone the decision they should have made, for humanitarian reasons, many days before. The frontier was thrown wide open from Cerbère to Bourg-Madame, and the refugees—men, women, children and soldiers — were allowed to stream into France with all their belongings. For a while the peasants were permitted to take in their carts and mules, even their goats and sheep, but a few days later all that was stopped, and everything was confiscated to be given to Franco. All war materiél was sequestered in fields near the frontier; soldiers were disarmed, and not only that, but their binoculars, cameras, pocket-knives and other personal belongings were ruthlessly taken away and dumped in a common heap. We learned of cases where even cigarettes were taken by *Gardes Mobiles*. Much of it was their plunder, and at least one guard retired and bought a café in Bordeaux with the proceeds. It was all done with a brutality that sickened those of us who had to watch the process day after day. . . .

By reading the Perpignan *Eclair* for the following day one can guess at the welcome the Loyalists received.

"Exhausted chauffeurs slept at their wheels," the newspaper wrote, "awaiting orders to go into the interior of France, which is so hospitable to the Marxist cowards. In one limousine a blonde and outrageously made-up woman could be seen, drinking avidly. . . .

"The number of Anarchist refugees in Perpignan has grown in an alarming manner. Certain of these bandits are circulating insolently. . . . Some of them submitted with bad grace to the search at the border. . . . It is truly scandalous that gasoline trucks have been allowed to come in which, at any instant, might provoke a catastrophe. Everything is permitted to Marxism. . . .

"One comes across police officers of the Russian Cheka, an organization well known under the initials S.I.M. . . .

"Perpignan is now infested with Spanish bandits. . . ."

And so it went. The Loyalists had thought they were incidentally defending France in their long and hopeless struggle, but they were now learning their mistake.

The French, much to their surprise, found that the "Marxist horde" gave them no trouble whatever as they came into France.

A few dozen New York traffic policemen, stationed between Le Perthus and the concentration camps would have sufficed as well as the huge military forces assigned to the task. The Loyalists simply wanted to know what to do and where to go.

The troops who came over acted like the disciplined soldiers they were. Two files of them crossed the frontier bridge at Le Perthus, one on each side of the road, while down the middle were driven automobiles and trucks, bearing the women, children, wounded and all others who had a right to be there. At the French end they were quickly and brusquely "frisked." Then they continued out of the village and along the road. A few places had been set aside between Le Perthus and Le Boulou as temporary camps, but most of the refugees were directed up the road toward Argelès. The good humor of the crowd would have been remarkable if one did not know Spaniards.

The British Minister, Stevenson, who was at Amelie-les-Bains, was making great efforts to induce the Negrín Government to sue for peace. Jules Henry, the French Ambassador, was likewise doing his best. The British had already begun arranging for the surrender of Minorca to the Rebels—an unnecessary bit of treachery, in the circumstances. It had not yet been learned that "peace at any price" is the equivalent of national suicide if continued long enough. Actually, there was no basis for negotiation. Franco demanded unconditional surrender, and it was obvious that the Government had to yield or fight. They chose to fight, although they knew it would be a lone, hopeless struggle.

To be sure, with the best will in the world, the French Government could not have coped with that sudden and overwhelming flood. On February 6 alone, some 40,000 came over at Le Perthus and about 25,000 at Cebère, without counting the minor passes. Then there were all the vehicles and all the materiél. One must blame the French, however, for the lack of preparation, and the heartlessness and bad grace with which the thing was done when it had to be done. By "the French" I mean the Government and Army, not the French people, who were kindly and considerate when they came into contact with the refugees. The thousands of women and children who were distributed throughout the villages of southern France received a genuine hospitality that was just as indicative of the true French character as was the callousness of its officialdom.

There was one last, great day—February 7—for which those who believe in Spanish Republicanism must be forever grateful. The stream of refugees, Carabineros, Assault Guards and deserters had flowed steadily across the frontier all the previous night, but by morning it had begun to dwindle, and soon became no more than a trickle. Then the French and the world discovered that they had made a gigantic mistake. Figueras had not fallen! The Army was still fighting twelve miles south of Figueras, fighting in good tactical order, with its artillery and other services functioning smoothly, with not only its General Staff, but its Government inside Catalonia.

The panic was in the rearguard, not in the Army, and it had been caused by the false report that Figueras had fallen. That report came from very high Spanish sources, and there were ugly tales about it, but the important thing was that the French believed it; the refugees believed it; the panic began, and the French threw open the frontiers because they thought all was over. It was just as well that they thought so, for it permitted the Army to protect their women, children and old folks, and left their rear free for a last, orderly retreat instead of a stampede. The French guessed wrong by only forty-eight hours, but that made all the difference.

And when everyone stood at the bridge in Le Perthus, looking anxiously down the road for the first signs of the fleeing army, what they saw was not a routed force, but a group of Internationals on parade, withdrawing with discipline and pride from Loyalist Spain—flags flying, songs on their lips, and fists raised in the Popular Front salute. Never had they been such a symbol of the ideals for which they fought as when they marched up, four abreast, to be reviewed by André Marty, Luigi Gallo, and Pietro Nenni, while the French officers looked on with respect and the Spaniards present cheered, and wept to see them go. . . .

Not even the members of the League Commission were permitted to talk to them, for the French authorities said that until the camp was properly organized the Internationals could not be visited. A few of us drove ahead and saw the camp, after which it was easy to understand why the French would prefer not to have League officials see it, and why the Spaniards felt so much humiliation and resentment.

The camp was several miles outside Argèles on sandy ground near the sea. Miles of barbed wire, in three concentric fences, had been strung around, with openings in four or five places, all strongly guarded by Senegalese and *Gardes Mobiles*. Senegalese soldiers were placed as guards at hundred-yard intervals, facing in toward the camp. That Senegalese should have been used was the crowning humiliation for Spaniards who had fought the Moors for more than two years and a half, and indeed, had a centuries-old tradition of fear and hatred of their African enemies.

Men, some women and children, civilians and soldiers, the wounded, the ill and the well, were all marched in, willy-nilly, and that was all. An attempt had been made to put up some flimsy barracks, but few were finished, and they did not hold more than a hundred of the refugees. Once inside, everyone fended for himself, although the wounded and ill got some elementary care from a first-aid station, which was as yet very inadequate.

Everyone slept on the ground, most of the men digging for themselves a slight depression for protection against the night winds. They could not dig more than a foot or so down because water would be struck quickly. That brackish water, incidentally, was the only water available in the camp, for either washing or drinking, and a plague of dysentery spread. There was not a single latrine for those 25,000 persons.

I could go on for pages, with the sickening details. At the time it was impossible to publish them in full, because the French in Washington protested, and some of us got reproaches from our editors. Since editors and readers were not there in France to see for themselves, we could do nothing to prove the truth of what we were writing. In time the facts became known, and are now beyond dispute. Like all neutral observers there at the time, I was hot with rage and helplessness. I suppose one could not expect newspapers to print details so utterly damaging to a friendly country whose diplomatic representatives were making violent, if unjustified, complaints. What we knew was so bad that when the story got around that the Spahis (French Moroccan cavalrymen) were using whips to herd the Spaniards into the concentration camps, we believed it. Certainly Spahis were used because I saw them, and that they should have been employed against proud, sensitive and courageous people was little short of criminal. The degradation was not theirs, but of the French, who could treat the most courteous and hospitable of races with such utter meanness.

By the afternoon of February 7 it could be said truly that the Army had performed its primary task of saving its women, children and useless units. That alone was a great accomplishment, but what thrilled all Spaniards on that day, and restored some of the pride and courage which the panic had taken from them, was the realization that the Army had not broken or fled in disorder. The idealism, the dignity, the traditions of Spanish soldiery, the reputation of the Popular Army—all these had never been lost. That screen of humanity had merely hidden the truth, giving full play to false rumor.

The beginning of the end came the next day, when the Rebels broke through to Llers, three miles northwest of Figueras, and the final orders were given to retreat into France. To Galán's 12th Corps was given the task of falling back through La Junquera, while Lister's 5th and Tagüeña's 15th, both under Modesto's command, withdrew toward Port Bou. The Government's last refuge of La Bajol was terribly bombed—raid following raid—until it was obvious that no one could stay there, so Negrín reluctantly departed, with Vayo, Mendez Aspe, Uribe, and Rojo.

Meanwhile, two Government promises were kept. As we drove into Le Perthus at ten in the morning, a ragged, bearded, wan-looking column of men marched sadly in. They were 2,000 prisoners of the Government, released to spare them the needless danger of being caught in the firing lines. It was a pity that the gesture, which was typical of the Government's policy, should have been more than wiped out by the murder of the Bishop of Teruel on that same day by some Anarchists who had been ordered to lead him, with other prisoners, into France. Something of the sort was bound to happen in those last bitter, confused days, and it would perhaps be more a matter of justice to wonder that there was so little of that sort of thing at the end of the war, compared to the beginning.

The other promise was kept when two more contingents of Internationals, 1,200 in all, paraded into France. I watched the first group of 800 Hungarians, Poles, Germans, and Austrians of the 11th and 13th Brigades come marching in, with songs on their lips, and flags flying. As they filed onto the frontier bridge they shouted "*Viva la República Española!*" They were "frisked" roughly by the *Gardes Mobiles*, and relieved not of arms, for they had none, but of cameras, field-glasses and typewriters. It was "Chapaieff" the commander of the 13th who had fought all through the war, who led them into France. Gustav Regler, German author and first Commissar of the Thaelmann Battalion, was in Le Perthus to greet his old comrades as they came over. Ludwig Renn was too ill to march, but not too ill to be put into a concentration camp by the French when he was carried out.

On that day there were still about one thousand five hundred Internationals unaccounted for, but they came through during the next few days, over the mountain passes and through Port Bou.

At one o'clock there was a tremendous explosion down the line, and a huge cloud of smoke rose on the horizon. A few days later Lister and others told me that it had been at the Castle of Figueras. The Loyalists had put all their remaining ammunition and explosives in it, something like 1,100 tons, and a million liters of gasoline. We had felt the concussion at Le Perthus, fifteen miles away.

High officers of the Loyalist Army began coming over, and I saw the commander of the Air Force, General Ignacio Hidalgo de Cisneros for the last time there, until we met in Mexico City in 1944. At three o'clock word came through that the Government's cortège was near. The commander of the *Gardes Mobiles* formed his troops, and as the cars drove up arms were presented and a personal greeting was extended by the commander. This was the last official courtesy extended to the Government of the Second Spanish Republic. Negrín and the other members of the cabinet, with Rojo, went into a three-story house on the Spanish-owned side of the street, between the bridge and the customs building in Le Perthus.

Walking back into Spain at about four o'clock I ran into "Paco" Galán, as cool and courteous as ever. "Can you hold for the night?" I asked. "Unhappily, no," he answered. "You know, we have an army with a big head and no body. It has nothing to function with. The men now have rifles, and we got some new American machine guns two days ago, but what can we do with them now except fight the last rearguard action?"

I wondered where those American machine guns had come from. But they had arrived too late.

And that was the end. Twelve hours later the Rebels had reached Le Perthus. Lister was still covering Port Bou, but it was only a question of hours there and at Puigcerda. The British were turning over Minorca to Franco. Only the central zone remained, and there was so much demoralization around Negrín and Vayo that despite their courage and optimism they were almost overwhelmed. It was only when they, and a few faithful supporters, who were later followed by Modesto, Lister, Galán, and other loyal officers, had shaken off the mire that surrounded them and flown to the Madrid zone, that one could feel sure the war was not over.

The duty to go on, as Negrín and the others saw it, was the necessity for protecting the lives of those whose very loyalty, patience and courage on the Government's behalf made their chances of escaping death or imprisonment very slight. As long as they fought on, there was always hope that a European war might come along and save them. It almost did. . . .

All the great figures of the Popular Army got out safely. I saw them all in the Spanish Consulate at Perpignan, and I was almost ashamed to go up and speak to them. They had been betrayed, and they had nothing to be ashamed of. Whatever soldiers could do they had done. Merino expressed their sentiments best, perhaps, when he said to me:

"We know the bitterness that awaits us here, but we also know that no human beings could have done more than we. Our resistance through these last weeks, when we never abandoned the struggle despite the hopelessness and odds against us, will surely do much to bolster the worldwide struggle against Fascism. You yourself have seen that the troops never lost courage or morale. They always did what we asked of them, and no army has ever been asked to do more than ours—to fight seven weeks, without materiél, without rest, without hope. And we fought! History must give us that credit."

That evening, at the hotel, a group of Nazi aviators, who had been prisoners of the Loyalists, but were set free so as to spare their lives, celebrated boisterously with a feast. They put a swastika flag in the center of the table, to which the fat little proprietor raised no objection, but one of the waiters remonstrated: "You must remember, this is still France!"

I was sick at heart that night when I wrote my last dispatch on the Spanish Civil War, but at least I, in my humble way, felt vindicated. "Countries do not live by victories alone," Negrín had said, "but by the examples which their people have known how to give, in tragic times. . . ."

From EDUCATION OF A CORRESPONDENT,
Harcourt, Brace, New York 1950
Excerpted From Lesson VII

You Have Not Fallen

RAFAEL ALBERTI

Dead in the sun, in the cold, in the bitter rain, the frost,
Beside the great torn holes which the guns have broken,
Under the drip of your blood, like harp strings, the fine grass
Sings again in the wind, your song, unsung, unspoken.

Torn from the sad bit of earth that bore you, you have become
Like proud seed, laid in a deep furrow of the land.
This furrow prepared for your sowing by war's plowshare
Receives your straight young bodies laid down with a ruthless
    hand.

It is not death, this sowing. There is a birth pang in your anguish.
Beneath the hard cover of the earth, life will quicken and stir,
Even as it pushes the thin blade, the ripening flower of the
    wheat field.
So youth shall rise again, youth shall become death's conqueror.

Who says that you are dead? Above the high sharp whistle
That marks the bullet's path, above the roar of guns,
Louder than rattle of the firing squad, the dirge of funerals,
Spain hears a chant of glory from her fallen sons.

Brothers, you are the living, and the living are not forgotten.
Sing with us now, facing life, facing the free wind, the sea;
Sing with our multitudes, from the hills, from the waving wheat
    fields.
You are not death, you are the new youth that shall make us free!

Translated by Katherine Garrison Chapin,
from AND SPAIN SINGS

402

> "Lifting up our hearts to the Lord, we give sincere thanks with Your Excellency for Spain's desired Catholic victory. We express our vow that your most beloved country, with peace attained, may undertake with new vigor the ancient Christian traditions which made her great. With affectionate sentiments we send Your Excellency and the most noble Spanish people Our Apostolic blessing."

PIUS XII IN TELEGRAM TO FRANCO,
April 1, 1939

"The Ancient Christian Traditions"

ANTONIO BAHAMONDE

THIS NARRATION, IN EVERY chapter, reflects the exact truth. Fully conscious of my responsibility before God, I am writing what I have to say only after careful meditation and with strict limitation to facts.

The clergy in Spain has rarely been found on the side of the people. The high dignitaries have never cared for the acrid smell of their miserable houses. They cannot relieve the pain, the anguish, the infinite suffering of the humble, because they avoid contact with them and only know them superficially. . . .

Consistently, the clergy from the very beginning of the movement, took the side of the "Nationalists." One of the first visits Queipo de Llano received was that of Cardinal Ilundain. The first act I witnessed of his definite collaboration was during the first month of the movement, on August 15, the feast-day of the Virgin of the Kings, patroness of Seville.

There was a morning mass in the cathedral for general communion organized by the Falange, which attended in large numbers, led by their chiefs, all in uniform, with arms of every kind —guns, pistols, daggers.

The altar of the Virgin was resplendent with surrounding bayonets. The general communion was administered. I saw a number of Falangists whom I knew to have had a direct hand in the massacres, approach the Holy Table with great fervor. Those were the days when the bodies of the dead were to be seen in the streets. A few days before, sixty-four corpses had been found along the walls of the piscina of the Remedies Convent.

I drew a sigh of relief. "Thank God, the assassinations are over! These people have repented for so much crime!" In my innocence it did not then occur to me, even remotely, to think that after they had partaken of Jesus Christ, those same Christian gentlemen, blessed by the Cardinal, were going to dedicate the night to the pursuit and murder of their brothers.

The following morning we witnessed the same spectacle as on all the other days: four bodies, two paces from the cathedral, in the street of García Vinuesa. The impression it made on me was so profound, the shock so great that even today it haunts my mind, and it will never be effaced so long as I live. It was a nightmare; it could not be. For my spirit it was a terrible blow which haunted me night after night and robbed me of sleep.

How could I explain the fact that, after having taken Communion, after receiving the God of Pardon, the Christ, the Love of Loves, these people could go right on murdering their brothers? I knew very well that it was the work of the Falange and of Queipo. I had seen all their leaders take Communion—and I knew that many of them were the actual executioners, who were responsible for the murders of that night and of all the nights that followed.

The unfortunates who were doomed to fall each night were gathered in Court No. 3 of the Commissariat of the greatly revered Jesus of the Great Power. A lady, as catechist, made a speech exhorting them to die worthily, and recited a series of clichés without revealing the slightest natural emotion at finding herself in the presence of human beings who were to be killed that night. She ended by begging them to confess and to repent of the crimes they had committed (ninety percent did not know why they were there); for, she said, if they repented, death would only produce a few moments of suffering and they would be delivered into life eternal.

The victims heard her in absolute silence. I have wondered many times how these wretched creatures endured that woman without strangling her. I have witnessed this scene many times. Some confessed. Those who wished to confess entered a small room in front, where there were two confessors.

One day two fathers of the Heart of Mary confessed the prisoners. Finding it monstrous to condemn so many innocent people to death, they went to see Diaz Criado, then Chief of Police, and they told him so. These ingenuous fathers believed he didn't know; they were convinced that many innocent people were being shot. Diaz Criado didn't let them finish. He told them they had allowed themselves to be deceived by Marxists, and that he knew very well what he was doing. So the good fathers, authentic religious and true Catholics, had the courage to see Queipo, explaining to him what they conscientiously believed.

Queipo promised to look into the matter and to take whatever measures were necessary to prevent the repetition of these lamentable cases. The "measures" were to send the two priests away, no one knows where. After that, the only priests who confessed the victims were Jesuits. There was no danger of their protesting, for they are the most convinced accomplices of the repression. I have many times, in the Commissariat of Jesus of the Great Power, watched these fathers come and go, bringing business to the offices which they settle according to their own whims. I have seen them, in the very presence of such persecution and grief, enjoying idle chit-chat with the police. Fathers Alonso and Uriarte, S.J., made daily visits to the Commissariat.

In Córdoba, confessions were received at first in the cemetery itself. The priest was driven there in an automobile, the window was opened to serve as a confessional, and there, in the darkness of night, the spiritual comfort was dispensed. I know a priest who begged insistently, and as a special favor, to have the executions postponed at least until he was out of ear-shot; a request that was often ignored. This priest became ill after witnessing a harrowing scene. One of the victims, after being shot and badly wounded, started to run—and took refuge in his car. He was dragged out and killed in the sight of the priest. The impression this made upon the priest was so profound that he was ill for nearly a month. He requested a leave of absence in order to recuperate, and went to Seville. He has not returned to Córdoba for fear of being forced to go to the cemetery again.

From the first days of the rebellion, the soldiers, the Falangists and the few Requetés* among them, displayed upon their chests a great number of religious medals, Sacred Hearts, scapularies and crucifixes. Within a few days the "fashion" became so widespread that there was not a soldier or civilian who did not have his lapels literally covered. To go out on the street without displaying some distinction of this kind was to risk arrest. The priests, far from putting an end to this absurdity, fomented it. They said it was beautiful to see how the religious spirit of the people had revived.

In consternation I saw all the Moors wearing their Sacred Heart of Christ, their medallion of the Virgin, their scapulary. Such a thing cannot be explained. Those who were true Catholics witnessed this farce with heavy hearts.

I have heard sermons in the villages that made me shudder. One Sunday I heard mass in Rota. The priest, from the altar and as though he were lecturing, said: "What did you think, that it was always going to be the same? Didn't men hesitate at the door of the church to see who was going to mass? And now? Now you are all very religious, all very humble. The most guilty and wicked have already given to God an account of their deeds; they are expiating their guilt for having fed the people the poison of Marxism, drawing them away from God. But there are still some others who think they are deceiving us. We shall discover them all; they shall all get what they deserve; not one shall escape; mark it well, *not one!* We must purge the country to the

---

* Requetés—armed bands organized by the followers of the Carlist pretender to the Spanish throne. Ed.

depths and rid it completely of all the putrefaction Russia has introduced into it. There are still some people who will have to settle their accounts—and soon.

"And the women who never used to come: here they are, every one of them devout. But you don't deceive me. I know you all very well indeed. And I give you this warning—every Sunday, all, all of you will come to mass; I will accept no excuse. Anyone who has little children can leave them shut up; anyone who has a sick relative can leave him alone. He won't die in a half-hour. On Sunday everyone comes to mass; don't let me have to repeat it. Anyone who doesn't come will suffer the consequences, for above all and before everything else comes obedience to the mandates of Holy Mother Church.

"And what about the children? What shall I say about them? There are some who don't even know how to cross themselves, and their former teacher, a wicked Mason, cannot pay, by the death he suffered, for the crime of not teaching the catechism to the little angels of God. They must all come to study the whole catechism and learn the doctrine which the new master will teach them."

On August 14, 1937 Badajoz commemorated the anniversary of the "liberation" of the city. This was the day chosen for putting into effect the unification of the provincial militia. It was done on paper, for in reality there is no such unification.

Various acts were celebrated. The first was the solemn mass. The wide naves of the cathedral could not accommodate the enormous throng. The first to enter were the Falangists, armed with rifles and fixed bayonets; then came the Requetés and last the civilian defense (National Militia) without uniforms or arms. The officers of these organizations took places in the presbytery, presiding with the religious dignitaries. On the right, the Falange placed their banner, unfurled and flanked by bayonets; on the left was the banner of the Requeté, and in the center the blue and white pennon of the civilian defense. It was escorted by a group of men in street clothes, who seemed very uncomfortable among so many uniforms. The "Pelayos" and the "Arrows," with their tin-plated bayonets, completed the picture.

A bugle call announced the entrance of the officiating bishop and the priests who assisted him. The mass began. "Peace unto men of good will." What an evil sound these words assumed in the midst of such war-like clatter. The evangel was followed by a sermon in patriotic and fiery tones:

"This is a moving scene; everyone is united under the command of the glorious Chief, to save the world from Marxist barbarism. It is a grave responsibility to sow discord and stir up disunity. For God and for Spain, antagonism must be laid aside. All, as one, must exterminate the enemies of God, who are the enemies of the Fatherland. One year ago today our troops entered in triumph, to free us from Marxism. The blood generously shed by our heroes and our dead, demands it of us. Unity, complete obedience to the Chief, to create a Spain like the Spain of Ferdinand and Isabel. The cross and the sword united will restore the days of glory to our Fatherland which, once again, is fulfilling its historic mission of saving the world from barbarism."

I rubbed my eyes. I thought, "Am I really in the House of God, listening to the holy sacrifice of the mass, or am I in some bull-ring listening to a patriotic harangue?" A bugle call disspelled my doubts. The Royal March resounded throughout the place and at the altar the priest raised the Blood of Christ, of Him who came into the world preaching pardon. I recalled His divine words as He died upon the cross: *"Father, forgive them for they know not what they do."*

At two o'clock in the afternoon a banquet was given by the municipality to the authorities and delegates who had come from Portugal to celebrate the anniversary.

There were fifty places. I attended, since I was a delegate of the government. The presiding officer was the bishop, who was attended by a priest dressed as a lieutenant of infantry, with a large Christ on his chest and a pistol in his belt. On his right sat the Governor of Elvas (Portugal). When His Eminence sat down, he read the menu, then rose and said in paternal and honeyed tones, "The hotel management seems to have forgotten that this is a fast-day. But, in order to cause the establishment no inconvenience, nor detract from this beautiful event, I will use the power vested in me by the Roman Pontiff and lift the prohibition against the eating of meat in return for an offering of alms."

He asked for a platter and went, himself, from one to another, taking the collection. He began with Canizares, who gave him fifty *pesetas*. We all felt obliged to give nothing less than five *duros*. When he was finished, he wrapped the offering in a napkin and handed it to Canizares, "for the wounded." Canizares opened the napkin, glanced at the contents and swiftly divided it into two equal parts, and said magnanimously, "For your poor, reverend bishop." The Portuguese were somewhat annoyed. Under our very eyes, these two gentlemen had divided up our money.

In my trips through the villages I had heard a great deal about the exploits of a certain priest of the regiment, although I did not know him personally. This was the priest whom the bishop chose to accompany him, the *only* ecclesiastic who attended the ceremony, a fact which is eloquent testimony to the regard the bishop felt for him, since it would have been more natural for him to have been accompanied by a lay familiar.

I was curious to meet him and asked the Governor to introduce me. He is about thirty years old, dark, with wavy hair, a common enough type, very talkative and rather congenial. I told him that, in my travels through the villages I had heard accounts of his acts of bravery. He told me his story.

He practiced his holy office in Safra (Badajoz), a town in which there was no fighting and there were no victims. He and all other Rightists were respected. When the troops arrived the town put up no resistance; it surrendered. When the regiment entered the town, he had joined it as chaplain. Before the troops left, he, knowing the town intimately, as well as the "Marxist rabble" who inhabited it, had the troops shoot a large number of people.

He left with the "colors" which took Badajoz and, when this company was destroyed, he joined the Eleventh Ensign, Second Regiment of the Legion, to which he is still attached. The two following scenes I heard from his own lips. In the cathedral of

Badajoz, on the day the regiment entered, a man had hidden in a confessional. The priest found him, pulled out his pistol and shot him on the spot.

He continued: "Don't imagine that we have an easy time in these villages. There are places that give us trouble. They resist and defend themselves. But they pay dearly for it. In Granaja de Torre-Hermosa, you know that dreadful barbarities and crimes were committed by the Marxists. They caused us many casualties. When we finally entered, I found four men and a wounded young woman hiding in a cave. I confiscated their two pistols and they were cynical enough to tell me that if these had been loaded, I wouldn't have captured them so easily. I made them dig a grave and I buried them alive as an example to the breed." In telling this he used many obscene expressions that he pretended to justify by saying that they were in common usage among the legionnaires.

Several days later I saw him at the Civil Administration, when he came to say goodbye to the Governor. We talked a bit. I asked him to show me the pistol from which he said he was never separated. He replied: "Here it is; this little pistol has rid the world of more than a hundred Marxists." We went out to have a beer. He gave me his address so that I could write to him. It is:

Juan Galán Bermejo
Chaplain of the Eleventh Ensign
Second Regiment

He is a native of Montanchez, where his family lives, and he was the priest of Safra until the arrival of the "liberating" troops. The bishop of his diocese shows him every consideration. As I have said, he is his favorite pastor.

Except for Málaga, in the territory held by the Government some churches were burned and priests were imprisoned without further molestation. But what has been the attitude of the "liberators" in this respect, these "liberators of the people," these rebels?

Their attitude has been totally different, not only because their deeds were done by men acting in their capacity of ministers of God, who condoned every crime, no matter how great, but also because they were active belligerents.

The clergy is the strongest bulwark of "Nationalist" Spain. Its highest dignitaries are the most zealous collaborators of the "liberating" movement. Anyone studying the problem will discover that the clergy, when persecuted, has not been persecuted as the representative of Christ, but for its acts in absolute and direct opposition to its ministry, and for its outright participation in the struggle against the people.

If the clergy had remained neutral, it would have suffered no harm. But they left their priestly ministrations to become belligerents, and should be treated as belligerents. They asked for it. The people discovered that upon the entry of the so-called "Savior troops," the priests whose freedom they had respected immediately became their most ardent persecutors. They believe that many laymen were shot down as the result of information supplied by the clergy. The responsibility is upon the clergy themselves, who, by their own acts, have unleashed the indignation and hatred of the people.

The attitude of the clergy in this tragic struggle that has undone Spain, should have been one of condemnation of the war and all its horrors. In an evangelic spirit they should have forgiven any attacks they may have suffered, and have made or at least attempted to make, peace the goal of their efforts. Certainly it was not their rôle to sow the seeds of hatred, nor to incite the fires of fratricidal passion, nor support and even bless the perpetrators of so many thousands of murders, against which, in no single case has there been any protest by the highest church dignitaries. With a vision that can only be called suicidal, they have openly taken the side of the "Nationalists."

How can they justify this attitude? It cannot be justified—there is no possible justification. They cannot plead ignorance. Those who live in the territory controlled by the "Nationalists" know very well that the crimes committed, by their very magnitude and monstrosity, are matters of common knowledge.

The "Nationalist" clergy has joined a political party. This is precisely their crime, a crime organized coldly and methodically. This is the party which is inspired by spurious and avaricious interest, against the legal power of the State, and which, aided by foreign nations, has mortgaged to those nations as a *quid pro quo,* the very soul of Spain itself. This is the party responsible for the destruction of thousands of homes. It is the party that has sown tears and death in all the families of Spain to such an extent that when the war is over it will be difficult to find anyone left who is not mourning the loss of one or all of his relatives.

It is disheartening to think that on the day when the legal government triumphs, irrefutable proof will be set before the world that hundreds of thousands of innocent victims have been created by this rebellion. Yes, innocent victims, gentlemen of the clergy. And the authors of these murders were helped and were blessed by the "Nationalist" clergy.

How can they justify themselves?

They have opened an abyss between the clergy and the people that will never be bridged. But the most terrible thing of all and one which constantly occupies my mind, is the fact that multitudes who were Catholics before the uprising, having witnessed the attitude of the clergy and its encouragement of crimes against people who were good Catholics and who were known by their priests to be innocent, have reacted by failing to distinguish between religion and men—have abandoned all faith and fallen into a state of stark despair.

The shock has been brutal. Today they believe nothing. They view the Christ with sarcasm and distrust. They know no peace.

The harm that has been done religion is incalculable and the responsibility tremendous before God and history. It can only be hoped that when the war is over and the prelates and clergy of the "Nationalist" party eliminated from Spain, a new group will come forth, animated by a spirit of truth, humility and love for the people, who will help us forget and pardon their predecessors and the crimes committed in their names.

An able and well-directed campaign has either suppressed these facts or gone to the opposite extreme of exploiting many of these crimes as acts of exemplary heroism! An attempt is also being made to demonstrate to the world that religious persecution is the work of the Republic. Among the more important sponsors of this propaganda is the Society of Jesus—the Jesuits. They are attempting to prove that a clergy that is animated solely by a spirit of grace and mercy is being persecuted by the Government for these very attributes. Nothing could be further from the truth.

On the other hand, why have they never uttered a word of condemnation of the infinite assassinations committed by the rebels? Obviously because the rebels have been supported and blessed by the clergy. It is a tragic spectacle to see cardinals participating in the rebel parades, making a grotesque parody of the Fascist salute! Spanish Catholics in the territory occupied by the "Nationalists" have a clear understanding of these truths.

No! Catholics of the world, no! The Catholic religion is not persecuted in Spain. Nor have priests, as such, been executed. What has happened is that certain reprobate priests have turned religion into an instrument of profit—they have turned the House of God into a shopkeeper's stand. There they have encouraged contributions. There they have trafficked in holy images, sacrilegiously despoiling the holy temples. Witness the incident of the Crown of the Macarena, the jewels of the Virgin of Pilár and many similar instances. Sacred precincts have been converted into rebel forts, from which the people have been shot down.

The Catholic clergy in rebel Spain carry pistols to assassinate their brothers and, what is a thousand times worse, they carry on their lips not words of pardon, but words of injury and insult. And we have seen that in the cases of the Canon of Córdoba and of the Jesuit Father Alonso, we find words of hate and vengeance in place of words of love. These ecclesiastics, Catholics of the world, have nothing in common with those who, scattered over the five continents, are self-sacrificing. They have nothing in common with those who, in hostile lands, spread the doctrine of the crucified Christ.

From MEMOIRS OF A SPANISH NATIONALIST,
United Editorial, London 1939
Excerpted from Chapter VI

Fifth Column

ART SHIELDS

Paris, April, 1939

I SAW THE FIFTH COLUMN betray Madrid last month while Franco was attacking on the Casa del Campo front. I was the only American correspondent in the city when the traitors struck down the Republic that Franco himself had never been able to conquer.

I barely escaped the massacre that followed.

The Fifth Columnists were a camarilla of Trotskyites, Anarchists, right wing Socialists and "Left" Republicans, who had not been uprooted in time.

Their military leader was Col. Segismundo Casado, commander of the central armies in Madrid, who left Spain on a British destroyer when his dirty work was done.

Casado struck at midnight, Sunday, March 4 after the Negrín Government had decided to remove him as a disloyal person. He executed the coup with several thousand fifth column troops, who had been diverted from the front, while loyal forces were holding back Franco.

The traitors had initial success, which was almost upset later. They took over the general staff headquarters at Jaca, near Madrid. They seized the key government buildings and the radio stations and telephone centers in the city. They opened the doors of the Modelo prison and freed 700 fascists, whom the Republican Government had arrested. And they confused many people with radio promises of "peace," "independence" and continued "resistance" as they prepared to surrender the city to Franco, Hitler and Mussolini without firing a shot.

I read the traitors' manifesto Monday morning in the Anarchist paper, "Castilla Libre." It was signed by the Fifth Column "Council of Defense," headed by Casado and his chief military aide, Col. Mera, the Anarchist commander on the Guadalajara front and by the Trotskyites Garcia, Pradas and Carrillo and the aged right wing Socialist leader, Julian Besteiro, and others.

The traitors were careful not to say a word against Franco. Their fury was directed solely against the Republican Government of Spain and the Spanish Communist Party.

The people struck back quickly under the leadership of the Communist Party. And Monday night Casado's star seemed setting. The people had captured the vast Ministry buildings on Avenida Castellana with the help of the great weapon—fraternization. In a lull in the fighting a commissar had stepped forward and called the troops in the buildings to join the battle against the pro-Franco traitors. Some soldiers began running towards him at once from their stations in front of the buildings. Others restrained Casado's officers from shooting the commissar down.

The traitors were driven out of other Government buildings by assault forces armed with tommy-guns and hand grenades.

By Tuesday morning Government forces had swept down the Avenida Castellana and Calle de Alcalá and other important streets and had cut across the northern triangle of Madrid from its apex at Plaza Independencia. The highways eastward from Madrid were in the hands of the Government and the traitors were isolated within the city.

The Government seizure of the key Jaca barracks on the road to Guadalajara seemed to be sounding the knell of the revolt.

The traitors were in despair.

I saw this despair reflected in the face of General José Miaja on Plaza Independencia on Thursday during a short truce in the fighting. Miaja, who had deserted the Negrín Government and joined the conspirators as a dummy "President" of the Casado junta (with no power), was gloomily standing between two tommy-gun guards. Men passed him without saluting or speaking. He looked miserable and futile. He fled Madrid that night and took no public part in the coup afterwards.

Meanwhile the Franco-Hitler forces were rushing aid to the traitors inside the city. I saw five of the Nazis' Junker planes bombarding the Ministry buildings that afternoon. And Franco himself began fiercely attacking the city on the Casa del Campo front that night.

Government forces hurled Franco back—but they took precious men from the anti-Fifth Column front inside the city to check the Falangist general's attack. So Franco accomplished his purpose. His attack was intended to divert Republican forces and to protect his ally Casado.

Prisoners admitted this. One high regimental Franco commander came over to the Government side during this battle with the text of military plans showing that Franco and Casado were working together.

Nevertheless Government forces continued to capture more buildings in Madrid for another day, and guards of the Radio del Norte station had begun negotiations for its surrender. And fascist snipers in the massive stone building of the Bank of Spain, which I passed every day, hardly dared to show their faces from sandbagged windows while Government artillery was pouring in fire.

But the traitors in Madrid were getting more help than the putschists of the Trotskyite P.O.U.M. had obtained during the Barcelona insurrection of 1937.

And while the masses of Communists and other loyal Government troops were holding the trenches against Franco in the suburbs of Madrid, I saw several thousand fifth columnists entering the city on Thursday. They came from Mera's forces in Guadalajara, and from the long front in Extremadura on the Portuguese border, where many officers were traitors.

Madrid food supplies were disrupted. Many families could get no bread or beans. The traitors' radio propagandists were blaming all the people's troubles on the "Communists." And Casado's forces began slowly cutting their way through Madrid.

416

The courage of Spanish girl Communists in those desperate days will always shine in my memory of Madrid. These girls were members of the United Socialist Youth League, which brought young Communists and Socialists together.

I watched them go out on the streets during the fighting to distribute anti-fascist leaflets to rank and file soldiers in the Fifth Column ranks.

The leaflets, signed by Gallego, the League's National Secretary, called for unity against Franco and the traitors within the city. [Now Gallego's bullet-riddled body is lying in some unknown grave . . . he was executed by Casado. And some of the girls were shot down, too. But others are still alive and at work for liberation, in Spain.]

My headquarters were in the fortress-like building of "Mundo Obrero," the only pro-Government paper appearing in this crisis, running off the presses in the basement of the building.

It was still more exciting to see the Communist battle organ loaded in bundles in the bellies of light tanks and armored cars by military "newsboys" on the way to the street fighting fronts.

But Franco was still attacking the Government troops in the Casa del Campo sector in support of his Fifth Column within the city. And the street battles were turning sharply against the Republic by late Thursday. The "Mundo Obrero" building was evacuated under heavy fire and I went to the Communist Party headquarters—one of the few buildings still in the hands of the anti-fascists—Friday morning.

I went there with four anti-fascist journalists from four separate lands, with whom I had been covering the fight against the Fifth Column. There was Heinz Massen, a blond young German writer; Bertha Manchet, a Belgian girl, with a rich dark beauty; Guiseppe Reggiani, a young Italian, who had spent four years in Mussolini's prisons in Rome; and Nicholas Gargoff, a young Bulgarian.

They were cool as ice under fire. We had hardly been in the massive building—which had once been used as a headquarters by Gil Robles, the fascist leader—for forty minutes, before the enemy attacked. A group of machine-guns and a light artillery piece went off together in a sudden scream. Bullets zipped through the windows. And then I saw the calibre of my companions. Bertha coolly stepped from the entrance room into shelter in a hallway. Gargoff's face didn't twitch as he finished a wispy cigaret. Massen and Reggiani looked at me and smiled.

I saw the courage of my friends again when the building was surrendered twenty-six hours later. The Fifth Columnists had met with one reverse when a sortie from the building wiped out five machine-gun nests outside. But enemy reinforcements finally crashed through. And the building was surrendered on Saturday afternoon, March 10—after some of the leaders inside had managed to escape.

We reporters filed out of the building under guard into a crazy-cat street scene, where twenty-five or thirty Fifth Column soldiers were dashing around with tommy-guns without a semblance of discipline. My comrades took it calmly as we were shoved against the wall and told to wait—and the next moment a frenzied fellow, with a contorted, maniac-like face leaped at us, throwing his tommy-gun into firing position. A soldier beside him jerked the barrel up before my diaphragm had time to give more than one twist.

I saw my friends at their best again that night at police headquarters, where three young anarchists, with guns on their hips, were trying to provoke us with scurrilous remarks. They spent three hours with us on two separate visits. Bertha and Massen knew how to handle them, mixing humor with dignified discussion until the provocateurs left.

Heavy guns boomed as we talked. And by grapevine we were getting the bad news that Casado was mopping up the rest of the city, while Franco continued his attacks and the radio stations spread confusion.

The Fifth Column firing squads were busy that week-end. From the basement cell, to which we were taken, we watched our comrades led out to execution. We saw the doomed anti-fascists file through the narrow prison corridor from the tiny ventilating holes in the door of our cell.

Fifteen hundred to two thousand men and women were executed that week-end, an American embassy spokesman told me. [These executions were the forerunners of the massacres of hundreds of thousands of anti-fascists that followed after Franco took power.]

New prisoners kept filling up the cells as the former inmates went to their death. Our little 11-by-5 foot cell had been occupied by others before us. Blood-stained bandages on the floor and "Vivas" to the "Gobierno de Negrín," that were scratched on the wall, were evidences of their stay.

We were saved from their fate in a curious way. On the third day we were marched to the Director's office on an upper floor. The guards had neglected to give us our usual meal of one tiny hard roll and a few mouthfuls of "bacalao" (raw salt codfish) that day and rumors were that we were to go against the wall. The police insisted first, however, that I tell them where I was staying, so that they could seize my baggage and "documents." I pretended I understood nothing until two policemen escorted me outside and warned me with threats to take them to my house. I told them to follow me. Our trip ended at the garden gate of the American embassy at Castellano Avenida. "*Embajada!*" the elder policeman angrily shouted. "Ring the bell!" I shouted back. And being an amateur cop, he obeyed.

No Americans were inside. The State Department had shifted the diplomats to Southern France and left a Spanish custodian in charge. To my good fortune the custodian was an anti-fascist. He told the policemen to let me pass in when I demanded admittance as an American citizen. The elder cop snarled "Comunista" as he denied the request. The argument went back and forth for several minutes. I was getting ready to jump past my guards and risk a shot in the back when another idea occurred to me. "I'm cold and have not eaten today," I said as I asked permission to step out of the wind inside the high garden wall by the gate. The custodian backed me up with a tornado of threats to the cops. They would be punished if they kept a sick American out, he said. I didn't stop near the gate, however, when the cop nodded. I was pulling the embassy door open twenty feet away before the cops caught me—too late. I was already partly inside.

"You would certainly have been shot with the others, if you hadn't escaped," my Spanish friend said. "Why should they let your story come out."

I asked a British journalist that night to do his best for the friends I left behind me. He warned Casado that it wouldn't do him any good to shoot journalists. The traitor kept them in prison for Franco, however. I have heard nothing since. [Note, ten years later: Reggiani was since shot by Franco. Nothing has been learned of Bertha Manchet and Nicholas Gargoff. But Massen escaped after seven years in prison and was helping to prepare the way for Socialism in Germany when I heard from him last.]

The Fifth Columnists opened the gates of Madrid for Franco several days ago. But the battle for Spain's freedom still goes on underground. It will continue until victory.

From the DAILY WORKER,
New York, April 1939

"Madrid will be the tomb of fascism"

(1939-19..?)

"Have them reserve me my table in the Café Gran Via; arriving Madrid next week."

RADIOGRAM FROM GENERAL MOLA,
November 1936.

. . . honour eternal is due to the BRAVE AND NOBLE PEOPLE OF SPAIN, worthy of better rulers and a better fortune! And now that the jobs and intrigues of their juntas, the misconduct and incapacity of their generals, are sinking into the deserved obscurity of oblivion, the national resistance *rises nobly out of the ridiculous details. . . . That resistance was indeed wild, disorganized, undisciplined and Al-*

gerine, but it held out to Europe an example which was not shown by the civilized Italian or intellectual German.

RICHARD FORD
Handbook for Travellers in Spain and Readers at Home, 1845.

The only thing in view of the circumstances surrounding our epoch that can keep the hope of better times alive within us is the heroic struggle of the Spanish people for freedom and human dignity.

ALBERT EINSTEIN

Reborn as a monarchy, Spain will be without significance: reborn as a republic, she will be great.

VICTOR HUGO, *1868.*

Andalucia

GENEVIEVE TAGGARD

Silence like light intense,
Silence the deaf ear of noise. . . .
The hid guerrillas wishing to commence
The big war, the war of the full voice.
In rocks, knives, guns, and dynamite,
. . . Or the scratch of scorpions ticking in the night;
And at the church door near the altar boys
One in black frowns with a boy in white.

Andalucía, land of naked faces.
Country of silver and green sky; lonely country, country of
    throngs.
Arabia and Africa in gardens and in arid places.
Country of essential dances and the song of songs.
Andalucía, place of the wine yellow light;
Place of wind too lucid for hissing in small tones.
Andalucía, where our dead comrades are young bones,
The color of old rock mountains, bone yellow and white.

In Andalucía, it is
Now a country of silences
Since the war; a hiss
Is the way of the wind,
And what a man says
Is also in his silences,
In the glance he gives behind,
In Andalucía, land of naked silences.

Andalucía, you too will feel
The wide wind that unlocks systems:
Franco to skid his heels and reel,
Men to shudder on the cluttered Thames.
A great rushing across the planet drives
Breath into bodies. Shouts and arms awake.
Andalucía, country of silver and green, shake
Like a reclaimed cloak, hum like a city of hives.

In Andalucía, it is
Now a country of silences
Since the war; a hiss
Is the way of the wind,
And what a man says
Is also in his silences,
In the glance he gives behind,
In Andalucía, land of naked silences.

From SLOW MUSIC, *Harper,*
New York, 1946

First Love

EDWIN ROLFE

Again I am summoned to the eternal field
green with the blood still fresh at the roots of flowers,
green through the dust-rimmed memory of faces
that moved among the trees there for the last time
before the final shock, the glazed eye, the hasty mound.

But why are my thoughts in another country?
Why do I always return to the sunken road through corroded
    hills,
with the Moorish castle's shadow casting ruins over my shoulder
and the black-smocked girl approaching, her hands laden with
    grapes?

I am eager to enter it, eager to end it.
Perhaps this one will be the last one.
And men afterward will study our arms in museums
and nod their heads, and frown, and name the inadequate dates
and stumble with infant tongues over the strange place-names.

But my heart is forever captive of that other war
that taught me first the meaning of peace and of comradeship

and always I think of my friend who amid the apparition of
    bombs
saw on the lyric lake the single perfect swan.

From FIRST LOVE, *Larry Edmunds*
Bookshop, Los Angeles, 1951

Ballad for Herman Bottcher

MILTON ROBERTSON

NARRATOR   He is one man.
His name is Herman Bottcher.
Some of you will know him,
and some of you will not,
but all will recognize him.
This is his story.
This is his ballad!
The Ballad for Herman Bottcher!

MUSIC   (*Guitar strums softly*)

VOICE   (*sings with guitar*)
Can you hear me calling, soft and low
soft and low?
Can you hear me calling soft and low?
Does my voice reach out to meet you
Does my voice reach out to greet you
Can you hear me calling soft and low?

NARRATOR   Somewhere, the moon is soft. (*Guitar under softly*)
A wind, touched by the sea
sings easy over the jungle.
Somewhere, a piece of moon, sliding on cool
silver feet, stops, where a twisting line of
blood is swallowed by the jungle.
A man died there with a dream.
A dream that races through the earth like a
spring rain.
A man died there with a dream.

A dream that is the root for a thousand wild
flowers.
A man died there with a dream . . .
a dream that calls. . . .

VOICE　　(*sings with guitar*)
Can you hear me calling, soft and low
soft and low?
Can you hear me calling soft and low?
Does my voice reach out to meet you
Does my voice reach out to greet you
Can you hear me calling soft and low?

NARRATOR　We hear you.
We hear you call. Your voice reaches out
and we hear you, and we know you,
and you will never be forgotten Herman
Bottcher.
You will never be forgotten!

SOUND　　(*sharp chord*)

MARINE　　I'll never forget him. He was the kind of guy I'd
follow through hell, carrying a bucket of ice water
for him all the way.

NARRATOR　One of your G.I. men, Herman Bottcher . . . he'll
never forget you.

OFFICER　　The Distinguished Service Cross for extraordinary
heroism against the Japanese in the Papuan campaign in Australasia.

NARRATOR　Major General William H. Gill, United States Army
. . . he'll not forget you!

VOICE 1   He was a sweet guy. A sweet, brave, simple honest guy. He hated the idea of the swastika. Started hating it way back when some of us still thought the twisted double-cross was an old Indian luck sign. He started hating it back in 1928 when he cleared out of Germany. He put that hate into action when he came to Spain in '37 to prove to Franco that you can fool some of the people . . . but not all of them.

NARRATOR   That was a member of the Abraham Lincoln Brigade talking. One of your old-time buddies. Anti-fascists with red blood corpuscles. Men who jumped the gun back in 1937. You were one of them, Herman Bottcher. And by the way, here's a thought. Maybe those Germans who might have taken Stalingrad . . . those Germans who might have stopped us at the Normandy Beach never got there because men like Herman Bottcher stopped them in Spain. I think Herman Bottcher would have liked to think of it that way. I think he would have liked the idea, but it's too late to tell him now. Captain Herman Bottcher died at Leyte!

VOICE   (*sings with guitar*)
Oh I died so lonely far from home,
far from home.
Oh I died so lonely far from home.
Oh the earth is full of sorrow
for I'll never know tomorrow
can you hear me calling soft and low?

NARRATOR   We hear you calling. We hear you Herman Bottcher. You'll know tomorrow. It's the day that belongs to you. We shall take that day and put it aside. We shall tie it in ribbons of bright sun and across it we will write these words;

VOICE 2 This tomorrow belongs to Herman Bottcher. This tomorrow belongs to him whose footsteps knew the rugged path to freedom. This tomorrow belongs to him who moved across the Pyrenees to the land of Spain. This tomorrow belongs to him who became familiar with a warm land and the warm names of the land. Belchite . . . Brunete . . . Teruel . . . Valencia . . . Benicasim . . . Ripoll. . . . This tomorrow belongs to him. . . to a man whose eyes loved the good clean look of the earth . . . whose lungs grasped the fragrance of the wind touched with the scent of oranges and the ripe grapes. It belongs to that man whose eyes reached up to look at the swastika planes that tore the sky . . . the planes that unloosed their death over Barcelona and Madrid . . . over Granollers and Guernica.

It belongs to the man whose finger pressed the trigger of his rifle hard because the fascist was at the end of that target sight.

It belongs to that man whose hands hurled rocks when the bullets ran out; who ate the hard bread of hunger and the bitter gall of defeat. It belongs to that man who left Spain with the hurt of a nation heavy on his heart . . . who left with the promise that some day the earth would be eased of such **pain.**

SOUND (*sharp chord*)

VOICE 3 (*Simple colloquial type*)
I knew Bottcher when he returned from Spain. He wasn't a big man. Not in size. He stood small and tight but his heart was oversize. His insides . . . something about him was bigger and better than most.

Not that he went around slingin out a special kind of big soundin talk. He just saw things kind of

429

simple and right. His bein a carpenter sort of makes you wonder too.

He couldn't stand to see folks wantin . . . when there was more than enough to go around.

He couldn't figure out how one man was better 'n any other cause of his color, or religion or where he came from.

He liked to think that kids were made for laughin and dancin and for eatin ice cream. Used to buy the kids ice cream cones and laugh with 'em.

But don't get me wrong. He had a man-sized temper. He could spit fire when someone upped with a wrong deal . . . and that meant wrong deal, nationally, internationally or just between you and me sort of stuff.

GIRL   I liked him because . . . well because of . . . well I liked him. He could tell you things about flowers or all the things that happened in the earth. He made it sound so mysterious and wonderful. He could take raw wood . . . and then shape it into something clever and useful—smooth to look at and touch. I only saw him a few times but I liked him. . . . I liked him because . . . well I liked him.

VOICE   (*sings with guitar*)
Oh the winds are blowing where I lie
where I lie
oh the winds are blowing where I lie.
Oh I hear my comrades talking
Oh I hear my comrades walking
can they hear me calling soft and low?

NARRATOR   They hear you. They hear you strong and sharp. They hear you and they know you and they'll never forget you!

1st GI   Ferget him? Like tryin to ferget me own right hand. Do yuh know there's a place called Bottcher's Corner? Out Buna-way. That's where he made the stand that cut the Japanese in two. . . . He with a coupla Joes like me.

2nd GI   I was there with him. He wasn't a Captain then. Just a staff sarge. But what a hunk of fightin' man . . . wasn't afraid of nuthin.

1st GI   That Buna Mission, that was only one story. The way he used to traipse out into the jungle like it was a picnic park or somethin . . . goin out solo behind the Japanese lines . . . brother that guy was made outa guts and a yard wide.

2nd GI   I remember once when he came back with a Japanese Captain. Some of us wanted to give him the works but it was no go. He said somethin about not havin to act the same way as the enemy.

1st GI   He said a lot of other things too. I never got around to figurin them all out but they stuck with me. About why he went to Spain frinstance. About why he went to war for a country he had no part of . . . fer democracy he said . . . always fer democracy. He used to talk about it tryin to make us catch on. Funny thing about the whole deal . . . he wasn't even an American citizen. Here he was talking to us about America and what made it run around and he was a German.

2nd GI   Maybe he was born in Germany but he didn't stay German long . . . he got transferred and fast after that Buna deal . . . they gave him his commission and Congress made him a citizen special.

431

1ST GI   And brother he was special. You know, when I
          was out on patrol with him, even when it was
          deep behind the enemy lines I always felt kinda
          safe . . . yeah . . . never a worry or nuthin when
          the old man was around.

2ND GI   I guess there wasn't one guy in the 32nd or any-
          where who felt different. You coulda got me to
          get into a rubber boat and row right up into Manila
          Bay if he was doin the orderin . . . and it would
          have been O.K.

SOUND   (chord)

NARRATOR Yes, they're talking about you Captain Bottcher.
          Your comrades are talking about you hard and
          long. The tough men with the sharp eyes. The
          jungle fighters who knew you well as leader and
          comrade.
          They're talking about you, remembering about you
          and remembering well. You're more than just one
          man now. You're an idea. You're an idea Captain
          Herman Bottcher and there's no forgetting your
          kind of idea.
          You step into a man's mind now and it's not just
          a chap they see but a step ahead to something
          good. You're not just another chap that happened
          along somewhere, you're a jungle legend with an
          accent on Spain. You're a fighting man and they
          remember you with your gun always pointed at the
          enemy . . . and there was never a mistake as to who
          was the enemy . . . anybody who threatened free-
          dom, dignity and honesty . . . that was the enemy.
          They're talking about you Herman Bottcher. They're
          whispering along the hills of Brunete and the cold
          peaks of Teruel. They're talking about you from

Spain to Frisco; along the mountain paths you climbed. They're talking about you at home. Many homes ... the chaps who knew you in one war ... they're remembering the times you shared those butts and a bottle of *vino rojo*. They're remembering the times you sang a song of Germans, that Germans died for ... and a song of Spain that you were willing to die for. And the others are remembering you. The men who fought with you on that last campaign ... they remember you. . . .

VOICE (*sings with guitar*)
Oh the night is ending where I lie
where I lie
Oh the night is ending where I lie.
Oh I feel the touch of sun
oh tell me is the battle won
can you hear me calling soft and low?

NARRATOR (*over music softly*)
The night is ending. The sun is shining soft and warm and the battle is almost won ... it is being won now. It is being shaped with your strength, shaped with your promise ... with the dream of you. The battle is being won, Herman Bottcher. And when it is finally won, we shall mount the victory like some proud flower, on the earth where you lie.
We shall mount it there close to you, and on it we shall write simple words.
We shall say the battle is over.
We shall say that all the lands that knew your step ... that knew the look of your eye ... that all the lands of the earth are free forever.
That little children shall be dedicated to laughter and song forever.

That the earth shall carry a sweet and wonderful
magic for all men . . .
that mountain paths and jungle ways and the broad
boulevards from New York to Madrid shall be forever free for the strong and happy step of all men.
these are the words we shall write for you Herman
Bottcher. . . . This we shall say for you beloved
comrade. . . .

VOICE   (*sings with guitar*)
Oh I hear your voices, calling low
calling low.
Oh I hear your voices calling low.
oh the sun is in my heart and
I am now no more apart,
oh I hear your voices calling low!

SOUND   (*chord to close*)

THIS BALLAD is DEDICATED TO THE MANY VETERANS OF THE ABRAHAM LIN-
COLN BRIGADE WHO DIED IN THE ANTI-FASCIST BATTLES OF WORLD WAR II.

The Undefeated

MARTHA GELLHORN

AT THE END OF THE gray unheated ward, a little boy was talking to a man. The boy sat at the foot of an iron cot and from this distance you could see that they were talking seriously and amiably as befits old friends.

They had known each other for almost six years and had been in five different concentration camps in France. The little boy had come with his entire family in the great exodus from Spain at the end of the civil war in 1939, but the man was alone. He had been wounded at the end of the war and for six years he had been unable to walk, with a wound in his leg that was never treated and had never healed. He had a white, suffering face and cheeks that looked as if the skin had been roughly stitched together in deep hunger seams and he had gentle eyes and a gentle voice.

The little boy was fifteen years old, though his body was that of a child of ten. Between his eyes, there were four lines, the marks of such misery as children should never feel. He spoke with that wonderful whisky voice that so many Spanish children have, and he was a tough and entire little boy. His conversation was without drama or self-pity. It appeared that the last concentration camp was almost the worst; he had been separated from his mother and father. Also the hunger was greater, although the hunger had always been there, and one did not think about it any longer.

In the last camp they all ate grass, until the authorities for-

435

bade them to pull it up. They were accustomed to having the fruits of their little communal gardens stolen by the guards, after they had done all the work; but at the last camp everything was stolen. And there were more punishments for the children: more days without food, more hours of standing in the sun; more beatings.

"The man who guarded us in our barracks was shot by the Maquis, when they came to free us," the boy said. "The Maquis shot him for being bad to children."

His mother was here with him, and three sisters, too. An older brother was somewhere fighting with the French Maquis.

"And your father?" I asked.

There was a pause and then he said, in a flat quiet voice, "Deported by the Germans." Then all the toughness went, and he was a child who had suffered too much. He put his hands in front of his face, and bowed his head and wept for his father.

There were other men in the ward, waiting for this day to pass, as six years of days had somehow passed before. They were all veterans of the Spanish Republican army who had either been wounded in the war or destroyed by the ill usage of the concentration camps. There were the faces of tuberculars among them, and men without arms, and one-legged men, and all of them were ravaged by the long hunger and the long imprisonment. They came around the bed now to comfort the boy.

"Come, man," one of them said, "courage! Thou must not despair. Here is this señora who knows more than we know, and she will tell you, the Americans will free your father in Germany. He will come back. The war is almost over, man, you will see your father." We all told the child consoling lies, speaking earnestly and with great conviction, and we all wished to believe what we said.

The child did not believe us, but he put his grief away where he kept it always, behind the anguished eyes and the lined forehead. His name is Fulgencio López and there are thousands like him; and no country, no government, no charity takes care of him. It is hard to know whether it is worse to be Fulgencio

López or to be his mother, who had had to watch those lines forming in his forehead and the pain growing in his eyes, and has been helpless and is still helpless.

Fulgencio wished to introduce me to his comrades in another ward. Having been removed from their last concentration camp a few weeks ago (because even though France was freed, there was no place to free the Spaniards in), they were now given temporary shelter in a Red Cross hostel in Toulouse. They could be considered lucky because there were cots and the building was not as cold as it might have been and there was food and no one would be cruel to them.

Other Spaniards were not nearly so fortunate; they slept on straw in cement huts that had no heating and no windowpanes; they lay wounded in hospitals that are tragic in their poverty; they lived in various cold empty schools, factories, barracks, surrounded by wastes of mud, and waited while tuberculosis gnawed the sick and threatened the sound.

By contrast, the gray wards of the hostel were a palace. So Fulgencio introduced me to his friends, about twenty of them. The youngest was six and the oldest was sixteen and they were all smaller than they should have been, but they were all wondrously alive and funny, and beautiful to look at, for the Spanish make lovely children. And also they make brave children, for if you are a Spanish Republican you have to be brave or die.

The children rocked with laughter as they told about climbing illegally into their barracks to get drinking water; the authorities locked the barracks all day long and the children were simply to suffer thirst between meals. The littlest ones wriggled in the windows and handed out water a cupful at a time. This was a huge joke apparently. Also they sang in the dark in their lonely barracks, separated from their parents, and when the guard came in to stop them and to punish the guilty ones, they acted as if they had been asleep all the time. (And how do you like that picture: the child voices inside the prison, singing defiantly in the night?)

There were two little blond characters of six, a girl and a

boy. The little boy had a pair of cheap goggles on his head (he planned to be an aviator one day), which was the only toy or semi-toy in the place. These two were called the fiancés! They had refused to be separated since they had been able to walk, and they knew nothing of life except jail.

The little boy's father had been killed in the war in Spain; the little girl's father had been deported in a German labor battalion. It must have seemed to them that only children could stay together in an unsafe world. When they went down the hall they held hands as if they were crossing a dangerous stretch of country, where enemies might fall on them and tear them apart.

The children wanted a bicycle: one bicycle for all of them. He who rides a bicycle is free and going somewhere. They said it must be a woman's bicycle so that even the smallest could ride it. If a bicycle was too much to ask they would like one Meccano set and one doll: these too would be shared amongst them all. They had never had any toys but they were full of hope, because some of them had ridden on the streetcar in Toulouse and for the first time had seen toys in shop windows. So, since these things existed, one day they might exist for them.

There are many Spaniards in Toulouse, and all up and down the Pyrenees frontier, and generally scattered in the villages and towns of France. You can go to a half-burned-out former French Fascist youth camp and see there the men who fought for their faith and their country, and in so doing became what is called *grands mutilés*—the armless, the legless, the blind. They lie on straw on cement floors, in cement buildings that are without heat or windowpanes, and in one building half the men—twenty-four out of forty-six—have tuberculosis.

But there are no vital statistics for the Spaniards in France for no one was concerned with their living or dying.

All we do know is that there were ten concentration camps in France from 1939 on. It is alleged that half a million Spanish men, women and children fled to France after the Franco victory. Thousands got away to other countries; thousands returned to Spain tempted by false promises of kindness. By the tens of thousands, these Spaniards died of neglect in the concentration camps. And the German *Todt* organizations took over seven thousand able-bodied Spaniards to work as slaves. The remainder—no one knows certainly how many—exist here in France. The French cannot be blamed for their present suffering since the French cannot yet provide adequately for themselves.

The Third French Republic was less barbarous to the Spaniards than was the Pétain government, evidently, but it would seem that all people who run concentration camps necessarily become brutal monsters. And though various organizations in America and England collected money and sent food parcels to these refugees, nothing was ever received by the Spanish. Furthermore, they were constantly informed by all the camp authorities that they had been abandoned by the world: they were beggars and lucky to receive the daily soup of starvation.

The only way to get out of these French concentration camps was to sign a labor contract: any farmer or employer could ask for two or ten or twenty Spaniards, who were then bound over to him and would have to work for whatever wages he chose to pay under whatever living conditions he saw fit to provide. If a Spaniard rebelled, he could return to the concentration camp. A well-known Barcelona surgeon worked as a wood-cutter for four years at twelve cents a day. He is sixty-two and there is nothing unusual about his case.

Behind the Spanish refugees were two years of a fierce and heartbreaking war, and most of them left their families locked inside their own country. They have of course not seen any of them for six years at least, and mostly they are without news. All they know is that there are a half million Republicans in prison in Spain and another million working at forced labor, and that the executions in the Spanish prisons have never stopped.

The generally accepted figure is 300,000 executions in the six years since Franco won power. The total present American casualties, killed and wounded in all theaters of war, are about

475,000. It is obvious that the only way to defeat these people is to shoot them. As early as 1941, Spanish Republicans were running away from their French employers and disappearing into the Maquis. From 1943 onward, there was the closest liaison between the French Maquis and the Spanish bands throughout France.

That the work of the Spanish Maquis was valuable can be seen from some briefly noted figures. During the German occupation of France, the Spanish Maquis engineered more than four hundred railway sabotages, destroyed fifty-eight locomotives, dynamited thirty-five railway bridges, cut one hundred and fifty telephone lines, attacked twenty factories, destroying some factories totally, and sabotaged fifteen coal mines. They took several thousand German prisoners and—most miraculous considering their arms—they captured three tanks.

In the southwest part of France where no Allied armies have ever fought, they liberated more than seventeen towns. The French Forces of the Interior, who have scarcely enough to help themselves, try to help their wounded Spanish comrades in arms. But now that the guerrilla fighting is over, the Spaniards are again men without a country or families or homes or work, though everyone appreciates very much what they did.

After the liberation of France, the Spanish Maquis in the southwest made the now famous forced entry into Spain, in the Val Daran section of the Pyrenees. This attack has been wildly reported and wildly misunderstood. It was a commando raid, purely and simply, and was never intended as anything more. The Spanish Republican soldiers involved were too few in number and too lightly armed to expect to overthrow Franco. But it was a gesture that worked.

It drove news into a country where there is no news, for inside those closed frontiers only word of mouth can travel. It was a call from the outside world where dictatorships were being destroyed and it was a call of hope to people who have lived in fear and misery for a long time. And though many of the Spanish Republican soldiers were killed, and though most of them withdrew into France as scheduled, many got through, and they have work to do inside their country. Because of that armed entry, the world was forced to remember the men who had started fighting Fascism in 1936. It is interesting to note that two thousand people suspected of Republican sympathies were arrested in Barcelona alone after the frontier attack.

Meantime the Spanish exiles in France are being criticized because there are two major parties, both clamoring to represent Spain. It is extraordinary how the ideas of Hitler have filtered through the world and diffused and altered themselves so you hear people saying the Spanish Republicans cannot get anywhere because they have no leader. People seem to forget that Franco calls himself the *Caudillo* or leader and that these Spaniards detest one-man rule. It is one of the strongest guarantees of their passion for a republic.

The major Spanish parties in exile agree that enough blood has been shed in Spain to last forever. The chiefs responsible for the uprising that started the civil war and for the years of repression after the civil war are to be punished. But after that, Spain is to belong to the Spaniards who must live together in it in a fiercely needed peace.

After the desperate years of their own war, after six years of repression inside Spain and six years of horror in exile, these people remain intact in spirit. They are armed with a transcendent faith; they have never won, and yet they have never accepted defeat. Theirs is the great faith that makes miracles and changes history. You can sit in a basement restaurant in Toulouse and listen to men who have uncomplainingly lost every safety and comfort in life, talking of their republic; and you can believe quite simply that, since they are what they are, there will be a republic across the mountains and that they will live to return to it.

From COLLIER'S *Magazine,*
March 3, 1945

Santa Espina

LOUIS ARAGON

I remember a tune we used to hear in Spain
And it made the heart beat faster, and we knew
Each time as our blood was kindled once again
Why the blue sky above us was so blue

I remember a tune like the voice of the open sea
Like the cry of migrant birds, a tune which stores
In the silence, after the notes, a stifled sob
Revenge of the salt seas on their conquerors

I remember a tune which was whistled at night
In a sunless time, an age with no wandering knight
When children wept for the bombs and in catacombs
A noble people dreamt of the tyrant's doom

It bore in its name the sacred thorns which pierced
The brow of a god as he hung upon the gallows
The song that was heard in the ear and felt in the flesh
Reopened the wound in his side and revived his sorrows

No one dared to sing to the air they hummed
All the words were forbidden and yet I know
Universe ravaged with inveterate pox
It was your hope and your month of Sundays. O

Vainly I seek its poignant melody
But the earth has now but operatic tears
The memory of its murmuring waters lost
The call of stream to stream, in these deaf years

O Holy Thorn, Holy Thorn, begin again
We used to stand as we heard you long ago
But now there is no one left to renew the strain
The woods are silent, the singers dead in Spain

I would like to believe that there is music still
In that country's heart, though hidden underground
The dumb will speak and the paralytics will
March one fine day to the cobla's triumphant sound

The crown of blood, the symbol of anguish and sorrow
Will fall from the brow of the Son of Man that hour
And man will sing loudly in that sweet tomorrow
For the beauty of life and the hawthorn tree in flower.

*Queremos que césen
tantas injusticias
y que disparesce
la desigualdád . . .*

Joe Hecht

ALVAH BESSIE

W HO WILL REMEMBER JOE? What does his name mean to you?
It is not Eisenhower, Rokossovski, Montgomery or De
Gaulle. He had no DSC, no Purple Heart . . . he never got the
time you need to earn one. I can tell you this about Joe Hecht.
Maybe it will mean something to you:

March 18, 1938: Some seventy-five replacements joined the
decimated remnants of the Lincoln Battalion up near Batea in
the Aragón. We had spent four days in boxcars and in *camions,*
marched forty kilometers the night before. What we found was
an outfit that had had the tar licked out of it at Belchite, Caspe,
Alcañiz. It had no guns, no food, no clothes on its back, no
shoes on its feet. It was camped on the side of a partly wooded
hill, crouched in the rain, licking its wounds, eating what grub
it could get off leaves instead of mess-kits. It was a bad time.

They lined us up and assigned us to what was left of Companies 1, 2, 3 and 4. A guy stepped out of the ranks when my
name was called. He looked like a walking corpse—hollow eye-
sockets, jutting cheekbones, sunken cheeks. His face was covered with hair and dirt. His eyes were red; his clothes in ribbons.
"Didn't you work on the Brooklyn Eagle?" he said to me. "I
think I met your kids one time."

That was Joe Hecht. A soldier. A man such as they come
once in awhile, and there seem to be more like him today than
there ever were before. His beaten face lit up like a light bulb
when I said I knew his name, remembered hearing about him
during the East Coast seamen's strike of 1936. He gave me a

444

cigarette—where did he get it? Joe Hecht had more parcels sent to him in Spain than any fifty men I ever knew. Why do you suppose that was?

How do you love a man? How does one man love another? Let me tell you. Wherever I went in Spain I met Joe Hecht. After that rout at Belchite, Caspe, Alcañiz, and after the second beating that followed at Batea, Gandesa and Villalba, when we staggered back on the Ebro River and across it, Joe Hecht was all worn out. He had been in Spain since January 1937. He had done more than his share of fighting. So they gave him an easy job; we envied him. They gave him a job driving a car, an ammunition truck . . . day and night, hour after hour. "It's better than walking," Joe said whenever I ran into him. And whenever I ran into him he had a cigarette for me, a piece of chocolate, chewing gum, a can of smoked sausages from home—from Brooklyn.

What he ever saw in me I'd like to know. But I discovered later that it wasn't only me. It was people. He loved them with a passion that is known to few of us—it devoured him. He could —and did—give more of himself than anybody I have ever met, and when he was through giving, he still had more than when he started.

We'd be dead-beat; marching through rain; spent the night out "sleeping" in the rain; come into a town. At the cross-roads I'd spot Joe Hecht with his *camion;* that grin on his face. "Come over here," he'd say. "I got something for you, baby."

He had something for me. Believe me, it was something more important to a soldier, more permanent, more satisfying than a butt, a half a bar of chocolate, a tin of condensed milk we could smear on bread. When I was low in the gut, Joe had good cheer. When I was confused, Joe Hecht had clarity. When I was lonely, Joe had understanding, comradeship. When I was ill, Joe nursed me—massaging my rheumatism-crippled limbs for hours, finding food that simply did not exist and cooking it himself, spoon-feeding me with his hands and with his love. He had these things for anyone who needed them.

Some of us came home from Spain and Joe went back to work. He never had a formal education. He worked as a garageman, a mechanic. He worked in drugstores and in a factory, making zippers. He had worked before that as an organizer, for unions, for the Workers' Alliance, for the Communist Party. That's what Joe was, a Communist. He wore the label like a banner; and that banner flashed in everything Joe was and everything Joe knew. With no "higher education," he was still the most widely read, the most deeply cultured man I ever knew. There was no field of art or science in which Joe had not plunged—alone, except for books—and in which he could not swim stoutly with the best.

He was the soundest critic of writing I have known; he knew music, classical and swing, and loved them both with equal passion; he knew painting from the Neanderthal caves of southern France to Picasso. He could point you out the errors —in conception or in execution—of actors, stage and screen, of playwrights, poets, painters, physicists, auto mechanics, dancers, novelists, radio technicians and philosophers. There was nothing human alien to Joe.

Does this sound like a superman to you? Joe was just an ordinary guy. I do not mean to make him sound unusual—he was common as dirt, a common denominator of mankind. He taught himself to speak fluent French and Spanish; he could speak German, Yiddish, Italian and some Russian. He could talk the language of any human being, black or brown or white or yellow he met from the Brooklyn waterfront to the halls of Congress—and somewhere and somehow he had met them all.

There was a time we don't like to remember, but I think we should recall it now. Because the times have changed and many people have changed with the times. It was a time when men and women who had been to Spain were regarded with suspicion here at home.

Joe went into the U.S. Army in 1942. He met with the reception that became a pattern with the Spanish vets. He was welcomed as a veteran, an expert in the science of war. He was asked to speak to his company, his battalion, regiment; he was interviewed by the Army papers and put on the local radio. Then they kicked him in the teeth.

Joe was only human; he got bitter. He wrote me letters, told how he had been recommended for officers' candidate school, and then turned down. He told how he applied for combat duty, got his transfer, then had it countermanded. He told how he was finally sent to an officers' preparatory school, made the best grades in his class—and was then sent back again.

His commanding officer called him in. "What happened up there, Hecht?" the CO asked. "I don't know," said Joe. "They say my grades weren't good enough." The CO was silent for a moment, then he went to the personnel file.

"This is none of my business, Hecht," he said, "but it wasn't your grades." He brought out Joe's card and showed it to him. Up in one corner there were two letters—SD.

"What does that mean?" said Joe.

"Suspected of disloyalty," the CO said. "I understand you're a Communist . . . but I never heard of you passing out any leaflets or agitating the men. I only heard you were a damned good soldier."

"I try," said Joe.

So his CO recommended Joe for combat duty again and he was transferred—to a hospital. There they set him to work scrubbing floors and polishing brass. He did such a good job of it that they promoted him—to keeping a filing system. Joe even learned something from this: he made a statistical breakdown of the percentage of psychoneurotic cases to the total, and he expressed his concern about the disproportionate number of "combat fatigue" patients. "Maybe they're not teaching the boys enough," he wrote.

Joe was transferred again—back to infantry. He wrote: "After two months of blundering about from one camp to another with nobody knowing where I belonged or why I was transferred here or there, I've finally reached a stopping place—I

think. Co.——, —— Infantry Regiment, —— Division, Camp ——.
That sounds good, doesn't it? In the infantry! I've been given a
rifle, I'm a soldier!"

Joe was the kind of soldier who didn't like things run
wrong. If the shavetail teaching the orientation class said that
Stalingrad had no strategic importance (which he did), Joe
was just as likely as not to ask for the floor and explain its importance (which he did). He trained the men under his charge
—for he was immediately made a sergeant—along the lines he
had learned in Spain where he had been a corporal, a sergeant,
a lieutenant, a captain.

He worked out infantry problems for them and solved them.
He argued and explained—it was a common thing for the guys
to call Joe in to settle their arguments—about anything, from
dames to Bible history. He led them in field maneuvers and won
the commendation of his officers. A general watching Joe demonstrate a combat problem with two infantry platoons, spoke to
him, said, "You're a good leader, young man." It made Joe feel
good.

So—after two and a half years in the Army, Joe finally got
shipped out, to France. Technical sergeant—in command of a
platoon. He wrote me from France—twice. He sent us the
French newspapers. He asked for "grub, candy, candles." He
wrote about the morale of the men. And this is the last thing
he wrote to us:

> *March 13, 1945*
> *Germany*
>
> *Lots to say but there is too much adrenalin in my blood-*
> *stream to permit the patience & relaxation to say it.*
>
> *This country of our enemy, the German, is desolate, de-*
> *stroyed, dead. Like the bastards' soul.*
>
> *One of these days you, my "dear diary," will receive a*
> *20 page letter from me. Till then, bear with me and my*
> *suprarenal glands.*

I'm well, kinda tired but OK. Write lots of letters and keep my morale up. Send me some candles if they still make them in the USA and brighten my days and nights. How are you doing in Hollywood? . . . Love to BV I & BV II. Wish me luck and cojones. Joe.

We had sent him grub; it didn't reach him. We didn't have time to send the candles. BV I is Joe's name for my wife—Blonde Venus I. (Silly, isn't it?) BV II is his name for my daughter whom he never saw. When he heard she was born he sent her a gift: a Spanish coin he had been carrying since 1937, called a *perro gordo.* It means "fat dog" in Spanish. And this is what Joe wrote:

Tell her it is a poor man's coin . . . that it was worn thin this way for over 50 years by the hands of poor, hard-working people. So she will understand, in time to come, what it means.

Joe was killed in action near Saarlautern, Germany, seven years to the day I met him on a hillside in the Aragón. The citation which accompanied the posthumous Silver Star reads like this:

"On the morning of 18 March 1945, a company rifle squad, commanded by Sgt. Hecht, was caught in the open by grazing fire from a German machine-gun emplacement which was also inflicting casualties on the entire platoon.

"Showing no hesitancy, and at the cost of his life, Sgt. Hecht charged the gun emplacement single-handedly in an effort to destroy it. As a result of his heroic action, his men were afforded the needed time to secure cover. His undaunted courage in sacrificing his life for the men of his squad reflects the highest credit upon Sgt. Hecht and the military service."

449

My wife wept and said, "It isn't fair; he never had any fun at all." But she was wrong, for Joe had lots of fun. And what he gave to others we are carrying around inside of us, and it will make us happier in the future, even if it aches today.

The coin Joe sent to my daughter is attached to a silver bracelet, and she plays with it every day. And when she is old enough to understand, we will tell her about Joe who sent it to her and whom she never saw. She will understand, Joe, who you were and what you did for her. She will remember your name and it will mean something to her, even if we never show her that picture of your beautiful ugly mug you sent us a week before you sailed.

Salud! Joe—*y suerte y cojones!*

From NEW MASSES, *New York,*
May 29, 1945

Spanish Lesson

I MET THIS GUY who was a veteran of Pearl Harbor on the "This Is the Army" radio program. They were doing a show from Camp Wheeler on "Why I like the Infantry" and we were waiting to go on to tell "why." It was the summer of '42 and the brass had just decided that infantry might come in handy if the U.S. Army happened to find itself in a spot where the Air Corps and the Navy found navigation impossible. So we got to talking and he told me how it was with the men when the Japanese came over that Sunday morning. He told me how they came pouring out of the barracks, hit the company streets and just kept running. So, many of them were clipped by the strafers, by bomb splinters and by flying debris—clipped because they were running instead of hitting the dirt and staying there.

They hadn't heard about hitting the dirt and staying put during an air raid at Pearl Harbor . . . they hadn't heard about the Lincoln Battalion at Jarama in February of 1937. A lesson lost.

The Americans who came to Spain to do battle that February ten years ago were somewhat surprised to discover that "doing battle" was a serious and a dangerous business. There they were deployed according to the book on a beautiful height when the fascist planes came over looking for them. The battalion staff had a serious discussion and decided that the wisest thing to do was to send the men running down the hill because moving targets are hard to hit. The order was given and the men ran and the fascists spotted them. One of the boys hollered "them bastards are trying to kill me." Afterwards we knew that the smart thing to do during a raid was to stay put and hug the earth. Too bad they didn't hear about that at Pearl Harbor.

The thing about Spain was that everyone got a hell of a lot

more out of it than they put into it. I mean the things that we saw there, the experiences we had, the people we got to know, the lessons we learned. I would like to write about a single man who came to Spain and what happened to him there and afterward. Let us consider him as a composite person.

He went to Spain in 1936 because he was an anti-fascist. He felt, although he did not know for sure, that if fascism were not stopped in Spain, it would sweep the world. He did not know beforehand what he was going to do when he got to Spain. Certainly he did not know anything about fighting or killing or dying; but he was a volunteer. In Spain he met a people who lived, slept and ate anti-fascism, who never tired of doing something about it. A people whose intense love of Spain and of freedom enabled them to make sacrifices without parallel. In Spain he also met men from almost every nation in the world, those who had fought fascism in their own country before Spain and those to whom fascism was just a word. Men who represented a complete cross-section of life; men from the ranks of the unemployed, from labor, from the professions, from the arts and sciences and even from the business world.

Then he went up to the front and met this thing called fascism. It became more tangible, it became a Moor screaming fiendishly in the attack, a machine gun rattling away, an Italian tank. It became planes overhead dropping bombs on hospitals, on schools, churches, women, children. And the lines of refugees pouring away from the front told him of fascism, told him of rape and plunder and pillage, told him of the slaughters in the bull rings, the mass graves, the concentration camps, and he, this International Brigader, became committed to the fight. He was a man of the shock brigades, and with the Spanish troops of Lister, Modesto, Durán, he fought in every decisive action, in every offensive and defensive battle and when he was wounded, he went back to the rear and there, as he recuperated, renewed his friendship with the Spanish people—with the mothers, the widows and the children.

And after Spain and after the bitterness of defeat when he came face to face with the treachery and the callousness and indifference of the appeasers, of the bureaucrats and diplomats of the governments, when he felt there was nothing but hopelessness and despair for mankind, he remembered Spain and it was too much a part of him to accept despair and hopelessness. The men who came to Spain and the Spaniards themselves were irrevocable proof that men knew how to fight and men could and would fight for truth and for liberty and that in the end fascism would not win. And so he went back home.

In the short time between the defeat of the Spanish Republic and the invasion of Poland, a period of months, he tramped up and down the face of the earth denouncing the fascists and the warmakers and the appeasers, urging collective security, fighting to prevent the coming war, to prevent the spread of Nazism. He was on the blacklist of the Gestapo, of the Fifth Column. He was a second-rate citizen in his own country. He was denounced as a false prophet, an adventurer, a bloodthirsty killer of priests and nuns, an anti-God pagan. He was hunted and persecuted, jailed and beaten but Spain was still with him and he never wavered. And when the war came and the *Wehrmacht* rolled over country after country, he was the man the people asked to lead the resistance because he had learned how to fight, because he had learned how to love and rely on the people. He had a vision of Spain and its hope for the future. And he was right. His France, Poland, Czechoslovakia were liberated from the Nazi yoke, his Italy hanged Mussolini in the square of Milan.

Now it is ten years since that first February when his antifascism was consecrated in the fire of Spain. In ten years he has seen people defeated, enslaved and finally victorious—but not yet in Spain. Spain remains the lesson not yet learned. The lesson of the strafing planes and the moving target, the lesson of unity whole and indivisible in the face of fascism. It is a lesson that Spain has given to the world. It is a lesson we must live by —if we're to live at all.

From 10TH ANNIVERSARY JOURNAL
of the Lincoln Brigade, New York, 1947

Monument

T. H. WINTRINGHAM

When from the deep sky
And digging in the harsh earth,
When by words hard as bullets,
Thoughts simple as death,
You have won victory,
People of Spain,
You will remember the free men who fought beside
    you, enduring and dying with you, the strangers
Whose breath was your breath.

You will pile into the deep sky
A tower of dried earth,
Rough as the walls where bullets
Splashed men to death
Before you won victory,
From the eating gangrene of wealth, the grey pus
    of pride, the black scab of those strangers
Who were choking your breath.

Bring together, under the deep sky
Metal and earth;
Metal from which you made bullets
And weapons against death,
And earth in which, for victory,
Across all Spain,
Your blood and ours was mingled, Huesca to
    Málaga; earth to which your sons and strangers
Gave up the same breath.

Bring to the tower, to its building,
From New Castille,
From Madrid, the indomitable breast-work,
Earth of a flower-bed in the Casa del Campo,
Shell-splinters from University City,
Shell-casing from the Telefónica.
Bring from Old Castille, Santander, Segovia,
Sandbags of earth dug out of our parapets
And a false coin stamped in Burgos by a traitor.

Carry from León, from the province of Salamanca,
Where the bulls are brave and the retired generals cowards,
From near the Capital of treason and defeat, bring now
Clean earth, new and untouched from the cold hills,
And iron from the gate, that shall now be always open
Of Spain's oldest school, where there shall be young wisdom.
From Extremadura, earth from the bullring
Where they shot the prisoners in Badajoz;
And lovely Zafra shall give one of its silver crosses;
Galicia, sea-sand and ship-rivets. From Asturias
Spoil from the pits that taught our dynamiters
To face and destroy the rearing tanks, and a pit-haft

That has cut coal and trenches, and is still fit for work.
From the Basque country, Bilbao, Guernica,
City of agony, villages of fire,
Take charred earth, so burnt and tortured no one
Knows if small children's bones are mingled in it;
Take iron ore from the mines those strangers envied;
And wash your hands, remembering a world that did so.

Navarre shall give a ploughshare and a rock;
Aragón, soil from the trench by the walnut-tree
Where Thaelmann's first group fought towards Huesca,
And steel from a wrecked car lying by a roadside;
Lukacsz rode in that car.

455

Catalonia, Spain and not Spain, and our gateway
(For myself a gateway to Spain and courage and love)
Shall bring a crankshaft from the Hispano factory
And earth from Durrutti's grave;
Valencia, black soft silt of the rice fields, mingled
With soil from an orange-grove, also
Telephone-wire, and a crane's chain.
Murcia, a surgeon's scalpel and red earth;
Andalucía, the vast south, shall pay
The barrel of a very old rifle found in the hills
Beside a skeleton; earth
That the olives grow from.
And Albacete, where we built our brigades:
Knife-steel and road-dust.

Take then these metals, under the deep sky
Melt them together; take these pieces of earth
And mix them; add your bullets,
And memories of death:
You have won victory,
People of Spain,
And the tower into which your earth is built, and
Your blood and ours, shall state Spain's
Unity, happiness, strength; it shall face the breath
Of the east, of the dawn, of the futures when there
         will be no more strangers . . .

From THE VOLUNTEER FOR LIBERTY,
Barcelona, November 7,1938

To the Heroes of the Spanish Resistance

Rendezvous With Spain

BERNARDO CLARIANA

NARRATOR   Fifteen years back, in the spring of 1931, the streets
and squares of every Spanish town were the scene
of great rejoicing. Without the firing of a shot, in
the same pure silence in which a ewe brings forth
her lamb, the municipal councils of Spain proclaimed the Republic. Like one who releases a dove
to the freedom of the sky, they deposited, in all
innocence, their white electoral ballots; and the
crowds sang and laughed and danced for joy, lifting up their eyes to the new flag of the Republic:
one red stripe transformed to violet.

First recollection: April 14

POET   See, a new color has come out on the flag!
How beautiful it is!
Color of violet.
Poppy, sunflower, and violet.
Come out, everyone, and see it!
How fine it is,
Our April flag!
   Ah, Captain Galán's
Fourteenth of April!
Set up a flag in Jaca,
For the winds of freedom breathe already
In the province of Huesca.

457

(Verbena all the mountain)
(All the air is violet)
See, how the crowds are dancing for joy!
They hurdygurdy through the streets, through the
   town!
Ayayayay, the Nobles are done for!
Ayayayay, the plow breaks the pasture!
Ayayayay, the Queen's in a faint!
Ayayayay, the King's packing up!

WOMAN   *singing*
   (*Mocking ballad to an ancient tune*)

Whither away, Thirteenth Alfonso?
Whither away, Sick & Sorry?
No more kinging: I never learned how to,
And it's me for exile in a hurry!
On your way, then, on your way
To the likeliest seaport you can find—
Cartagena's good, they say—
And make it fast, if you'll be so kind:
Spain has declared the rule of the people,
And you don't want to be found staying behind.
Scram, Alfonso! Scram, Alfonso!
Pick up your feet and run, run, run!
And while you're about it, King Alfonso,
Take along Juan, your princely son.
Here's an end to the Habsburg rubbish,
Sickly calf of a rickety breed.
When we inherited you to rule us,
That was Spain's hard lines indeed:
Not 'by the grace of God,' for His Grace
Never can sin in will or deed.
Two dictatorships you gave us,
Berenguer's and that other one,
And a mess of misery's all you brought us:

Blood in buckets, but never a bun.
From the Rif, Arruit sent up a cry,
Annual re-echoes back the noise;
King, if you listen attentively,
From Lobo Gulch you will hear a voice:

POET   *declaiming*
King Alphonsus Africanus,
Off in exile you will die.
In your fall we see the finish
of the Habsburg monarchy.
In your Oriente Palace
Listen: you can hear them say
Hard luck, King Alfonso Thirteen!
Thirteen means you're on your way!
Sick with fear, our old friend Bourbon
Leaves his royal throne behind,
Takes the bus to Cartagena,
Headed for a healthier clime.
As he passes up the gangplank
Back he rolls a wistful eye:
Never a hanky waves to speed him,
Never a voice bids him goodbye.
Safe on shipboard, under hatches,
Still he can hear that dismal cry:
In your fall we see the finish
Of the Habsburg monarchy!
And as the thirteenth King Alfonso
Sails across the bounding main,
He can hear the people's slogan
Borne on the wind from far-off Spain:
Hard luck, King Alfonso Thirteen!
Thirteen means you're on your way!
If you're really a two-balled he-man,
Sink your crown where the mermaids play!

NARRATOR   That was the way our Spanish Republic was born, an April virgin, fairer even than the Republic pictured on the calendars. And when night fell, the crowds went on singing and dancing through the streets of Madrid, through streets all over Spain. No one wanted to sleep: for that day ought never to end, and the eyes should be wakeful that were to watch the march-past of justice in the great pageant of the dawn. No; the Spaniards had no desire to sleep on that Fourteenth of April; they were not tired of watching their flag as it streamed in the wind, and they were awaiting the final burning of the effigies of the past. Their gay Spanish chatter bubbled beneath the fireworks of the springtime stars, the pinwheel moon, and the tricolor rustling of the new flag.

POET AND PEOPLE   Who gave it that color?
The whole Spanish people!
Who brought the violet-spray?
All those of the Left!
Ayayay, the weeping Nobles!
Ayayay, the praying Churches!
Ayayay, the grunting Silk Hats

REVOLUTIONARY CHORUS OF WORKERS AND PEASANTS

The earth will belong to him who works it.
We shall have diplomatic relations with the Soviet Union.
Spain is a republic of all the workers.
We shall plant our trees on the estates of the rich.
Arid Extremadura will glitter with canals.
Our children will go to school
With new sandals.
We shall have cheap and attractive houses.

Decent wages.
Clean clothes on Sundays.
Mothers will bear their children in peace.
Our little ones will have bread.
The arena bulls of the big ranchers
Will turn into horses.
Into museums, the palace salons.
Children will have their swings
In the Casa del Campo,
And the poor will take their walks in cleanliness
Through the Pardo Park.
The landlord will cry like a lizard:
Oh my acres, my fat interest, my whips!
The bishop will cry like a crocodile:
Oh my tithes, my firstfruits, my poorboxes!
The general will cry like a cat:
Meow, my military dictatorship!
Help, Narváez!
Oh my coup d'état, *my jangling sabres!*

NARRATOR It might have been like that, but it wasn't. Friendliness was bitten by mad-dog hatred. One July day in 1936 a triple hurricane of uniforms, cutaways and cassocks began to batter at the doors of the poor.

Second recollection: July 19

POET, AND VOICES

(*within*)

Who is it comes knocking, knocking at our door?
The Civil Guard and Franco.
The Requetés, the Church.
Who is it comes knocking, knocking at our door?
Mola. Sanjurjo. Doval.
Aranda. Yagüe. Varela.

Who is it comes knocking, knocking at our door?
  Queipo de Llano and the Moors.
  Millán Astray and the vultures
  Of the Foreign Legion.
What is it, what is it those wild beasts are crying?
DEATH TO INTELLIGENCE!

Poet *solus*
  Attention, Spanish people,
  Spanish fighters: this is war!
  They are taking our pastures,
  Burning our crops.
  They are closing down the schools.
  They are beating our comrades,
  Hunting them down like beasts.
  They are insulting our women,
  Cropping their heads, outraging, disfiguring.
  In Badajoz they are baiting
  Leftists like bulls in the ring
  With their lances and banderillas,
  Their machine-guns on the sand
  Of the arena.
        Ah, the horror!
  Vengeance, fiercest vengeance!
  Their hyenas howl around us,
  Their panthers swill our flesh:
  Let our sheep-fleece pierce them
  Sharp as tusks or horny bristles!
  Vengeance, fiercest vengeance!
  Their hyenas howl around us!
  Worker-fighters, to the battle!
  Bring your sickles, bring your guns,
  Bring your hearts, your nails, your rocks and
  Stones, whatever arms your hands find
  Fit for service in this combat!
  For if Right makes Might, our cause will

Triumph, since the right is with us.
But before Madrid they gather,
And in Badajoz they taunt us,
They're the masters now in Cabra,
They advance on Andalusia.

Here Begins the Ballad of Enrique Vásquez

From the olive country
A great cry goes up,
Men ponder the distance,
Women their household things.
A howling is heard
From Andújar to Cabra.
The Moors are on the march,
Their slogans are sorrow.
Enrique Vásquez hears their
Threat to his country;
He leaves his woman behind him,
His imploring daughters.
From the land of Jaén
To gallant Andalusia
Peasants like Vásquez
Feel their blood turn to flame.
If Montoro is in danger,
The hour has come.
Brigades of Juan Garcés,
Vásquez commanding,
You were forced to fall back
When evil night shut down.
The year was dying on the field
Along the long trenches;
Vásquez had been captured,
A prisoner since dawn.
If he had not fallen from his horse
To the frosty ground!

Rivers would rise up
Horsed on white chargers
To rescue the guerrilla
From his deadly danger.
O luckless fall
That betrayed the commander!
Ah Casas de Pedro Abad
That saw him at dawn
Dragged bleeding along
To the grim dark walls!
Long live the Republic!
He cried, and fell dead.
A lamentation is heard
From Andújar to Cabra.
Jasmine and gilliflower
Take the sad rosebay guise.
Black doves fly
From the tragic bells
That jubilate his death
From the town spires.
Commander Enrique Vásquez,
Your death will be avenged.
Ah Casas de Pedro Abad
That saw him at dawn!

NARRATOR: That is how it was. And like the eyes of this ballad
hero, the fists of countless Loyalists closed forever
in death. Listen to what Franco said, standing on
the last tomb.

FLUTING EFFEMINATE VOICE

The Republic is done for.
Spain is a graveyard.
The oranges are cypresses.
The canals, stiff moons.

The children go barefoot.
The bulls own the parks again.
The jails are the workers'
Cottages. No strikes now!
Close up the schoolrooms.
Let everyone go to church.
Up Spain! Are you deaf?
Can't you hear me say *Up Spain?*
You, dead man, *Up Spain!*
You, prisoner, *Up Spain!*
You, widow, *Up Spain!*
Whoever doesn't say *Up Spain!*,
I'll shoot him on the spot.
(Bang, bang, bang, bang)
When they die, how bravely
Their hands go up!

NARRATOR: So died the Republic of the Fourteenth of April,
parched by the gunpowder glare of dusty July. For
seven years it has been sleeping underground—or
above it, cooped up in more than a million prison
cells. For seven years it has gone groaning beneath
the yoke of the Falange,—a nation of bulls that they
tried to turn into a nation of oxen! Seven years of
hatred and sighs beating at the prison walls, at
the earth of the common ditches where our dead
lie, their eyes open, their fists clenched. Seven years
that the flag of Monte-Arruit has floated above a
people lost in a maze. But now, little by little, one of
its stripes is turning violet, is becoming as purple
as the bruised flesh of the beaten, as the livid vio-
lets of their flesh.

POET   The old fount
Bubbles in the tiny square.
And an old refrain is heard

From near and far.
(*Franco can not sleep.*)
The song is a soul in pain,
Soul of the old fountain
That sings and waits.
(*Franco can not sleep.*
The water drowns him, the song burns him.)
A song whose meaning
Is spring and a flag.
Hear it and remember it,
For the Republic is at hand:
Our April banner
Will dawn early as the almond:
People of Spain,
Hold it fast in the blowing wind.

Translated by Dudley Fitts,
from RENDEZVOUS WITH SPAIN,
Gemor Press, New York, 1946

"I Have Been Kissed by the Snake"

ILYA EHRENBURG

WE HAVE SEEN a great deal, yet at the very word "Spain" the blood still rushes to one's face. Spain was the first to take on herself the blows of the two fascist empires. Only the Soviet Union then stood for support of the government of the Spanish Republic.

For nearly three years she resisted, but fell in the unequal struggle. Having finished bombing Madrid and Barcelona, the Germans turned their attention to Paris and London.

In the war years, the English, Americans and French vowed they would destroy fascism all over the world. The war has ended. Hitler is no more. Mussolini has disintegrated. Yet Franco is still sitting in Madrid, and gestapo-like men are torturing Spanish patriots.

Recently M. Blum's newspaper *Populaire* published a report about the torture chambers of Spain in 1947. We learned that arrested persons were beaten in these chambers with truncheons across the mouth and groin, that they were hung up by the feet, that their bodies were scorched and that, to quote *Populaire*, "the interrogations are conducted by Germans; all the evidence is translated for them, and the Germans indicate the course the examination must take."

So nearly three years after the collapse of Hitler Germany, Hitlerites are torturing people in Spanish cities and French Socialists, who are supposed to be outraged by it, open up the closed frontier with Spain, hastening to Franco's aid.

Is this not a mockery? I would not allow a single respectable chatterer to open his mouth without exclaiming: "Sir, and what about Spain?"

They say there was only a civil war in Spain. But can one call the struggle of the French partisans against Laval "only a civil war"? Can one call the struggle of the Norwegian partisans against Quisling "only a civil war"? In Spain there were the people and the traitors, the state and the fifth column, the republic and the hirelings.

Spain was attacked by Italy and Germany. A peace treaty has been signed with the new Italy. There is talk of a peace treaty with Germany. But in Spain the Anglo-Saxon peace-makers have left the Iberian Laval-Quisling, Franco. It is no good pretending to be legitimists and peace-lovers. On them lies the blood of Spain.

I saw German bombs exploding in the narrow streets of Madrid, Barcelona and Valencia, narrow streets perpetually full of children. The blood of Spanish children was Hitler's first voucher. Has England forgotten how the Junkers, Heinkels and Messerschmitts destroyed the cities of Spain before they bombed London? We remember Coventry. But before Coventry was Guernica.

I shall never forget my first meeting with a fascist airman. They called him *Oberleutnant* Kaufman. Asked why he had bombed the little town of Puerto Llano, where there were neither soldiers nor factories nor warehouses, he replied: "We were testing the effect of bombs dropped from different altitudes." I was not surprised when five years later I came across Kaufman in Byelorussia. There was consistency in his behavior.

But what can be said of those people who first whispered to Kaufman, "Please do your bombing—we won't intervene," then cursed him roundly in Paris and London air raid shelters, and now, while thousands of such *oberleutnants* are torturing Spaniards, speak again of the advantages of non-intervention? Is it levity? No, it is cold calculation. They are not afraid of Kaufman; now they are afraid of the Spanish people.

During the war Franco served his masters honestly. Officially Spain did not come out on the side of the Axis, but actually she became a vulgar satellite of Germany. Out of hangmen and riff-raff Franco formed his "Blue Division" and sent it to the Eastern Front. We know the Spanish people are not responsible for the crimes of the Falangists, but London and Washington are responsible. It was they who saved the scoundrels who hanged Russian girls, killed Novgorod collective farmers, took part in the blockade of Leningrad, destroyed the palaces of Pushkino.

There is nothing surprising in the fact that the fascist Franco was supported by the fascist Hitler. But it is surprising that so-called "democrats" and "socialists" are defending him. Indeed, it is more than surprising. It is disgusting.

Altogether different was the behavior of the Spanish people. Abandoned by sham friends, bled white by foreign and home-grown gestapo men, they have all these years continued to fight fascism.

I was on the Spanish-French frontier when the Republicans retreated. Terrible was that exodus. Daladier's government had placed Senegalese on the frontier, and they did not understand what sort of people were before them. The heroes, defeated but valiant, were treated like criminals, and put in concentration camps differing little from those of Germany. But the Spanish knew the French people were not responsible, and two years later there was not a *maquis* detachment in which Spaniards were not fighting side by side with Frenchmen.

Many Spaniards, especially children and young people, found refuge in our country. When the Germans attacked us, some of these Spanish children had already grown into young men. Among the names on a list of partisans who had received decorations I noticed José, Juan, Rodrigo, Fernando, Pablo, interspersed among the Russian names. It is not merely a matter of the military help they gave; of what significance was a handful of men in that gigantic battle? But there is another reckoning besides the arithmetical. There is the reckoning of the human heart.

Spain, which is regarded as backward, will never consent to go along with the baggage train of history. Spaniards are noted for their disinterestedness, for their courage and cult of human dignity. Even the poorest, often illiterate peasants of Castille or Aragón, are politically more enlightened than American farmers. The workers of Barcelona or Seville are not fooled by Marshall's sermons.

Crossing the Pyrenees, one sees another world. One becomes aware of the peculiarities of Spain's historical development, the remnants of feudalism, the burden of a fanatical church, the relation between the ruling caste and foreign capital, the deep democratism of the people, the fusion of the idea of national independence with the idea of social emancipation.

English correspondents, describing Madrid, say that nowhere in Europe today can one see such luxurious motorcars and such wretched, hungry people. The ruins of three years of war and new prisons, ten lackeys to each *caballero*, and a thousand rebels to each lackey, such is Spain in our day. Aware of that fire of indignation in the heart of the Spanish people, the Anglo-Saxons carry on negotiations with the pretender to the throne of the Bourbons, with Gil Robles, with generals and bishops, with the cunning Prieto. They are over-eager to substitute a more modest jailer for the conspicuous Franco, but are afraid of stirring up the fire.

Spain is not a country of ministerial combinations. It was a country of military juntas and all-powerful priests, a country of conspiracies, of silent sorrow, of long roads, long songs, a long destiny. But that Spain is no more. It vanished with the king, with the ephemeral careers of garrulous lawyers and generals who for an hour hastened to join the Republicans.

In 1931 it was still possible to lull Spaniards to sleep with talk of "a republic of toilers of all classes." The Spanish people paid too dearly for its credulity: with the blood of Asturian miners, with years of bleak reaction, with the agreement between Franco and foreign fascists, with the terrible war and the fascist terror. Now, in the mountains of Asturias, Catalonia and Castile, detachments of guerrillas are fighting against Franco and his Falange.

Who supports Franco? Dollars, English diplomacy, the anathemas of the Vatican and the nurslings of Himmler who fled from Germany. But the partisans are supported by the Spanish people. I have no desire to underestimate the enemy's forces —they are the black hundreds of the whole world. But I have no doubt that the people will conquer, and they will conquer not in order to replace Franco by a king, Gil Robles, or Prieto.

*   *   *

When I saw Spain for the first time (it was sixteen years ago) I wrote: "Spain is not Carmen, or the toreadors, or King Alfonso, or the diplomacy of Lerroux, or the novels of Blasco Ibañez. Spain is none of the things exported abroad and given out as genuinely Spanish, together with Argentine dancers and imitation Málaga. No. Spain is twenty million ragged Don Quixotes; she is barren rock, grievous wrongs, songs as sad as the rustle of dry olive leaves; she is the sound of strikers among whom you will find no scabs; she is goodness, kindness and compassion. A great country, she has managed to preserve the fire of youth notwithstanding all the efforts of the inquisitors, parasites, Bourbons."

Later I saw the Spanish in the years of their terrible trial. I saw kind-hearted old peasants marching with sporting guns to fight against tanks. I saw the heroism of youths and young girls who defended Madrid. I saw how people who said "*No pasaran*" died and did not retreat.

I was at the last session of the Spanish Parliament. It was held underground in the cellars of an old castle in the little frontier town of Figueras, which the fascists were bombing day and night. A little old man brought a scrap of carpet into the dark cellar; he wanted to embellish the agony of freedom. He was killed by a bomb.

Not once while I was in Spain would a peasant allow me to pay for fruit or cheese or wine. One said to me: "A smile is worth more than a *peseta*." The men in Wall Street can hardly be expected to understand this, or to reconcile themselves to the emancipation of people who, while respecting men, honestly

471

and deeply despise money.

Spain has given much to humanity. Her art and literature are immortal. It is enough to mention Cervantes and Lope de Vega, Quevedo and Calderón, Velasquez, Zurbaran, El Greco and Goya to gauge the extent of her contribution. The architecture of Córdova, Toledo, Segovia, Salamanca, Granada, Seville have delighted and will always delight people of all countries. How can a people which has created such art support Franco, with his Prussian thugs and American bankers?

The writer of a brilliant work on Don Quixote, Miguel Unamuno, for a long time could not find his way about politics; in politics his naiveté was akin to blindness. Yet before his death he flung these magnificent words in the face of the fascists: "You will conquer, but you will not convince." (*Venceréis, pero no convenceréis!*)

The Falangists shot the talented young poet García Lorca. An old and great poet, Antonio Machado, traversed the whole painful road of the defenders of the Republic, and died crossing the French frontier. Now in exile are the poet Rafael Alberti, the writer José Bergamín and many others. In the years of the Spanish war, Pablo Picasso created "The Ruins of Guernica" and an album called "The Fantasies and Falsehoods of Franco."

Franco has no poets or painters. His praises are sung by contributors to *The Daily Mail*, and his eye is gladdened by the green banknotes from Washington.

Even before the war I saw with what love the simple people of Spain regarded the great past of their country. The chairman of the local council of the village of Escalona, a laborer and a Communist, showed me some 12th century manuscripts. His predecessor, a fascist, an "upholder of tradition," had thrown them out of the cupboard in which they were kept, but the Communist said, "We'll send them to a museum."

*   *   *

In Madrid lived a great physician, Prof. Manuel Marques. When the war began and the fascists were approaching Madrid, he evacuated his home. On the door of his house he placed a note: "In the files of Professor Manuel Marques are the fruits of thirty years' work."

Several months later he received this letter: "Professor: Your house, a real temple of science, has been destroyed by the fascists, but the 'red ignoramuses' have saved your thirty years' work. Rest assured that we shall rebuild your house. All your instruments and eighty-five folders of papers are being taken care of. Red Soldier Gabriel Hernández Rinsón."

What can be added to this? It is true that the red soldiers have not yet rebuilt the professor's house. Franco has built not a few prisons, and sitting in these prisons are the friends of the professor and of the soldier Rinsón. But prisons do not last, whereas the people are immortal.

Today Spain is shut off from the world. Faintly, from afar, we hear the sound of volleys of the executioners as partisans are shot. But we know this people, we know that the fire of its creative force will never be quenched. For us Spain is not only a museum, not only a land where there are many graves dear to us. It is a land with many children, where growing up even now is the genius of its future.

General Franco is frightened. He realizes that his days are numbered. He will have to answer for everything: for the ruins of Madrid, for the blood of children, for the "Blue Division." He may have an Anglo-Saxon absolution for his sins, but the Spanish people have not absolved him.

An ancient Spanish epic tells a striking story of King Rodrigo who, having lost Spain, wandered about the country. An anchorite enjoined him, in God's name, to lie down living in his grave and place a snake upon his breast. For three days and nights the king waited for death, and at last said with relief: "I have been kissed by the snake."

General Franco says nothing, but he has been kissed—not by a common copperhead, but by a golden American viper. For Franco Spain exists no more. It is a new Anglo-Saxon colony. It may be said that all Spain has been converted into a Gibraltar with an Anglo-American façade and German storm-troopers fitted out in new suits of Scottish tweed.

But the Spanish people did not consent to this guardianship. The struggle continues.

According to an old Spanish anecdote, three languages were used in Paradise. In dulcet Italian the serpent tempted Eve; in Spanish, God banished man from Eden; and in polite French, Adam asked God to forgive him.

Now, Spaniards do not listen to the serpent, even when he speaks in English. Nor have they need of the French tongue, in which the Blum socialists offer excuses to the world for supporting Franco. Spaniards will throw out Franco in Spanish. And Spaniards must know that there is a people which believes in them, which has never betrayed them, and never will—the Soviet people.

In the mountains of Asturias march the guerrillas, singing an old song: "My adornment is my weapon, my rest is to fight, my bed—the hard stones, my dream—to banish sleep."

And we respond—*"Salud y victoria!"*

From THE DAILY PEOPLE'S WORLD,
San Francisco, California, April 18, 1948;
original title: THE TRAGEDY OF SPAIN

> *"Having been helped to power by Fascist Italy and Nazi Germany, and having patterned itself along totalitarian lines, the present regime in Spain is naturally the subject of distrust by a great many American citizens. . . . Most certainly we do not forget Spain's official position with and assistance to our Axis enemies at a time when the fortunes of war were less favorable to us. . . . These memories cannot be wiped out. . . ."*
>
> FRANKLIN D. ROOSEVELT (letter to Ambassador Armour in Madrid, March 10, 1945.)

Two Speeches

1.   ROBERT THOMPSON

FRIENDS: YOU WHO ARE here tonight are but a small section of multitudes throughout the world who are determined that peace shall triumph over war. Listen, then, to the flat, cynical opinion of one of your sworn enemies. I quote: "Peace does not exist. Peace is a constant preparation for war."

Was this Hitler speaking—the man who destroyed Germany? Was it Mussolini, whom the Italian people hung up by the heels in the streets of Milan? It might well have been either but those particular lines were spoken by their ardent admirer, Francisco Franco, the new puppet of American imperialists. By their friends shall ye know them.

Yes, Francisco Franco is now the friend of the Truman administration. No one can say today that the evil road down which the men of Wall Street are trying to drive us is not fully illuminated. Its windings and twistings, its ultimate destination, are fully exposed to public view.

Franco is the butcher of the Spanish people. And American reaction has finally lost touch with reality when it considers such a man a potent ally. Yet it must be said that he is a logical addition to the motley crew of Wall Street puppets. He is a worthy cohort of Synghman Rhee, Chiang Kai-shek and the defeated Nazi Wehrmacht generals.

Every last one of this crowd screams for war against the Soviet Union and the peoples' democracies. Why? Because it is only through imperialist war that they can hope for survival in the face of their own peoples' struggle for a better life. Say this about Franco—at least he is consistent. He has not changed his line. His regime is still the same as when the General Assembly of the United Nations condemned it in 1946 in these words.

I quote: "In origin, nature, structure and general conduct the Franco regime is a fascist regime patterned on, and established largely as a result of aid received from Hitler's Nazi Germany and Mussolini's Fascist Italy." It has not changed one iota since May 12, 1949 when Dean Acheson said, and I quote: "It was and is a fascist government and a dictatorship."

So it is not Franco's policy that has changed. It is *our* policy that has changed—from a Roosevelt policy for peace and against fascism to a Truman policy for war and against democracy. And now the ruling class of our country is desperately wooing not only Franco but all his old comrades in arms.

It is a commentary on our times that the wooing is not without its set-backs. These fugitives from Stalingrad marched once before against the peoples of the world under the banner of anti-Communism and they are a little skittish about marching again. The Wehrmacht generals would, of course, dearly love to strut again before their troops. But where are their troops? The great truth of 1951 is that the troops—or the people who could make up these troops—do not want war; they want peace.

The majority of the world's peoples, in fact, want no part of American imperialism and its drive toward war. They are not afraid to fight but they will fight only for their own liberation—not to enslave others. The Koreans, the Chinese, the Indonesians, the Greeks and the Spanish guerrillas have proven that, and they will continue to prove it till their freedom is won. It is these people and people like them who are our allies in the struggle to prevent a third world war. As they sustain their fight for liberation, they retard the outbreak of general war. As they match their skill and courage against the mechanized imperialist armies, they puncture the chauvinist delusions of the would-be war lord, MacArthur.

However, to utterly frustrate the plans of our own imperialists, to save the lives of millions of young Americans—men like those dying so uselessly in Korea—to keep atomic destruction from raining upon our own cities, we Americans must be as persistent and as courageous as these partisans of peace and freedom in other lands. Yes, as persistent and as courageous in our fight for peace as were the men of Valley Forge in their determination to win freedom.

Friends, only he who fights for peace has faith in mankind. We have such faith. Because we have it we know that the drive of our ruling class towards atomic world war can be frustrated. The world of 1951 is closely knit. It is too closely knit for the comfort of those who would dismember it with atomic bombs.

The Spanish guerrilla fights for us and for world peace when he fights Franco. We fight for him and for world peace when we call the American people to defeat every deal with the fascist butcher, Franco. If the cause of world peace is important to us, we cannot relax, but rather must we intensify our support to the anti-Franco struggle of the Spanish people.

2. JOHN GATES

FRIENDS: WE WHO FOUGHT in Spain learned early and well what fascism is. We learned that fascism can exist only through a policy of "Divide and Conquer." Above all, we learned that fascism can be defeated and that a united people can easily frustrate the aims and objectives of the fascists. Therefore it is no accident that we who fought in Spain were among the first to suffer attack by those reactionaries who would drive our country into war.

Dr. Edward K. Barsky, who ministered to the wounded in

Spain, recognized immediately that the attack upon the Joint Anti-Fascist Refugee Committee was a concrete step toward an American fascism. For his resistance to this attack he and ten fellow members of the executive board of that organization went to jail.

Almost immediately thereafter, the Hollywood Ten were attacked because they insisted that their political opinions were their own. For exercising this fundamental constitutional right they received sentences of from six months to one year in prison. And again, it was no accident that one of these gallant ten fought honorably on behalf of the democratic government of Spain.

Bob Thompson and I are proud to be members of the National Committee of the Communist Party. We are facing sentences of up to five years in prison for our progressive thoughts. If this attack upon Communists for what they think is not defeated by the American people, a period of thought control will be initiated in America. The thinking of every democratic and peace-minded American will be censored. Today those who rule our nation are determined to outlaw even the very thought of peace.

The differences between the repressive actions of our government and those of Franco Spain are rapidly disappearing. In Spain they outlawed the Stockholm Petition that demands the outlawing of the atomic weapon. Yet even there, thousands of signatures were collected. Here in America the Petition was also outlawed—not by governmental decree but by terrorizing and intimidating those who signed and those who organized the collection of signatures.

And what is behind the declaration of a state of "national emergency"? Does an emergency really exist? Are our shores being attacked? Are the vital interests of the American people really in danger?

The answer is obvious. No. One of the major reasons for the declaration of an emergency is the government's determination to suppress the ground swell of popular opinion which is

demanding that we withdraw our troops from Korea and nego-
tiate a peaceful settlement with China and the Soviet Union.

No matter where one looks in America today, the signs of
repression are blatant. The efforts of the workers to improve
their standard of living in the face of soaring prices are restricted
by the Taft-Hartley law. The Un-American Committee harasses
and imprisons those who fight for a decent life for all Americans. The attacks upon the Negro people are on the increase.
A Negro veteran is murdered by a cop on the streets of New
York. The cop goes free; but innocent Negroes are sentenced,
every day, to twenty years at hard labor—or to death. The basic
American rights of free speech and free thought are being denied.

This is the road to fascism. This is the road which, if it is
not blocked, will lead to the establishment of a Franco-like
regime in America. To you who are gathered here tonight it must
be clear that Spain is not only a horrible symbol of what our
American future will be like if fascism should come to power
here, but that Spain is, above all, a noble and heartening example
of the will and the ability of a people to resist fascism.

Though defeated by the overwhelming aid given Franco
by Hitler and Mussolini, as well as by the refusal of the Western
powers including the U.S.A. to aid Republican Spain, the Spanish people have continued the struggle against Franco for eleven
long years. They have shown that so long as the will to resist
exists, a people cannot really be conquered.

Franco may brag of his readiness to serve as a Wall Street
mercenary in a third world war, but there is a tremendous gap
between his promises and his ability to perform. The unceasing
activity of the Spanish republicans guarantees that the Spanish
people are our allies for peace, and that they deserve and need
our support. The fight for civil rights and against creeping
fascism in our own country is a part of that same fight.

> *"These two speeches were delivered by transcription at a
> meeting under the auspices of the Veterans of the Abra-
> ham Lincoln Brigade in San Francisco, California, on
> January 5, 1951."*

> *War in Spain has, from the days of the Romans, had a character of its own; it is a fire which cannot be raked out; it burns fiercely under the embers; and long after it has, to all seeming, been extinguished, bursts forth more violently than ever.*
>
> THOMAS BARINGTON MACAULEY *1833*

"I Am Still Alive"

JOSE GOMEZ GALLOSO
La Coruña, Spain, September 6, 1948

DEAR AUNT:
I have no assurance that this or another letter I have written will ever reach you. However, I am making another effort although you will note by my handwriting that my hands are in no condition for writing.

I was arrested in La Coruña on July 11, while directing the organization of the resistance movement. Upon entering a house on Calle Real where I was to meet Antonio Seoane, leader of the Guerrilla Army of Galicia, I found the police waiting inside. The aforementioned person had been arrested the night before. A woman accompanied me—Maria Blazquez.

Upon knocking at the door, we were taken by surprise by the police. Maria, with supreme courage and serenity, and without fear, lunged at the nearest officer and pushed me back, hoping that I would thus manage to escape. She was felled by a shot in the stomach.

I managed to reach the second floor and upon readying my pistol for any eventuality, I was fired on from above. The bullet hit me squarely in the face, knocking out one eye and shattering my nose and face. Despite this I managed to reach the street and escape. However, the loss of blood was so great that one-half hour later I was caught, as the police were able to trail me to my hiding place through the bloody tracks I left behind.

After thirteen days in the hospital, half-cured, I was taken to the headquarters of the Civil Guard, where the so-called "interrogations" were begun. It is not necessary to relate what they did to us, especially to Antonio Seoane and myself.

I am practically a skeleton. From July 11 to September 1, when I was released from the dungeon and interned in a semi-isolation cell, I lost fifty-five pounds. My stomach and intestines are practically ruined and for many days I did nothing but spit up large chunks of blood. It is humanly impossible for me to roll a cigarette. Seoane is in practically the same state. This is fascism!

However, I have never lost spirit. They are now rushing matters in order to liquidate us as soon as possible. I believe that, at the very latest, we will have been executed by November 1. They are in a hurry, a great hurry, for although we are prisoners, we are still dangerous to them.

They thought that, with our capture, they would destroy the guerrillas, but they have failed completely. Despite the great mobilization of forces on their part, the whole guerrilla movement remains firm. Moreover, since our capture, the activities of the guerrillas have increased, and daily dozens of new partisans join their ranks. This, dear Rosa, is what really matters. The rest, our lives hanging by a thread, and the knowledge that this thread will soon be cut by the butchers of our people, is a secondary matter.

During four and a half years, those of us who returned from exile have put our sparse intelligence, but all of our heart and conscience at the service of the cause of the liberation of our beloved homeland. We have fallen? We only regret that we cannot do more! However, it is comforting to know that nothing and no one will be able to undermine the struggle. How great and how brave are our people! What indestructible faith they have in victory! With such faith and such people, and for so noble a cause as that which we defended and will continue to defend to the last moment, we are ready to give not one but a hundred lives without vacillation. I am only sorry that I did not give more, that I was not capable of accomplishing the task entrusted to me with confidence and honor when I was sent to Spain. All of Galicia and Spain are a volcano of struggle which shall never be extinguished by Franco.

Because of my condition, my being isolated and surrounded by provocateurs and police disguised as prisoners, I am not certain that I will be able to leave behind my last letter to you, and to Pasionaría. However, if this letter should reach you, please send her a copy. Tell her we will hold aloft the banner of struggle until death; that she may rest assured that the resistance movement of Galicia remains firm; that the struggle will not cease, because the love and respect our people have for us cannot be extirpated even with rivers of blood by the cowardly fascists. This is being demonstrated daily and hourly.

The four women who fell victims of fascism merit special mention. They all carried on as they were taught by our beloved Pasionaría. They are: Maria Blazquez del Poxo, Josefina González Cudeiro, Clementina Gallégo Abelado, and Carmen Orózco. Their physical condition is very grave. The bullet has not yet been removed from Maria Blazquez's stomach. Carmen Orózco is suffering from a grave cardiac ailment. Clementina Gallégo is partly paralyzed in one leg.

Eight of us await trial. They are trying to include a pair of provocateurs, common criminals and highwaymen, for the purpose of discrediting us and making us appear adventurers and common thieves before the military tribunal. Two or three death sentences will be demanded for at least three of the eight accused. These are: José Gomez Galloso, teacher; Antonio Seoane Sanchez, worker; Juan Romero Ramos, cabinet maker. The others, although also in grave danger, may be spared the death penalty if the campaign of solidarity is intensified. They are José Bartrina, doctor; José Rodriguez Campos, worker; José Ramos Diaz, tailor, and Juan Martínez, peasant.

It took me four days to write this letter. To you and to her, whom even more than aunt and cousin I have always loved as mother and sister, I request that you remain firm. No grief! For you, may my death be an inspiration to help, more and more, the liberation of our people. If it is possible and there is still time, send me a few lines.

And nothing more. If my friends can help me, ask them to cable me. I have no relatives and thanks to the kindness of the other prisoners, I am still alive. My address is: José Gomez Galloso, Prision Provisional, Galeria 1, Celda 4, La Coruña, Spain.

A very, very strong embrace—my very last—in which my heart is entwined.

JOSE

NOTE: *José Gomez Galloso was executed on November 7, 1948, eight weeks after this letter was written. November 7 is the anniversary of the defense of Madrid by the International Brigades.*

To the Veterans of the Abraham Lincoln Brigade

GENEVIEVE TAGGARD

Say of them
They knew no Spanish
At first, and nothing of the arts of war
At first:
   how to shoot, how to attack, how to retreat
How to kill, how to meet killing
At first.
Say they kept the air blue
Grousing and griping,
Arid words and harsh faces. Say
They were young;
The haggard in a trench, the dead on the olive slope
All young. And the thin, the ill and the shattered,
Sightless, in hospitals, all young.
Say of them they were young, there was much they did not know,
They were human. Say it all; it is true. Now say
When the eminent, the great, the easy, the old,
And the men on the make
Were busy bickering and selling,
Betraying, conniving, transacting, splitting hairs,

484

Writing bad articles, signing bad papers,
Passing bad bills,
Bribing, blackmailing,
Whimpering, meaching, garroting,—they
Knew and acted
                          understood and died.
Or if they did not die came home to peace
That is not peace. Say of them
They are no longer young, they never learned
The arts, the stealth of peace, this peace, the tricks of fear;
And what they knew, they know.
And what they dared, they dare.

From THE LONG VIEW,
Harpers, New York, 1946

ACIER, MARCEL (ed.), *From Spanish Trenches,* New York, Modern Age, 1937.

AGUIRRE, JOSE ANTONIO DE, *Escape Via Berlin,* New York, Macmillan, 1945.

ALLAN, TED, *This Time A Better Earth,* New York, William Morrow, 1939.

ALLEN, JAY (& ELLIOT PAUL), *All The Brave,* New York, Modern Age, 1939.

ALTABAS, JULIO YUS, *Struggles of Spain,* New Orleans, Dameron-Pierson, 1938.

ARRARAS, JOAQUIN, *Francisco Franco: The Man and His Times,* Milwaukee, Bruce Publications, 1938.

ATHOLL, DUCHESS OF, *Searchlight on Spain,* London, Penguin Books, 1938.

AUDEN, WYSTAN HUGH, *Spain,* New York, Ryerson Press, 1938.

AZANA, MANUEL, *Spain's War of Independence,* New York, Spanish Information Bureau, 1938.

AZPILIKOETA, ALBERTO DE, *The Basque Problem,* New York, Basque Archives, 1938.

BAHAMONDE, ANTONIO, *Memoirs of a Spanish Nationalist,* London, United Editorial, Ltd., 1939.

BALLOU, JENNY, *Spanish Prelude,* Boston, Houghton-Mifflin, 1937.

BAREA, ARTURO, *Struggle For The Spanish Soul,* London, Secker & Warburg, 1941.

    Garcia Lorca, The Poet and His People, London, Faber, 1944; also New York, Harcourt Brace, 1944.

    Spain In The Post-War World (& Ilse Barea), London, Fabian Society, 1945.

    The Forging of a Rebel, New York, Reynal & Hitchcock, 1946.

    The Clash (drama), London, Faber, 1946.

BATES, RALPH, *Lean Men,* New York, Macmillan, 1935.

    The Olive Field, New York, Dutton, 1936.

    Sirocco, New York, Random House, 1939.

    The Miraculous Horde, London, Cape, 1939.

BENARDETE, M. J. (ed.), *And Spain Sings,* New York, Vanguard Press, 1937.

BERNANOS, GEORGES, *A Diary of My Times,* New York, Macmillan, 1938.

BESSIE, ALVAH, *Men In Battle,* New York, Scribners, 1939.

BLANKFORT, MICHAEL, *The Brave and The Blind* (one-act play), New York, Samuel French, 1937.

    The Brave and The Blind (novel), New York, Bobbs-Merrill, 1940.

BLASQUEZ, JOSE MARTIN, *I Helped to Build an Army,* London, Secker & Warburg, 1939.

BLYTHE, HENRY, *Spain Over Britain*, London, Routledge, 1936.

BORKENAU, FRANZ, *The Spanish Cockpit*, London, Faber, 1937.

BORROW, GEORGE, *The Gypsies in Spain* (1841).

The Bible in Spain (1842).

BREA, JUAN, *Red Spanish Notebook*, London, Secker & Warburg, 1937.

BRENAN, GERALD, *The Spanish Labyrinth*, New York, Macmillan, 1943.

The Face of Spain, New York, Pellegrini & Cudahy, 1951.

The Literature of the Spanish People, New York, Cambridge University Press, 1952.

BRENNAN, FREDERICK HAZLITT, *Memo To A Firing Squad*, New York, Knopf, 1943.

BRENNAN, TERRY, *Death Squads in Morocco*, London, Low, 1938.

BRERETON, GEOFFREY, *Inside Spain*, London, Quality Press, 1938.

BRIFFAULT, ROBERT, *Fandango*, New York, Scribners, 1940.

BROWN, IRVING, *Deep Song*, New York, Harper Brothers, 1929.

BROWNE, FELICIA, *Twenty Drawings*, London, Lawrence, 1936.

BUCKLEY, HENRY, *Life & Death of the Spanish Republic*, London, Hamilton, 1940.

BURDIN, RUTH, *Incident* (drama), New York, French, 1937.

CALMER, ALAN (ed.), *Salud!*, New York, International, 1938.

CAMPBELL, ROY, *Flowering Rifle*, London, Longmans, 1939.

CAPA, ROBERT, *Death In The Making*, New York, Covici-Friede, 1938.

CARASA, PILAR FIDALGO, *A Young Mother in Franco's Prisons*, London, United Editorial, Ltd., 1939.

CARDOZO, HAROLD G., *The March of a Nation*, New York, McBride, 1937.

CASADO, SEGISMUNDO, *Last Days of Madrid*, London, Peter Davies, 1939.

CASTILLEJO, E., *The War of Ideas in Spain*, London, Murray, 1937.

Causa General, The Red Domination in Spain, Ministry of Justice, Madrid, 1946.

CERVANTES, MIGUEL DE, *Don Quixote*, New York, Modern Library, 1930.

CHALMERS-MITCHELL, SIR PETER, *My House in Málaga*, London, Faber, 1938.

CHARLTON, LIONEL EVELYN OSWALD, *The Military Situation in Spain*, New York, Georgian Press, 1938.

CHASE, ALLAN, *Falange*, New York, Putnam, 1943.

The Five Arrows, New York, Random House, 1944.

CHILDS, RICHARD STORRS (ed.), *War in Spain* (photohistory), New York, Modern Age, 1937.

CLARIANA, BERNARDO, *Rendezvous With Spain* (trans. Dudley Fitts), New York, Gemor Press, 1946.

CONZE, EDWARD, *Spain Today*, New York, Greenberg, 1936.

CORWIN, NORMAN, *They Fly Through The Air*, New York, Holt, 1942.

COT, PIERRE, *The Triumph of Treason*, New York, Ziff-Davis, 1944.

487

Cox, Geoffrey, *The Defense of Madrid,* London, Gollancz, 1937.

Crabites, Pierre, *Unhappy Spain,* Baton Rouge, Louisiana University Press, 1937.

Davis, Frances, *My Shadow In The Sun,* New York, Carrick & Evans, 1940.

Dingle, Reginald James, *Russia's Work in Spain,* London, Spanish Press Services, 1936.

Documents on German Foreign Policy (*On German-Spanish Relations During the Civil War*) Series D. Vol. III, U.S. Government, 1950.

Dos Passos, John, *Adventures of a Young Man,* New York, Harcourt Brace, 1938-9.

Journeys Between Wars, New York, Harcourt Brace, 1938.

Duff, Charles, *Key To Victory: Spain,* London, Gollancz, 1940.

Dundas, Lawrence, *Behind The Spanish Mask,* London, Hale, 1943.

Dzelepy, Eleuthere Nicolas, *The Spanish Plot,* London, King, 1937.

Britain in Spain, London, Hamilton, 1939.

Ellis Havelock, *The Soul of Spain,* Boston, Houghton-Mifflin, 1937.

Elston, Peter, *Spanish Prisoner,* New York, Carrick & Evans, 1939.

Espinosa, A. M., *Second Spanish Republic & The Causes of the Counter-Revolution,* San Francisco, Spanish Relief Committee, 1937.

Fieldhouse, H. N., *Spanish Civil War,* New York, Macmillan, 1937.

Feis, Herbert, *The Spanish Story,* New York, Knopf, 1948.

Fischer, Louis, *War in Spain,* New York, The Nation, 1937.

Men and Politics, New York, Duell, 1940.

Flores, Angel (ed.), *Spanish Writers in Exile,* Sausalito, Cal., Bern Porter.

Foltz, Charles, Jr., *The Masquerade in Spain,* New York, Houghton-Mifflin, 1948.

Fonteriz, Luis de, *Red Terror in Madrid,* London, Longmans, 1937.

Ford, Richard, *Gatherings From Spain,* New York, E. P. Dutton, 1906.

Foss, William, *The Spanish Arena,* London, Gifford, 1938.

Fox, Ralph, *A Writer In Arms,* New York, International, 1937.

Franco's Rule, London, United Editorial, Ltd., 1938.

Frank, Waldo, *Virgin Spain,* New York, Boni & Liveright, 1942.

Gannes, Harry (& Theo. Repard), *Spain in Revolt,* New York, Knopf, 1936.

Garratt, Geoffrey T., *Mussolini's Roman Empire,* New York, Bobbs-Merrill, 1938.

George, Robert Esmonde Gordon, *Spain's Ordeal,* New York, Longmans, 1940.

Gerahty, Cecil (cf. Foss, William), *Road to Madrid,* London, Hutchinson, 1937.

Gautier, Theophile, *A Romantic in Spain,* New York, Knopf, 1926.

GIRRI, ALBERTO (& WM. SHAND), *Poesia Inglesa de la Guerra Española*, Buenos Aires, Liberia y Editorial 'El Ateneo', 1947.

GODDEN, GERTRUDE M., *Conflict in Spain 1920-1937*, London, Burns Oates, 1937.

GREAVES, HAROLD RICHARD GORING (& DAVID THOMPSON), *Truth About Spain*, London, Gollancz, 1938.

GREENE, GRAHAM, *The Confidential Agent*, New York, Viking Press, 1939.

GREENE, HERBERT, *Secret Agent in Spain*, London, Hale, 1938.

GREENWALL, HARRY JAMES, *Mediterranean Crisis*, London, Nicholson & Watson, 1939.

GRIMLEY, BERNARD, *Spanish Conflict*, St. Anthony Guild, 1937.

Guest, David, A Memoir, London, Lawrence & Wishart, 1939.

HAMILTON, THOMAS JEFFERSON, *Appeasement's Child*, New York, Knopf, 1943.

HANIGHEN, FRANK CLEARY (ed.), *Nothing But Danger*, New York, McBride, 1939.

HARDIN, FLOYD (ed.), *Spanish Civil War & Its Political, Social, Economic Ideological Backgrounds*, Bibliographical Center for Research, Denver Public Library, Denver, 1938.

HAY, JOHN, *Castilian Days*, Boston & N. Y., Houghton-Mifflin, 1904.

HAYES, CARLETON J. H., *Wartime Mission in Spain*, New York, Macmillan, 1945.

The United States and Spain, New York, Sheed & Ward, 1951.

HELINE, THEODORE, *Spain, World Ideas in Turmoil*, Los Angeles, New Age, 1938.

HEMINGWAY, ERNEST, *All the Brave* (cf. JAY ALLEN).
The Spanish War, London, Fact, 1938.
The Spanish Earth (film commentary), Cleveland, Savage, 1938.
The Fifth Column (play), New York, Scribner, 1940.
For Whom The Bell Tolls, New York, Scribners, 1940.

HERICOURT, PIERRE, *Arms For Red Spain*, London, Burns Oates, 1938.

HISPANICUS (pseud., ed.), *Foreign Intervention in Spain*, London, United Editorial, 1938.

HOARE, SIR SAMUEL, *Complacent Dictator*, New York, Knopf, 1947.

HUGHES, EMMET J., *Report From Spain*, New York, Holt, 1947.

HUXLEY, ALDOUS (ed.), *They Still Draw Pictures*, New York, Oxford, 1939.
(ed.), *The Complete Etchings of Goya*, New York, Crown, 1951.

IBANEZ, VICENTE BLASCO, *The Shadow of the Cathedral*, London, Constable, 1909.

IBARRURI, DOLORES (*La Pasionaria*), *Speeches & Articles*, New York, International, 1938.

INTERNATIONAL BRIGADES (pub.), *Los Niños Españoles,* Barcelona, 1938.
Canciones de las Brigades Internacionales, Barcelona, 1938.
The Book of the XVth Brigade, Madrid, 1938.
IRVING, WASHINGTON, *The Alhambra,* New York, Putnam, 1868.

JELLINEK, FRANK, *The Civil War in Spain,* London, Gollancz, 1938.
JOHNSTONE, NANCY, *Hotel in Spain,* New York, Longmans, 1938.

KESTEN, HERMAN, *Children of Guernica,* New York, Longmans, 1939.
KLINGENDER, F. D., *Goya in the Democratic Tradition,* London, Sidgwick and Jackson, Ltd., 1948.
KNICKERBOCKER, HERBERT RENFRO, *Siege of Alcazar,* Philadelphia, McKay, 1936.
KNOBLAUGH, H. EDWARD, *Correspondent in Spain,* London & New York, Sheed & Ward, 1937.
KOESTLER, ARTHUR, *The Spanish Testament,* London, Gollancz, 1937.
Dialogue With Death, New York, Macmillan, 1942.

LANGDON-DAVIES, JOHN, *Behind the Spanish Barricades,* New York, McBride, 1937.
Air Raid, London, Routledge 1938.
LARREA, JUAN, *Guernica; Picasso,* New York, Curt Valentin, 1947.
LAST, JEF, *Spanish Tragedy,* London, Routledge, 1939.
LAWSON, JOHN HOWARD, *Blockade* (screenplay), Walter Wanger Productions, 1938.
LEHMAN, JOHN (& STEPHEN SPENDER, eds.), *Poems For Spain,* London, Hogarth Press, 1939.
LEWIS, NORMAN, *Spanish Adventure,* New York, Holt, 1935.
LEWIS, WYNDHAM, *Count Your Dead: They Are Alive,* London, Davies, 1939.
LORCA, GARCIA, *Lament For The Death of a Bull-Fighter,* London, Oxford, 1937.
Plays, New York, Scribners, 1941.
Selected Poems, London, Oxford, 1939.
LOVEDAY, ARTHUR F., *World War in Spain,* London, Murray, 1939.
LOW, MARY (cf. BREA, JUAN).
LOWENSTEIN, PRINCE HUBERTUS VON, *A Catholic in Republican Spain,* London, Gollancz, 1937.
LUNN, ARNOLD, *Spanish Rehearsal,* New York, Sheed & Ward, 1937.

MACKEE, SEUMAS, *I Was a Franco Soldier,* London, United Editorial, 1938.
McCABE, JOSEPH, *Spain in Revolt 1814-1931,* New York, Appleton, 1932.
McCULLAGH, FRANCIS, *In Franco's Spain,* London, Burns Oates, 1937.
McNEILL-MOSS, GEOFFREY, *The Siege of the Alcazar,* New York, Knopf, 1937.
The Legend of Badajoz, London, 1937.

490

MADARIAGA, SALVADOR DE, *Spain*, New York, Creative Age Press, 1943.

MALRAUX, ANDRE, *Man's Hope*, New York, Random House, 1938.

MANNING, LEAH, *What I saw In Spain*, London, Gollancz, 1935.

MANNING, WILLIAM ROY, *Diplomatic Correspondence of the United States*, New York, Carnegie Endowment, 1932-37.

MANUEL, FRANK, *The Politics of Modern Spain*, New York, McGraw-Hill, 1938.

MARTIN-BLAZQUEZ, JOSE, *I Helped To Build An Army*, London, Secker & Warburg, 1939.

MASSIS, HENRI (& ROBERT BRASILLACH), *Cadets Of The Alcazar*, New York, Paulist, 1937.

MATTHEWS, HERBERT L., *Two Wars and More To Come*, New York, Carrick & Evans, 1938.

Education of a Correspondent, New York, Harcourt-Brace, 1946.

MEDIO, JUSTO (ed.), *Three Pictures of the Spanish Civil War*, London, Hutchinson, 1937.

MERIN, PETER, *Spain Between Death and Birth*, New York, Dodge, 1938.

MENDIZABAL, ALFRED, *The Martyrdom of Spain*, New York, Scribners, 1938.

MITCHELL, MAIRIN, *Storm Over Spain*, London, Secker & Warburg, 1937.

MONTAVON, WILLIAM FREDERICK, *Insurrection in Spain*, Washington, National Catholic Welfare Conference, 1937.

MORA, CONSTANCIA DE LA, *In Place of Splendor*, New York Harcourt-Brace, 1939.

MORROW, FELIX, *Civil War in Spain*, Labor Book Shop, 1936.

MOWAT, ROBERT BALMAIN, *Fight For Peace*, London, Arrowsmith, 1937.

NEHRU, JAWAHARLAL, *Spain! Why?* London, Indian Committee for Food for Spain, 193-?

Nazi Conspiracy In Spain, by the Editor of the *Brown Book of the Hitler Terror*, London, Gollancz, 1937.

NEXO, MARTIN-ANDERSON, *Days In The Sun*, New York, Coward-McCann, 1929.

NOEL-BAKER, FRANCIS EDWARD, *Spanish Summary*, New York, Hutchinson, 1948.

NOGALES, MANUEL CHAVEZ, *Heroes and Beasts of Spain*, New York, Double-Day Doran, 1937.

O'BRIEN, KATE, *Farewell Spain*, New York, Doubleday Doran, 1937.

O'DONELL, PEADAR, *Salud! An Irishman in Spain*, London, Methuen, 1937.

O'DUFFY, EOIN, *Crusade in Spain*, London, Browne & Nolan, 1938.

OLIVIERA, A. RAMOS, *Politics, Economics and Men of Modern Spain*, Crown, 1948.

ORMSBEE, DAVID (pseud. STEPHEN LONGSTREET), *Chico Goes To The Wars*, New York, Dutton, 1943.

491

ORTEGA Y GASSET, JOSE, *Invertebrate Spain*, New York, Norton, 1937.

ORWELL, GEORGE, *Homage to Catalonia*, London, Secker & Warburg, 1938.

PADELFORD, NORMAN JUDSON, *International Law and Diplomacy in the Spanish Civil Strife*, New York, Macmillan, 1939.

PALENCIA, ISABEL DE, *I Must Have Liberty*, New York, Longmans, 1940.
Smouldering Freedom, New York, Longmans, 1945.

PALMER, NETTIE (et al), *Australians in Spain*, Sydney, Current, 1948.

PAUL, ELLIOT, *Life and Death of a Spanish Town*, New York, Random House, 1937 (cf. also ALLEN, JAY).

PECK, ANNE MERRIMAN (& E. A. MERAS), *Spain in Europe and America*, New York, Harper Brothers, 1937.

PAYNE, PIERRE S. R., *Song Of The Peasant*, London, Heinemann, 1939.

PEERS, EDGAR ALLISON, *Spain*, New York, Farrar & Rinehart, 1930.
The Spanish Tragedy, New York, Oxford, 1936.
Catalonia Infelix, New York, Oxford, 1940.
Spain in Eclipse 1937-1943, Saunders, 1943.

PEYRE, JOSEPH, *Rehearsal in Oviedo*, New York, Knight, 1937.
Glittering Death, New York, Random House, 1937.

PIDAL, MENENDEZ RAMON, *The Spaniards in Their History*, New York, W. W. Norton, 1950.

PITCAIRN, FRANK, *Reporter in Spain*, London, Lawrence & Wishart, 1936.

PLENN, ABEL, *Wind in the Olive Trees*, New York, Boni & Gaer, 1946.

PRIETO, CARLOS, *Spanish Front*, London, Nelson, 1936.

QUINTANILLA, LUIS (cf. also JAY ALLEN), *All The Brave*, New York, Modern Age, 1939.
Franco's Black Spain, New York, Reynal & Hitchcock, 1946.

REGLER, GUSTAV, *The Great Crusade*, New York, Longmans, 1940.

REID, JOHN T., *Modern Spain and Liberalism*, London, Oxford, 1937.

RIEHM, HELEN, *Still Alive With Lucas*, London, Davies, 1940.

RIESENFELD, JANET, *Dancer in Madrid*, New York, Funk & Wagnalls, 1938.

ROBINSON, IONE, *A Wall To Paint On*, New York, Dutton, 1946.

ROGERS, FRANCIS THEOBALD, *Spain: A Tragic Journey*, New York, Macaulay, 1937.

ROLFE, EDWIN, *The Lincoln Battalion*, New York, Random House, 1939.
First Love, Los Angeles, Larry Edmunds Bookshop, 1951.

ROLLINS, WILLIAM, JR., *The Wall of Men*, New York, Modern Age, 1938.

ROMILLY, ESMOND, *Boadilla*, London, Hamish Hamilton, 1937.

ROTVAND, GEORGES, *Franco Means Business*, London, Paladin, 1937.

RUST, WILLIAM, *Britons in Spain*, New York, International, 1939.

SALTER, CEDRIC, *Try-Out In Spain,* New York, Harper, 1943.

SEDGEWICK, HENRY DWIGHT, *Spain, A Short History,* Boston, 1937.

SELDES, GEORGE, *The Catholic Crisis,* New York, Messner, 1939.

SENCOURT, ROBERT ESMONDE, *Spain's Ordeal,* London & New York, Longmans, 1938.

SENDER, RAMON, *Pro Patria,* New York, Houghton-Mifflin, 1935.
   Seven Red Sundays, New York, Liveright, 1936.
   Counterattack in Spain, Boston, Houghton-Mifflin, 1937.
   War In Spain, London, Faber, 1937.
   Mr. Witt Among the Rebels, New York, Houghton-Mifflin, 1938.
   The King and The Queen, New York, Vanguard, 1948.

SHAND, WILLIAM (cf. GIRRI, ALBERTO).

SHEEAN, VINCENT, *Not Peace But a Sword,* New York, Doubleday, 1939.
   The Eleventh Hour, London, Hamilton, 1939.

SHOLLEY, HAZEL H., *Night Falls on Spain* (drama), Boston, Baker, 1939.

SINCLAIR, UPTON, *No Pasaran,* Pasadena (pub. by author), 1937.

SLATER, HUMPHREY, *The Heretics,* New York, Harcourt Brace, 1947.

SLOAN, PAT, *John Cornford: A Memoir,* London, Cape, 1938.

SOMMERFIELD, JOHN, *Volunteer in Spain,* New York, Knopf, 1937.

SORIA, GEORGES, *Trotskyism in the Service of Franco,* New York, International, 1938.

Spanish White Book, Spanish Embassy, Washington, D.C., 1937.

SPENDER, STEPHEN (cf. LEHMAN, JOHN).

SQUIRES, ALMA M., *What Of Spain?,* Los Angeles, David H. Schol, 1939.

STAVIS, BARRIE, *Refuge* (drama), New York, French, 1939.

STEER, GEORGE LOWTHER, *Tree of Gernika,* London, Hodder & Stoughton, 1938.

ST. EXUPERY, ANTOINE DE, *Wind, Sand and Stars,* New York, Reynal & Hitchcock, 1939.

STRONG, ANNA LOUISE, *Spain In Arms,* New York, Holt, 1937.

TENNANT, ELEONORA D., *Spanish Journey,* London, Eyre & Spottiswoode, 1936.

TIMMERMANS, RODOLPHE, *Heroes of the Alcazar,* London, Spottiswood, 1937.

TINKER, FRANK, *Some Still Live,* New York, Funk & Wagnalls, 1938.

TODRIN, BORIS, *At The Gates,* Prairie City, Decker, 1944.

TORRES, MANUEL, *Social Work of the New Spanish State,* New York, Peninsular News Service, 1938.

TREND, JOHN BRANDE, *The Origins of Modern Spain,* New York, Macmillan, 1934.

UHSE, BODO, *Lieutenant Bertram,* New York, Simon & Schuster, 1944.

UNITED NATIONS, *Report of the Sub-Committee on the Spanish Question,* New York, Hunter College, 1946.

493

United States State Department, *The Spanish Government and The Axis*, Washington, 1946.

"Unknown Diplomat," *Britain in Spain*, London, Hamilton, 1939.

Van Paasen, Pierre, *Days Of Our Years*, New York, Hillman-Curl, 1939.

Vayo, J. Alvarez del, *Freedom's Battle*, New York, Knopf, 1940.
The Last Optimist, New York, Viking Press, 1950.

Vilaplana, Antonio Ruiz, *Burgos Justice*, New York, Knopf, 1938.

Vollenhoven, Maurits Willem Raedinek van, *Tragedy of Spain*, London, Burns Oates, 1938.

Volunteer For Liberty, pub. Veterans of the Abraham Lincoln Brigade, New York, 1949.

Wall, Bernard, *Spain of the Spaniards*, New York, Sheed & Ward, 1938.

Watson, Keith Scott, *Single To Spain*, New York, Dutton, 1937.

Werth, Alexander, *France and Munich*, New York, Harper, 1939.

Wertheim, Barbara, *The Lost British Policy*, London, United Editorial Ltd., 1938.

Westerman, Percy F., *Under Fire in Spain*, London, Blackie, 1937.

Wet, Oloff de, *The Patrol is Ended,,* New York, Doubleday, 1938.

White, Freda, *War In Spain*, London, Longmans, 1937.

Willis, Jerome, *It Stopped At London*, London, Hurst & Blackett, 1944.

Wilson, Francesca M., *In The Margins of Chaos*, New York, Macmillan, 1945.

Wintringham, Thomas Henry, *English Captain*, London, Faber, 1939.
Deadlock War, Ryerson Press, 1940.

Wolfe, Bertram D., *Civil War in Spain*, New York, Workers Age, 1937.

Woolsey, Gamel, *Death's Other Kingdom*, London, Longmans Green, 1939.

Worsely, Thomas Cuthbert, *Behind The Battle*, London, Hale, 1939.

Writer In A Changing World, New York, Equinox, 1937.

Writers Take Sides, New York, League of American Writers, 1938.

Ydewalle, Charles d', *Interlude in Spain*, London, Macmillan, 1945.

Zglinitzki, Helen de, *The Painted Bed*, New York, Dodd Mead, 1938.